Tilly Stood on a Railed Dais

Gazing Toward the Bench...

"You have heard what the other witnesses in this case have said. To their mind you are the cause of Mrs. Ellen Ross being present here today and being charged with manslaughter. One of them has definitely stated that you have some . . . well"—the judge now looked down at the bench, then over it and on to the head of the clerk standing below before he raised his eyes to the witness box again—"occult power. You understand what I mean by that?"

"No . . . o, no . . . o, sir."

"Well, in ordinary terms it means that you dabble in witchcraft."

Everyone in the courtroom had their gaze fixed on Tilly waiting for her answer, but she didn't reply, not even to make a motion of her head, and Simon, gazing at her, cried voicelessly, "She knows as much about witchcraft as an unborn child. Oh, Tilly! Tilly!"

"Well, do you dabble in witchcraft?"

"No, sir. *No! No!*" Her words were slow but emphatic now. "I . . . I never . . . never have, never. I . . . I don't know nothing about witchcraft."

CATHERINE COOKSON

Tilly

PUBLISHED BY POCKET BOOKS NEW YORK

Originally published in Great Britain in 1980 by
William Heinemann Ltd. under the title *Tilly Trotter*

POCKET BOOKS, a Simon & Schuster division of
GULF & WESTERN CORPORATION
1230 Avenue of the Americas, New York, N. Y. 10020

Published by arrangement with William Morrow & Company, Inc.
Library of Congress Catalog Card Number: 80-16627

ISBN: 0-671-45219-3

First Pocket Books printing October, 1981

10 9 8 7 6 5 4 3 2

POCKET and colophon are trademarks of Simon & Schuster.

Printed in the U.S.A.

Contents

PART ONE

The Old Life

1

He urged his horse up the rise, then stopped at the summit as he always did and sat gazing about him. The sky was high today, clear and blue, not resting as it usually did on the far low hills away to his left, or on the masts of the ships not so far away that lined the river. From this point he could see the town of South Shields lying in a bustling huddle along the banks of the river right to where it made its way into the North Sea.

From Tyne Dock to where the village of Jarrow began the land was bare of all but a cottage and a farmstead here and there, but once his eyes lit on Jarrow itself he had the feeling of bustle again, even if it were in a lesser way: the little shipyard he knew would be busy, and at the salt pans along the river where the work would be ceaseless.

Then came Hebburn. He knew it to be there, but it was obscured from his view by a series of hillocks. Always a shadow of pity rose in him when he looked upon any town, even the great Newcastle, for he could never understand how men, given the choice, would want to live among the bustle and hustle and, for the majority of them, stink and muck. But then again the majority of them had little choice. Yet if the chance were given them would they want to live out here in the open country? . . .

Open country! The words were now scornful in his mind. He looked down toward the earth. There was a mine underneath his horse's feet. How often did the miners enjoy the open country? Once a week? Some of them were so worn out that all the Sunday privilege meant to them was bed.

He urged on his horse again, impatience in his "Get up there!" Now why was it that on this monthly visit to William Trotter he should, winter or summer, pause on that knoll and ask himself questions that had nothing whatsoever to do with him or his life? Here he was a prosperous farmer, well set-up; oh yes, he knew his own value. He would have liked another inch or two to his stature but five foot ten and a half wasn't bad, not when you had breadth to go with it; and the hair on his head was as thick as a horse's mane, and the color of chestnut into the bargain. As for his face, well, the looking-glass had told him there were handsomer men but they were only to be found among the fops. His was a strong manly face; all strong faces had big noses. His mouth in proportion was large, and that was as it should be. And he had all his teeth; the bottom set as wide as they were high and as white as salt would make them. It wasn't everybody who could reach twenty-four and brag that he hadn't as yet had one tooth broken or pulled. Jeff Barnes had three missing in the front and him not twenty yet, all because he couldn't stand a bit of faceache, and him the size of a house end! No, his face, as his mother used to say, would get him past in a crowd . . . but only just. He used to laugh at his mother: she had been a joker.

At the bottom of the knoll he was still on a rise and as he turned the horse on to a narrow bridle-path he was now looking over a mass of woody land where in the far distance a row of ornamental chimneys pierced the sky, and on the sight of them he again pulled his horse to a stop; and as he did so he now asked himself: Could the rumor be true? Was the Sopwith mine finished, or running out? Because if it was that would be the finish of the family and the Manor. But in a way it could be the making of himself, it could bring about the realization of a dream. Yet if the place and the land and farm

4

went under the hammer could he go to Mr. Mark and say, "I have money to buy me farm"? He couldn't for there was very little left of the big lot and the first thing Mr. Mark would likely say would be, "Where did you get such money from?" and what would he say to that? "An uncle died in Australia"? People did say things like that. He hadn't an uncle in Australia and Mark Sopwith would know that. There had been Sopwiths in the Manor for the last three hundred years and there had been Bentwoods on Brook Farm for as long, and each knew the history of the other.

He urged his horse on again and the thought in his mind now was, I hope to God it is just a rumor. Aye, I do, for all their sakes.

He entered a narrow belt of wood and when he emerged a few minutes later it was as if he had come into a new country, so changed was the scene. Beyond the stretch of moorland lay a huddle of houses known as Rosier's Village. They were mean two-roomed, mud-floored, miners' cottages housing the workers in the mine that lay half a mile beyond, and the land between the houses and the mine seemed to be dotted with black coal mounds. Although there were only three of them, they nevertheless dominated the landscape.

As his eyes dwelled on the panorama of industry he wondered how it was that one mine owner, such as Rosier, could flourish when a man of more ability and stature such as Sopwith could go to the wall. He supposed the answer could be given in two parts: first, although, so he understood, Rosier had his troubles with water and explosions and the like, as every mine owner had, his was a shaft mine whereas Sopwith's was a drift mine; and the second part of the answer lay in luck, which, in the coal industry, meant good seams and bad seams, although it was said that luck, bad luck, was just an excuse for poor prospecting.

Even when he was well past the village the stench of

it still clung to his nostrils. He had ridden a further two miles or more before he came in sight of his destination. It was a thatched cottage, and it lay just off the bridle-path sheltered in a flat-bottomed hollow, and within the boundary of the Sopwith estate. It had a large square of cultivated garden in front and a paddock behind, all neatly railed in. Away to the left of him the land dropped slightly before rising to a grass-covered hill which halfway up leveled itself into a narrow plateau, then rose upward again and on to an apparently flat head.

He rode down to the cottage, dismounted and tied his horse to the gate-post. When he unlatched the gate and went up the path the geese in the paddock set up a chattering and screeching, and this seemed to be the signal for a door to open. When he reached it he spoke to the old woman standing there, saying, "They're as good as watch-dogs those two."

"Oh, hello, Simon. 'Tis good to see you. Come away in. Come away in. Isn't it a beautiful day?"

"It is, Annie. It is," he said, following her inside.

"I was just saying to William there"—she thrust her hand out toward the bed that was inset in the wall at the far end of the room—"give us one or two more days like this an' we'll have him outside."

"Why not. Why not indeed. . . . How are you, William?"

The man in the bed pulled himself up out of the feather tick and leaned forward, holding out his hand. "As you see me, as you see me, Simon; no better, no worse."

"Well, that's something."

As Simon Bentwood spoke he opened the buttons of his double-breasted coat and inserted his finger in his high neckerchief as he exclaimed, "It's been a hot ride."

"I've got something for that. And take your coat off. Ginger or herb?"

6

Simon was on the point of saying, "Ginger," when he remembered that the last pint of ginger beer he'd drunk here had filled him with wind and he'd been up half the night. She had put so much root ginger into it it had burned his innards. "Herb," he said. "Thanks, Annie."

"Herb," she repeated; "I thought you liked ginger."

"I like them both, but I can have a change, can't I?" He flapped his hand toward her, and, laughing, she turned from him and hurried across the long stone-floored room, her humped hips swinging her faded serge skirt.

When she disappeared through a door at the far end of the room Simon took a seat by the bed and, looking at the old man, he asked quietly, "And how goes it?"

"Aw." William Trotter now lay back into the denseness of the feather-filled pillows and muttered slowly, "Not so good at times, Simon."

"Pain worse?"

"I can't say it is, it's always been worse." He gave a wry smile now through his bewhiskered face.

"I might be able to come by a bottle of the real stuff shortly; I understand the lads are going out again."

"That would be good, Simon. Aw, that would be good. There's nothing like a drop of the real stuff. But it's funny that the real stuff has to come from foreign parts, now isn't it?"

"Aye, it is when you come to think of it, William; yes, it is. But then of course brandy has to come from foreign parts."

"Aye, aye; yes, I remember the last lot, I slept like a baby for nights." The old man now turned and looked toward Simon and, his words slow and meaningful, he said, "Sleep's a wonderful thing you know, Simon, it's the best thing that God has given us, sleep. I think He bestowed it on us as an apprenticeship to death, 'cos that's what it will be, death, just a long sleep."

"Yes, William, yes, I . . . I agree with you there, just a long sleep. Ah . . . !" He turned, on a forced laugh,

7

and greeted Annie Trotter as she came back into the room carrying a gray hen by the handle: "There you are then. Mind, you've taken your time."

"Away with you. Taken me time! I'm not as young as I used to be; it's difficult to get under the house, Tilly usually does the crawling."

"Where is she, by the way?"

"Oh, out gathering wood as usual. She's for ever sawing branches off and sawing them up. I'd like to bet there's not a cleaner line of trees in the country than those in Sop's Wood. It's a good job Mr. Mark doesn't mind her stripping the trees head high, but I must say this for her she does it properly, as good as any man, for there's no sap runs after she's finished; she tars every spot."

"I'm worried."

Simon now looked at William again and he asked, "Worried? What about?"

"Her . . . Tilly. Fifteen gone, coming up sixteen, she should be in place, in good service learnin' to be a woman 'stead of rangin' around like a half-scalded young colt; it wouldn't surprise me if one day she decided to wear trousers."

"Ho! I don't think you need worry about that; she'll never do anything silly, not Tilly, she's got a head on her shoulders."

"Oh, I know that, I know that, Simon. The trouble is she's got too much head on her shoulders. Do you know, she can read and write as good as the parson hissel."

"And dance."

Simon turned quickly to Annie who was in the act of handing him a mug of herb beer and he said, "Dance?"

"Aye. You don't know the latest. It's the parson's wife, Mrs. Ross."

"The parson's wife?" Simon screwed up his face.

"Aye, aren't I tellin' you? She must have thought that Tilly needed some gentlewomanly accomplishments or some such, and so what does she do? She shows her how to dance. Takes her into the vicarage indeed! Plays a tune on the spinet, then down into the cellar they go and there she takes her through a minet . . . no, minuet. That's it."

"Mrs. Ross, the parson's wife!" Simon's face was stretched now in one wide grin.

"Aye. But oh, Simon, don't let on. Now don't say a word 'cos once that got about, God help her. Well, I mean if it was anybody else they could dance until their toes wore down to their knees, but she's the parson's wife and as ignorant, so I hear, poor dear, of how to be a parson's wife as I am to be the lady of the manor." Now she was laughing. Her two forearms underneath her flagging breasts, she rocked backward and forward for a moment, and the tears were spurting from her eyes as she asked, "Have you seen her?"

"Yes, oh yes; she's there sitting in the front pew every Sunday and that front pew hasn't seen anything so pretty for many a year, I can tell you."

"Is she bonny then?"

He put his head on one side, then thought for a moment before answering. "Aye," he said, "she's more than bonny. But she's not beautiful. What she's got is an air about her, she's alive. . . . Aye, that's the word. Now that's funny"—he wagged his finger now at Annie—"she's got the same quality about her as Tilly has."

"Like our Tilly? And her a parson's wife! Aw no!"

This had come from the bed, and Simon turned to the old man and said, "Aye, William, it's a kind of glowing quality, spritey. Aw, I'm not the one for words, I can only say she looks alive."

"Well"—William nodded his head slowly—"all I can say is, if she looks and acts like Tilly she shouldn't have married a parson."

"Oh, I don't know, William, Parson Ross had a pretty thin time with the other one. She'd have frightened the devil in hell, she would, and did sometimes I think. But I must confess I meself have wondered if he's been wise with his second choice. She comes from quite a family I hear. Oh yes, quite a family. Got a cousin or some such in the new young queen's household, high up at that, so they say. I'm also told that both families were neighbors years ago, away in Dorset. He was the youngest of seven boys, and thereby thrown into the church. Anyway, I can tell you this, she's made a different fellow out of him. He's not so much blood and thunder these days, more love thy neighbor. You know what I mean? An' you know something more? She never takes her eyes off him all the time he's preaching. I've watched her. But on the other hand he never looks at her. He daren't. . . . I think the fellow's in love." He threw his head back and laughed, but it was a self-conscious laugh.

Annie stood looking at him, her face straight; then she said, "But about this dancing. It's the last thing on God's earth I would have thought our Tilly would have wanted to do, 'cos as you know she's only happy when she's got a saw in her hand or an axe. She can get through a log better than I ever could, an' she's dug every inch of that ground out there as well as William ever did. She's always wanted to do the things that a lad would want to do, an' it's worried me. But I think it's gona worry me more now that she wants to dance."

"She's a girl, Annie." Simon's face, too, was straight now. "And she might grow into a bonny one I've been thinking."

"Aw, I doubt it; she hasn't a bit of figure to her frame. Comin' up sixteen, she should be developin', but look at her! Like a yard of pump water, as straight as a die."

"There's plenty of time . . . and some fellows like them thin." He was smiling now, but Annie shook her head at him as she said, "I've yet to meet one. Nobody buys a cow with its ribs sticking through if there's a fat one aside it."

"She's no cow and don't you refer to her as such, Annie Trotter!"

Annie turned her face sharply toward the bed and cried, "An' don't you bark at me, William Trotter, else I'll give you what for! I've got you where I want you. You'll keep a civil tongue in your head." She now bounced her head at him before turning and winking at Simon; then glancing toward the window, she said, "There she comes over the top."

Simon now bent his back and looked out of the small window away toward the mound and to where a young girl was leaping down the hill as a wild goat might. Of a sudden she came to a stop, and the reason was evident for there emerged from behind a clump of gorse the figure of a young man.

"Who's that with her? Can you see, Simon?"

Simon made no reply but he narrowed his eyes, and it wasn't until the two figures were half-way down the lower part of the hill that he said, "McGrath. Hal McGrath."

"Oh no! Him again?" Annie straightened her back, and as she did so Simon turned from the window and put his hand into his pocket; he drew out a sovereign and, handing it to her, said, "Better take it afore she comes."

"Oh thanks, Simon. Thanks." She nodded up at him.

He stared at her for a moment, bit on his lip, then said, "What do you think he's after? Do you think he's got his eye on her, or is it the other thing?"

"Hopes to kill two birds with one stone I should say." They both looked toward the bed. "He's been around here every Sunday for months past."

Simon looked at Annie again and his voice came from deep in his throat as he muttered, "He won't give up, will he?"

"Not while there's a breath in him, if I know anything about Hal McGrath. He's his father over again, an' his father afore him."

"Does she ask any questions, I mean about . . . ?" He pointed toward her hand that was now clutching the sovereign against her breast, and she blinked her eyes and looked away for a moment before she said, "A year or so ago she asked where we got the money from to buy the flour, meat and such. She provides our other needs from the garden and, as you know, she has done since William took to his bed, so I . . . I had to give her some sort of an answer. I said it was money you borrowed from us some years ago. Well, not you, your father."

"That was as good as anything. Did she believe you?"

"It seemed to satisfy her. I remember she said, 'I like people who pay their debts.'"

"Huh! debts." He turned again toward the window and, once more bending his back, he said, "She's left him; she's running like a hare and he's standing like a stook."

When a few minutes later the cottage door burst open it was as if a fresh wind had suddenly blown into the room. Tilly Trotter was tall for her age, being now five foot five and a half inches. She was wearing a faded cotton dress and it hung straight from her shoulders to the uppers of her thick boots, and nowhere was there an undulation. Her neck was long and tinted brown with wind and weather, as was her face; yet here there was a flush of pink to the tint of her high cheekbones. Her eyes, now bright and laughing, looked as if they had taken up the color of her skin, the only difference being that the brown of her skin was matt while the brown of her eyes was clear and deep. Her hair was dark, darker than brown and thick, and it should at her age have been either piled high on the top of her head or in a decorous knot at the back, but it was hanging in two long plaits tied at the back of her neck with what at one time had been a piece of blue ribbon and joined at the ends with a similar piece. Her mouth, full-lipped, was now wide with welcome as she gabbled breathlessly, "Hello, Simon." Then without pause she said, "Why didn't you come and rescue me? Do you know who I've just been accosted by, an' that's the word, accosted, which means waylaid?" She now nodded toward the bed. "That Hal McGrath's been at me again. You'd never guess, not in a month of Sundays, what he's just asked." She now dropped with a flop on to a wooden chair by the side of the long bare wooden table that was placed in the middle of the room; then leaning her head back on her shoulders, she looked up toward the low ceiling and pulled her nose down as if in an effort to meet her chin before she brought out, "He wants to court me. Him, Hal McGrath! And you know what I told him?" She rolled her eyes from one to the other. "I told him I'd sooner walk out with one of Tillson's pigs. I did! I did!" She was now laughing loudly.

"Court you!" Sitting straight up in the bed and his voice a loud growl now, William repeated, "Court you!"

"Yes, Granda, that's what he said. He wanted to court me because he thought—" The laughter slid from her face, her voice dropped as she lowered her chin on to her chest, and she ended shyly, "He said I . . . I was ready for it . . . courtin'."

"That bloody gormless clot!"

Annie was now bending over the bed pressing her husband down into the pillows, saying soothingly, "There now! There now! Don't frash yourself. Didn't you hear what she said? She'd sooner walk out with one of Tillson's pigs. There now. There now. Settle down, settle down."

Simon now stood pulling on his coat; his face was set and stiff, and when he fastened the last button he looked down on Tilly where she was still sitting at the table, her hands clasped on it in front of her now, and he said, "Keep clear of him, Tilly."

She looked back at him and, her voice as sober as his, she said, "Oh, I keep clear of him, Simon, I dodge him whenever I can, but he's been around here a lot lately—"

Annie's voice cut in on her now, saying, "Go and get me some water, we're nearly run dry."

Tilly got up immediately from the table but stopped in front of Simon and said, "Ta-rah, Simon," and he answered, "Ta-rah, Tilly"; then moving his head to take in both the old man and woman he brought out on an embarrassed laugh, "I came over with me news today but here I am on the point of going and never spilled it. . . . I'm going to be married."

"*Married? No!*" Annie moved two steps toward him, then stopped; William sat up in the bed again but said nothing; and Tilly looked up into his face and after a moment asked quietly, "Who you marryin', Simon?"

"Mary . . . Mary Forster. You wouldn't know her, she's not from this part, she's from over beyond Felling way."

"So far away from your farm!" It was Annie speaking again, and he turned his head to her and said, "Oh, it's only five miles or so and you know what they say, a warm heart and a galloping horse can jump that."

"When is it gona be, Simon?"

He was again looking at Tilly. "We're calling the banns next Sunday," he said.

"Oh!" She nodded her head and smiled faintly, and there was silence in the room until he broke it with a laugh, and his voice was loud now as he bent toward her, saying, "And you can come and dance at me wedding."

"Yes." She nodded at him now, answering his smile. "I'll come and dance at your wedding, Simon."

"But don't bring the parson's wife with you." He had

spoken in a mock whisper and he shot his glance toward the two old people before letting his eyes rest on her again; and she too glanced sharply toward her grandparents before she said soberly, "Don't say nothing about that, will you, Simon, because the Reverend doesn't like her to dance, I mean Mrs. Ross."

"Oh, your secret's safe with me." He had bent forward until his laughing face was on a level with hers, but as he looked into her eyes the smile slid from it, and when he straightened up his voice was hearty and loud once more as he cried, "Well now! I must be off, cows can tell the time better than me."

"Have you still got Randy?"

He turned to Annie, saying as he made for the door, "Oh yes, yes; but he's so damned lazy, he falls asleep with his head in their ribs and his slobbers almost dripping into the milk. But young Bill and Ally are good lads, they'll come on with the years. Oh, by the way." He turned and directed his gaze now toward William, saying, "I forgot to tell you, you'll never guess who applied to me for a job. He did it on the quiet like, on the side—he'd have to of course—Big McGrath's youngest, Steve, the fourteen-year-old you know. He waylaid me one night last week and asked if there would be any chance. I had to laugh at him. I said, 'Does your da know you're asking to be set on?' but he only shook his head. And then I said to him soberly like, 'It's no use, lad. I'd set you on the morrow because you look strong and fit, but you know what would happen; your da would come after you and haul you out. You are all in the pit, and for good.'

"And you know what he answered to that?" He looked from one to the other now. "He just said, 'Not me, not me for good, I'm getting out,' and turned on his heels. It's funny, that young 'un isn't like any of the others, he's not like a McGrath at all; not as we know McGraths, eh, William?"

"All McGraths are the same beneath the skin, Simon. Never trust a McGrath."

"Perhaps you're right. Keep rested now." He nodded toward the old man, and William said, "Aye. Aye."

"Ta-rah for now," he said, his glance taking them all in, then went out, closing the door behind him.

Annie was the first to move. She went toward the open fireplace where the kale pot was hanging from a spit and, reaching up to the mantlepiece above it, she took down a wooden tea caddy and placed the sovereign gently in the bottom of it; then replacing the caddy, she turned and, looking at Tilly, said, "I thought I told you to go for water."

"You only said that to get me out of the room, Gran; the butt's half full outside, you know it is. What's it you don't want me to hear?"

"Now don't you be perky, miss."

"I'm not being perky, Gran." Tilly walked toward the table, then around it to the side that faced the fire and her grandmother who was now opposite to her, and her grandfather who lay in the bed to the left of her, and, looking from one to the other, she said, "You're always tellin' me I'm comin' up sixteen and that I should act like a young woman, yet there's things you keep from me an' always have done. Like the sovereign up there that Simon brings every month. And did you know he was gona be married? Did it come as big a surprise to you as you let on it was?"

"Of course it was a surprise to me, an' to your granda there." Annie's voice was harsh now. "It's the first breath of it we've heard. We never knew he was even courtin', did we, William?" She turned and looked toward the bed, and William shook his head slowly and looked at Tilly as he said, "No, girl, it was news to us. Now if it had been Rose Benton, or that Fanny Hutchinson, yes, her who's been after him for years, I could have understood it, but I've never heard of this one. What did he say her name was?"

"Mary Forster."

They both looked from under their lids at Tilly, and after a moment Annie, too, said, "Mary Forster." Then shaking her head, she added, "Never heard one of any such name."

"Well, that's explained that!" The tone of Tilly's voice was such that her grandparents gaped at her in surprise as she went on, "But about the other thing." She nodded her head toward the tea caddy. "And don't tell me again that Simon's paying back some money he's owin' you. I could never imagine you havin' that much to lend him that it would take all those years for him to clear his debt, so what's it all about? I'm entitled to know. . . ."

William now began to cough, a racking tormented cough, and Annie, going to him quickly, brought him up on the pillows and thumped his back and as she was doing it she turned her head toward Tilly and cried, "See what your niggling pestering's done! It's days since he had a turn. Scald some honey and bring it here, sharp! . . . You an' your entitled to know. Huh!"

Tilly, her whole attitude changed now, ran toward an oak dresser at the far end of the room and, taking a jar from it, she quickly returned to the table and scooped out two spoonfuls of honey into a mug; she then went to the fire and after dipping the mug quickly into the kale pot of simmering water she stirred the contents with a small wooden spoon, before going to the bed and handing the mug to her grandmother.

Between gasps the old man sipped at the hot honeyed water; then lay back on his pillows, his chest heaving like bellows all the while.

Tilly stood by the bed, her expression contrite and her voice equally so as she said, "I'm sorry, Granda. I'm sorry if I've upset you."

17

"No, no"—he took hold of her hand—"you'd never upset me, me dear. You're a good girl; you always have been, and I'll tell you something else . . . when I can get me breath." He pulled at the air for some seconds; then smiling at her, he said, "You've been the joy of me life since you came into it."

"Oh, Granda!" She bent now and laid her face against his hairy cheek and there was a break in her voice as she again said, "Oh, Granda!"

Then the emotion and sentiment was shattered by her grandmother's level tone, saying now, "I didn't want water but I did want wood an' I'll have to have it, that's if you two want a meal the night."

Tilly moved from the bed and as she passed her grandmother the old woman turned toward her and they exchanged glances that held no resentment on either side.

At the back of the cottage, a roughly paved open yard was bordered on one side by two outhouses: one had been a stable and the other a harness-room. The harness-room was now used for storing vegetables and the stable for the storage of wood. Outside the stable there was a sawing cradle and on it lay a thick branch of a tree that she had brought down from the wood only that morning. She put her hand on it and, turning her body half around, leaned against the cradle and looked across the paddock and beyond to where the land dropped far away before rising again to the woods that edged the Sopwith estate; and for once, looking over the landscape, she didn't think consciously, by! it's bonny, because she was feeling slightly sick inside.

Simon was going to be married. She was still under the shock of the announcement; she had never imagined Simon getting married. But why hadn't she imagined it?-A good-looking strapping farmer like him with his kindness and sense of fun. She had loved him for so many things, but mostly for his kindness and sense of fun.

18

She could remember the very first day she had seen him, it was the day her mother had brought her to this cottage. She was five years old. She could remember what she was dressed in, a black serge dress and a short black coat and bonnet; she was wearing black because her father had fallen over a steep cliff in Shields and was drowned. Her granda took off her coat and sat her on a chair; then together with her grandmother, he helped to get her mother up the steep stairs and to the bedroom because her mother was sick.

She was sitting by the fire when the door opened and a man and boy entered, and the boy came over to her and said, "And who are you when you're out?" And he laughed down on her; but she didn't laugh back, she began to cry and he said, "There now. There now," and brought a barley sugar from his pocket and gave it to her.

And when her granda came down the stairs he and the man talked. It was on that day too that she first heard the name McGrath spoken, and also a swear word, for the man said, "Bugger me eyes that for a tale, your Fred to fall over a cliff!"

The boy then asked her name, and when she told him "Tilly," he said, "Tilly Trotter! Now that's a daft name, Tilly Trotter." And she remembered her grandfather shouting at the boy, saying, "Don't you call the child daft, Simon! Her name's Matilda," and the man said to the boy, "Get outside! I'll deal with you later. It's you that's daft."

But the boy didn't go outside. She could see him now standing straight and looking at her grandfather and his father and saying, "I heard tell Mr. McGrath was there waiting for the boat an' all, he wasn't on his shift, he had slipped it. Bill Nelson heard his father talking." And at that the two men came up to the boy, and somehow the boy no longer seemed a boy but a man.

From that time she had always looked upon Simon as a man and someone who belonged to her. But he was no longer hers. She felt a desire to cry, and the desire was strange for she rarely cried. She'd had nothing in her life to make her cry, her days had been free, happy, and filled with love; moreover she hadn't been sent into service, or into the fields—or yet down the mine.

She was seven when her mother died, and she had scarcely missed her for the two people back in that room had wrapped her around with loving care from that day until this moment, and she had tried to repay them not only with love but with work. Even so, she knew that they could not have survived these past few years since her grandfather had taken to his bed had it not been for that monthly sovereign.

But why? Why did Simon feel bound to bring that money? He must do, for to her knowledge he had never missed a month during the last six years. And before that he had accompanied his father on similar missions. There was something here she couldn't understand. And look what happened when she probed, it forced her grandfather to have a turn.

Would Simon's wife probe? She could give herself no answer.

She turned quickly about and went into the stable and, picking up a straw skip, she flung in small logs; then, scooping up handfuls of chips from a wooden bin, she threw these with equal force on top of the logs. With a heave she lifted up the weighty skip and with her arms stretched wide gripping it she went toward the back door. Here, she pressed the basket against the stanchion and, her head turned over her shoulder, she once again looked at the wide landscape, but now as if saying good-bye to it, for there had come over her a foreboding feeling as if she had suddenly stepped out of one life into another, and she felt that never again would she know the lightness of spirit that had caused her to run down the hills, or skip the burns like a deer; nor yet sit in the moonlight on the knoll and let the day seep from her and the night enter into a silent patch that lay deep within her and from which there oozed understanding—understanding which in turn she could not understand, for she had not as yet served her time in tribulations. But in this moment she sensed that that time was not far ahead.

As she pushed open the door and went through the scullery her mind skipped back a step into the long childhood she had just left and she said to herself, "Perhaps if my breasts had developed more he would have noticed me."

2

Simon stood with his back against the farm gate and looked up at his landlord, Mr. Mark Sopwith, and he returned the smile of the older man, nodding as he said, "'Tis true, 'tis true; tomorrow as ever was I let the halter be put about me neck." He turned now and nodded toward the head of the horse, and Mark Sopwith, laughing too, said, "There's many a worse situation; it all depends on the temper of the rider."

"Oh, I know the temper of the rider; I can manage the rider."

"Oh well!" Mark Sopwith now pursed his lips and made a slow movement with his head from shoulder to shoulder. "You can't wear the halter and be the rider, that's an utter impossibility."

"You're right there. You're right there." Simon jerked his chin upward now, and the action spoke against himself and he said, "I've always been one to have me cake and eat it. By the way, sir, may I ask, is it true what I'm hearin'?"

"It all depends, rumors always have a spice of truth

in them." Mark Sopwith's face was straight now. "What have you been hearing?"

"Well—" Simon now kicked at a pebble in the road so raising a cloud of dust, and he watched the pebble skitting away over the surface before looking straight up into Mark Sopwith's face and adding, "They're saying the mine's all but finished since the water's come in."

Mark Sopwith did not answer but he stared down at Simon, then presently said, "There's such things as pumps. The water did come in, but it's gone. And you can set another rumor around; my mine isn't finished, nor likely to be."

"I'm glad of that, sir, I really am."

"Thank you. Ah well!" The stiffness went out of his face and tone again as he said, "I must be off now, but you have my best wishes for a happy life after tomorrow."

"Thank you, sir."

Mark Sopwith was just about to press his knees into the horse's flanks when his action was checked by the sight of a rider coming around the bend in the road a few yards ahead. The rider was a girl—no woman, and she sat her mount as if molded to it. A few trotting steps of the horse and she was abreast of them, and she drew the beast to a stop and looked at them, and both men returned her look, their eyes wide with interest.

"Good-morning."

"Good-morning, ma'am." They both answered her almost simultaneously. Mark Sopwith raised his hat but Simon, hatless, didn't put his fingers to his forehead.

"I'm speaking to Mr. Sopwith?" She was looking directly at Mark now and he inclined his head and said, "That's so, ma'am."

"I'm Lady Myton."

"Oh, how do you do? I'm . . . I'm sorry I haven't been able to call on you yet, I . . ."

The lady now smiled, then gave a chuckling laugh as she said, "I've called on you just this very morning but I was told that you were out and that your wife was indisposed."

Simon, standing straight, stared from one to the other of the riders. He noted that Mr. Sopwith's face had lost its sallowness and was now a warm pink; he also noted that the lady was amused. He had heard that a lordship had taken over Dean House and that he was an oldish fellow with a young wife. Well, from what he could see she wasn't all that young, nearing thirty he would say, but by! she had a figure on her; and the boldness in those eyes was what one would expect to see in the face of some wench sloshing out the beer in an inn.

With almost a start he realized her eyes were being leveled on him and the head was being held inquiringly to one side, and he also knew that his landlord was being put to a little disadvantage wondering whether or not he should introduce him. He felt his spine stiffening a little, and the action became registered in his expression as he looked up at his landlord.

"This is Farmer Bentwood, a tenant of mine."

She was again looking at Mark Sopwith, and it was a number of seconds before she inclined her head toward Simon, but he still didn't, as he should have done, raise his hand to his forehead and say, "Good-day, me lady," but returned her the same salute, inclining his head just the slightest, which action seemed to annoy Mr. Sopwith for, backing his horse, a maneuver which caused Simon to skip to one side, he brought its head around in the same direction as that of Lady Myton's mount and now level with her and, his knee almost touching her skirt, he said, "Have you any destination in view or are you just out for a canter?"

"I'm just out for a canter." She accompanied her words with a deep obeisance of her head.

"Then perhaps you'll do me the honor of riding with me back to the house and there make the acquaintance of my wife?"

"Surely."

As they both started their horses Mark Sopwith turned and looked down on Simon, saying, "Good-bye, Bentwood, and a merry wedding tomorrow."

At this Lady Myton pulled up her horse and twisted around in the saddle. "You're going to be married tomorrow?"

He paused before he said quietly, "Yes, me lady."

"Well, may I too wish you a merry wedding, Mr. . . . Farmer . . . what did you say your name was?"

"Bentwood, Simon Bentwood." He stressed his name. His face was straight, but hers was wide and laughing as she repeated, "Simon Bentwood. Well, again I say a merry wedding, Farmer Simon Bentwood," and on this she spurred the horse sharply forward, leaving Mark Sopwith to follow behind her; that was until they reached the end of the winding road, for there he shouted, "Turn right here on to the bridle-path." He himself now took the lead, putting his horse into a gallop and then knowing a feeling of satisfaction and of not a little amusement that though she was close on his tail she would, he guessed, even from this short acquaintance, be annoyed that she couldn't pass him and show off her horsemanship because he had recognized at once she was one of those women who once seated on a horse would go hell for leather over walls, ditches, fences . . . and over farmlands. Yes, they were no respecters of farmlands. Likely, that was what Bentwood had recognized in her that had made him act out of place, because his manner had not been respectful.

When the path eventually widened out he drew his horse to a walk and as she came abreast of him he looked at her, but she gave him no indication of annoyance. She was looking away to the right, down toward a cottage, and she remarked, "That's a pretty cottage and a well-tended garden. That's something I've noticed in the short time I've been here"—she glanced at him now—"the cottages have very untidy gardens; some with a few vegetables, nothing pretty."

"That's the Trotters' place. It's within the boundary of my land. Old man and woman Trotter live there. It's their young granddaughter who keeps the place tidy. There she is now coming up from the burn. She does the work of a man. She can fell a tree as good as the next; she's got one of my copses as clean as a whistle."

"You allow her to saw your trees down?"

"No, only limb so far up; it's good for them."

As they drew nearer the cottage the girl came closer into view, and Lady Myton said, "She looks very young, rather fragile."

"Oh, I shouldn't judge her on her thinness, she's as strong as a young colt."

When the girl saw them she didn't stop but went on toward the back of the cottage, carrying the two wooden buckets full of water, and as they passed the paddock Lady Myton said, "So this is all part of your estate?"

"Yes, what's left of it." There was a wry smile on his face as he said, "Half our land was sold to enhance your property about fifty years ago."

"You must have been very short of money."

"We were."

"And now?"

"Things haven't altered very much."

"But you have a mine?"

"Yes."

"Doesn't that make money?"

He sighed. "The only way mines seem to make money is if you go abroad or live in London and leave them to managers. If you stay at home and look after the people's interests you lose all along the line."

"The Rosiers, I understand, do very well."

25

His face became straight. He leveled his glance now toward his hand that was gripping the reins as he muttered, "Ruthless people generally do . . . do very well."

There was silence between them for a moment. They reined the horses away from each other to avoid a deep pothole in the road and when they came together again she said, "You sound as if you don't care for the Rosiers, why?"

It was on the point of his tongue to say, "Whether I care for them or not, madam, is no business of yours," for of a sudden he was realizing that he hadn't been in the company of this woman for half an hour and she was questioning him as any close friend might. But when he turned and looked at the expression in those large deep blue eyes it wiped away any sting with which he might have threaded his next words. "You're a most inquisitive lady," he said.

Her answer was to put her head back and let out what he considered a most unladylike laugh, and, her eyes twinkling now, she looked at him and said, "You know some people are with me a full day before they realize what a very nosy person I am."

He was now laughing with her, but his was a gentle chuckle, and as he kept his eyes on her he felt a stirring in his blood that he had never imagined he would experience again, for here he was, forty-two years old, with a son of twenty by his first wife, three sons and a daughter by his second, and she in decline, a mortgage on his estate that was choking him, a mine that was barely meeting his men's wages, and a household that was in chaos because it had no controlling hand. He had imagined there was no space left in him wherein was harbored a remnant of the emotions of youth; desire of the body yes, but not the excitement with which it had first made itself known. It was in this moment as if the spring of his manhood had just burst through the earth.

26

When she now suddenly put her horse into a gallop and they entered another bridle-path that led toward the back drive, which in its turn led toward his house, he allowed her to take the lead.

At the beginning of the nineteenth century the account books showed Highfield Manor's staff amounted to thirty-two people in all; this included six gardeners and four in the stable yard. Today the account books named only thirteen on the staff, which numbered a coachman and three gardeners but did not take into account Mr. Burgess, the tutor, and Miss Mabel Venner Price, who was Mrs. Sopwith's companion-maid.

The depletion of the staff showed itself not only in the ornamental gardens that surrounded the house but in the house itself. Mr. Pike, the butler, who had been with the family for sixty years no longer appeared in the hall whenever Robert Simes, the footman, answered the doorbell, for he was mostly otherwise engaged doing, as he mournfully stated, the work of lesser men; nor did Mrs. Lucas, the housekeeper, make her appearance from nowhere, as her predecessor would have done, to greet her master. When Mrs. Lucas appeared it was usually to say in her own stiff, polite, guarded way that she could get no help from the mistress or that she herself couldn't be expected to run an establishment like this on such a depleted staff; or, would he order Mr. Burgess, the tutor, to come down to the staff room for his meals? It would be one less to take up to the nursery floor. But generally when she waylaid him it was to complain about the children: they were entirely out of hand; the nursemaid had no control over them, nor for that matter had the tutor. Would he speak to Master Matthew because where Matthew went the others followed?

Of late, Mark had dreaded entering the house because from the ground floor to the top he was met with complaints. He looked back with deep nostalgia to the time when in London, or abroad, or even at the mine, all he longed for was to get back to his home. Now at the mine, all he wanted was to get away from it; and the same feeling was in him with regard to his home.

He stood aside and opened the door to allow his elegant visitor to enter the hall, and as he did so he looked about him. Then calling across to where the footman was disappearing into the dining-room, he shouted, "Simes!" and when the man turned and walked toward them across the marble-tiled floor he pointed to Lady Myton who was holding out her riding crop and gloves, then asked, "Your mistress, is she still in her room?"

The man blinked once before he answered, "Yes, master," and Mark knew he could have added, "Does she ever leave it?"

"Will you come this way?" He now led the visitor across the wide hall and up the broad faded red-carpeted staircase and on to a wide gallery, also carpeted in the same fading red, and of which the walls were almost obliterated by ornately framed paintings, mostly portraits. He glanced at her as they crossed the gallery and there was a twinkle in his eye as he noted the fact that she wasn't, as was usual, carrying the train of her riding habit over her arm, but was allowing it to trail the floor. She was determined to be different, this lady.

He was about to lead the way down a long corridor when a succession of high squeals caused them both to look toward the far end from where a staircase led upward; and now scampering down it and into their sight came three children. Two were boys, the third, a smaller girl. It was she who was screaming the loudest, and apparently she had cause to, for from the top of her head streaming down her face and on to her frilled pinafore was a thick blue substance.

"Matthew! Luke! Jessie Ann!"

For a moment he appeared to forget about his

companion and, striding to the children who seemed oblivious of them and who were now making for the main staircase, he brought them to a halt with another loud bellow: "Stop! Stop this minute!"

As if governed by one mind, they skidded to a stop that brought them into a huddle, and the younger of the two boys, Luke, a dark-haired, dark-eyed, mischievous-faced seven-year-old, now flapped his hand wildly in the air to get rid of the blue substance that he had picked up from being in contact with his sister's pinafore.

"What is this? What is the meaning of this? Jessie Ann, what have you done?"

"Oh, Papa. Papa." She came toward him now, but, backing slightly from her, he cried, "Get yourself away! Where is Dewhurst?" He was now speaking to his elder son Matthew and he, endeavoring to keep a straight face, muttered, "In the nursery, Papa, crying."

Mark closed his eyes, then was about to issue another order when Lady Myton's voice, threaded with laughter, broke in. "Somebody's been having a game," she said. She was standing by Mark's side now, bending slightly forward, looking into the three upturned faces, and Jessie Ann stopped her sniveling for a moment when the lady said, "Was it from the top of the door?"

As Jessie Ann nodded slowly the boys shrieked in chorus, "Yes, yes, ma'am! It was for Dewhurst, but she had Jessie Ann alongside her." They remained now staring their admiration at the lady who had been clever enough to guess how Jessie Ann had become covered with the paste.

"I never thought of using paste, I never got beyond water."

The boys now giggled and the small girl sniffed, then screwed up her face and sneezed violently in an effort to rid her nostrils of the paste.

"Get upstairs, all of you! And don't dare leave the floor again until I see you. Understand?"

"Yes, Papa."

"Yes, Papa."

Jessie Ann couldn't make any retort, she was still sneezing, but her brothers, each grabbing an arm, pulled her toward the nursery stairs again and as they did so Mrs. Lucas appeared at the end of the corridor.

Going quickly toward her and his voice seeming to be strained through his narrowed lips, he said, "Mrs. Lucas, will you kindly attend to your duty and contain that commotion upstairs"—he pointed toward the disappearing figures—"and also see that they don't come down on to this floor unless they are escorted. You may remember that we have been over this particular matter before."

Mrs. Lucas, her hands joined at her waist, pressed them into it so causing her already full breasts to push out her black alpaca bodice and puff out a small white apron that appeared like a patch on the front of her wide skirt, and looking straight at her master and ignoring the visitor as if she weren't there, she said, "My various duties take me from one end of the establishment to the other, sir; I cannot spend my time in the nursery. Moreover, there is a nursemaid, and a tutor there."

"I'm well aware of that, Mrs. Lucas"—he endeavored to control the tremble of anger in his voice—"and I was under the impression that the nursemaid at least came into your province. But no more! No more!" He wagged his hand almost in front of her face. "Go up there this moment and restore order!"

The housekeeper stretched her neck out of the narrow white-starched collar that bordered her dress; she inclined her head just the slightest; then with a step that expressed her ruffled indignation, she passed between her master and his guest and went toward the staircase.

Now Mark, turning and walking slowly toward a deep-bayed window in the corridor, stood for a moment with his hand across his eyes; then turning again and looking toward where Lady Myton still stood, he made a helpless gesture with his shoulders and out-stretched hands as he said, "What can I say? I'm . . . I'm very sorry you have had to be subjected to this scene."

"Don't be silly!" She moved toward him and when she stood opposite him she smiled openly into his face as she said, "I've enjoyed every minute of it. It took me back; I used to do the same. I loathe nursemaids, governesses and all their kin. They were always chang-ing my nursemaids. I led them a hell of a life."

He was looking into her eyes and seconds passed before his chest jerked and there came from the back of his throat a low rumbling, and now he was laughing with her. But it was a smothered laughter, and after a moment, still looking at her, he said softly, "You're a very refreshing person. But I suppose you know that?"

"No, no . . . well, I've never been called refreshing before; it sounds like one of those fizzy drinks. And that takes me back to the nursery too because when I used to belch, and I did often and on purpose"—she nodded her head now—"I had a nurse who used to squeeze a lemon into a glass of water, then put a great dollop of bicarb in, and when it fizzed, which it did straightaway, she used to make me drink it, almost pouring it down my throat. But no, I haven't been referred to as refreshing; exciting yes, enticing yes, amusing yes, and—" she paused, and pursing her lips ended, "and one great lump of a bitch. The last, I may say, is a purely female comment."

He said nothing but continued to gaze at her, with open admiration in his look now, then giving a little huh! of a laugh he took her arm and turned her about and led her further along the corridor, and when he drew her to a stop opposite a gray-painted door he glanced at her for a moment before tapping twice on it with his knuckles.

Having entered the room, he immediately stood aside to allow her to pass him, and he closed the door deliberately before leading her across the room toward the window where, on a chaise-longue, lay his wife.

Eileen Sopwith was thirty-seven years old. She had a fair complexion, gray eyes, a delicate tint of skin, and hair that had once been a very fair blonde but which was now of a mousy hue. She had taken to this couch four years ago, and had not put her foot outside her apartments since. She only moved from the couch to be helped to the water closet and to bed in the adjoining room at night. She passed most of her time reading or doing embroidery—she took great pains in embroidering pinafores and dresses for her daughter—and the most trying moments of her day were when her four children were filed decorously in to greet her. It took only five minutes for them to say their "Good-morning, Mama. How are you, Mama?" and for her to answer them and to add, "Be good children," but even this exhausted her.

The expression on her face rarely altered, mostly showing a patient resignation, as did also her voice. Her visitors were few and far between, and then they were nearly always members of her own family.

So when her husband now ushered into her room the startling looking stranger in a riding habit, her mouth was brought slightly agape and her head up from the satin pillow. For a moment she was on the point of calling, "Mabel! Mabel!" because very few people got past Mabel, but here was her husband leading a woman, a healthy, vigorous striding person, toward her.

She wasn't called upon to speak because Mark was saying, "This is Lady Myton, Eileen. She had called earlier but you weren't quite ready for visitors, so when I came across her on my way home I assured her you would be pleased to see her. They have taken Dean House you know."

As Eileen Sopwith took her eyes from her husband and lowered her head in a slight acknowledgement of the visitor, Agnes Myton held out her hand, saying, "I'm delighted to meet you. I had called to bring you an invitation to a little dinner we are putting on next week but perhaps it would be too much for you."

"Yes, yes, I'm afraid it would."

"That's such a pity. You being our nearest neighbors, I had hoped—" she shrugged her shoulders. "Well, what's a dinner party, I can always call."

"Please be seated."

She turned and smiled her thanks at Mark as he pressed a chair under her thick riding skirt and after she was seated there was a moment's silence before, laughing now, she said, "I've made the acquaintance of your charming family."

Eileen Sopwith now turned a quick inquiring glance on her husband and he, smiling down at her, said, "Yes. Yes, they made their presence felt, up to some prank." His head bobbed.

"Have . . . have you any children?"

"No, I'm afraid not. But there's plenty of time, I've only been married just over a year." She ended on a laugh as if she had expressed something amusing.

Eileen Sopwith stared at her visitor but said nothing, while Mark put in quickly, "I suppose you find this part of the country very stale after London. I am, of course, taking it for granted you did live in London?"

"Yes, yes, we had a house there, and another in Warwickshire, but he sold them both up, Billy, you know. His people originally came from this part, so I understand, a hundred years or so ago. He's always wanted to live up here, he says he finds more to do here than in London. He came up at the back end of last year in all that terrible weather just to be here for the Mansion House sale in Newcastle; there were some pieces he wanted for our place you know. Moreover, he's very interested in engineering; and there were some bridges going up at the time. I've forgotten the name of them." She shrugged her shoulders and glanced up at Mark, and he said, "Oh yes, the railway viaducts over the Ouseburn and Willington Dean."

She nodded at him and said, "Yes, those are the places; I can never remember names. . . . The first place he took me to when I came up here was the New Theater at Newcastle, rather splendid, and it was a great evening. I've never laughed so much for a long time, not only at the play but at the people. Really" —she glanced back up at him—"you'll likely get on your provincial high horse when I say this, but I could hardly understand a word any of them said."

When Mark made no immediate reply to this because the word "provincial" had annoyed him somewhat she cried loudly, "There! there! I told you."

"Are . . . are you returning to London soon or are you making this your permanent home?"

The quiet question from the chaise-longue cut in on her laughter and she answered, "Oh no, no, we've just come from there, well, only a fortnight ago. We were to come up much earlier but then the King died and the Queen was proclaimed and Billy had to be there. I think Billy is going to love it here, in fact I'm sure of it, but as yet I cannot speak for myself, except I know I am going to enjoy the riding, the land is so open and wild . . . like the people." She turned her head again and glanced up at Mark and her expression invited contradiction.

It was at this point that the door opened and the companion entered, and her hesitation and the look on her face as she stood with her hand still on the door handle showed her surprise, and also her displeasure.

The latter was immediately evident to Mark, who, bent on mollifying her, put out his hand toward her while looking at Lady Myton, and saying, "This is Miss Mabel Venner Price, my wife's companion, Lady Myton."

The title "lady" seemed to have little effect, for Miss Price's countenance didn't change; her mouth opened, the square chin dropped and she dipped the smallest of curtsies as she said, "Your Ladyship."

Lady Agnes acknowledged the salute by a mere inclining of her head, which gesture reminded Mark of the look she had bestowed on young Bentwood. Apparently she had a manner she kept precisely for menials, and the condescension was, to his mind, overdone.

She was a madam all right, but a very likable madam, oh yes, a very likable madam.

He watched her now making her farewells to Eileen and it was apparent that Eileen had been stirred slightly out of herself by her visitor. Well, that was a good thing an' all. There were times when he had his doubts about his wife's malaise, yet both Doctor Kemp and Doctor Fellows had said she must have no more children, something to do with her womb; and the man he had brought down from Edinburgh had gone further, stating that the pain she had in the sides of her stomach was from her ovaries and that there was really no cure unless nature took a hand and settled things internally, which it often did. Well, nature was a long time in taking a hand and he had asked himself often of late, would he know when it had? He missed the warmth of her body—she no longer allowed him to lie beside her at night. When he explained he could love her without taking her she had been shocked.

How was it, he wondered, that the common woman managed to carry on. There were women in his mine crawling on their hands and knees, pulling and shoving bogies full of coal less than a week after giving birth. Often when he had gone down the mine with the manager they had come across couples sporting and more in a side roadway on the bare rock earth, and while Yarrow scattered them, crying, "I'll cuddle you! Begod, I'll cuddle you!" he himself had been filled with envy. He often thought about the word "cuddle." It was a beautiful word, warm in itself.

"Shall we be going then?"

"Oh yes, yes."

He hadn't been conscious of staring at her all the while he had been thinking, but he was now conscious of his wife's eyes being tight on him as he turned to her and said, "I'll be up shortly."

When Mabel Price opened the door for them he smiled at her but her cheeks made no answering movement.

They had reached the main hall before they spoke again. Looking at her, he said, "I feel very embarrassed, you have been offered no refreshment whatever," and she put out her hand and gently tapped his sleeve with two fingers as she said, "Please don't apologize, there is nothing to apologize for. The visit itself has been refreshment enough." Then her head on one side, she asked, "Can I depend upon you coming to dinner a fortnight tonight?"

There was the slightest pause before he answered, "Most certainly. I shall be pleased to."

Their eyes held for a moment longer, then she turned about, walked toward the door where the footman was now standing with her crop and gloves, and taking them from him as if she had picked them up from a hallstand she went out and on to the broad terrace, then walked down the three shallow steps on to the grass spattered gravel and to where Fred Leyburn, the coachman-cum-groom-cum-handyman was holding her horse.

Mark himself helped her up into the saddle; then taking the reins from the coachman, he dismissed him with a lift of his head, and handing the reins up to her, he said, "Until today fortnight then," and she, looking down at him, her face unsmiling now but her gaze steady, replied, "Until today fortnight . . . if not before." With that, she spurred her horse and was gone galloping along the drive, and he stood and watched her until she disappeared from his sight before turning and running up the steps and into the house again.

At the bottom of the main staircase he paused a moment, his fingers pressed on his lower lip. He knew he should go straight to the nursery, take Matthew's breeches down and thrash him—he had promised him that the very next time he played a dirty prank on Dewhurst he would lather him—but were he to do so there would likely be screaming, and when the sound reached Eileen, as it surely would because Matthew had a great pair of lungs on him, she would either have one of her real bad turns or punish him with her weapon of hurt silence for the next few days.

Running once more, he took the stairs two at a time. He was panting when he reached the gallery and as he drew himself to a walk he asked himself why the hurry.

When he entered his wife's bedroom again, Mabel Price was adjusting a light silk cover over her mistress's knees and she turned an unsmiling face toward her master before walking past him and leaving the room.

"What's the matter with her?" Mark looked toward the closed door.

"She didn't like your visitor."

"My visitor! She came to see you."

Eileen Sopwith ignored this remark and went on, "She has heard rumors."

"Yes, yes, I bet she has. If there's any rumors to be sifted out our dear Miss Price will be the first down the hole."

"You mustn't talk like that about her, Mark, she's a very good friend to me, quite indispensable."

"And does that allow her to be rude to guests?"

"Lady Myton wasn't a guest, Mark, she came here uninvited."

"She came here as a neighbor, hoping, I think, for a neighborly response. She likely wants to make friends."

"By what I hear she's quite adept at making friends."

He stood looking down at his wife while she

37

smoothed out a fine lawn handkerchief with her forefinger and thumb. "Did you know she'd been married before?"

"No, I didn't. . . . But you knew I'd been married before"—he now leaned toward her—"didn't you, Eileen, and that didn't stamp me as a villain."

"It is different with a woman, and I'm not blaming her for being married before, but I do now understand the reason why they came here in rather a hurry. Her name was coupled with that of a certain gentleman in London, and her husband was for thrashing him."

He screwed up his face now as he said, "You've learned all this in the last few minutes, and may I ask where Price got her information?"

"Yes, you may ask, Mark, that is if you don't shout." There was a pause now while she stared at him before continuing, "It should happen that their coachman is a distant relation to Simes, second cousin or some such."

"Really!"

"Yes, really."

His head took on its bobbing motion as it was apt to do when he was angry or annoyed, and he said, "I suppose Lord Myton challenged some young fellow to a duel because he admired his wife? . . . Oh!"—he flung one arm wide—"why do you listen to such clap-trap, Eileen? Myton, I understand, is well into his sixties and past thrashing anyone or anything, even his dogs." He sighed, then said quietly, "Why do you listen to Price?"

He watched her lips quiver and when she brought out in a thin piping voice, "I have no one else to listen to, you spare me very little of your time these days," he dropped down on to the edge of the couch and, taking her hands in his, he said patiently, "I've told you, Eileen, I can't be in two or three places at once, I'm up to my neck at the mine. There was a time when I could leave everything to Yarrow but not any more, things are critical. Come on, smile." He cupped her chin in his hand, then said brightly, "You'll never guess who is being married tomorrow. . . . Young Bentwood, the farmer, you know."

"Really!" She smiled faintly at him and nodded her head as she repeated, "Young Bentwood. Dear! Dear! I haven't seen him for years. He . . . he was quite a presentable young man."

"Oh, he's that all right. A bit cocky, knows his own value, but he's a good farmer. He's made a better job of that place than his father did."

"Do you know whom he's marrying?"

"A girl, I think." He laughed and wagged her hand now, and she turned her face from him, saying, "Oh, Mark!"

"No, I don't really know anything about her."

"Do you think we should make them a present?"

"A present? Yes, I suppose so. But what?"

"Yes, what?" She put her head back on the pillow and thought for a moment, then said, "A little silver, a little silver milk jug or sugar basin. There's a lot in the cabinets downstairs, one piece would never be missed."

"No, you're right, and it's a nice gesture." He moved his head down toward her and kissed her lightly on the cheek, then repeated, "A nice gesture, very thoughtful. When I come back later I'll bring some pieces up and you can choose."

"Yes, do that. Oh, by the way, Mark"—she put out her hand to him now in a gentle pleading gesture as he moved from the bed—"Go up to the nursery and speak to Matthew but please, please, be gentle. I know he's been naughty. Mabel tells me she went up and remonstrated with him. He's upset Dewhurst again. But the girl is weak, she has no control over the children. I . . . I don't know what's going to be done."

He turned fully about now and in a manner that swept away his easy-going kindliness of the moment before, he said, "I know what should be done, I've known what should be done for some time, and we'll have to talk about this, Eileen. That boy should be sent away to school."

"No, no, I won't have it, I've told you. I won't even discuss it. And . . . and anyway, boarding schools cost money and you're continually telling me that the household expenses must be cut down. No, no, I won't have it. Leave me. Please leave me."

He left her with her hands thrashing the top of the silk coverlet, but he did not go up to the nursery. Running down the stairs once more, but his haste now conditioned by acute irritation, he burst out of the house, hurried across the courtyard and to the stables, and within minutes he was mounted and riding now toward the mine.

He couldn't understand the woman, he couldn't. She could only bear to see the children for a few minutes each day, yet the very mention of sending them away to school upset her. . . . No, no; he just couldn't understand the woman. Or any woman for that matter. Lady Myton who seemed to see life as a joke, or perhaps more accurately as a stage on which to play out her affairs and the cuckolding of her husband. Women were enigmas, and botheration, the lot of them.

3

"Aye, you do look bonny. Doesn't she, William?"

"Aye. Aye, she'll pass."

They both looked smilingly at Tilly standing straight but with head slightly bowed.

"You should have gone to the church. Shouldn't she, William?"

"Yes, I should have thought you would have liked to see Simon wed because there's no one been kinder to you since you first set foot in this house."

"No, you're right there, William," Annie put in, nodding her head. "An' you would have got a ride in one of the brakes, both there and back. An' that treat doesn't come upon you every day, now does it? And I'm sure Simon would be puzzled and a bit hurt likely. I wish I'd had the chance, I do, I do."

Tilly's chin drooped a little further toward her chest. She knew that they were both staring at her waiting for an explanation which she had refused to voice over the past days because she could not say to them, "I couldn't bear to see him married," but she knew she had to say something, so what she said, and in a mumble, was, "It's me frock."

"Your frock!" They voiced the words, one after the other. "What's wrong with your frock? You look as fresh as a sprig in it."

"Aw, Gran!" She had lifted her head now and also had caught hold of the skirt of the dress at each side pulling it to its full width as she exclaimed somewhat reproachfully, "It's washed out! It's been turned up and turned down so many times it's got dizzy an' doesn't know if it's comin' or goin'."

At this there was silence for a moment. Then as William eased himself from his elbow and lay back on his pillows and let out a deep grunt of a chuckle, Annie put her fingers across her mouth while Tilly, her head once again drooping, joined her smothered laughter to theirs.

As she had said, her dress was washed out. Its original color of deep pink was only to be seen now under the ten rows of pintucks that ran shoulder to shoulder across her flat breast. When it was bought five years ago in the rag market in Newcastle for ninepence, the sleeves had been much too long; even after the cuffs had been turned up twice they still reached her knuckles; as for the gored bell-shaped skirt, its six-inch hem had been turned up another nine inches. There had been no thought at that time of cutting off either the bottom of the dress or the ends of the sleeves because Tilly was sprouting "Like a corn stalk gone mad," as Annie was apt to exclaim almost daily. And so as Tilly grew the dress was lengthened, until the day came when the six-inch hem was reduced to three inches and the dress was now of an embarrassing length reaching only to the top of her boots; in fact she knew she would be indecent if she had been wearing shoes, for her ankles would have been entirely exposed.

"Go on, get yourself off, lass, else you'll be late. The jollification will be over afore you get there. And look—" Annie reached up toward Tilly's bonnet, saying, "Loosen some of your hair, a strand or two to bring over your ears."

"Oh, Gran! I don't like it fluffed around me face."

"I'm not fluffin' it around your face. There"—she patted the two dark brown curls of hair lying now in front of Tilly's ears—"they show up your skin, set if off like."

"Aw, Gran!"

"And stop saying, Aw, Gran! There you are." She turned her about and pushed her toward the door. "Enjoy yourself. Take everything in because we want to hear all about it the morrow. And tell Simon again that we wish him happiness. Tell him we wish him everything that he wishes for himself, and more 'cos he deserves it. Away with you."

Tilly turned in the open doorway and, looking toward the bed, said softly, "Bye-bye, Granda."

"Bye-bye, lass. Keep your back straight, your head up, an' remember you're bonny."

"Now, now, now, don't say, Aw Gran or Granda again, else I'll slap your cheek for you."

One final push from Annie sent Tilly toward the

gate, and there she turned and waved her hand before hurrying along the bridle-path.

She hurried until she knew she was out of sight of the cottage, and then her step slowed. It would be all over now; he'd be firmly wed, and to that 'girl! Woman. Twenty-four, he said she was, but she looked older. Her round blue eyes and fair fluffy hair didn't make her appear like a young woman. Not that her face looked old, it was just something in her manner. She had only met her the once when coming out of church and she knew she hadn't liked her. And it wasn't only because she was marrying Simon, she was the kind of woman she would never have liked. She had hinted as much to Mrs. Ross.

Wasn't that funny! She was always telling herself it was funny, how she could talk to the parson's wife openly, even more so than she could to her granny. Sometimes she thought that the parson's wife and herself were about the same age, but Mrs. Ross was all of twenty-six, she admitted so herself. She had never known anyone quite like her, life would be very dull without her, without their reading lessons and their talks. She wondered if she would dance the day. Perhaps not, not in the open. And anyway she mightn't be there for the wedding had taken place in Pelaw. Still, if the parson should happen to be there and Mrs. Ross joined in the dancing, wouldn't that cause a stir?

For a moment she forgot the sickness in her heart as she imagined the straight faces and nodding heads of some of the villagers should the parson's wife forget herself so far as to allow her feet to hop.

She was glad she didn't live in the village, there was always bickering among one or other of them, mostly the churchgoers. She knew that Simon had come in for quite a bit of gossip because he had chosen a girl from so far away when all around him were, as her granda had said, lasses like ripe plums waiting for him to catch them falling.

She came to the burn. It was running gaily today, the water gurgling and struggling to make its way in between the rocks. She crossed it carefully because the water had risen slightly during the last few days owing to recent rainfalls, and was lapping over some of the stepping stones.

As she reached the further bank and bent forward to pull herself up on to the path she espied the head and shoulders of a boy half hidden by the bushes that bordered a small pool to the side of the burn. As she straightened up the boy rose from the bank but didn't come toward her, and she looked at him over the top of the bushes, saying, "Hello, Steve."

"Hi there, Tilly!"

"You fishin'?"

"No, no, just sitting watchin'. There's a salmon here. I don't know how he got up this far."

"Oh!" She went round the bushes, her face eager. "Are you going to catch him?"

"No." He shook his head.

"No?" She was looking at him in surprise now, and again he said, "No; I just like watchin' him. I don't think anybody knows he's here."

"I'm sure they don't else he wouldn't be here long."

"You're right."

She stared at him. His face was solemn, unsmiling. He didn't look like any one of the McGraths, he didn't talk like any one of the McGraths, he didn't act like any one of the McGraths. She had at one time wondered if he had been stolen as a baby, but her granda had disabused her of that idea for he remembered the day Steve was born because he had helped to carry his father home drunk from the hills. There had been a still going and the hard stuff was running freely.

"You goin' to the weddin'?" he asked.

"Yes." She moved her head once and while he stood looking at her she looked at him. He wasn't very tall for his age. He had a long face and sandy-colored hair that

looked strong, even wiry in parts for strands of it stood
up straight from the crown of his head. His shoulders
were thick but his legs looked thin, even skinny, below
his moleskin knee pants. His movements were quick,
jerky; yet when he spoke his words always came slowly,
as if he had to think up each one before uttering it.

He didn't speak further, and so she said, "Well, I'll
have to be goin', else it'll be over."

"You look different the day."

"Do I?"

"Aye, bonny."

She half turned away, then faced him again, and she
smiled rather sadly at him as she said, "Ta, thanks,
Steve, but I don't believe you. I'll never look bonny
'cos I've got no flesh on me."

"That's daft." His words came surprisingly quickly
now, and he added to them, "You haven't to have loads
of fat stickin' out of you like a cow's udders to be
bonny."

For a moment her face remained straight, and then
her mouth sprang wide and her head went back before
drooping forward, and as she laughed his chuckle
slowly joined hers.

"You are funny, Steve," she said, taking out a
handkerchief and drying her eyes. "I didn't feel like
laughin' the day, but it was the way you said it."

"Aye"—he jerked his head to the side—"I can be
funny at times, that's what they say, but mostly I keep
me mouth shut, I find it pays." His face was straight
again, as was hers now, and she folded her handkerchief carefully and tucked it in the cuff of her dress
before saying, "Well now, I must be off this time.
Ta-rah, Steve."

"Ta-rah, Tilly."

She had gone beyond the bushes when his voice came
at her in a hissing whisper, calling, "Don't let on about
this fish," and she called back, "Why, no! I won't say a
word."

45

But as she went on she wondered why he should be sitting watching a fish, especially a salmon. He was a funny lad, was Steve, but nice. She had always liked him. She wished that the rest of his family took after him.

She had just reached the coach road when a brake full of people passed her, and they waved their hands and shouted unintelligible greetings to her. But the driver didn't pull the horses to a stop to give her a lift, and she stood where she was well back on the verge of the road until the vehicle disappeared into the distance because she didn't want to walk in the dust that the horses and the wheels had thrown up.

The sounds of jollification came to her while she was still quite some distance from the farm, and she slowed her step. She wished she needn't go, she didn't want to see Simon, or his new wife. She had been thinking over the past week that it would be better if she never clapped eyes on Simon Bentwood again, but she knew this would be difficult because they never knew which day he would pop in with the monthly sovereign. That business was still troubling her; she even lay awake at nights now wondering about it.

As she went through a gateless gap in the stone walls and crossed the farmyard toward the front of the house she saw that the whole place seemed transformed. It wasn't only that there were a lot of people milling about, but on the lawn there were two long tables set in the form of a T, both weighed down with food; and there was a tent at the far end of the lawn and the open flaps showed the big head of a beer barrel and a laughing man busily filling tankards.

She stood shyly by one of the long windows that were on each side of the front door. Simon's father had had these put in some years ago at his own expense and had had to pay tax for doing it, so she had been told. As she stood looking on the gay milling scene she chided herself for wondering at this particular moment if the money for the windows had come out of the same coffer as the monthly sovereign, and she was telling herself to stop it, because the matter seemed to be getting between her and her wits, when she heard her name being called loudly, and she turned to see Simon coming down the two steps that led from the front door. The next minute he was holding her hand and she was looking into his face. His eyes were bright, his mouth was wide. "Where've you been?" he cried at her. "I thought you weren't coming. And why didn't you come to the church, eh?" He was bending toward her, his face level with hers. "Come"—he was pulling her now—"come and see Mary."

. He tugged her up the steps and into the farm sitting-room to where his bride was standing in her white dress.

Tilly mouthed her good wishes as her granny had told her to. "I hope you have a very happy life," she said, "and never want for nothing; an' that's from me granny and granda an' all."

"Oh thank you. Thank you." The words were polite, stilted. The lids blinked rapidly over the blue eyes and as the bow-shaped mouth moved into a wider smile Tilly thought grudgingly, She's bonny, I suppose, and I can see what got Simon. Oh aye. Her look went to where the white lace dipped deeply between the full breasts, then swept downward to the tight-laced waist, and as her eyes lowered toward the floor her practical mind told her that there was all of ten yards of satin or more in the skirt of the dress.

"Oh, how kind of you."

She found herself nudged aside by the churchwarden and his wife, Mr. and Mrs. Fossett. Mrs. Fossett was being gushing, as usual. "Oh, you do look beautiful, Mrs. Bentwood. And what a wedding! what a spread! The village has seen nothin' like it for years." Then came the sting as it always did from Mrs. Fossett's barbed tongue. "'Twas . . . 'twas a pity though you couldn't have been married in our church. Oh, that would have given the stamp to the day. But there, there . . . I would like you to accept this little gift. It's really nothing, although it's very old, it belonged to my great-grandmother."

As she spoke she was unwrapping a small parcel, and when the paper fell away it showed a flower vase of no apparent attraction.

"Oh, thank you. Thank you."

As Tilly looked at the bride she was asking herself if that was all she was ever going to say; but she was wrong, for now the new Mrs. Bentwood led the way to a table at the end of the room and there, from amid a number of presents she picked up a fluted sugar basin and, holding it up for all to see, she said, "Mr. Sopwith himself called in earlier on and brought us this. It's a present from his wife." There was a pause before she ended, "It's solid silver; it's from their collection."

"Oh! Oh!" Mrs. Fossett's voice was cool. She nodded her head, then said, "Very nice. Very nice."

"Enough. Enough of presents for the time being. Come on, it's time we had something to eat . . . Mrs. Bentwood—" Simon now playfully caught hold of his bride's arm and in a masterful voice demanded, "Aren't you going to see to my victuals, woman?"

There was general laughter and the company in the room followed the bride and bridegroom outside on to the lawn. All except Tilly. She remained behind for a moment and looked round the room. She had often been in this room. She'd had her dreams about this room. It was a bonny room; it wasn't like other rooms in the house, dim because of the small windows. Old Mr. Bentwood had known what he was doing when he'd had these windows put in.

She turned and made for the door and as she did so she saw Mrs. Ross, the parson's wife, passing, and Mrs. Ross saw her and, coming quickly up the steps, she said, "Hello, Tilly," and not waiting for Tilly's greeting, she added in a voice that was low and rapid and was backed by a mischievous gurgle, "Have you seen the vicar? I should have been here an hour ago but I got caught up with a class." Her voice sank even lower now and her eyes seemed to sparkle more as she brought her face close to Tilly's and whispered, "I've got three pitmen. Aha! Aha!" Her head moved in little jerks now. "What do you think of that? Three pitmen!"

Tilly's voice was as conspiratorial as hers and her eyes shone as she repeated, "Three . . . for learnin'?"

"Ssh!" The parson's wife now looked from side to side. "Not a word. They came of their own accord, said they wanted to learn their letters. Of course it's dangerous"—she straightened her back—"I mean for them. Should Mr. Rosier get to know they'll be dismissed their work. Dreadful. Dreadful, when you come to think of it."

"'Tis, 'tis awful." Tilly nodded vigorously. "Just because they want to learn their letters!"

"They were as black as the devil himself." The parson's wife was gurgling again. "They hadn't washed, you see. Well, if they had got tidied up to come to the vicarage someone would have noticed. But they were supposedly on their way home from their shift, as they said."

"But where did you learn them? I mean, where did you take them?"

"In the summer-house at the bottom of the garden."

"Oh, Mrs. Ross!" Tilly had her hand over her mouth now. Then her face straight, she said, "What about the parson?"

At this Mrs. Ross cast her eyes toward the ceiling and said, "Heigh-ho! nonny-no! skull, hair and feathers flying."

"He'll be very vexed?"

Mrs. Ross now turned her head to the side as if considering, then said, "I really don't know, Tilly. I've thought about it and somehow I think he might even turn a blind eye . . . seeing they are men. Oh, it's different for men. As you know he doesn't hold with women learning. I can't understand that about Geor . . . Mr. Ross, because he is wide you know, Tilly, very wide in his views."

"Yes, yes, I know, Mrs. Ross. Yes, I know. Oh my!" She looked past the parson's wife out on to the lawn as she whispered now, "They are sitting down at the tables. Should we be going?"

"Dear! dear! yes." Mrs. Ross swung around so quickly that the skirt of her gray alpaca dress formed itself for a moment into a bell and it looked to Tilly as if she were about to run down the steps and across the lawn. This thought made her want to laugh; just think of the faces if the parson's wife was seen running across the lawn! She loved Mrs. Ross. She did, she did . . . Could you love a woman? Yes, she supposed you could, like you loved God. And she was the nearest thing she knew to God. Eeh! that somehow sounded like blasphemy. Yet she was. Yes, she was; she was better and kinder than anybody she knew. What's more, she was of *the class*, and you didn't get much kindness from *the class*, did you? Not really. You usually had to work for the kindness you got from *the class*. And yet *the class*, in the form of Mr. Sopwith, had been kind to her granda and her great-granda by letting them have the cottage. But then her great-granda had worked for the Sopwiths from he was six years old, and her granda had worked in the Sopwith mine since he was eight. Still, he hadn't got the cottage because he had worked in the mine, because so many men worked in the mine and they didn't get cottages, he had got the cottage because he had dived into the lake in the bitter cold weather and saved Mr. Mark Sopwith, as he was now, from drowning. The lad had gone out in a boat when he shouldn't and it had capsized and he couldn't swim, and his father had been on the shore and stood there helpless, and her granda had dived in and brought him out almost dead.

The young lad had survived without hurt, but her granda had always had his chest after that. Her granda shouldn't have been in the Sopwith grounds that day, he was after a rabbit and could have been had up for poaching, but old Mr. Sopwith, who was religious, said that God had sent him, and for saving his son's life he had let him have the cottage free for as long as he should live.

Her mind was wandering. Everybody was laughing and shouting all up and down the tables and all toward the bride and bridegroom. Someone pushed a great chunk of hare pie in front of her. She didn't like hare, it was too strong, but she nibbled at it out of politeness.

She lost count of the time she sat at the table. Everybody was talking, but she hadn't much to say. Mrs. Ross was now at the top table seated next to the parson, and she herself was stuck between Mr. Fairweather and Bessie Bradshaw, the wife of the innkeeper. She didn't know Mrs. Bradshaw very well, only that no one ever called her Mrs. Bradshaw, it was always Bessie. She knew Mr. Fairweather because he was one of the sidesmen at the church, but she had never liked him, he always sang the hymns louder and longer than anybody else, and his amens were like an echo, they came so long after the prayer was finished. But now he was laughing a lot; he'd had his tankard filled four times to her knowledge. There was a tankard of home-brewed beer in front of her, too, but she had only sipped at it because it was bitter; it had a different bitterness to the herb beer her granny made, she liked that.

The whole table now seemed to rock to its feet as somebody cried, "The fiddlers! The fiddlers!" and there at the other side of the lawn two fiddlers were dragging their bows across the strings while the man with a melodeon began to pull it in and out.

She was glad to get to her feet, but as she was lifting one booted foot decorously over the form she squealed and almost jumped in the air; then turning angrily about, her face flushed, she stared at Mr. Fairweather and in no small voice she cried, "Don't you dare do that to me, Mr. Fairweather!" whereupon Andy Fairweather, the usually staid church sidesman, put his head back and laughed, saying, "'Tis a weddin', girl. 'Tis a weddin'."

"Wedding or no"—she backed from him, her hand to her bottom—"you keep your hands to yourself."

There was much laughter from the bottom of the table and as the company made toward the far end of the lawn somebody chokingly spluttered, "Andy Fairweather put his finger in her backside."

"Never! Andy Fairweather? Ho! Ho!"

"'Tis the wedding. 'Tis the wedding. There'll be more than backsides probed the night."

She wanted to go home, she wasn't enjoying this wedding, not a bit. But she had known she wouldn't before she came.

"Here, Tilly! what you looking so solemn about?" It was Simon, and once again he had hold of her hand. "Not a smile on your face. I saw you at the bottom of the table. And what was that business with Andy Fairweather?"

She turned her head to the side, then looked down as she simplified things by muttering, "He nipped me . . . my . . ."

"Oh! Oh! . . . Andy Fairweather nipped your . . . ? Well! Well?"

As she looked into his face she saw that he was straining not to laugh; then his mouth springing wide, he said, "See the funny side of it, Tilly: Andy Fairweather nipping anybody. My! the ale must have spread right down to his innards for him to do that. Next time you see him in church claiming kinship with the Almighty, just think of him the day, eh?" He jerked her hand in his and she bit on her lip and began to laugh. "Come on, there's a nice lad over here, his

52

people are neighbors of Mary's. Come on, give him a dance."

"No! no!" She pulled back from his hand, but he held on to her tightly, saying, "Look, I won't enjoy me wedding if I see you sitting with a face like a wet week-end. Come on." But as he tugged her across the lawn, weaving in and out of the company, his wife's voice suddenly arrested him, saying, "Simon! Simon! Come here a minute."

He stopped and looked over the heads of the group surrounding her and, his chin up, he called to her, "In two ticks, Mary. Be with you in two ticks." The next minute he had pulled Tilly to a stop opposite a young boy of seventeen. "Bobby, this is Tilly, a great friend of mine. Now I want you to look after her, give her a dance. What about it?"

"Aye, yes, yes, Simon."

Simon was now peering down into Tilly's face. His own mock stern, his voice imitating a growl, he ordered her, "Enjoy yourself, Miss Tilly Trotter. Do you hear? Enjoy yourself." Then on a laugh he patted her cheek and turning from her hurried to his bride.

Tilly looked at the boy and the boy looked at Tilly, and neither of them found a word to say to each other.

When in embarrassment she turned from him and went and sat on a weather-worn oak bench that was set against a low hedge bordering the lawn, he paused for a full minute before following her and taking his place by her side.

Then together they sat in silence and watched women clearing the tables and carrying the remnants of the food around the side of the house and into the barn where later in the evening the jollification would continue.

The lawn finally cleared, the fiddlers and the melodeon player struck up a lively turn, and almost immediately Simon, leading his bride into the middle of the lawn, cried, "Come on, let's go!" And this was the signal for the men to grab their partners and start the dance.

The musicians played polkas and jigs, and the dancers danced, some in step and some out of it, stopping between times to refresh themselves from the barrel. Once Simon waved to Tilly telling her to get to her feet, but she shook her head.

She was on the point of getting up and walking away from her tongue-tied companion when she saw Simon weaving his way toward her. Then he was standing over them, looking from one to the other and demanding, "What's the matter with you two? This is a wedding not a funeral! Come on." He pulled her up, and the next minute he was whirling her over the grass. One, two, three, hop! One, two, three, hop! They went into the polka and laughing, he cried to her, "By! you're as light as a feather." Then bending his mouth down to her ear, he said, "She taught you well."

She had no breath for speaking and so she just shook her head at him and went on lifting her feet: One, two, three, hop! One, two, three, hop! When he almost swung her into the air, so light did she feel she could imagine she hadn't any boots on.

At last the music stopped; he held her tightly against him for a moment; then looking down into her face, he said, "What about that, eh?"

"'Twas wonderful, Simon. Wonderful."

"Well, you go on now and take Bobby."

"No! No! I'm not going back to him, he's never opened his mouth."

"Well, did you open yours?"

"No."

"Well then . . . I've got to go, but enjoy yourself." His face became straight for a moment as he ended, "I want you to enjoy yourself, Tilly, and be happy with me the day."

She could find no answer to give him, not even to say politely, "I will, I will. Don't worry, I'll enjoy meself."

"Simon!" A man was pulling at his sleeve. "Your missus is calling you. By! you're going to get it."

"Oh aye. Oh aye. Comin' George. I'm comin'." Without further words he turned from her.

She watched him but he did not make directly toward where his wife was sitting below the house steps; instead he went toward the beer tent, and when he was handed a tankard of beer she saw him put it to his mouth and almost drain it at one go.

He would be drunk before the night was over. Men usually got drunk on their wedding night, at least those who drank did. Would she like the man she married to get drunk on her wedding night? A stupid question to ask herself 'cos she would never marry. With or without the chance she would never marry.

She looked about her. What could she do? Who could she talk to? There were three old village women sitting alongside the wall at the far end of the house; she'd go and talk to them, she was used to talking to old people. She got on well with old people; likely it was having lived with her granda and grandma all these years . . .

Two hours later, when the light was beginning to go, she knew she could now make her excuses and go home. She had talked to the old women, she had been in the kitchen and helped to wash up, she had been in the barn and filled plates with odds and ends and carried empty ones back into the house. The guests had now sorted themselves out, those who were going home had already left such as the parson and Mrs. Ross and the old people who were tired. One brake-load had set off an hour ago back to Felling. She went up the steps into the house to say good-bye to Simon and his wife. There was nobody in the front room. She went out into the passage, then into the hall; and there they were, he had his arms around her and was kissing her.

Her muttering, "Oh, I'm sorry!" brought them apart, yet still holding.

"'Tis all right, Tilly, 'tis all right." His voice was slurred and he held out one hand toward her, but she remained standing, saying, "I'm off now; I just wanted to say thank you." She didn't look at Simon but at his wife. "It . . . it was a lovely wedding. Good-night." She was about to add, "I wish you happiness," when Simon made to come toward her but was stopped by his wife, her hand on his arm. He remained still, asking now, "You'll be all right?"

"Yes, yes. Aye, of course, thank you. Thank you." She nodded to both of them, then backed into the doorway before turning and going hastily out.

She had begun to make her way toward the farmyard when she saw Mr. Fairweather and Mr. Laudimer, another sidesman at the church, standing together. They were laughing and had their hands on each other's shoulders. She didn't want to pass them. She looked toward the far end of the lawn. There was a gate that led into a meadow, and further on there was a bridle-path that would bring her out near the toll bridge and the coach road, and from there she could pick up her usual route home.

A few minutes later she had let herself through the gate and had walked across the meadow and swung herself over a low stone wall and so on to the bridle-path that ran alongside it.

She must have gone about a mile along the path when she saw galloping toward her a horse and rider. Jumping to the side she pressed tight against the hedge to allow them to pass, but the man drew the horse up almost opposite her. She recognized him as Mr. Sopwith, and he, recognizing her, said, "Hello there."

"Hel . . . Good-evenin', sir."

"You're some way from home, aren't you?"

"Yes. Yes, sir; I've been to Mr. Bentwood's wedding."

"Oh, the wedding. Oh yes, yes." He nodded down at

her smiling. Then casting his eyes about him, he asked, "Did you happen to see a lady on a horse further along this road?"

"No, sir, no; I haven't met anyone but yourself."

"Oh. Well, thank you. Good-night."

"Good . . . good-night, sir."

He rode on again, putting the horse into a gallop, and she watched him for a moment before going on her way . . .

As Mark came to the meadow he took the horse over the stone wall, then again drew it to a stop, and once more he looked about him; then settling himself in the seat, he brought his teeth tightly together for a moment before muttering aloud, "Damn!" She was playing cat and mouse with him: she was very much the cat and he didn't like being put in the position of the mouse. "All prizes must be won" she had said, doubtless considering herself as being a very big prize. Well, he'd had enough; he would return home. He had ridden like an escaping hare hither and thither for the past hour, and likely she was back in her house laughing up her sleeve.

What was the matter with him anyway? Why had he allowed himself to get in this state? She was coming between him and his sleep. He felt he would know no peace until he'd had her. But then what? Would the taste of her consume him or would he be brought to his senses and the fire in him quenched? It had happened before. Many years ago, he had become enamored of a woman, so much so that he had thought life would be worthless without her. Janet, his first wife, had known. He had hurt her terribly but he hadn't been able to help himself. Once he had conquered, however, the woman had gone sour on him and he had sworn never again, never, never again. Yet here he was galloping the countryside after a will-o'-the-wisp, she was a full-blooded, alluring, maddening woman.

He rode along by the wall, jumped a hedge, and

came on to the coach road, and in the distance he could hear the faint sound of a fiddle being played . . . Farmer Bentwood's wedding was still in full swing.

As he put his horse into a gallop he damned and blasted Lady Agnes Myton. He was tired, as he also knew was his mount, and he doubted if he would make home before dark. Again he damned her.

Then at a turning in the road his horse shied from one side to the other as the figure of a boy came bursting through the hedge.

"What the hell!" Mark Sopwith pulled himself straight in the saddle and, glaring, bent toward the boy who had paused in his run and was gasping as he spluttered, "Sorry, mister. Sorry," and quickly drawing in one long breath, he raced off down the road, leaving Mark still glaring after him.

Now what had he been up to? Poaching? But if someone was after him he wouldn't have stopped to say he was sorry. He turned the horse around, allowing it to move at a walking pace now. . . .

Steve McGrath was a good runner. He had won a race at the hill fair last year, beating lads three and four years older than himself, but that race hadn't taken it out of him like this one was doing. The sweat was running down his groin and his short moleskin breeks were sticking to his buttocks.

He didn't seem to hear the music until he stopped to hug the end of the brick wall that bordered the farmyard and the gateless drive-in. There was a pain in his chest, his feet were sore and his legs at this moment were like jelly and threatening to give way beneath him. He tried to call out to someone crossing the yard, but his voice came out as a croak.

A minute later he stumbled into the yard and, catching hold of a man's arm, said, "Mister! Mister! Where will I find Mr. Bentwood?"

The man turned a laughing face down on him.

"With his bride, lad, with his bride, where else? Tripping the light fantastic." He pointed toward the barn from where was coming the loud noise of the fiddles and the whining of the melodeon.

"Will you get him, mister, will you get him for me?"

"Get him for you?" The man peered down at him. "You're young McGrath, aren't you? Aye yes, young McGrath. What do you want with him?"

"I must get him, talk to him, I've got somethin' to tell him."

"You can tell him nowt this night, lad; I should say he's past listenin'."

"Mister! Mister!" He was clutching at the man now. "Tell him, will you? Tell him somebody is going to get hurt, somebody he knows. Ask him if I can see him a minute. Go on, will you, will you? Please! Please!"

"Who's gona get hurt?"

"Just . . . just somebody, somebody he knows."

"Oh! Oh, well, well, if that's it." The man turned about and with a gait that spoke of his having imbibed not a little from the barrel, he made his way into the barn.

Steve moved to the side to get out of the way of people who were coming and going, all laughing and joking. He stood with his back pressed against the stone wall of the cow byre but keeping his eyes on the great open doors of the barn and, fascinated, he watched the scene within.

The whole place was lit with lanterns. Some people were dancing, and some people were standing drinking, and some were sitting round the walls eating, but all had their mouths open and were laughing.

So immersed had he become for the moment in the scene that he didn't realise Simon was coming toward him, nor that the bride was standing just within the barn and that she alone wasn't smiling.

"What is it boy? What do you want?"

"Oh. Oh, Mr. Bentwood, it's . . . it's Tilly. She needs somebody to see to her. I . . . I couldn't, I mean on her way home, because there's three of them."

"What on earth are you talkin' about, boy?" Simon's brain was not very clear, it was fogged with ale and not a little with happiness and expectation of his wedding night, and his voice now was full of impatience as he demanded, "Speak clearly, boy! what you gettin' at?"

Steve swallowed a mouthful of spittle before he said slowly, "She'll . . . she'll have to have somebody to guide her home, perhaps more than one, 'cos they're gonna net her."

"Net her?" Simon was now bending over him and he repeated, "Net her? What you on about, lad?"

"It's . . . it's our Hal and Mick and Ned Wheeler. Our Hal said, well, she wouldn't have him the clean way so she's gona have him t'other way." He bit his lip and his head drooped.

Simon straightened his back and looked around him. In his glance he saw his wife staring enquiringly toward him, and he raised his hand as if to say, "I'll be there in a minute," then taking the boy by the shoulder, he pushed him into the cowshed and seeming now to sober up, he said, "Make it quick, boy, explain yourself!"

"They're waitin' for her. They've a net rigged up in a tree. She's strong, Tilly, wiry, an' our Hal knew she'd fight like a chained bitch, an' so they're gona net her an' . . . an'—" He turned his head to the side, bit hard on his lip again, then muttered, "He's gona take her down, then she'll have to have him."

"What!"

The boy looked up into Simon's face which was now twisted in disbelief and he said, "He'd murder me if he knew I'd split. But it was our George, I heard him tellin' me dad and me dad was for it. George wouldn't go along with them and me dad went for him and said he was soft. And then he said—" He stopped and shook his head, and Simon cried impatiently, "Yes! yes! what did he say?"

"I don't know what it meant, it . . . it was about somethin' they wanted to find out, it seemed to be mixed up with money, and if he got Tilly he'd find out. It was double Dutch . . ."

"My God!" Simon now pushed his hand up through his hair.

"You'll take her home?"

"She's gone, boy, this fifteen or twenty minutes or more . . . Come on! . . . No, wait. Where are they going to do this?"

"Billings Flat near the wood. Eeh! God, they could have her by now." He put his hand to his mouth, then muttered, "But I . . . I can't come along of you 'cos he'd . . . he'd brain me."

Simon didn't hear the boy's protest, he was already running toward the barn where his bride was still standing. When he reached her he took her by the hands and pulled her aside, out into the yard, across it and into the dairy, and there, holding her hands against his chest, he said, "Listen, me dear, there's something come up, I've . . . I've got to leave you, but I won't be a half-hour or more."

"Where . . . where are you going?"

"It's"—he closed his eyes and shook his head—"it's nothing, just a little bit of business."

"Business? Business that can't wait on this special night! What did that boy want?"

"He had come to tell me something. I'll . . . I'll explain it all when I come back. I tell you I won't be more than half an hour. Keep things going. Anyway I won't be missed, only by you I hope." He jerked her hard against him and kissed her upon the lips. Then looking at her again, he said, "It's been a grand day, and it's not over yet, is it?"

"I hope not." She was smiling at him now. "Don't be long."

"I won't, I won't, I promise." He kissed her again quickly; then pulling her out through the door, he pushed her gently toward the barn before he himself turned and ran into the stable.

Simon was quite used to riding bare-back though not in tight breeches; but there was no time to stop and saddle the mare, and within minutes he was out of the yard, causing some of the guests to stand and gape as if they couldn't believe their eyes, for wasn't that the bridegroom riding out on his own!

Billings Flat was all of two miles from the farm and about half a mile from the cottage. To anyone for whom the name conjured up an open area, this particular piece of land was misnamed, for the path ran at the bottom of a shallow stretch of land bordered on each side by trees which were intertwined here and there with great shrouds of ivy, the Flat itself being more than twenty yards in length and only in winter when the trees were bare did full light penetrate it.

Simon knew that he could cut off a further mile by taking his horse straight across his fields. This would be against his principles for he hated even the hunt to cross his fields either on horse or on foot; but this was a case of needs must when the devil drove, and the devil was driving him now because he swore inside himself that if Hal McGrath had taken Tilly down then he wouldn't live long to enjoy his victory.

Tilly hadn't hurried on her way home. Again as of late, she'd had the desire to cry, and that was something she mustn't do, not until she got into bed because else how would she explain her red eyes to her granny and granda: she was returning from a wedding and they were sitting up waiting to hear all the news. And she knew that she'd have to make things up, at least about herself, how she had eaten a grand tea and drunk Simon's home-brewed ale, and danced. And then she would have to tell them what the bride looked like and how Simon, too, had appeared. Well, she could be truthful about Simon for she would say to them he looked happy.

She stepped out of the twilight into Billings Flat. She blinked her eyes and turned her gaze toward the ground, being careful where she placed her feet for the roots of the trees spread across the path in places and had tripped her up many a time before today. She had never been afraid passing through Billings Flat. Many people were; the village women in particular would never come this way after dark, for it was said that the long hollow had once been a burial ground, and that at one time it had been dug over and the bodies carted away. But her granda said that this was all nonsense because it would take a few hundred bodies lying side by side to fill the Flat.

She was half-way along it and could see through the dim funnel where the trees ended and the twilight in comparison showed almost bright, when something came flying out of the heavens at her like a bird with extended wings and brought a high piercing scream from her. The thing now had her on the ground trapping her arms and legs and she continued to thrash and scream until the wind was knocked completely out of her as a body, a human body, pressed down on her and fingers digging into her cheeks clamped her mouth shut.

Her eyes, wide in a petrified gaze, were now peering through the mesh of a net and into a face, and she knew the face. There were other figures at each side of her holding her arms tight to the ground. She wanted to yell out in agony because one forearm was being bent over a rut in the path.

She couldn't believe this was happening to her until Hal McGrath, his breath fanning her face now, said between gasps, "You've got some fight in you, skinny

as you are, that's your choppin' 'n sawin', I'll . . . I'll
put that to use an' all. Now listen . . . listen, Tilly
Trotter. I asked you squarely, I wanted to court you
proper, I gave you a chance but you'd have none of it.
Well now, you wouldn't take it the decent way, you'll
take it t'other an' when your belly's full I'll come an'
claim me own. Your two old 'uns won't last much
longer, then what'll you do? You know what happens to
lasses who get taken down, it's the house or the whore
shop. . . . Go . . . God Almighty!"

This exclamation was wrenched from him as Tilly,
gathering every fraction of strength she had left in her
body, surprised them all by getting one leg free from
under the side of McGrath's body and, twisting herself,
brought her knee up with all the force she could muster
into McGrath's groin, so causing him for a moment to
release the pressure on her mouth; and now, her strong
teeth going through the net dug into the side of his
hand.

"You bloody vixen you! God!" He thrust his doubled
fist between his legs. Then as the men on each side of
him scrambled to hold her thrashing limbs she let out
another blood-curdling scream. But this was throttled
at its height by a hand again clapping itself over her
mouth. And now McGrath was growling, "Get the net
off her; it'll be here and now. By God! it will. It will."

When her skirt was flung over her head the hand left
her mouth and again she screamed, but once more the
wind was knocked out of her body.

It was as somebody laughed that she cried from the
essence of her soul *"Oh God! No! No! No! Please. No!
No! No!"* and it was as if instantly He had heard her
prayer, for her hands were released and she heard a
voice that hadn't spoken before gabbling, "Somebody
comin'. Ha! Ha! man! stop. Stop! somebody comin'. A
horseman an' more than one about somewhere, I
know, I know, I can hear 'em. Let's be gone! Let's be
gone!" Then another voice, full of panic now, said,

"Give over, Hal man. Listen, they're comin'. I'm off. I'm off."

The next minute the weight was wrenched from her. She lay inert, the skirt and petticoats still over her head, her body trembling from head to foot, aware of her indecent_appearance yet not able to exert the strength needed to pull her clothes down and see what was happening about her.

She had a strange feeling on her and felt that she must be going to faint. But she had never fainted before, only ladies fainted, and then only when in church. Dimly she was aware of the sound of thuds and groans and curses and of horses' hooves trampling quite near her. She heard a woman's voice and a man's voice, both strange, then her skirt and petticoats were pulled down from her face and her shoulders were brought upward, and the woman saying, "Really! Really! They're savages! Hadn't I just said they were savages." Then turning to the man, she said, "Stop him before he kills him, whoever he is."

Mark Sopwith now ran toward where Simon had Hal McGrath pressed against a tree, his fingers around his throat, while McGrath's hands were gripping the wrists in an endeavor to free himself.

"Leave go! Leave go, man! you'll choke him to death. Leave go, I tell you!" Mark Sopwith brought the side of his hand sharply down across Simon's forearm, and as if a spring had released his hands Simon dropped them away from McGrath's throat and stumbled backward.

His face was bleeding from a cut above his eye; the sleeve of his wedding coat was wrenched partly from the shoulder. His head thrust forward, his hands hanging limply by his side now, he stood gasping, his eyes tight on McGrath who, with hands clutching his own throat, sidled drunkenly from the tree.

It was Mark Sopwith who spoke now. Peering through the dusk he said in some surprise, "You're

McGrath, aren't you, the blacksmith at the mine? Yes. Yes. Well! I'll deal with you later. Now get! Clear out. Go on!"

Hal McGrath didn't immediately obey the order but, looking from one to the other of the men, he said, "'Twas nought to do with either of you, nowt! I was courtin' her. 'Twas family business, courtin'."

"And her screaming her head off? Go on, on your way before I myself decide to have a go at you. And by the way"—he held up his hand—"show yourself at the office on Monday; my manager will have something to say to you."

McGrath's face twisted as he stared at the mine owner; then muttering curses, he turned from them.

Both men now went to where Tilly was still sitting on the ground, but Lady Myton was no longer bending over her, she was standing dusting her gloved hands together. Looking toward them, she said, "She's got the shakes, she's been badly frightened."

Simon passed her without a word and, dropping on to his hunkers at Tilly's side, he put his arm around her shoulders, saying hesitantly, "Are . . . are you all right?"

The words "All right" had a twofold meaning, and after a moment, as if she were considering, she moved her head slowly downward.

"Come on, I'll get you home."

When he lifted her gently to her feet her legs threatened to give way beneath her and she leaned against him, her head pillowed on his breast.

"The farmer, isn't it?"

Simon turned and peered at Lady Myton, but he gave her no answer, just stared at her as she continued, a chuckle in her voice now, "It's your wedding day, I understand. What brought you here, you couldn't have heard her screaming from your farm?"

"No, me lady, I didn't hear her screaming from my

farm"—his words were slow and heavy—"I was warned of what was going to happen to her."

"Oh, and you got here just in time . . . I think so anyway."

"Come." He now turned from them and led Tilly toward where his horse was standing calmly munching at the grass on the side of the bank, and after he had lifted her on to its bare back he turned his head and looked toward Mark Sopwith, saying, "Thanks. Thanks for your help, sir."

"I was no help, except to stop you killing him. You just could have you know."

"Pity I didn't." He now bent his knees, then with a heave of his body he, too, was sitting astride the horse, his arms around Tilly gripping the reins. Slowly he urged the animal forward and when it passed Lady Myton he did not look toward her or give her any word of farewell, although she was standing looking up at him . . .

Mark Sopwith went back along the road and, gathering up the reins of the two horses which had also been contentedly munching at the grass on the bank, he brought them forward, and when he reached Lady Myton she lifted her gaze from the departing figures and, looking at him, she said, "Well! Well! an interesting interlude." Then after a moment's pause she added, "The interruption came at a most crucial part of our conversation. If I remember rightly"—her head drooped to one side now—"you were about to extract your winnings, Mr. Sopwith."

As he handed her the reins of her horse he could scarcely make out the outline of her face but he knew that she was laughing at him, and he also knew that she didn't think he would be ungentlemanly enough at this stage to, as she said, extract his winnings from her.

Well, she was mistaken for there would be no better time than the present, nor place for that matter, to prove her wrong, and if it lay with him he would extract his winnings to the full before the night was out because she had led him a dance. It was as if she had been in a position all evening to watch his every move for when, disgruntled, he had been making his way home she had stepped out on him, elegantly straight in the saddle, some little distance from the Flat, and what she had said was, "Good-evening, Mr. Sopwith. Were you looking for me?"

When, having dismounted, he had gone to her she had extended her arms toward him and he had helped her down from the saddle. Having lifted her to the ground, he had kept his hold on her as he answered her, saying, "No, Lady Myton, you weren't even in my thoughts."

He had still been holding her, their faces close together, their eyes telling each other that a certain kind of relationship was about to begin, when a girl's scream brought them apart.

It could have been a girlish scream of delight, but neither of them was sure, and they waited for it to be repeated, then were about to resume their own affairs when it came again.

When he moved from her and held his ear cocked, she had inquired coolly, "What do you think it might be, some yokel causing his lady love to squeal with delight?"

"That was no squeal of delight."

A few minutes later another scream was abruptly cut off and so he quickly helped her to mount, then turning in the direction of Billings Flat, he said, "Follow me."

"What? What did you say?"

He had turned toward her and said slowly, "I said follow me."

"Oh, I thought that was what you said."

He knew that she was annoyed, yet once they reached the scene in which the Trotter girl was involved her attitude changed, and he had the idea she had really been amused by it all.

And now she was awaiting developments. Well, he wouldn't keep her waiting any longer.

At the end of the Flat he took the reins from her and now quickly urged the horses toward a low bank. Once up it, he doubled them back and now led them along the higher ground beyond the belt of trees that bordered the Flat.

Here the belt thinned out into saplings and scrub land, and after not more than a minute's walk he tied the horses to a tree, then turned and waited until she came stumbling toward him. He could see her face now. Her eyes were wide and filled with amusement, her mouth was laughing. She didn't speak, but he did and what he said was, "I'm ready for the prize-giving."

He knew that she was about to laugh and loud, but just as Tilly's scream had been smothered, so was her laughter now as he, putting his arms about her, swung her from her feet. The next minute they had both tumbled on to the ground, and there they lay staring at each other for a moment, but only for a moment.

As often happened in his life, the prize turned out in the end to be somewhat of a surprise holding a negative quality, because, whereas he knew who was master in the beginning, at the end he was not at all sure, and he was made to wonder how an elderly man like her husband coped with such passion, that was if he attempted to cope at all. Perhaps it was lack of his coping that made her so ravenous.

It had been a very unusual night, but strangely he wasn't feeling elated, not even temporarily happy.

As Simon helped Tilly into the cottage Annie, turning in her chair before the fire where she had been dozing, put her hands to her lips and muttered, "God in heaven! what's happened?"

In a matter of seconds she was pulling herself from the chair and glancing toward the bed where William was now easing himself on to his side, his face showing the same amazement as hers, and turning, she said again, "What is it. What is it? What's happened?" She was now standing in front of Tilly, and Tilly, throwing herself into the old woman's arms, began to sob, spluttering as she did so, "Oh Gran! Gran!"

Holding her tightly, Annie looked up at Simon, at his blood-smeared face and at his rent coat, and in a voice that was a mere whisper she asked him again, "What's happened, lad? What's happened you? And why are you here this night of all nights?"

Simon, dropping into a chair at the side of the table, didn't answer her directly, but looking toward William, he said, "Doesn't take long in the telling. McGrath tried to take her down, the dirty bugger! But besides that, he netted her in order to do it."

"Netted her?" William's face was screwed up.

"Aye, you know the old game, the net slung up atween a couple of accommodatin' trees, with a slip knot and a pole. The last time I heard of it being used was years ago when they wanted to trap a good pony. Safer way than chasing your guts out across the moor."

"Netted her?" William looked toward where his beloved child, as he thought of her, was now sitting crouched low on a cracket before the fire, and Annie, standing by her side, stroking her hair. "God above! if I only had the use of me legs."

He turned his head now and looked at Simon and ended, "They'll stop at nothin', they're so sure it's here."

"Yes, William, yes, they're sure it's here."

They both started somewhat and Annie actually stumbled backward as Tilly, swinging her body round from the stool, cried now, "What's here? He isn't only after me, it's somethin' else and . . . and I've got a right to know; after tonight I've got a right to know.

Granda!"—she appealed to him, her head thrust out and falling to the side and the tears raining down her face—"this business of the money, I've a right to know."

There was silence in the room for a moment, except for the wind blowing down the chimney, and when the fire hissed and the log of wood parted in the middle and dropped gently away to each side of the hearth, William, lying back on his pillow, drew in a short painful breath before he said, "Aye, aye, lass, you've got a right to know. But I think you've had enough for one night, we'll talk about it the morrow."

"No, no, you're always sayin' never put off till the morrow what can be done the day, or the morrow never comes, or some such. The morrow, you'll have another excuse. And you an' all, Gran," she said, her voice breaking as she turned and looked at her grandmother.

Annie bowed her head as if against a piercing truth.

"Come; sit down." Simon had risen from the chair and now, his arm about her shoulders, he brought her to the end of the table and pressed her down into a chair that was facing the bed, and he said, "Go ahead, William; or . . . or shall I tell her as I know it?"

William's eyes were closed, his head was turned slightly away as he muttered, "Aye, Simon; aye, 'tis best."

Simon now pulled his chair toward the end of the table and, sitting down, he leaned his forearm on it and looking at her, where she had turned her face half toward him, he said, "It's some thirty years this August. That correct, William?"

William made no verbal reply; he merely acknowledged with a small movement of his hand, and Simon went on, "Well, it was on this summer's day, a Sunday it was, your granda there was taking the air because that was the only day in the week the pitman had to himself. He had walked a good way and was hot and tired and he lay down amidst some gorse and dozed off.

Now, as your granda said, when he heard the commotion beyond the gorse he lay still thinking it was a courting couple having a tussle. But then he realized he wasn't listening to a tussle but to a man gasping as if he were struggling with something heavy. Your granda then turned on his side and carefully edged himself along by the scrub until he could see just beyond it. Well, he found himself looking on to part of the fell that was covered with boulders; he had just earlier on become acquainted with these boulders when he had walked in between them before coming to the grassy patch where he had lain down, and what he saw then stretched his eyes, so he's told me many times, and I can believe him, for there was McGrath, Hal McGrath's father you know, who was blacksmith in the village then as he still is today, struggling with one of the outcrops of rock. Eventually he moved it; but he moved it in the direction in which your granda was looking, so he couldn't see what was going on beyond. But after a time, Big McGrath struggled with the rock again and placed it where it was before, then straightened up, dusted his hands, and walked calmly away into the fading light.

"Your granda there"—Simon now nodded toward the bed—"was naturally set to wondering. He stayed where he was for some time to let McGrath get well away, then he went around and examined this great lump of rock. And he marveled that any one man could move it. He himself tried but he couldn't even rock it. Then your granda got to thinking.

"Well, things were very bad in the country about this time; jobs were scarce; farmers, such as my father, had had to dismiss some of their hands because of taxation and the like; the whole country was in a state of unrest. We think it's bad enough now but around that time two men not a mile from this spot were sent to Botany Bay for stealing a sheep. One of them had lost two children in three months through starvation; but that was no excuse, he was lucky to get off with his life. The village, our village, was one of the hardest hit around these parts because half of the workers were on the land and four farmers went broke within one year. There were near riots. You know the big houses that still lie between here and Harton village, well, they used to put guards round them at nights with dogs to stop the peasantry, as they called them, raiding the vegetable gardens or the chicken runs. It had been said there wasn't a rabbit to be seen between Westoe village and Gateshead not for many a year . . . So how, your granda asked himself, did the McGraths always appear to manage, always appear to be well fed and well shod, because fewer farms meant not only fewer farm workers but also fewer horses to be shod and Big McGrath worked the forge himself. The Rosier mine and Sopwith's had their own blacksmiths, so how did it come about that the McGraths were not only surviving but surviving well? The answer, your granda considered, lay under this stone. But how to move it?

"Now you knew, didn't you, William?"—he inclined his head toward the bed—"that should you go into the village and ask one of your neighbors to come and help you find out what McGrath had hidden under that stone, and should the findings show money, because money was the only thing that bought food in those days, for people had nothing left to exchange; well, you knew that should they help themselves the change in their fortunes would soon be noticed."

Simon looked at Tilly again. Her face white, her eyes wide and unblinking, held his for some seconds, until he wetted his lips and went on, "You see, men like the miners were working for starvation wages. Often a husband and wife had to go down below just to keep themselves alive. Aye, and take their young 'uns with them, five or six years old. There were about three dozen Sopwith's men in the village at that time living in hovels; and as you know some of them are still there; and your granda was one of them.

"Anyway"—he inclined his head again toward the bed—"your granda was determined to see what Big McGrath had got buried, but he was at a loss to know where to go for help. Well, he began to walk home. Now on his road he had to pass our farm; and it didn't look as it does today. My father, so I understand, was at the end of his tether both financially and domestically. You see my mother had had five miscarriages before she had her sixth child, and that had lived only a month. Moreover, it was only five months to Christmas and the rent to the owner, Mr. Sopwith, was then due. Now old Sopwith was going through hard times too, at least so he gave out; he wasn't as lenient as the present one, with him it was no rent, no farm; and what was more he was badly liked because he had enclosed some free pasture on the north side of his land. People said it was because his own father had had to sell half the estate in order to keep going. But hard times with the gentry and hard times with the people were horses of a different color. The gentry could still have their servants by the dozen, go up to London Town, lavish presents on their wives and children; but what was more important in the eyes of the ordinary man, they could still eat.

"Anyway, I'm going off the subject, which your mind is apt to do because these issues are still with us the day. Now who should your granda see when passing the farmyard but my own father. Now it says in the Bible, cast thy bread upon the waters and it shall be returned to you a thousandfold; well, I translate that, Tilly, in this way, do a good turn for anybody and if they're decent folk they'll repay you in some way. So it should happen that a few years afore this when there was a strike at the mine my father had given your granda there free milk, mostly skimmed of course, nevertheless free milk every day during the time they were off; he had also thrown in a stone of taties every week. Your granda there never forgot this, so when he saw my father coming toward him across the yard, to use his own words, he thought, here's a man who is as much in need of an extra shilling or two as anybody in these parts, and so what did he do, he told him what he had seen. And my father, after listening to him in silence, simply said, 'Come on, show me.'

"It was a good mile back to the spot and it was getting dark, and when there it took them both every ounce of their strength to budge the stone an inch. But gradually, gradually, they moved it to the side, and there in the dim light below them was a hole, and in it was a tin box. Not an ordinary tin box you know, but one of those that travel on coaches, steel bound and locked; the gentry sometimes use them for carrying jewelry or money in when traveling from one estate to another, or in a mail coach when hundreds of pounds had to be taken to where they were building the railroads. Anyway"—Simon's voice dropped now— "that box wasn't only full of golden guineas but round it there were a number of leather bags also full. But these ones were mixed with silver.

"Well, your granda there and my father peered at each other, and it was my father who said, 'What about it, Trotter?' and your granda answered, 'We'll take it. But where will we put it?'

"My father thought a minute and then said, 'I've got the very place, the dry well.' It's a well that drained out in my father's time after he had made an extension to the seed room and had roughly slabbed over it. It is three or four years ago since I looked down it. It was still dry then, a bit soggy at the bottom but that's all. Anyway, water or not, guineas don't melt.

"So they cleared the hole of its secret and they replaced the stone and in the now dark night they skitted along that road, keeping to the hedgerow like two highwaymen with their loot." For the first time Simon's face went into a smile as he added, "There's little more to tell. They counted the money. There was close on a thousand pounds. They were both amazed and slightly drunk with the happening, but when they sat down and thought things out they faced a snag, and that was, they wouldn't be able to use the money, not openly, not in any way that would show a difference in their style of living. It was easier for my father because any extra money he had a mind to spend he could put out as profit from the farm, but not so William there. William was getting twelve shillings a week; even a shilling spent extra could bring suspicion on him because they knew that McGrath, once he made the discovery, would have his sons taping everybody in the village and beyond. And so your granda decided to have five shillings a week for as long as it would last, but he would spend it far afield, like in Shields . . . So there you are, now you know why I bring the sovereign every month." Simon let out a long, slow breath and leaned back in the chair and ended, "And what McGrath's after an' all."

Tilly's eyes were wide, her mouth was slightly agape. She stared at Simon for some time before she turned her head slowly and looked toward her grandfather, then toward her grandmother who was seated at the top of the table. But now it was Annie who spoke. Sadly, she said, "The times, hinny, I've been tempted to ask for more in order to buy you some decent clothes. An' I might have chanced it except that I made a mistake one day. 'Twas some weeks after they had brought William back from the pit. They thought he would die an' I couldn't leave him and we were in need of meat, candles, and flour an' such, an' you being on ten years old and a sensible child into the bargain, I told you what was needed. And so I wrapped the sovereign in a rag and pinned it in the pocket of your petticoat an' gave you a penny for the carrier cart into Shields. Well, you came back as proud as punch with all the messages an' the change intact, an' when I asked you how you got on you told me that one woman at the bacon stall wanted to know how a little thing like you had come by a sovereign, an' you said your granny had given it to you to do the messages with. And then you caught sight of Bella McGrath at another stall an' simply to point out to the woman your honesty you said, 'That's Mrs. McGrath from the village, she knows me an' me granny.' An' you went to her and brought her to the bacon stall an' said to her, 'You do know me an' me granny, Mrs. McGrath, don't you?' An' Bella McGrath said, 'I do, I do indeed. But what for are you askin'?' An' you explained to her about the sovereign." Annie now sighed and shook her head as she ended, "It was from then, hinny, that this business all started. The McGraths knew, like everybody else did, that William being bad, there'd be no money coming in, so from that day to this they've never let up. You see, they think we've got it hidden here. They've worked it out that there must still be a good deal left. That's why Hal McGrath's bent on having you; it's one way of getting his hands on the remainder of it."

Tilly could find no words to express what she was feeling. The whole business sounded too fantastic to be believed, yet she knew it was true, too true. They had been living on stolen money for years. They had stolen it from McGrath, but whom had McGrath stolen it from? All that money, all those sovereigns, and she had been the means, the innocent means of giving her grandfather away and of bringing on herself the raping attack tonight. She shuddered visibly and bent her head. She would feel his body on top of her for the rest of her days, and his hands clawing at her bare flesh. Instinctively, she brought her legs tight together under the table.

"Don't worry, he won't come near you again."
Simon's hand came across the table and covered her
joined ones.

As she looked back into his face she thought, I've
spoiled his wedding. And yet the question she asked
him now had nothing whatever to do with his wedding:
"Where did Mr. McGrath get the money from? Was he
a highwayman?"

"No, not him"—Simon shook his head—"he would
never have the guts. But his cousin was transported
three or four years previous. He was one of three men
who held up a coach on its way to Scotland, it was on
the road between Gosforth and Morpeth, a lonely
stretch. One of the men was shot by the guard, the
other two escaped. McGrath's cousin was picked up
from a description some weeks later when he was at the
hoppings in Newcastle; one of the gentry who had been
in the coach spotted him and informed the constables.
It couldn't really be proved against him, it was only
hearsay, but still it was enough to send him to Botany
Bay; otherwise it would have been his neck. William"—he looked toward the bed again—"you remember him, don't you, McGrath's cousin?"

"Aye, aye, I do indeed. He was a small fellow, quiet,
dark, quick on his feet. Around that time there were
two or three big hold-ups. They never found who did
them, but the money in that box told the tale all right.
The only thing I can't understand, and never have been
able to, is why he let Big McGrath have the keeping of
it 'cos he himself lived in Glasgow in one of those
tenements they said that you wouldn't house a rat in."

"Here"—Annie was now standing by Simon's side,
she had placed a dish of water on the table—"let me
clean up that cut. You are in a mess. My goodness!"
She dabbed at his face with a wet cloth. "This needs a
needle and thread else you're going to have a scar
there. Here, dry your face." She handed him a rough
towel, then added, "I'm sorry I can't do anything with

your coat, that's a tailor's job. By! your wife will go mad when she sees you. And this to happen on your wedding night. 'Tis sorry I am to the heart, Simon."

He stood up and, handing her the towel back, he smiled and only just in time stopped himself from saying, "It isn't every man who saves another woman from being raped on his wedding night and gets his face bashed into the bargain" because Tilly wasn't a woman, she was a girl, still a girl, a sweet girl, a lovable girl. He looked at her and as he met her wide, warm, troubled gaze, he turned on himself: Aw, to hell! Let him get out of here and back to Mary. Aye, back to Mary. And what would she say to him? Aye, what would she say? Would she overlook his running off like that and greet him with open arms when he turned up like this? Huh! he doubted it. Well anyway, the quicker he got back and tested her temper the better.

"Good-night, William. Good-night, Tilly. Good-night, Annie."

William muttered, "Good-night, lad, and thanks, thanks for what you've done the night."

Tilly gave him no farewell. She just stood and watched him as her grandmother handed him a lantern, saying, "You'll need this now."

"Aye, yes I'll need it now."

She opened the door for him and as he stepped out into the dark, she said, "Tell your wife I'm sorry you were fetched away and are going back to her like this. I . . . I hope she understands."

He made no answer, but as he went swiftly down the path toward the gate and his horse he thought, I hope she does an' all.

But Mary Bentwood was never to understand this night, nor to forgive him until the day she died.

4

The light of the candle lantern set in the middle of the vestry table illuminated the six faces gathered around it, those of the churchwarden Mr. Septimus Fossett and the five sidesmen: Burk Laudimer the wheelwright, Andy Fairweather the carpenter, George Knight the cooper and grave-digger, Tom Pearson the painter and odd-job man, and Randy Simmons, Simon Bentwood's cowman.

Mr. Fossett had just finished speaking, and it was Andy Fairweather who answered him, saying, "Aye, 'tis as you said a serious business. And that's why we're here, we're responsible men, responsible for the conduct of the church. Well, what I mean is to see that those who run it act decent like."

"But she doesn't run it"—Tom Pearson's voice held a note of protest—"be parson that is responsible."

"Aye, but he's responsible for his wife." Two voices came at him now, Andy Fairweather's and George Knight's.

"Aye, well, yes, you're right there." Burk Laudimer was nodding his head now. "But she be different class. We knew that from the start. She comes from the gentry, an' we all know what they're like. Like bitches in season they skitter about."

"Aw, shut tha mouth!" Tom Pearson not only nodded angrily toward Burk Laudimer, but he thrust his pointing finger across the table at him, crying, "We're not talkin' of bitches but of the parson's wife."

". . . One an' the same thing p'raps."

"Now, now, Burk"—Septimus Fossett nodded his head disapprovingly down the table—"This is no time to be funny, 'tis no light subject we're dealing with. Now tell us, you're sure what you saw?"

"As true as God's me judge. An' as I said, you haven't only got to take me word for it, there was Andy. You saw them with your own eyes, didn't you, Andy?"

"Aye, aye, I did, Burk. You're right, I did. There they were in this very room, this table pushed back to the wall there, an' dancin' they were." The carpenter's voice now dropping to a low mutter, he went on, "Astonishin' it was to see in a place of worship an' all, their arms about each other. And her singin'! An' no hymn. Oh no! no! No hymn. A lilt she was singin', a dancin' lilt, and as Burk here has told you—I saw it as well as him—when they parted they up with their skirts like a pair of whores on the waterfront at Shields. Half-way up their calves they pulled them, and started prancin' about. Now 'twould have been bad enough if it had been in a barn or in the room across yonder"—he thumbed over his shoulder—"where she holds what she calls her Sunday school, but I suppose that was too small a place for them to have their fling. . . . But now listen." He rolled his eyes from one staring member to the other. "I'll tell you somethin', I don't blame the parson's wife altogether. No, no, I don't, 'cos I think she's been led astray, aye she has, and by that young Tilly Trotter."

"Ah, don't be daft man."

"Now, Tom Pearson, don't you tell me I'm daft, I know what I'm talkin' about."

"Well, you're the only one." Tom Pearson turned his head away from the table and looked into the deep shadows as he said, "Led away by Tilly Trotter! She's only a bit of a lass, not yet on sixteen."

"She's no bit of a lass, not in the ordinary way I'd say. An' what's more, she's above herself, has been for

81

years. There's always been something fishy about her; an' about her old grandparents an' all. Old Trotter's never done a hand's turn for years, but they never seem to want. Have you ever thought of that? An' can you tell me another thing"—he now cast his glance again around the table—"why should Simon Bentwood ride off on his weddin' night to see that she was all right just 'cos he heard that Hal McGrath was for takin' her? Leaves his bride he does an' all the bridal party; in the midst of the jollifications he rides off and comes back hours later, a slit brow, a black eye, an' his clothes torn off his back through fightin' Hal McGrath for her. Now I ask you, is that usual goin' on for a groom on his weddin' day? An' look at the rumpus that came after. Randy there"—he pointed down the table—"said there was hell to pay. An' the lads didn't see them up to bed that night. An' moreover there was high jinks in the house the next day. That girl, I'm tellin' you, is a creator of trouble, in fact she's witchlike in some ways. Have you ever seen the way she looks at . . . ?"

"Oh, for goodness sake!" Tom Pearson got to his feet. "I've never heard such bloody rubbish in me life."

"No language in here, Tom. Remember where you are." The churchwarden's voice was stern.

"Not so much rubbish, Tom." It was George Knight, the grave-digger now.

His thin piping voice seemed to check the anger of the two men and they both looked at him, and he, nodding from one to the other, said, "That was a strange business about Pete Gladwish's dog, now you must admit that. It was strange that was. It was."

"Aye, it might have been"—Tom Pearson's voice was also quiet now—"but what has that to do with young Tilly Trotter?"

"More than something, Tom, more than something, so some folks say. Pete's dog was a ratter, you know that yourself, an' one of the best terriers for miles. An' the old fellow lived on his winnings, didn't he? Saturda' night in the pit I've seen that dog kill fifty rats in as many minutes, or less. Aye, or less. Then comes the night that he's takin' him over Boldon way, and they meet up with young Tilly on the road, an' you know what happened? She stroked the dog. Talked to it, Pete said, and the bloomin' beast then didn't want to come along of him, tugged to follow her. An' that night he didn't even want to go in the pit. Can you imagine a terrier seeing a rat an' not wanting to go after it? Why, when they see them swarming down in the pit they nearly go mad to get at 'em. But, Pete said, that dog just stood there, dazed like. Well, he knocked the daylights out of it and took it home and chained it up, and what happened? Well, you live in this village as well as I do an' you know what happened, the dog was gone the next mornin', wasn't it, and it's never been seen hilt nor hair of since. It wasn't until this business of the weddin' an' the sort of enticing away of Farmer Bentwood on the most special night of his life that old Pete got thinkin' about the night Tilly Trotter stroked his dog; he hadn't linked it up afore. And to my mind there's something in it. . . ."

"To your mind, George, there's always something in it, even in an empty pea-pod."

"Pity the stocks are no longer in the square."

"Why, are you thinkin' of sitting in them?"

Burk Laudimer now turned on Tom Pearson, crying, "I don't know why you were asked in on this meetin', you're for her, aren't you, for the pair of 'em? When they're dancing on the altar next and drinkin' out of the font you'll say that ain't witchery. Just high spirits, you'll say."

"Aye, I might an' all." Tom Pearson nodded at them; then looking up the table to where the churchwarden sat, his face grim, he said, "Well, I've got a job to finish, I'm off, but have you made up your mind what you're gona do?"

Mr. Fossett put the palms of his hands flat on the

table before him and surveyed the five of them for a moment before he said, "Yes, I've made up me mind, an' being churchwarden 'tis me duty as I see it to carry it out."

"And what are you gona carry out?" Tom Pearson asked.

The churchwarden's head swung from side to side before he answered, "Just the fact that the parson will have to put a stop to her gallop, he'll tell her she must behave or else. . . ."

"Or else what?"

"Well"—again Mr. Fossett's head was wagging—"we can't have disgrace brought on the church, an' his wife acting like a light woman can bring nothin' but disgrace on the church."

"You're right. You're right." His supporters nodded confirmation of this; then simultaneously they rose and the meeting was at an end. . . .

Outside in the churchyard they dispersed to go their separate ways, with the exception of Burk Laudimer and Andy Fairweather. As if of one mind they both stood looking up into the darkening sky, then they turned together and walked down by the side of the church and, cutting across between the gravestones, made for a small gate in the low stone wall that surrounded the cemetery. But before going through it, Burk Laudimer came to a stop and, looking at his companion, said under his breath, "Do you remember the tale of old Cissy Clackett?"

"Cissy Clackett? . . . You mean Cissy Clackett over there?" He pointed to the right of him where the tall grass was almost obliterating the small headstones.

"Aye, that Cissy Clackett." Burk Laudimer now turned from the gate and made his way into the long grass until he came to a side wall close to which was a headstone so green with moss that the inscription on it was almost obliterated, and he turned to Andy Fairweather and, his words slow and low, he said, "She was buried seventeen twenty-four and as the story goes she just escaped being burned, they had stopped doing them then. But now, listen here"—he now bent his head close to that of Andy Fairweather—"Old Annie Trotter was a Page before she married, wasn't she?"

"I don't know."

"Well, she was; and you should know 'cos you've lived in the village as long as me, and your people afore you. Anyway, the Pages took their names from the male side, didn't they, but on the female side they were the Clacketts and they went back right to old Cissy here." He now went to clap his hand on top of the headstone but stopped suddenly as if in fear, and he rubbed his palm up and down his thigh again before he went on, "This thing runs right through families, the female side—always the female side—and from all the evidence we've heard the night, an' what I've suspected for a long time, young Tilly Trotter's picked up the thread."

"Eeh! Well, 'tis a funny thing to say, Burk."

"'Tis true, these things run in families, like boss eyes and harelips."

"Aye, I've got to agree with you there; aye, you're right there."

They both turned now and made their way back to the gate, through it and into a sunken road that led down into the village.

Presently Burk Laudimer said, "Gona call in?"

Andy Fairweather hesitated, saying now, "Oh, I don't know the night; I'm not feelin' too clever, heavy tea I think."

"Aw, come on, a mug of Bessie's brew will cure that."

"I don't think we should, Burk. If Fossett gets to hear about it he won't like it."

"Damn Fossett I say! I do what I like in me own time.

I pay me respects on Sunday, I do me duty, but there's nobody goin' to stop me wettin' me whistle when I want to."

Andy Fairweather lowered his head for a moment, then gave a shaky laugh and turned with Burk Laudimer round the curve of the narrow street where the houses seemed to bow to each other from each side of the road and into an open square in the middle of which was a round of rough grass, and at the center of this a flat stone measuring about six foot square.

On the far side of the green was a row of cottages sitting well back and fronted by small gardens, and on the near side, that to which the two men were now making their way, was a crescent of what appeared to be workshops. The end one gave evidence of being the blacksmith's shop by the faint glow coming through the open doorway. The wheelwright's next door was distinguished by its swinging board with its trademark painted on it. A space divided it from the baker's shop, and another opening beyond the baker's provided space for the vehicles belonging to the patrons of the inn. Beyond the inn were two cottages, stone-faced and sturdy looking, one occupied by the cobbler, the other by a breeches maker who was also a hosier, for he could knit stockings as well as any woman, better in fact some said. But then of course he wasn't really a man, having been stunted in his youth and only four foot in height. The grocer's shop took up the space of two cottages, and it needed every inch because with the exception of meat, it sold most things necessary to the village life.

The crescent now straggled away in an untidy end covered by a row of small cottages which housed the drover, who was also the mole catcher, the thatcher whose wife was the district midwife, and also the families of Andy Fairweather, George Knight, Tom Pearson, Burk Laudimer and lastly the McGraths.

Mr. Septimus Fossett, as behoved his standing in the church and the fact that he owned the draper's shop on the outskirts of Harton village, had a house fifty yards away. It possessed all of five rooms and had wooden floors, even in the kitchen. Moreover, the railings on the south side of his back garden touched on the grounds of the first of the gentlemen's residences which led toward Harton village, then on to Westoe village. But unfortunately and irritatingly so, its back windows looked on to the row of cottages lying down in the valley below. These were the habitations of Rosier's mine-workers.

As Burk Laudimer and Andy Fairweather entered the inn it was the adult section of the McGrath family that their eyes encountered, for Big Bill the father, Hal, and Mick were seated side by side on an oak settle that ran at right angles to one side of the deep based open fire, and opposite them on a similar settle sat four men, two being middle-aged and two decidedly old-aged. It was the elder of the latter, Charlie Stevenson, now turned eighty, who, wiping his ale dripping unkempt moustache with the back of his hand looked toward the newcomers and croaked, "Hie! there, Burk."

"Hello, Charlie." Burk Laudimer nodded at the old man, then at his companion, saying, "Evenin', Peg-Leg," and the man with the rough crutch by his side grinned at him toothlessly and bounced his head two or three times but made no reply.

It was toward the younger of the other two men that Andy Fairweather spoke, saying, "Why, Billy, don't often see you round here," and Billy Fogget, the carrier, replied, "Visitin' me sister, Andy, visitin' me sister."

"Who's lookin' after your cart?"

"Oh, me lad is for the next few days, he's got to learn."

When Bessie Bradshaw now called from behind the rough counter, "What's it to be?" Laudimer and Fairweather looked at each other; then it was Andy Fairweather who said, "Mild."

Having pulled two stools from under a rough table, they brought them to the front of the fire, placing them between the settles, and the conversation became general, in the course of which most of the attention was given to the carrier for he traveled places and knew about goings on. He told them about taking cart loads of folk up to the New Theater in Newcastle that had just been opened; that he only charged half as much as they would have paid by coach, but that they paid extra when it was raining for then he supplied covers for them, penny for sacks, tuppence for oilcloth. He told them he had spoken to people who had been to London and had glimpsed royalty; and when he told them he was in Newcastle on June 21st when news had come in that the King was dead and that the young Princess Victoria was now Queen, the four men on the settle sat open-mouthed.

The three McGrath men, too, seemed interested, because Fogget, being a natural story-teller, had the art of holding his audience; that was until Peg-Leg Dickens, speaking for the first time, said, "Wonderful thing 'tis to travel. Me, I traveled world till I got this." He patted the stump of his leg. "But now times 're different, nowt happens here, one day like t'other, nowt happens here."

He was shaking his head as Billy Fogget's companion Joe Rowlands, who was the hedger and ditcher, put in on a grunt of a laugh, "Aa wouldn't say that. It all depends what you're after for amusement; aye, it does. I get mine. Things I see nobody'd believe"—he nodded now toward Burk Laudimer—"but Dick and Bessie there." He turned his head to include the host and hostess now. "They know 'tis right, don't you, Bessie? Don't you, Dick?"

"About Sopwith?" Bessie Bradshaw heaved up her flagging breasts with her forearms, then laughed and said, "Put nowt past the gentry. Never put nowt past the gentry. As for the new 'un, she's a flyer if I ever saw one. Went past here like the divil in a gale of wind yesterday. Thinks she owns the county that one, an' not in it five minutes."

"What's this all about?" Andy Fairweather now looked at Joe Rowlands who, sensing he had the attention of the company, appeared in no hurry to explain further. Taking a long drink from his mug, he then wiped each side of his mouth with his knuckles before directing his gaze down to the floor. And there he let it remain for some seconds; then slowly raising his head he looked around the company from under his brows before saying, "I see things on me travels, I see things you'd never believe. First time you see 'em you think you're mistaken, but not second time. No, not second time."

"Well, go on, go on, you're lettin' it drip like treacle in the workhouse."

There was a guffawing now at Burk Laudimer's remark and old Charlie Stevenson spluttered, "Aye, go on, go on, Joe, it's spice you've got in your gob I can tell, I can tell, so spit it out, man, spit it out."

Joe Rowlands was laughing now at the old man. Nodding his head toward him, he said, "Aye, spice. Aye, spice, Charlie, 'twas spice all right. Well—" his eyes again traveled around the company and, his voice dropping now, he brought them into the circle of expectation by beginning, "It was on this night, the night that this village won't forget, Farmer Bentwood's wedding, you mind . . . what's been said about it, an' the divil's fagarties that took place. Well, I see some of what happens but only at the end of it. I heard the shoutin' an' the bashin' from a distance. I was takin' a short cut over from Lord Redhead's place, you know where our Fanny's man works on the estate, an' he had a bit of something for me"—he nodded and winked knowingly—"'twas in the shape of a bird, you understand." He pressed his lips together for a moment. "So there I was comin' back pathways, never expecting to

89

meet anybody 'cos I was goin' to drop down into Billings Flat. Anyway, there was this hullabaloo, an' me with what I had with me, well, I didn't want to show me face. I stayed up top of bank. There's rough ground there, you know round top of Billings Flat." He was nodding to each one in turn now. "I couldn't hear exactly what was going on but it was a rumpus right enough an' voices shouting and horses gallopin'. Then things went quiet and I was just about to get up and continue on me way when I hear the sound of horses coming toward me, and so I lay doggo and there who did I see, eh? Who did I see?" He paused, but no one broke the silence. "Mr. Sopwith himsel'. An' who was with him? The new lady from Dean House, Lady Myton." He paused again. "Now there they were right in front of me, an' I could see them plain from where I was lying atween two boulders. He said something to her which I couldn't catch; then as if he were picking up a sack of corn he had her off her feet and on her back. But it was no rapin' 'cos God she was willin'. Aye, God! I'll say that for him, she was willin'."

There was silence in the room now; then for the first time one of the McGrath men spoke. It was Hal. His voice quiet, soft and flat, he said, "You sure of this?"

The insult to his integrity brought Joe Rowlands to his feet and he barked at Hal McGrath, crying, "I'm not a bloody liar! What do you think I've been tellin' you, you think I made it up?"

"No, no—" Hal McGrath's voice was quiet, even pacifying—"only it's a night of tales goin' round." He cast his glance toward the carrier.

"'Tis no tale," Joe Rowlands interrupted him. "'Twas as I said, I could hardly believe me eyes the first time but when I came across it again then there was no mistakin'. No, it was no mistakin'. They passed me on the road they did with never a glance in my direction. I touched me cap but neither of them seemed to see me. I was in the ditch when they passed, but happenin' to go up the bank a few minutes later I saw them cutting up on to the fells an' it struck me where they were makin' for, the same place again. Well, I couldn't beat them to it an' get there afore they did 'cos it was a good half mile away an' there were three stone walls to jump, an' me jumping days are over. But what I did do was to skitter up through Fletcher's Copse and up to the mound near Trotter's cottage, and from there if I couldn't see exactly what they were up to I could tell the time of their goin' in and their comin' out. Well, from the time they reached the outcrop to the time they came out of it was a full half-hour, and as I guessed they didn't go out the way they came in, but they came out t'other end. They were a good way off from the mound but I could see them clearly although they were protected on each side by trees, and their parting was not 'Good-bye, Mr. Sopwith.' 'Goodbye, Lady Myton,' for she was hanging on to him like a bitch in heat and he was over her likewise. So there it is, the truth."

He looked full at Hal McGrath, who said, "Well! well! Aye, as you said, Joe, the things what happen round here, it isn't as quiet as you think."

"No, you're right there." Burk Laudimer was nodding in his direction now, and not to be outdone in the tale-telling he said solemnly, "Things happen in the open and beyond closed doors, which is the worse I wouldn't know. Andy and I here have just come from a meetin' in the vestry, an important meetin', and the result could have percussions on this village. Aye yes; yes, indeed."

"What kind of percussions?" Dick Bradshaw's voice came from behind the bar and his mind they all knew was linking the percussions with business, and Burk Laudimer, looking toward him, said smarmily, "Oh, it wouldn't affect you, Dick, it wouldn't affect you. But the vicarage it would. Aye, yes, it would that, the vicarage."

"The vicarage?"

"Aye, the vicarage."

"The vicarage?"

The question came from different throats now, then Peg-Leg Dickens said, "What's wrong with parson then?"

"'Tisn't parson, Peg-Leg, 'tisn't parson, 'tis his wife."

"His wife?"

"Aye." He nodded at him; then bending forward and his voice dropping a number of tones, he murmured, "She and that young Tilly Trotter up to larks in the vestry."

"Up to larks?" The carrier's round eyes were bright, his face was poked forward. He looked from one to the other; then his gaze resting on the three McGrath men sitting straight and silent, he laughed as he repeated, "Up to larks?" expecting them to join in his amusement. However, they neither smiled nor moved but waited for Burk Laudimer to continue, and he did.

"Dancin' they've been, dancin' together, their skirts almost up to their thighs, kickin' their legs up."

There was a murmur of "Never! never! not parson's wife."

"Aye, parson's wife." His voice was louder now. "But I don't blame parson's wife, no, no, 'tis young Trotter that I blame, as has been mentioned by Joe there. There was divil's fagarties to play on Farmer Bentwood's weddin' night, weren't there, but who started it?" He now turned his head and looked at Hal McGrath and said, "No blame attached to you, Hal; no, no, courtin's courtin' all the world over, an' as you said you tried to do it honest with her 'cos she had led you on; if she hadn't asked for it you wouldn't have attempted to give her it, would you now? No, no; so no blame's attached to you. And for Sopwith to sack you, 'twas a bloody shame, 'twas. She's trouble that girl, she's trouble. You're best off without her. Aye, I'd say, 'cos I was just pointin' out to Andy here back in the cemetery that old tombstone of Cissy Clackett, you know. Remember Cissy Clackett?" His head was again bobbing from one to the other; and the bobs were being returned, particularly from the two old men. "Well, she comes from that stock, young Trotter does. An' the thread runs strong in the female. As I said an' all back there in the vestry, it's a pity the stocks are not in use no more. Aye, it is that, for I'd put her in meself, I would that. An' as I was sayin' to Andy here an' all, there was Pete Gladwish's dog. That was a funny business now, wasn't it? Eh, wasn't it?"

When a silence fell on the room again, Big Bill McGrath turned his head slowly toward the counter and said quietly, "Fill 'em up all around, Bessie, small 'uns."

"Good, good. Oh, that's kind of you, Bill." They all stirred on their seats.

"Aye, aye, 'tis."

After half pints of ale were distributed among the men the conversation flagged somewhat, but when Burk Laudimer and Andy Fairweather rose to take their leave, the three McGrath men rose too, saying it was time for them to hit the road, and they all went out into the dark night together. They did not, however, immediately make their ways to their respective homes, but stood outside the inn talking for quite some time.

5

Parson Ross was only thirty-five years old but his slightly stooped shoulders, long face, and thinning hair made him appear a man in his middle forties. He was tall and thin, and usually had a sallow complexion, but at this moment his skin was suffused to a dull red, and his wide straight lips trembled slightly as he pressed them together, at the same time shaking his head as he looked at his wife.

Ellen Ross at twenty-six was what could be called petite. She hardly reached her husband's shoulder. Her hair was light brown, her eyes a startling clear blue; her manner and speech were quick and when she talked she had the habit of moving her hands, each gesture seeming to add emphasis to her words, as they did now. "They are spiteful, those men are spiteful. I've never liked them from the first. And churchwarden or no churchwarden, Mr. Fossett's an old granny. As for the wheelwright, well!" She grimaced and threw her arms wide as if pressing something away to each side of her.

George Ross now closed his eyes for a moment as he said with strained patience, "You are getting away from the point, Ellen. Were you or were you not dancing with Tilly Trotter in the vestry?"

"*Yes! Yes! Yes!* All right if you say we were dancing we were dancing, but as I've already told you, it was the first time it had happened there, and . . . and it was all over in a matter of seconds. And we didn't move the benches back; we went around the table once."

Ellen looked at her husband as he closed his eyes again while his head slowly drooped toward his chest and, her voice pleading now, she whispered, "Oh! George, George, I'm so sorry if this has distressed you, but it all started so innocently. One day in the summer-house after I had taken Tilly for her letters I remarked that there was a barn dance being held outside of Westoe village and I asked her if she was going, and sadly, that was it . . . that was it, George. There was so much sadness in her voice when she replied she never went to barn dances, that in fact she couldn't dance at all, she had never danced. Well, George, you know yourself what used to happen on birthdays and anniversaries at home when Mother played the spinet and

Robert the violin, you were there, and you enjoyed it you did. Our drawing-room was gayer than any court ball; you said so yourself."

The vicar slowly raised his head now and looked with infinite sadness at his wife as he said softly, "That was before we were married, Ellen. When you agreed to become my wife you knew there would be responsibilities, and these responsibilities would be heavily laden with decorum. We talked about this, didn't we?"

"Yes, George." Her voice was flat, her hands remained still, joined tightly together at her waist now.

"The first Mrs. Ross was . . ."

"Oh! Oh no! George." Her hands had sprung apart and her head was shaking widely. "Please, don't tell me again of the first Mrs. Ross's qualities. If you do I shall scream."

"Ellen! Ellen! Ellen! Calm yourself. Dear! Dear!" He stared sadly at her. "I wasn't going to do any such thing except to admit that an excess of decorum can have its drawbacks when it impinges on happiness."

"Oh, I'm sorry. I'm sorry, George." She moved a step nearer to him and, putting out her hands, she gripped his and, looking up into his face, she said softly, "I will try, George. Honestly and faithfully, I give you my promise that from today I will try to be different."

The parson stared down into the face he so dearly loved. Then his nose twitched, his eyelids blinked, he wetted his lips and his voice now soft and unlike its previous tone, he said, "Oh, Ellen, Ellen, I do so want you to be happy, and . . . and, I would like to add, I want you to be free to take the line your active mind directs, but . . . but I am hampered, my very position hampers us both."

"I know, I know, my dear."

"Well now, Ellen, I'm sorry to have to say this, but you must stop seeing Tilly."

Now it was her eyes that blinked and her whole face

twitched and she glanced to the side before she said,
"Not even teach her her letters?"

"Not even that, my dear. They . . . the villagers,
they have strange ideas about Tilly, weird, stupid ideas,
but these ideas could make them dangerous."

"What . . . what kind of ideas?" Her head had
swung quickly around toward him again.

"Well—" he became embarrassed for a moment and
his lips worked in and out before he answered, "She is
apparently a descendant of an old lady who . . . who is
buried in the churchyard. Her name was Cissy Clackett
and she was . . . well, they seem to think she had
supernatural powers."

"A witch?"

"Yes, yes, I suppose she would in those days have
been called a witch."

Ellen's hands jerked quickly away from her husband's and her body bristled with indignation as she
cried, "And they're saying that Tilly is a witch! Tilly
Trotter a witch!"

"My dear, you must have realized yourself that most
of the villagers are ignorant people and ignorant people
thrive on superstition. . . ."

"But Tilly a witch, huh!" She gave a mirthless laugh.
"I have never heard anything so stupid in my life. She's
a sweet, kind, quite innocent girl, and I've never heard
her say a wrong word about anyone, not even about
that horrible McGrath man." She paused for a moment
while they stared at each other; then in a high, clear
voice, like someone asking a question of the platform,
she said, "Are they intending to burn Tilly Trotter,
sir?"

"Don't be silly, Ellen."

"I am not being silly, at least not any more silly than
the villagers or anyone else who takes notice of them."

"Ellen!"

Although his voice held a stern reprimand it seemingly had no effect on her now for, swinging round from

him and walking to the far end of the drawing-room, she looked out of the window for a moment before turning again with the same swinging movement and facing him across the room as she cried, "And what sentence are they likely to put on. me should they discover that I sit alone for an hour at a time in the summer-house with three coal-begrimed pitmen?"

"What! What did you say?"

"I think you heard, George, what I said. I sit alone at least one hour a week, sometimes two hours a week, with three very dirty, ignorant miners from Mr. Rosier's pit."

The vicar's long face seemed to take on inches. His mouth dropped into a gape, his eyebrows moved up toward his receding hair, and as he walked toward her his gait could have suggested that he had been indulging early in the day. An arm's length from her he stopped and his head moved with a small unbelieving motion as he said, "No! no! Ellen, you couldn't, not Mr. Rosier's men. Do you know what you're doing?"

"Yes, yes, I do. I am helping them to express themselves; I am pushing them through the thick barrier of ignorance, the ignorance that you yourself say is prevalent in this village. But these men are different, they've had enough of ignorance, they have at last realized the power that lies in the pen, and in being able to read the written word."

The parson now drew in a long breath and let it out slowly before he said in a flat unemotional tone, "And of what help, may I ask, will this knowledge be to them when they are dismissed from their work, and not only dismissed but more probably they and their families turned out of their cottages?"

Her lids were blinking again and it was some seconds before she said, "They . . . they know the risk they are taking and, as one of them has already said, except for the cold they'd have to endure during the winter he'd rather sleep on the hillside, in fact bring his family up there, than in the hovels that Mr. Rosier provides for the men who work for him."

The parson's face was a deep red now, there were beads of sweat on his brow, and he seemed to find difficulty in speaking. "This must stop and at once. You have gone too far, Ellen. You are young, you know nothing about the privations of these men, what can happen to them when they are without work. Outside this very parish last year a man died on the road through starvation. He was found stiff in a ditch. He was one of Rosier's men. You haven't as yet seen people standing for hours waiting for a bowl of weak soup; you haven't as yet seen a child tugging at the breast that held no milk. You have a lot to learn, Ellen. Now tell me, when are you seeing these men again?"

It was some time before she answered him. Her hands hanging slack by her sides, her head bent, she seemed for the moment defeated as she whispered, "They're . . . they're waiting for me now in . . . in the summer house."

"Dear God! Dear God!"

Ellen's head came up slowly. The fact that her husband had used God's name outside of prayer or when in the pulpit showed how deeply troubled he was, and so she was torn inside between the hope of bringing the glory of reading and writing to the poor and the love, the deep passionate love, she had for this man.

Sensing some of her feelings, his manner softened. He put his hand out and gently took her arm, saying, "Come, we will settle the matter now at once. They will understand. Put on your cloak and bonnet."

His last command brought a slight stiffening to her body. Put on her cloak and bonnet to go down to the summer-house! But it melted away on the thought that, as he said, she was the parson's wife, she was going out in the open and her head must be covered, as must her dress.

A few minutes later they were walking side by side

over the stone flags of the large hall, through the heavy oak door, across the narrow terrace and down the six broad stone steps that led on to the gravel drive.

The drive curved away to the iron gates that gave on to the road, but since they were going to the bottom of the garden they took the path along past the three mullioned windows and were about to go under the topiary archway leading into the flower garden when the sound of running steps and a voice calling "Parson! Parson!" brought them to a stop, and they both looked to where Tom Pearson hurried panting up the drive toward them.

When the painter came to a stop in front of them he was unable to speak, and the parson said with some concern, "What is it, Tom? Something wrong?"

"Don't know, parson, don't know for sure yet, but I fear something could go wrong, and badly so."

"Your family?"

"Oh no! No! No, not me family." Tom Pearson now glanced toward Ellen and muttered in a gasping shy manner, "'Tis young Tilly Trotter I fear, ma'am."

"Tilly! What's happened to her?"

"Don't know, ma'am, not yet, but things could."

"Speak up, Tom." The parson's voice was brisk now. "What can happen to Tilly?"

"Well—" Tom swallowed deeply, drew some spittle into his mouth, made as if to get rid of it, changed his mind, swallowed again, then blurted out, "'Tis the stocks, the old stocks that used to be on the slab in the center of the village years gone by; been lying in Tillson's barn this age. I wouldn't have believed it, wouldn't have known nowt about it but for young Steve McGrath. I found him crying, poor little devil, in the wood, Hal had thrashed the daylights out of him, I think he's broken the boy's arm. I told him to go to Sep Logan, he knows more about bones than most, but the lad had been and Sep, like everybody else seemingly, was away to the fair, except the three concerned, Burk

Laudimer, Andy Fairweather, and Hal McGrath himself."

"But . . . but what about Tilly? What about her?"

"I'm comin' to that, ma'am. They set up the stocks again in the old barn and Laudimer sent his young Frank with some sort of a message; apparently young Steve was on his way to tip Tilly the wink but Hal McGrath sensed what he was up to and by! he has lathered that lad, there won't be a place on him that's not black and blue the morrer. But . . . I knew it was no good me goin' on me own, I couldn't tackle the three of 'em and . . . and it's authority they want"—he was looking at the vicar—"brawn alone won't stop 'em, Parson."

Again Ellen heard her husband murmur. "Dear God! Dear God!" Then without further words the three of them were going through the garden at a pace between a trot and a run.

It was when they came to the side path which would lead them into the vegetable garden and so into the meadow beyond that Ellen, glancing over the long lawn which ran right up to the very steps of the summer-house, stopped and cried, "The miners! George. I'll bring the miners."

"No! No!" He paused in his walk and again said, "No, no." Yet there was a doubt now in the words and she, sensing it, ran from him lifting her skirts above her shoes as she did so, and when she burst into the summer-house the three grimed men rose slowly from the slatted wooden bench while their caps remained on their heads and were nodding toward her when she startled them by crying, "Come! Come quickly. You can help us. My . . . my friend, I mean a young girl, she's in trouble with some men. The vicar and I would . . . would be obliged if you would come and . . . and help us."

"Is it a fight, ma'am?"

They were out of the door now, following her

running steps toward the parson and Tom Pearson, and she had almost reached her husband before she answered them, saying, "It well might be. It well might be."

The parson gave no explanation to the miners; instead, after glancing at them with a look of dismay, all he said was, "We'd better hurry."

A wall separated the boundary of the vicarage from the meadow. It was a low wall and the men were over it in a moment and the parson, about to follow them, turned and looked at his wife and said, "Run to the gate, my dear." He pointed to the far end of the meadow, but for answer Ellen caused a shiver of shock to run through him while at the same time evoking a thrill of admiration from the men as she sat on top of the wall, pausing a moment as if in deference to her husband's feelings to spread her skirts over her ankles before swinging them to the other side.

They were all running again now. "Where we making for, sir?" One of the pitmen turned his head and shouted toward the minister, and George Ross called back, "The barn. Tillson's Barn. It's in the far end of the other field. We . . . we must cross the road."

Having crossed the meadow, this time they went through a gate, over the road, jumped a narrow ditch, climbed a bank, they were now in a large field. It was rutted here and there with outcrops of rock which made it unsuitable for farming and the sparse grass in between the outcrops hardly afforded enough grass even for a few sheep, yet at the far side of this field there had at one time been a farmhouse. But all that remained of the house now were the foundations buried among long tangled grass. Many years previous a fire had destroyed the house and most of the outbuildings, leaving only the barn whose timbers had stood the outrage of time for two hundred years and were still persevering; only time it seemed was now winning the battle, for the roof had fallen in a number of places, and the owner of the barn, Mr. Tillson, who now farmed about half a mile away, did not consider the place even worth attention. If it was used at all it was as a questionable shelter for those traveling the road or at some season in the year when the village children would decide to scramble over it.

That a commotion was going on inside the barn became evident to them all as they neared it, and when the parson, with the help of the miners, dragged open the half-door they were all brought into a moment's amazed silence at the scene before them.

Their entry also brought to a frozen halt the three men who were in the act of aiming something they had cupped in their hands at the bedraggled and gagged figure pinioned by arms, legs and head in the stocks.

Again the parson said, "Oh my God!" but now it was merely a whisper on a long soft outgoing breath, but the exclamations from the three pitmen were anything but soft. Their curses rang round the barn as they cried, first one, "Why you bugger in hell!" Then "You bloody maniacs!" And lastly as they seemed to leap forward of one accord the smallest and broadest of the three men yelled, "Stocks! Bloody stocks!"

What followed was a melee of blows and curses and figures slipping on the overturned box of rotten apples.

The parson was yelling now, his voice higher than ever he had allowed it to go in his life before; he was screaming at the combating men, "Give over! Cease I say! Stop it this moment all of you, stop it!" But when no one paid any heed to him he edged himself along by the barn wall, closely followed by Tom Pearson. They were making their way toward the top end and the stocks but before they reached them they were both thrown together by the combined force of the joined bodies of Andy Fairweather and one of the pitmen.

Ellen Ross had remained standing in the open doorway, her hands clapped tightly over her mouth, and moving from one foot to the other as if she was doing a standing march, but now seeing that her husband was being impeded in his efforts to reach Tilly, she ran blindly from the doorway and, weaving her way between the battling men, reached the end of the stocks, and as she moaned "Oh Tilly! Tilly!" she reached out and touched the bent shoulders pressed against the wood.

As her eyes darted over the back of the stocks she saw that the top section, which clamped Tilly's head down, was held in place by long wooden spikes set in sockets at each side. Gripping one of them she wrenched it back and forward and when she managed to ease it upward it came away so quickly that she stumbled backward. It was at this moment she saw, within an arm's length of her, that her brightest pupil was about to be given a final blow by Burk Laudimer. Laudimer had his fist upraised and her instinct told her that if it reached its aim Sam Drew would fall to the floor because his body was only being kept upright by the fact that Laudimer had him held by the front of his jacket.

Ellen never remembered turning the long peg in her hand, nor could she ever believe that even in her anger she had enough strength to fell a man, but when her swinging arm, her hand now gripping the narrow end of the peg, came in contact with Laudimer's neck, he became quite still for what appeared a long second. His left hand was still holding Sam Drew by the coat while his right arm, fist doubled, was raised in the air. So many things happened in that second, blood spurted from a hole in his neck, he screamed a high wild scream, at the same time loosening his hold on Sam Drew and swinging round to confront the parson's wife.

Ellen was still standing, her arm half extended; her hand was open now and the peg was lying across it but there was no blood on it, not what you could see.

Following the scream there fell on the barn a silence; then the parson and Tom Pearson came rushing toward the stocks, not to release Tilly, but for both to stand stock-still. Their eyes darted between the huddled prostrate figure on the barn floor and Ellen looking like a piece of sculpture carved in stone presenting an offering of a stock peg.

"What . . . what have you done?" The parson was now kneeling by the side of Burk Laudimer and, tearing a handkerchief from his pocket, he thrust it around the man's neck, then cried, "Give me something quick! A scarf, anything to bind him."

Tom Pearson wasn't even wearing a scarf or a neckerchief, he had on a high-breasted coat buttoned up to under his chin. Andy Fairweather was in no position to offer any assistance for he was lying slumped against the far wall. It was Hal McGrath who stumbled forward tearing at his white knotted neckerchief, and as he handed it down to the parson, the parson let his eyes rest on him for a moment and in a voice that no one in that place had ever heard him use before he said, "You've got a lot to answer for this day, Hal McGrath."

McGrath looked down on him where he was now tying the neckerchief around Burk Laudimer's neck in an effort to hold the pad of the handkerchief in place, and he said, "I ain't the only one likely who'll have a lot to answer for, ours was only a bit fun."

"Do you call this a bit fun?" It was Tom Pearson speaking now as he wrenched the pegs from out of their newly made sockets.

"Enough to turn anybody's reason. Fun you call it? You should be strung up, the lot of you."

When at last Tom Pearson, with the help of one of the miners, had Tilly free, they laid her down on the rough floor. Her eyes were closed, her face looked ashen, she could have been dead. Tom Pearson clasped her hands, then tapped each cheek, saying, "Come on. Come on, Tilly. Wake up. Wake up."

"Is . . . is she all right?" It was a small voice above

them and both Tom and the pitmen looked up at the parson's wife. Her face, too, was white and all her perkiness, as Tom Pearson called her vivacity, seemed to have left her.

"Tom." It was the parson calling now, and when Tom Pearson rose from his knees and went and stood by his side he noted that the parson too, in some subtle way, seemed strange. He would even have put the word frightened to the look in his eyes, and there was no command now in his voice as he said, "I . . . I can't stop the bleeding and . . . and I don't think it would be safe to move him at this stage. Will . . . will you go and get the doctor?"

"But it will take me all of an hour, parson, to get to Harton and back."

"Run to the vicarage. Get Jimmy to harness the trap." His voice was still quiet, flat, it was as if he were saying "Hurry" but at the same time implying that his errand would be fruitless.

As Tom Pearson now turned to run out of the barn he glanced toward the pitmen still kneeling by Tilly's side and called, "Will you see to her, see her home?" and one man answered, "Don't worry; we'll see her all right."

It was as the pitman spoke that Tilly opened her eyes, and she stared into the man's face for a full minute before, her lips trembling and her memory returning, the tears sprang from her eyes and rained down her brown mushed-apple-smeared face.

"There, there! It's all right. Can you stand, hinny?"

She made no answer, and the man helped her to her feet and as she stood wavering on her shaking legs Sam Drew said, "Come on, let's get out of here" and to this his companions said, "Quicker the better."

As they went to turn away, Sam Drew paused and, looking at Ellen, who was standing silently gazing toward her husband who was still on his knees, said, "Thanks, missis, you saved me bacon; he could have done for me. An' he would have an' all if he had got the chance, I could see it in his eyes." Then looking toward where his late opponent lay by the side of the parson's kneeling figure, he added, "Don't worry, missis, he'll be all right, 'tis only the good die young," and on this the three men turned away, two of them supporting Tilly, and went out of the barn.

Ellen stood and watched them. There was a non-reality about herself and the whole proceedings. She had never spoken to Tilly, never commiserated with her. It was strange but she had the feeling she was saying good-bye to her forever.

"Oh God above! what's happening to us? 'Tis the money. It all started with the money. Money's a curse. I've always said it, money's a curse. But lass! lass! to do that to you, to put you in the stocks. Why God above! there's been no stocks used for many and many a long year. Then to even make a place for your head. Oh dear God! Oh me bairn! Me bairn!"

They were sitting on a box in the woodshed and Annie had her arms around Tilly, cradling her head and rocking her as if she was indeed a bairn again. Presently she released her and, passing her fingers gently around Tilly's smeared face, she said, "Wash yourself. Go down to the stream and wash yourself and tidy yourself up. But for God's sake don't let an inkling of this get to your granda 'cos it would finish him off. He's bad, you know he's bad, if he has another turn like yesterday, it'll be the end of him. I'll . . . I'll tell him that the message that came from the parson's wife"—she now gritted her teeth together as she repeated —"supposedly from the parson's wife," and it was a second or two before she went on, "I'll tell him she wanted a hand with her scholars like, eh?"

Tilly made no response, she just rose to her feet and walked to the door of the woodshed where she leaned against the stanchion and looked up into the clear high sky. And her thoughts sprang upward too. She asked God why, why was He allowing all these things to happen to her? She had done no harm to anyone, she wished no harm on anyone—except to Hal McGrath, for added to the other business she would always remember the feeling of his hands again on her body after he had thrust her legs through the holes of the stocks.

It came to her now as she stared upward that she would never know happiness until she could leave this place. . . . Yet she could never leave it as long as it held the two people she loved and who needed her. She was like the linnet in the cage hanging outside the grocer's shop in the village which sang all day to the world it couldn't see: they had poked its eyes out because they said blind linnets sang better.

She walked down through the back garden, crossed the field and when she reached the burn she lay down on the grass and, bending over the water, she sluiced handfuls of it over her face and head. That done, she took a rag from her pocket and after wetting it in the burn she went into a thicket and there, lifting her skirt, she washed her thighs in an endeavor to erase the feeling of Hal McGrath's hands at least from her skin if not from her mind. . . .

When she returned to the house she endeavored to go about her duties as usual, but William noticed the change in her and he remarked, "You look peaky, lass, bloodless somehow. You're not eating enough, is that it?"

"I . . . I suppose so, Granda."

"It's a pity you don't like cabbage, and you grow them fine, there's a lot of goodness in cabbage."

"Yes, Granda."

"Are you feelin' bad, lass?"

"No, Granda."

"Are you tired then?"

"Yes; yes, I'm feelin' a bit tired."

"She's growin'." This was Annie's voice from where she was placing some griddle cakes on the hanging black griddle pan.

"Aye, yes; yes, she's growin', and into a bonny lass, a bonny, bonny lass." His voice faded away and his head sank into the pillow, and Tilly and her granny exchanged glances. . . .

It was almost dark when there came a knock on the door and it was opened before either Tilly or her granny could get to answer it. To their surprise they saw Simon standing there.

Annie's first words to him were, "Anything wrong, Simon?"

He made no reply for a moment but looked through the lamplight from one to the other, then turned his gaze toward the bed and William, and Annie, sensing trouble, said quickly, "William's not too clever, he . . . he had a turn yesterday."

"Oh. Oh."

"Anything . . . anything wrong, Simon?" William's words were slow and halting, and Simon called to him, "No, no; just on me way back from the fair, I thought I'd look in, see . . . see how you were doing."

"Aha." This was all the comment William made before closing his eyes again.

"You all right?" Simon now asked softly looking full at Tilly, and after a moment she answered, "Yes, yes, I'm all right, Simon."

"Well, that's fine, that's fine. I . . . I just thought I'd look in." He glanced again toward the bed and making sure now that William's eyes were closed he made a quick motion with his hand toward both Annie and Tilly, and they understanding the motion followed him to the door, which he opened quietly and went outside.

In the deep gloom they stood peering at him, and it was Tilly he looked at as he said, "You had a bad day then?"

"Yes; yes, Simon." She turned her head away.

"They're devils. I'll do for that McGrath yet."

"No, no, Simon"—Annie put her hand on his arm—"no violence like that. No, no."

"No violence, Annie?" His voice had a strange note to it now. "No violence you say! Well, I haven't only come to see if Tilly was all right, I've come with some news, violent news, bad news." He was again looking at Tilly. "Tom Pearson said you were dazed and you mightn't have taken in what happened. Do . . . do you remember the fight that took place?"

"Just . . . just dimly, Simon. I think I fainted like. I must have 'cos everything went black."

"Well, I must tell you because you'll know soon enough, they'll . . . they'll be coming to question you."

"They? Who's they?" Annie's voice was sharp.

"The police, Annie. The police."

"What!" They both said the word, Annie sharply and Tilly in a whisper.

"Apparently three pitmen that the parson's wife was teaching their letters to, went with them, I mean the parson and missis, when Tom Pearson told them that Hal McGrath, Burk Laudimer and Andy Fairweather had Tilly in the old barn in the stocks, and apparently from what I can gather there was a fight, and Laudimer was knocking daylights out of one of the pitmen, who was almost at his end, when Mrs. Ross who had taken a peg out of the stocks to release you Tilly, saw this little fellow being knocked silly by Laudimer and God knows why, because she's a refined lady, but she hits him on the neck with the peg. But of course she didn't know that there was a nail in the top end, it was placed there I suppose to stop the peg slipping further into the socket. Well, it went into Laudimer's neck." He stopped, swallowed, looked from one side to the other, and now in a mumble, he finished, "He . . . he bled to death."

"No! No!" Tilly backed from him, her head shaking.

"No! Mrs. Ross could never have done that. No! no! She's small, not strong."

"It's all right, Tilly, it's all right. Now, now stop trembling."

Both Simon and Annie had hold of her now, but so violently was her body shaking that they shook with her.

"Get her around to the back, Simon, William . . . William mustn't be disturbed. . . ."

Once more they were in the woodshed, and Tilly was crying loudly now, "Oh no! no! they'll hurt her, they'll do something to her. She's lovely, lovely, a lovely woman. An' all through me, all through me."

"Hold her fast, Simon. I'll go an' get a drop of William's laudanum, she'll go off her head else."

In the dark he held her while, with her arms about him, she clung to him, crying all the while, "Because of me, because of me. There's a curse on me. There must be, there must be, Simon, there must be a curse on me."

"Ssh! Ssh!"

And with one arm tightly around her waist and the other cupping her shoulders he thought, And there's a curse on me, a blind curse. Why in the name of God couldn't I see where me heart lay. Oh Tilly! Tilly! There, there, there my love, my love.

6

"Why don't you go and live across there?"

"Look, Mary. . . ."

"Don't look Mary me. Yesterday you went to the old fellow's funeral. He was buried at ten o'clock in the morning but you never landed back here until almost dark. Do you think the farm can run itself?"

"No, I don't think the farm can run itself." Simon's tone now had changed from one pleading for understanding to an angry yell. "I was born and brought up on it and for the last ten years have worked from dawn till dusk, and far into the night. I've made it what it is, so don't you say to me do I think the farm can run itself. And what's more, let's get this out into the open once and for all, the Trotters are my friends, our families have been close for years. . . ."

"Huh! a miner and a farmer friends?" Her words were a mutter but he picked them up and cried at her, "Yes, a miner and a farmer; but not an ignorant miner, William Trotter was one of the wisest men I've ever known. Well, now he's gone and his wife, an ailing old woman, and Tilly, but a lass, are alone. . . ."

"But a lass!" Mary Bentwood flounced around so quickly that her heavy wool skirt billowed; then as quickly again she turned toward him, her voice as loud as his now as she cried, "That girl's a menace! From the day I wed she has got into my hair. I've got her to thank for my wedding night and the week that followed and this thing that's been between us ever since. They're saying roundabout that she's a witch and not a good one, a bad one, one that creates trouble. A man is dead, and it wasn't really the parson's wife who brought him low, that poor woman would have had no need to go to the barn that day if it hadn't been for that . . . that creature."

"Don't"—Simon's voice was low now, his words thick—"don't speak of her like that. She's naught but the victim of circumstances. She's too attractive for her own good, and women, aye women like you Mary, sense this. Yes, yes"—he nodded at her, his head bouncing on his shoulders now—"I'm telling you the truth, and men, aye, men, although they mightn't know it, want her. She's got something about her that they want and because she won't give it their feelings turn to hate."

"Aw! Oh!" Mary Bentwood's face was now wearing an unpleasant smile that slowly mounted into a broad sneer, and after staring at her husband for a moment she asked, "Are you speaking of your own feelings, Simon?"

"Oh my God! woman"—again his head was shaking, but slowly now—"you'll drive me mad afore you're finished."

"Huh! Huh! Five months we've been married and now I'm driving you mad. All right, I'm driving you mad. Well, what I'm going to tell you now might add to it, and it's just this, Simon Bentwood, when you're away from the farm I don't work, the milk can go sour, the churns green, but I don't do a hand's turn when you're gone from this house other than the days you're at market. Now there you have it. And I'll add to that, I didn't promise to be your wife in order to be a slavey."

He stared at her for a full minute before he inclined his head toward her once, saying now, "Very well, have it your way. You don't work, then I get someone in who will, and I'll hand the housekeeping over to her every week. You can sit on your backside and pick your nails, or sew fine seams for your frocks, as you seem to have done all your life. Anyway, now we know where we stand. I'm away to give me men their orders and they'll see that the farm, at least outside, doesn't drop to pieces until I return from Newcastle."

Simon now turned from his wife and went across the room and as he opened the door into the hall her screaming voice seemed to thrust him forward as she cried, "I hate you, Simon Bentwood! I hate you, and your old farm and everything about you and it."

He closed the sitting-room door quietly, then standing still, his shoulders hunched, he screwed up his eyes tightly and bit on his lip before straightening up again and, this time thrusting back his shoulders, he crossed the hall, went through the kitchen and out into the yard to where his trap was waiting for him.

Simon loved Newcastle. The first time he had visited it he had gone on foot. As a lad of thirteen he had walked the ten miles to watch the hoppings on the town moor; but even on that day his interest had been caught by the sight of the amazingly beautiful buildings. He remembered he had left the town moor in the early afternoon and wandered through streets and crescents and terraces, imagining that they couldn't be real because no man could build so high and so decoratively with great lumps of stone. In the village it took the masons and the carpenters all their time to erect a double-storied house. Of course around about the village were the big houses of the gentry, but at that early age, he didn't imagine these had been built by the hand of man either.

Since those days he had not once visited the city without leaving himself time, if only half an hour, to wander about; and now in the twelve years that had passed the changes that had come about were amazing. The bridges he found fascinating, but the streets even more so because these were where people actually lived.

There was the new Jesmond Road and the Leazes Crescent with its rounded gable ends, and the beautiful Leazes Terrace, four great windows high; as for Eldon Square, he always imagined that Mr. Dobson, the designer, must have thought it up during the period of his life when he was happiest. And Mr. Grainger, who built the Square, well, what had *he* thought when he put the last touches to the long handsome wrought-iron balconies?

Strangely, after each visit to the city he would experience a day or two of unrest. Although within himself he was aware that he had been born to farm the land, he realized there were other avenues in life that could give a man intense satisfaction, for once a street, a terrace, a church was built it was there. You could move on to other things, greater things, express greater dreams, but on the land life covered but one year at a time, your long efforts were whipped up with the scythe or ended when you struck the fatal blow at an animal you had come in a way to like—he wouldn't go as far as to say love. . . .

But here he was in Newcastle today and it would be the one time he wouldn't walk its elegant streets that spoke of wealth and comfort, but which he recognized in his heart housed only a small portion of the population, for at the other end of the city there were rows of hovels that he wouldn't put his pigs into.

As he drove the trap toward the courthouse his mind was a turmoil of emotions, private emotions. His marriage had gone sour on him right from that first night. He knew he had made a mistake in picking Mary for a mate, but he also knew he'd have to live with his mistake.

His horse was brought to a standstill in the midst of a mêlée of traffic. There were gentlemen's coaches, beer drays, ragmen's flat carts laden with stinking rags and their horses with heads bent as if in sorrow at their plight. There were meat carts and vegetable barrows; there were fish carts and knackers' vans, the latter displaying their trade by the legs of the dead animals sticking out from the back, one animal piled on top of the other as if they had been instantly massacred, which he hoped was the way they had died, for some men made killing a slow business.

The din was indescribable; Simon's call to his horse to be steady was lost to his own ears. The pavements along each side of the road were full of people. These in a way were fortunate because they were walking on flagstones, a new acquisition to the streets, but the road where the traffic was jammed was still made up of mud and broken stones.

When at last there was a movement and Simon

turned his horse's head toward a lane that led off at the top of the street he found his passage again blocked. Standing up in the trap he could see that the hostelry ahead where he usually left his horse was jammed full. He looked to the side of him where a man in a similar trap to his own shouted, "The town's out, it must be the case at the courthouse, the parson's wife," and he nodded; but Simon didn't return the nod. He glanced behind him. No one had turned in from the main road to block his return passage and so, jumping down from the trap, he took the horse's head and eased her backward, to the main road where he mounted the trap and rode onward.

Agitated inside, he pulled out a lever watch from his waistcoat pocket. It said quarter past eleven. The case would have already begun and Tilly, looking around for just one friend, would encounter nothing but the hostile gaze of the villagers. And these would undoubtedly be making a day of it. Oh yes, they'd be making a day of it all right.

He did not at this moment think of what might happen to the parson's wife; she had lawyers and big men on her side, her family were important. Anyway, she was only being charged with manslaughter, not murder, and whatever her sentence, one way or another, she'd be gone from the village after today. But not so Tilly, Tilly had to live there, as long as her granny was alive Tilly would stay there. But what would happen to her? Apart from Tom Pearson and himself, aye, and young Steve, there wasn't one soul in that whole place that had a good word for her. After Laudimer died they would have killed her. Now that was strange for it wasn't she who had struck the blow; but they'd worked it all back to the beginning: the parson's wife was in the pickle she was because of Tilly Trotter.

My God! if only he could get out of this jam.

It was a full half hour later when he found a stable

where he could leave the horse and trap, and from there it was all of a ten minute run back to the court-house. And run he did; but when he tried to enter the building his way was blocked by the spectators. The outer hall was a mass of people, yet all strangely quiet, until he began to thrust himself between them, when there were angry murmurs. But he took no notice. Some made way for him, thinking he was some kind of an official, that was until he came to the main doors leading into the courtroom itself, and there he was confronted by an officer of the law.

"How . . . how far is it on?"

"Over half-way I should say, sir."

"The main witnesses, have they . . . ?"

"Yes, I think so. The young lass is on the stand now."

"Please let me in." Simon brought his face close to that of the officer, saying again, "Please, let me in. You . . . you see I"—he gulped in his throat—"I'm about the only friend she has."

They stared into each other's eyes for a moment; then the officer said, "Well, even if I could sir, I doubt if you'd make it, it's as bad in there as it is out here, it's crammed."

"Let me try, please." His hand came out of his pocket and slid unobtrusively in front of him and pressed something into the officer's hand and the officer, not taking his eyes from Simon's now, said, "Well, you can have a try, sir," and on this he turned the big handle of one of the double doors, and as he opened it a number of people almost fell backward. Simon, pressing himself forward with the aid of the policeman, forced himself into the throng, and the door was pushed slowly behind him; and there he was looking to where Tilly stood on a railed dais gazing toward the bench and the man who was speaking to her. . . .

"You have heard what the other witnesses in this case have said. To their mind you are the cause of Mrs. Ellen Ross being present here today and being charged with manslaughter. One of them has definitely stated that you have some . . . well"—the judge now looked down at the bench, then over it and on to the head of the clerk standing below before he raised his eyes to the witness box again—"occult power. You understand what I mean by that?"

"No . . . o, no . . . o, sir."

"Well, in ordinary terms it means that you dabble in witchcraft."

Everyone in the courtroom had their gaze fixed on Tilly waiting for her answer, but she didn't reply, not even to make a motion of her head, and Simon, gazing at her, cried voicelessly, "She knows as much about witchcraft as an unborn child. Oh, Tilly! Tilly!"

"Well, do you dabble in witchcraft?"

"No, sir. *No! No!*" Her words were slow but emphatic now. "I . . . I never . . . never have, never. I . . . I don't know nothing about witchcraft."

"It has been stated that you enticed the parson's wife to dance in a place that is usually considered part of holy ground, namely the vestry. Did you do this?"

For the first time Tilly took her eyes from the judge and looked toward Ellen Ross and when Ellen shook her head at her she looked at the judge again, then mumbled, "We did a step or two, sir."

"She didn't! I taught her to dance." Ellen Ross's voice ringing through the courtroom caused the whole place to buzz; and now there were two men standing in front of her and talking to her.

The judge struck the bench with a mallet and after the hubbub had slowly died away he, looking at Tilly again, said, "You danced in the vestry?" and after a moment Tilly said, "Yes, sir."

"What else did you do in the vestry?"

"Nothing, sir, only a few steps up and down."

Looking at the bench once again, the judge was heard to mutter to himself, "Only a few steps up and down"; then raising his head his next question was,

"Do you hold yourself accountable for being here today? Do you in any way think that you are responsible for the death of Burk Laudimer?"

"No, sir. No, sir."

"But you have heard the prosecuting counsel say that you are responsible inasmuch as the accused, Mrs. Ellen Ross, would never have gone to your assistance had you not been put in the stocks, and you would not have been put in the stocks had you not been seen to be dancing on holy ground. So can you still say that you don't feel at least partly responsible for what is happening in this court today?"

As Tilly drooped her head Simon groaned inwardly. These men with their words and their cleverness, they could make out black was white. He allowed his own head to hang for a moment, or was it two or three, but he brought it up sharply as the judge said, "Mark my words well, young woman. Now you may stand down."

He watched her stumbling down the two steps, then being led to the end seat of the front row, and when she sat down he could no longer see anything of her. But the courtroom became astir again. "Call Hal McGrath . . . Hal McGrath."

McGrath dressed in his Sunday best, his hair brushed back from his low forehead, a clean white neckerchief knotted below his Adam's apple, his gray worsted coat tightly buttoned across his chest, stood with his cap in both hands, his mien that of a quiet country man.

"You are Hal McGrath? You are said to be the man responsible for putting the girl, Tilly Trotter, into the stocks?"

There was a pause before McGrath spoke, and then he said, "Yes, sir, 'twas me."

"Why did you do this?"

"Just . . . just for a joke, sir."

"Nothing more?"

"Well"—McGrath's head swung from side to side – "I'd been a-courtin' her and she'd egged me on like;

then she threw me off so I suppose, sir, 'twas, 'twas a bit spite in it."

"You're honest, I'll say that for you."

Again Simon hung his head and missed something that was being said by the judge, but McGrath's answer to it was, "Yes, sir, I'd heard of things she'd done like an' 'twas a bit odd, but I thought, well, when we were wed I'd knock that all out of her."

This answer evoked loud guffaws and brought the eyes of the judge on all those present.

"Do you in any way hold yourself responsible for the death of Burk Laudimer?"

"Well"—McGrath looked from one side then the other—"no, sir. No, sir, 'tain't me what hit him."

"No, it wasn't you that hit him"—the judge's voice was stern now—"but had you not put that girl in the stocks then Mrs. Ross would have had no need to go to her rescue, nor to call in the aid of three miners, nor in defense of one of them to strike a blow that inadvertently brought about the death of a man." There was a pause now before the judge asked, "Do you still want to marry this girl?"

There was another pause before Hal McGrath muttered, "Aye, sir."

"Then I hope it may come about, and it could be the making of her. Stand down."

Simon leaned against the door and closed his eyes. He was raging inside. Marry Hal McGrath and be the makings of her. He would do for him first before he saw that happen to her.

"Call Mrs. Ellen Ross."

The parson's wife was on the stand. After the preliminary questioning by the counsel the judge addressed her and it was evident to everyone in court that he was speaking to her in a manner that he hadn't used to any previous witness that day.

"You are very interested in education, is that not so, Mrs. Ross?"

"Yes, my lord." Ellen's voice came as a thin whisper.

"It is your desire to educate the laboring classes?"

There was a pause, and again she said, "Yes, my lord."

"Have you now come to the conclusion that your decision to do so was ill-advised?"

"No, my lord." Her voice was stronger, her manner slightly more alert, and undoubtedly she had non-plussed the judge for again he looked down at the bench, then on to the head of the clerk before continuing, "You don't think it ill-advised that because you desired to teach three pitmen their letters they are now out of employment?"

When she made no reply to this the judge waited a few minutes before going on, "Well now, tell me, do you not think it would have been wiser if you had refrained from teaching the girl, Tilly Trotter, her letters and attempting to coach her into refinements that are far above her station, such as dancing gavottes and such like?"

The whole court stared at Ellen as, her chin coming up now, she said, "Country people dance, your honor, farm laborers and such, as do the people in the lower end of this city."

It was evident now by the judge's tone that his sympathy for the parson's wife was waning a little, for his voice was crisp as he said briefly, "There's dancing and dancing as you well know; as the classes differ so do their types of recreation, and this, I think, has been proved by the very fact that this case is being tried in this court today."

The assembled people watched the judge purse his lips, then look toward an object lying on the bench; and, pointing to it, he seemed to address it as he said, "This is the implement that caused the death of a man. Had you any idea that it had a nail in its end when you picked it up?"

He was now looking at her, and her voice trembled a

little as she answered, "No, my lord, of course not, no."

"Why did you aim the blow at the deceased man? Was it because he was one of the men that put the girl in the stocks or was it because he was attacking one of the workmen you had come to look upon as a sort of protégé?"

Some seconds passed before Ellen gave her answer, and then she said, "I don't know, my lord. My intention was to thrust the man aside because I could see that Mr. Drew was in a bad way and . . . and the further blow would have felled him to the ground."

"Yes, yes." The judge was now looking down at the bench again. The court waited; then lifting his head he said abruptly, "You may stand down."

As the defense counsel stepped forward to present his side of the case there was a stir in the middle of the court as a woman fainted, and when they brought her limp body toward the doors Simon was pressed outside into the hall once again, and when he attempted to return into the courtroom it was only to find that the door was closed with someone else having obviously taken his place and pressed against the door. The policeman, remembering the tip, spoke apologetically, saying, "Sorry, sir, that's how things go. You couldn't get another pin in there."

Seeing it was no use trying any further persuasion, Simon turned about and pushed through the throng and out into the open air. All he could do now was wait until the case was over. . . .

It was almost an hour later when the courtroom doors opened and the people surged through the hall and into the street. It was now that Simon forced his way back through them and into the courtroom. The bench was empty, but before it he saw the parson standing, his wife enfolded in his arms, and about them a number of men. But standing alone at the far end of the long front seat was Tilly, and he made his way straight toward her and without preamble took her hand and said, "I was outside, I didn't hear how it went."

Tilly looked up into his face and muttered slowly, as if coming out of a dream, "She's free. Thank God!"

"Come." As he turned her about and went to walk up the aisle, he glimpsed from the side of his eye the parson's wife turning from her husband's arms and looking toward them.

But Tilly didn't notice for her head was down, and she kept it down until they were well away from the court walking up a comparatively quiet street and then she stopped and, looking up at Simon, she said, " 'Twas awful, Simon, awful, to say I was a witch. Simon, what has come upon me?"

"Nothing, nothing, me dear. Don't let it trouble you."

She shook her head hard now as if throwing off his soft words as she said bitterly, "But it does trouble me, Simon, it does. I've . . . I've never done any harm to anyone, not even to wish them harm, that is not until the last business, then I wished, I even prayed, that God would strike Hal McGrath, I did. But that is the one and only time I've ever wished bad on anybody. They're even saying I spirited Pete Gladwish's dog away. Can you understand it, Simon?" Her voice had risen. "What'll they say I've done next? I'm afeared, Simon."

"Now! now!" He gripped her hands tightly. "No one's going to do anything more to you; I'll keep a look out."

"No, no, don't." She now pulled her hands away from his and began walking up the street again, and she had her head turned from him as she went on, " 'Tis best if you keep away from me, they're sayin' things."

"Who's sayin' things?" His voice was grim.

"Oh, all of them." She moved her head wearily now.

"Well, what are they saying?"

Her voice harsh again, she cried, "They're sayin' I'm the cause of your marriage going wrong."

He pulled her to a sharp stop, demanding now, "Who said my marriage is going wrong?"

"Oh, it's no matter, I just heard."

"You must have heard it from somebody. Who said it?"

She lifted her head and looked him in the eyes now as she replied, "Randy Simmons has put it about that you're always fightin' and it's 'cos of what happened on your marriage night. Oh, Simon, Simon, I'm sorry."

"Damned lot of rot! Never heard such idiot talk in me life. Don't you believe a word of it." He bent toward her now. "Do you hear! don't you believe a word of it. You know, it's funny"—he straightened up—"I've read things like this, about every now and again a village going mad. They've nothing to do except their grind, nothing to interest them after, so they hatch up something like a—" he had almost brought out "a witch hunt" but substituted quickly, "a scandal and run a gossip shop."

Slowly she turned from him and began to walk again, and presently she said quietly, "If it wasn't for me granny I would leave the place an' go miles away. I could get work, perhaps in a big house, somewhere where I wasn't known."

"Well, you can't leave, you know you can't, you've got your granny, and she needs you, more so now than ever before 'cos she's lost William."

They walked on in silence until she broke it by saying, "I miss me granda, Simon. He was always kind to me. He never gave me a harsh word in his life. I . . . I suppose"—she dropped her head slightly to the side as if thinking back—"between them they spoiled me. I was lucky to have been brought up by them. Aye, I was."

He cast his glance toward her. Lucky, she said, and here she was walking through the streets of Newcastle dressèd as the poorest of the poor would be in this city. Her short blue coat was green in parts; her serge skirt had been darned in various places near the hem; her hat was a flat straw one and unadorned; her boots had seen better days, one toe showing it had recently been very roughly cobbled. He would like to take her into a restaurant and give her a meal but her appearance might suggest he had picked her up from the street. He wished also he were able to take her into one of the fashionable new dress shops with their huge glass windows and say, "Rig her out"; but were he to do so he wouldn't now be able to pay out of his own pocket. What the old couple didn't know was that the money had run out some time back, for his father had not only spent his own share, he had dipped into William's side too; and so he himself had sworn that as long as they needed it the sovereign a month would be forthcoming. Up to the time of his marriage the carrying out of this resolution had been easy, but since, what he had discovered, among other things, was that his wife had a nose for keeping accounts, and he knew that in the future he was going to be hard pushed to explain where the regular payment went.

And so he said, "There's a shop not far from here, would you like some pies and peas? They're good; I generally have a plate when I come into the city."

She hesitated, then said, "I'm not hungry, Simon."

"Aw, come on; you'll be hungry when you smell these." He took her arm and hurried her forward now and within a few minutes they were standing among others scooping up the hot pies and peas, and he smiled at her, saying, "Good?" and she answered, but without a smile, "Yes, very tasty, Simon, very tasty."

As he was finishing the last mouthful of pie, Simon, glancing over the mingled customers toward the open door, saw white flakes falling and exclaimed on a mutter, "Oh, not snow!" then looking at Tilly who had only half finished her food, he said, "We'll have to be moving, Tilly; look, it's starting to snow."

"Aye; I don't really want any more, Simon." She put the plate down.

"Are you sure?"

"Yes; 'twas nice but I'm not hungry."

"Come on then. . . ."

Fifteen minutes later they were crossing the bridge into Gateshead amid heavy falling snow and it was almost an hour later before they came to the outskirts of the village. It was still snowing but not so heavily here, although the ground showed a good spread of it. It was at the point where the roads branched that Tilly said, "Stop here, Simon; I'll make my way over the fields."

"You'll do no such thing."

"Simon—" she leaned forward and gripped the hand that held the reins and her voice no longer sounded like that of a young girl but of a knowing woman as she said, "You know what will happen if you're seen drivin' with me through the village. They'll say. . . ."

"What'll they say?" He jerked his finger toward her. "Well, let them say, but you're not going to end up stiff in the fields because of their dirty tongues, so sit tight."

She sat tight with her head bowed, in fact she crouched down on the seat hoping that she'd pass unrecognized. Because of the state of the weather there was no one in the village street, but that wasn't to say that the sound of a neighing horse or the muffled tramp of its feet didn't bring at least some of them to their windows.

When they eventually reached the cottage gate it was to see Annie with her face to the window, and as Tilly got down from the trap she said, "Are you comin' in, Simon?" and he answered, "No, I'd better be getting back while the going's good. But listen." He bent toward her where she was standing in the road now, her hand extended on the back rails, and he leaned sideways and covered it with his own as he said, "At the slightest sign of trouble, make for the farm . . . I'm going to have a word with young Steve on the quiet; he'll keep me in touch."

"No, no!" She shook her head. "Don't ask Steve to do anything more, Simon. The poor lad, look at the state he was in; and his arm will never be the same again."

"Well, in spite of that he's still for you, very much for you. He's a good lad, is Steve. How he came to be bred of that crew, God alone knows. Now look, get yourself in, there's your granny at the door, you'll catch your death in this."

She stared up at him for a moment longer; then in pulling her hand from underneath his she let her fingers rest against his for a moment as she said, "I don't know what I'd . . . we'd do without you, Simon; but please, for your own sake an' . . . an' your wife's, keep your distance."

He blinked some snowflakes from his eyes before he answered, "That'll be up to me. Go on; good-night to you."

"Good-night, Simon."

Annie had the door open and her first words were "Oh, lass, I thought you were never comin'." Then she added, "That was Simon; why didn't he come in?"

"He's got to get back, the roads are gettin' thick."

"Here, give me that coat off you, you look frozen. Come to the fire."

Tilly had only one sleeve out of her coat before Annie was tugging at her arm and pulling her forward toward the fireplace where she pushed her down into a chair, saying, "I've got some broth boiling." She inclined her head toward the spit. "It's been on the bubble these past two hours. Ah, lass!" Her voice suddenly sank deep into her chest and, the tears springing from her eyes, she said, "I . . . I thought they

126

had done somethin' to you, kept you or somethin'. I thought you were never coming. I . . . I didn't know how I was goin' to go on without you. Aw! me bairn."

"Aw, Granny." It was too much on top of all that had happened, and Tilly leaned forward and laid her head against Annie's breast, and the old woman held her tightly while they both cried. Then Annie, recovering first, muttered, "This won't get any broth down you an' you're as cold as clay." This latter remark seemed to remind her of William for she now added, "Me poor lad. Me dear lad."

It wasn't until after she had served up the plate of broth and Tilly had forced herself to eat it that Annie now asked, "How did it go?"

"She got off."

"Thanks be to God! What did they ask you?"

"Aw, Granny." Tilly now put the bowl on to her knees and she bent her head over it as she murmured, "It was awful, awful. All of it was awful, but . . . but when the judge asked me had . . . had I practiced witchcraft. . . ."

"*What!*"

"Aye, Granny. They're makin' out in the village that I'm a witch. It isn't just the McGraths now, 'tis everybody, and they're blamin' me for the lot."

"They're mad, stark starin' mad."

"And you know what, Granny"—Tilly's voice rose now—"the judge asked McGrath did he want to marry me and he said aye, and he would knock the witchcraft out of me. And the judge said it was a good thing. Aw, Granny, I thought I would die."

Annie looked at the face before her, the beloved face, and all she saw in it was purity. Her bairn was bonny, lovely; aye, too much so really, and in spite of having no figure to speak of, she had something, an air about her, a quality, something she couldn't give a name to. But . . . witchcraft! What would they say next? But this was serious, very serious, much more so than McGrath's thinking they had money hidden here. Oh aye, more so. Feeling suddenly weak she sat down on the settle by the side of Tilly, and after a moment she said, "Thank God we've got Simon. As long as he lives he'll let nothing bad happen to you." And to herself she added, "Married or no."

The fire had been banked down. Tilly was lying by the side of her grandmother in the walled bed. She had lain there each night since they had boxed William and set him out on the table in the middle of the room until it was time to take him to his last resting place.

Her granny was quiet; she didn't know whether she was asleep or not but for herself sleep was far away, her mind was going over the details of the day from the moment she had got off the back of the carrier cart and Mr. Fogget, the carter, had pointed out the way to the courthouse. But he had done so without looking at her, and the other passengers from the village had remained seated in the cart and let her go ahead. No one had spoken to her on the journey, in fact Mrs. Summers, whose husband worked in the Sopwiths' gardens, had pulled her skirt aside when she sat down beside her.

The thought of wanting to die had been in her mind a lot of late but never more so than at the moment when she entered that courthouse. It was as if she was the person about to be judged, and she knew that in a great many minds this was so.

She lay wide-eyed in the stillness. There were no night sounds tonight, the snow had muffled them. The fire wasn't crackling. The only sounds were the short soft gasping breaths of her granny.

Then she was sitting bolt upright in the bed, her hand pressed tight against the stone wall to her side. Someone was coming up the path. She wasn't dreaming. No, she wasn't dreaming. They had stopped outside the door, and now her heart seemed to leap in her breast when there came two short raps on the door.

She was immediately aware that her granny had not been asleep because now she was resting on her elbow and whispering, "Who in the name of God can this be at this time?"

As Tilly went to crawl over her to reach the edge of the bed, Annie's hand stayed her, saying, "No, no; stay where you are."

When the raps came again and a soft murmur came to them, saying, "Tilly! Tilly!" Tilly turned her head to stare down at her grandmother, and although she couldn't see her face she knew that her granny was staring at her, and she whispered, "I think 'tis Mrs. Ross."

"Mrs. Ross at this time of the night! Dear God! Dear God! what now?" Annie was muttering as she painfully swung her legs out of the bed. By this time Tilly was at the door and, pulling her coat over her nightgown, she paused before calling, "Who's there?"

"Me, Tilly, Ellen Ross."

Tilly turned the key in the lock, withdrew the top and bottom bolts and pulled the door ajar.

The world outside looked white and against the whiteness stood the small dark form of the parson's wife. "Come in. Come in."

When the door was closed and they were standing in the dark room, Tilly said quickly, "Stay where you are, ma'am, stay where you are till I light the lamp."

When the lamp was alight it showed Ellen Ross leaning against the door and Annie standing supporting herself against the edge of the table.

It was as if the heightening of the flame drew Ellen Ross toward the table too and as she came within the halo of the light Tilly glanced at her for a moment; then turning quickly, she grabbed the bellows and blew on the dying embers of the fire. Immediately these flared she turned toward the table again, saying, "Come and sit down, ma'am, you look froze. Take your cape off a minute;" and she put her hands out to take the hip-length fur cape partly covering the long gray melton cloth coat. But Ellen Ross shook her head and, putting her gloved hands to the collar, gripped it as she said, "I . . . I can't stay, but I had to come and see you to . . . to say good-bye."

It was Annie who now spoke, saying, "Well, sit down a moment, ma'am."

Ellen nodded at the old woman, then took a seat by the side of the reviving fire and as she looked at it her head drooped on to her chest and the voice in which she now spoke was tear-filled. "I . . . I had to come and say how sorry I was, I am . . . I am for all the trouble I have brought on you."

Tilly walked slowly toward her now and, standing before her, looked down on the bent head as she said, "There's no blame attached to you, ma'am; there's only one person who bears the guilt for this and that's McGrath."

"Yes, yes, I think that's right, but . . . but my interference hasn't helped; oh no, no, it hasn't helped." She now looked up at Tilly. Her face was wet as she said, "I have ruined George . . . my husband's life; he can no longer follow his vocation, at least not in this country. He has already arranged that we should go abroad; he is to be a missionary."

"Oh, ma'am!" There was a break in Tilly's voice, and again she muttered, "Oh, ma'am!"

Ellen now looked toward Annie, who was on the settle opposite to her, and she addressed her as if she would understand what she was now about to say. "My . . . my people want me to return home but . . . but that would mean separating from my husband. As much as I would love to, because my family are very understanding people, I feel I must abide with my husband, for that is as little as I can do for all the trouble I have caused him. Where he goes I go, I must go."

"And you're right, ma'am, you're right."

"Yes, yes, I think I am. But . . . but life will never be the same again. I shall carry the burden of that man's death with me to my grave."

"You weren't to blame for that, ma'am. That part of the business links straight up with Hal McGrath."

"Yes, I suppose you're right, Tilly. But . . . but tell me, he won't get his own way? I mean you will never marry him, will you Tilly? No matter what happens you couldn't. . . ."

"Oh no! No!" Tilly was shaking her head in wide sweeps. "Never! Never! I'd sooner die first."

"And I'd sooner see her dead first." Annie was nodding her head violently now. "I'd kill him afore he'd lay a hand on her."

The fire suddenly blazed upward, the lamp flickered, there was a whining of wind around the chimney. Ellen Ross shivered; then getting to her feet; she said, "I . . . I have to return."

"It must have been dangerous for you coming, ma'am; the roads are bad, an' you didn't carry a light." Although Annie had referred to the roads her words also implied there was danger from another quarter, and to this Ellen answered, "I'm safe in the fact that not many people will venture out tonight, and the snow has made it quite light."

"I'll put my things on me and go back with you to the crossroads."

As Tilly spoke the protests came from both Annie and Ellen Ross saying, "No! No!" and Ellen now added, "I'm warmly wrapped and I'm not afraid. Believe me, I'm not afraid. I don't think there's anything could happen to me in life now that could make me really afraid. The last few weeks I have lived with fear and I have faced it, and conquered it."

"Well, it's good-bye, Mrs. Trotter." Ellen walked

toward the old woman and took her outstretched hand. "I used to think it would be nice to grow old here-abouts, but it wasn't to be."

"Good-bye, me dear, and God go with you."

Tilly had walked toward the door, and when Ellen came up to her she suddenly put out her arms and drew Tilly tightly into her embrace, and after a moment's hesitation, Tilly returned the embrace with equal inten-sity. Then Ellen kissed her on each cheek and, her face again flowing with tears and her voice breaking, she said, "Promise me one thing, promise me you'll keep up your reading and your writing; no matter what happens you'll do a little each day. Promise me, Tilly."

Tilly had no voice with which to answer that promise but gulping in her throat and screwing up her eyes tight, she made a deep obeisance with her head.

"Good-bye, my dear, I'll never forget you. I . . . I would like to say I will write, but I . . . I may not be able to because I . . . I prom. . . .' Her voice ended abruptly and she turned blindly to the door and, slowly opening it, went out into the night and she didn't look back.

Tilly watched the dark figure seeming to glide over the snow; she watched her go through the gate; she watched her until she became lost in the night; then she closed the door, locked it, bolted it top and bottom, and, leaning against it in the crook of her elbow, she sobbed aloud.

7

A week went by; then a month; then two months, and nothing happened. Tilly never went into the village, and only from a distance did she see any of the villagers, except Tom Pearson and young Steve. On the day she found a couple of dead rabbits in the woodshed she thanked Steve on the Sunday afternoon when she went down to the burn and saw him sitting on the bank. Sunday being his only free day from the pit he had made it a rule, she knew, to be at the burn in the afternoon; and she was glad of this because it was someone to pass a word with, someone young. But on that particular Sunday afternoon after she had thanked him for the rabbits he had said that it wasn't he who had put them in the woodshed but he had a good idea who had; it would be Tom Pearson because he was known to be a dab hand at poaching. She had felt slightly warmed inside that day knowing that besides Simon and Steve she had another friend, one who apparently wasn't afraid of the villagers.

One person she hadn't seen even a glimpse of over the past weeks was Hal McGrath, and she wondered if Simon had gone for him. However, she had not asked him because the subject she felt was best buried; and deep in her mind she wished that McGrath could be buried with it.

Yesterday Simon had brought the sovereign. His face had looked frozen and pinched, and there was a kind of sadness about him. But perhaps it was due to the weather. For the past fortnight it had hardly stopped raining, and even under better weather conditions farmers always found this a heavy time. He'd had little to say, just asked them if they were all right and if they had been troubled by anyone. When she had said, "No," his answer had been, "Well, that's as it should be."

When he left without even having a drink of hot ginger beer her granny had said, "He's more troubled than we are, he's not happy, you can see it in his face."

This morning the rain had stopped but the wind was high and the air biting, and when she was pulling her coat on Annie said, "Don't put your hat on, it'll be blown away afore you get out of the gate. Look, take my shawl"—she pulled the shawl from her shoulders— "put it around your head and cross it over and I'll tie it behind your waist."

"No, no, Granny"—she put out a protesting hand— "I'll be all right. I've got me scarf, I'll put that around me head."

"Don't be silly, girl, that piece of wool wouldn't keep the wind out of a flute. Here"—she was already putting the shawl over Tilly's head; then crossing it over, she turned her around and knotted it under her shoulder blades—"There, at least you'll be warm."

"What about you?"

"I'm in the house, aren't I, an' there's a roarin' fire there and enough wood in to keep me going for a week; you've got a four mile walk afore you each way."

"I don't mind the walk, Granny."

And she didn't mind the walk. She no longer took the carrier cart into Shields for the necessities because it would already be laden with villagers. Instead she now went into Jarrow for her shopping.

The shops in Jarrow were of poor quality compared with those in Shields because Jarrow was little more than an enlarged village, nor was the quality of the food as good as that which could be purchased in the market place in Shields. Still, they could live without bread, substituting potato cake in place of it rather than sit that ride out among the villagers, or even walk along the road into Harton village just to get flour; for that way she was sure to bump into one or the other she knew, and someone who didn't want to know her.

Ready now for the road, she stood waiting while her granny went to the tea caddy on the mantelpiece and took out the sovereign, and as she handed it to her she said, "What would we do without Simon? Although I've cursed that money many a time of late, it helped to put my William decently away." Then her chin jerking, she said, "That'll be another thing to puzzle them, where we got the money for an oak coffin. Well, let it puzzle 'em; he wasn't going to his last bed in any deal box. Now away with you, and get back well afore dark, won't you?"

"Yes, Granny. An' mind you don't go outside, or it'll be you who'll catch your death, not me. Sit warm aside the fire. I won't be all that long." She leaned slightly forward and touched her grandmother's cheek, letting her fingers linger on it for a moment; and Annie put up her hand and gripped it tight, and, her lips trembling slightly, she muttered, as she was wont to do when her feelings were troubled, "Aw! lass. Aw! lass."

Turning quickly away, Tilly went out, but she was no sooner on the path than the wind caught her skirt and swirled it up to the bottom of her coat and when she reached the gate she turned, laughing, and waved her hand to Annie who was at the window and indicated what the wind had done to her skirt. And Annie waved back.

The shortest cut to Jarrow led through Rosier's village but she always skirted that; news spread, at least bad news and who knew but the Rosier villagers would hold her responsible for the three pitmen losing their jobs, and their cottages. The Rosier pit lay about a mile from the village, and she skirted that too. Once or

twice when she had seen the men coming out of the
gates following their shift, to avoid running into them
she had swung herself over a wall or hidden in a thicket,
until they were past.

But this morning, on a narrow path, her head down
against the wind, she glanced upward to see a solitary
pitman coming toward her. He wasn't a man but a
young boy, and when he came nearer she stopped, as
he stopped, and as she exclaimed brightly, "Why!
hello, Steve," he said, "Hello, Tilly."

"Just finished a shift?"

"Aye, but it's been over half an hour or so. I . . . I
had something to see to, that's why I'm late gettin'
home . . . Where you goin'?"

"Into Jarrow for some groceries."

"Oh, aye. Aye." He nodded his head in understanding; then looking about him, he said, "How long will it
take you?"

"Oh, I should be there in another twenty minutes or
so and I spend about half an hour in the shops. It takes
me about three hours altogether."

He shook his head as if that wasn't what he was
meaning, then said, "Would you like me to come along
of you?"

"Oh no, no." She gave a small laugh. "An' look at
you, you're dead on your feet. Have . . . have you
been on a double shift?"

"No, no; just the twelve hours."

Some part of her mind repeated, Just twelve hours.
Twelve hours down there! She said, " 'Tis a long time to
be down below, an' you must be hungry an' want a
wash."

"Aye, both." He laughed now; then his face becoming suddenly serious, he stepped close up to her and,
half turning his back against the wind, he asked, "Has
anybody been about your place lately, Tilly?"

Her face and voice were serious as she answered,
"No, nobody."

136

"You haven't seen our Hal or Mick, nor our George?"

"No, no, none of them. Why?" She swallowed deeply now before she could ask the question, "Are they up to something again?" She watched him droop his head; and now she was looking down on to his greasy black cap as she again said, with a tremble in her voice now, "Are they?"

The wind carried his answer away and she bent down and said, "What did you say?"

He lifted his head to the side and the whites of his eyes seemed to grow larger in his black face and she watched his mouth open and shut twice before he said, "I think they're hatching something, Tilly. What, I don't know. They're wary of me, never say nowt in front of me. An' since our Hal gave me this"—he lifted his arm upward—"he hasn't touched me again because me ma threatened him. But . . . but I think you'd better be on your guard, Tilly. I . . . I think you should get in touch with Farmer Bentwood and tell him what I've just said."

Her stomach seemed to be loose within its cage, her whole body was trembling, she had the desire to be sick.

"Try not to worry. I . . . I might just be imaginin' things but I thought it best to put you on your guard. Anyway, I'd hurry up now and get back afore dark."

"Aye, aye, Steve. And . . . and thanks."

"You're welcome, Tilly. I wish I could do more, I wish —" he put his dirty hand out toward her, then withdrew it sharply and saying, "Take care. Go on now, an' take care," he turned from her and hurried away.

She, too, turned and walked along the road, but she didn't hurry because of a sudden her legs seemed to have lost their power. Like a child who didn't know which way to turn, she wanted to sit down on the side of the road and cry until someone should come to her aid. Well, there was only one person who could come to her aid and as soon as she got back she would go to him. She'd risk annoying his wife, but she'd go to him.

Her arms were breaking. Although she had only bought a half stone of flour, a pound of bacon ends, a pound of hough meat, a marrow bone and a few dry goods, each mile she walked seemed to add to the weight, and she had just passed the Rosier village and was within the last mile home when she smelled the smoke. At first she thought it was Mr. Sopwith's woodman burning the scrub; he liked his places kept clear did Mr. Sopwith. Of course he hadn't the men now to do all he would like on the estate and some of it was like a jungle, so he seemed pleased that she kept the little wood clear of brambles and undergrowth. She stopped for a moment and changed the half stone of flour over into the crook of her left arm and picked the bass bag up with her right hand. But as she went to walk on again she put her head back and sniffed. The smell of burning was heavy, not like brushwood or leaves burning.

She had gone another hundred yards or so when she paused for a moment; then some instinct rising in her, she actually leaped forward and ran. Leaping and stumbling, she came to the beginning of the bridle path that led to the cottage, and there, her head back and her mouth open, she cried aloud, "Oh Lord! Lord!" for a great pall of smoke was blotting out the road and the surrounding sky.

When she came in sight of the cottage she let out a high cry, dropped her packages, oblivious at the moment that the flour bag had split, and raced toward the blazing building. There were a number of people standing on the pathway and one of them caught her arm and said, "It's no use. Everything possible's been done, but it's no use."

Her wild agonized glance looked up into the face of Mark Sopwith, then at the other three men standing near. One she vaguely recognized as the pitman Mrs. Ross had defended and the other two looked like Mr. Sopwith's men. She actually grabbed at Mark Sopwith's coat as she cried, "Me granny! Me granny!"

"It's all right, she's safe. It's all right. Come"—he took her arm—"she's around the back with the farmer."

When he went to draw her over the vegetable patch giving the blazing cottage a wide berth, she pulled herself to a halt for a moment and, looking at the flames leaping heavenward through the aperture that had once been the roof, she moaned aloud, and Mark Sopwith said, "Come. Come."

At the back of the house she looked toward the woodshed. All the wood had been dragged outside, but she recognized that only half of it was lying about. The byre door was open but there was no one in there. She glanced at Mark Sopwith again and he motioned his head down toward the bottom of the garden where stood a rickety outdoor closet and next to it an equally rickety shed in which, over the years, unused or worn out household objects had been thrown.

She now pulled herself away from Mark Sopwith's grasp and raced toward it.

Gasping, she stood gripping each side of the doorway. Lying on some sacks was her granny, and kneeling by her side and almost taking up all the remaining space were two people: one was Simon and the other was a young girl she hadn't seen before.

Simon immediately got to his feet and, holding her arms, said, "It's all right. It's all right."

"What . . . what have they done to her?" Her voice was high, almost on the point of a scream, and now he gripped her shoulders as he shouted at her, "It's all right! It's all right! I'm telling you."

"They . . . they burned her?"

"No, no"—he shook her again—"we found her down here. She's . . . she's had a bit of a seizure."

139

"Oh God! Oh God!" She thrust past him and dropped on to her knees beside the inert figure and tenderly now she cupped the wrinkled face between her palms and whimpered, "Oh, Granny! Granny!"

The girl kneeling opposite her said in thick rough tones, "Don't frash yourself, lass; you can't do nowt by frashing yourself. She's alive. It's just likely a stroke she's had. Me Aunt Hunisett, she got a shock when they told her her man was drowned, she went just like this, but she's alive the day and well, as well as can be expected. There now. There now." The girl put out her hand and patted Tilly's shoulder and Tilly, looking through her streaming eyes at her, whimpered now, "They're cruel. They're cruel."

"Aye, those are the very words our Sam said; cruel buggers, the lot of 'em. 'Twas him an' me saw the fire first an' the poor old girl going mad outside. We tried all we could with buckets from the rain barrel but it was like spittin' against the wind. Then the old lady here up and had a seizure, fell at our feet she did. 'Twas no use puttin' her into one of your outhouses, they were too near the house, this was the only safe place, and I stayed alongside of her while our Sam ran back to the big house. An' it was fortunate Mr. Sopwith was just mountin' to go to the mine, an' he galloped along here. But what could he do? Nowt, because the whole place looked like hell let loose. But he was in a state 'cos he thought you were inside, miss, an' he gallops off again to the farmer, so our Sam said, an' he comes tearing up with his men, an' that's the whole of it. Except the farmer there." She nodded her head toward the opening of the hut. "They had to stop him going in. And I think he would have gone, only a lad from the village said you had gone shoppin', and at the news he went down like a pricked balloon. There now. There now, I talk too much. But I always do in cases like this, accidents like. When me dad was killed in the pit two years gone I never stopped talkin' for a week."

Tilly looked at the girl. She didn't look much older than herself but she sounded like a woman. She said to her now as if she could give her the answer, "Where am I going to put her? She can't stay here, she'll die of cold."

The girl considered for a moment, her head on one side, then said, "Well, we're packed like sardines since we got the push from Rosier's an' the cottage; but we were lucky to get into Mr. Sopwith's row. They're a bit cleaner his cottages, but no bigger. One room's got a stone floor and that's something. But there's nine of us there still." She smiled. "As me ma says, if you can't lie down to sleep tack yoursel' to the wall. We'd find a corner for you; as you say, the old girl can't stay out in this."

"You mean . . . you mean your mother wouldn't mind?"

"No, me ma won't mind; she takes life as it comes. As she says, she had to take us an' we've been far from God's blessin'." Her smile had turned into a wide grin and for the moment Tilly almost forgot she was in the midst of tragedy. Here was someone kind, a stranger, an utter stranger offering to take them in, and making light of it.

Her attention was brought from the girl as Annie stirred and slowly opened her eyes. Her hand came up and grabbed at Tilly's arm, and her mouth opened and shut but no sound came from it.

"It's all right, Gran, it's all right. It's going to be all right. I'm here, I'm here."

Again Annie's mouth opened and shut but still no sound came from it, and the girl at the other side from her remarked, "Aye, she's had a stroke an' I bet it's down the left side." She now lifted Annie's left arm and when it dropped lifelessly back on to her skirt she nodded at Tilly and said, "Aye, I thought so; it's usually on the left side."

At this point Simon's voice came to her, saying,

"They're not going into the house, neither of them, I'll take them back home with me." And Mark Sopwith's reply was, "That's good of you, I'm glad of that. They were a decent couple and they brought the girl up well."

When Simon entered the hut again Tilly looked at him with the feelings of her heart shining through her wet eyes, and he said to her, "Move out of the way a minute." Then nodding at the girl at the other side of Annie, he added, "You'll both have to get outside because I've got to lift her up."

"But you can't carry her all the way."

"I'm not aiming to." He glanced at Tilly as she made for the door. "I've got the farm cart outside. I was on the road to the miller's when I met Mr. Sopwith. The cart's at the end of the bridle path." He stooped down and gently gathered Annie up into his arms and, his body bent, he eased himself out of the hut doorway; then hitching his burden close up against his breast, he cut across the vegetable patch, round the side of the blazing cottage and through the gate into the road where there were now a number of villagers standing, and when, passing through them, he heard the remark, "'Tis a blaze, isn't it?" he paused and cried at the man, "Yes, 'tis a blaze, and somebody's responsible for the blaze, and by God! he or they'll suffer for it."

Their faces shamefaced, some of them looked away, while others continued to stare at him; but no one gave him any answer. And when Mark Sopwith led Tilly through the gate they had the grace to turn their heads away; that was until, as if digging her feet into the ground, she pulled herself to a halt and, looking around them, she cried, "You've given me a name, you say I've the power to curse, well, if me granny dies, I'll curse each and every one of you. Remember that. You'll do no more to me or mine without paying for it! No, by God! you won't."

The eyes blinked, here and there a head bowed as if

in fear, one or two turned away; then, her glance full of scorn sweeping over them, she hurried on, without the aid of Mark Sopwith now, and he, turning and looking at the villagers, said sternly, "She's right. Someone will pay for this."

When one man dared to voice his opinion and say, "Fires are apt to start in thatched cottages, sir," he turned on him, saying, "This fire was deliberately set. There was almost a bonfire blazing in the center of that room when I first saw it. It was a prepared fire, and the scattered wood from the shed adds proof to this. Now you can go back to the village and tell them what I said, someone will pay for this, not only because it is my property but because of the damage that has been done to two people, whose only crime was to keep themselves to themselves. Now get away with you, all of you, you've seen enough . . . I hope."

Without further words they obeyed him, some hurrying along the bridle path; but when these came in sight of the cart with the inert figure lying along it and the girl kneeling beside it, they stayed their step. Mr. Sopwith was one thing but Simon Bentwood was another, for hadn't he put it around that should anyone lay a finger on the pair up at the cottage they'd have to answer to him; and they guessed what the result of his answer would be, it would be the horsewhip, and he had a thick, strong arm. So they climbed the banks and made their several ways back to the village by varying routes.

But Simon drove straight through the village, straight through the main street that had as many people in it as was to be seen on a fair day, but no one called to him; no one passed any remark, but all their eyes noted the girl in the back supporting the head of the old woman who looked dead. . . .

"What in the name of . . . !"

Mary Bentwood's voice was cut off by Simon saying, "Get out of that! Out of the way!"

"What did you say?"

Walking sideways through the kitchen door with Annie in his arms, he almost yelled now, "You heard. I said get out of the way."

"What do you think you're doing?" Her voice was a hoarse whisper now as she followed him up the long, stone-flagged kitchen to the door at the far end. But he didn't answer her, he simply turned his back to the door, thrust it open with his buttocks, stumbled across the hall and into the sitting-room, and there he laid Annie on the couch. Then straightening his back, he turned to his enraged wife, saying a little more calmly now, "They've burned them out."

"Burned them out?"

"Yes, that's what I said, right down to the ground. It's a wonder they spared her." He looked down at the inert form of Annie.

"And the other one?" Mary Bentwood now jerked her head backward toward the door, and Simon, putting stress on the name, said, "Tilly? Tilly was in Jarrow shopping, and she came back to find a blazing house."

"I hope her conscience is pricking her then."

"Oh, woman!" he glared at her now; then walking sharply across the room he said, "She's got to have a doctor."

"Here"—she reached the door before him and she stood with her back to it facing him—"let's get this straight, Simon Bentwood. What do you intend to do with these two?"

"What do you think? They're staying here for the time being."

"Oh no! no! they're not. A sick woman like that and her, that girl!"

"Mary"—he leaned toward her, his voice deceptively soft now—"I've told you before, they're my lifelong friends. Until I can get them fixed up some place they're staying here."

. Mary Bentwood pressed her flat hands to each side of her against the door now and, her broad chest heaving, she said, "I'll not have that girl in my house."

"Well, that's where we differ. I'm going to have her in *mine,* Mary. And if I'm not mistaken, you've been grumbling for weeks that you haven't enough help in the house so she can come to your assistance in that way."

"I'll . . . I'll walk out, I'll go home."

"Oh well, that's up to you. Now get out of my way!" He took her by the shoulder and thrust her aside almost overbalancing her, leaving her standing in the doorway glaring after him as he hurried across the hall; her face was red, her eyes wild with temper that touched on fury.

In the kitchen Tilly was standing near the dresser. Her face was devoid of all color, her eyes looking like saucers in her head, and when she said, "Can I go to her?" he said, "In a minute, Tilly. I'm going to send Randy for the doctor. Just take your coat off and sit down by the fire. Make a cup of something, Peggy."

The woman standing at the far end of the kitchen peeling potatoes turned her head in a nonchalant way and said, "Aye, master, aye."

When Tilly hesitated to walk toward the fire he took her arm and, his voice a whisper now, he said, "It'll be all right, it'll be all right. I'll . . . I'll explain things to you in a minute." And then he left her.

She was standing by the fire looking down on the big black pan simmering on the hob when the far door opened and Mary Bentwood came slowly into the room, and walking past Tilly as if she weren't there, she spoke to her woman, saying, "Leave that and see to the churn in the dairy."

"But I've just come from there, ma'am," Peggy Fullbright said.

"Then go back again."

"Aye, ma'am."

145

As soon as the woman left the kitchen, Mary Bentwood walked toward the fireplace and, standing in front of Tilly who had been awaiting her coming, she ground out between strong white clenched teeth, "You're not staying in my house, girl! You understand? Your granny can stay until she's fit to be moved but you'll find some place else to sleep."

"Aye, she will, and it'll be upstairs for the present."

They both swung around toward the door where Simon was standing. He moved to the table and, looking at his wife, his voice harsh and deep, he said, "Let's hear no more of it. She's staying; they're both staying until I can get them fixed up in a place of their own. This much I'll grant you, I'll see to the business right away."

He hadn't looked at Tilly, but now he said, "Go in to your granny, she's in the front room."

Tilly looked from one to the other before, her head bowed, she turned and went hastily from the kitchen. But no sooner was the door closed on her than Mary Bentwood cried, "By God! I'll make you pay for this day. You see if I don't. Oh! you see if I don't." Her last words were slow and ominous and to them he replied on a long sigh, "Everything in life has to be paid for and I've never been in debt yet, so there's no doubt, my dear, that you will, and with interest." He turned and he, too, went out of the kitchen and toward the sitting-room.

PART TWO

The New Life

1

Four days later Annie died. She died without speaking except through the pain and love she expressed with her eyes whenever she looked at Tilly; and she was buried three days afterward. A very short laying-out, as the men said in the yard, but the quicker the old 'un went the quicker the young one would leave and things would get back to normal.

Besides the new parson the Reverend Portman, George Knight the gravedigger, the master, and that Tilly Trotter, there was one other person whose presence surprised them as much as did the presence of Tilly, the latter only because everyone knew it wasn't right for a female to attend a funeral, especially that of a relative. But Mark Sopwith's appearance in the cemetery just as, with the help of Tom Pearson and the hedger, they were carrying the coffin from the cart, caused eyebrows to be raised. He had ridden up to the gate, left his horse there, then joined the small cortège to the graveside.

When the first clod fell on the coffin Tilly closed her eyes tightly and her mind gabbled, Oh, Granny! Granny! What am I gona do without you? Oh, Granny! Granny!

She wasn't really aware of someone turning her from the graveside until she was once again standing by the farm cart, then through her blurred tear-streaming eyes she saw Simon and Mr. Sopwith standing apart talking.

Presently, Mr. Sopwith went to his horse and Simon came back to her. It was when he said, "Come on, get up," that her tears stopped flowing. She took out her handkerchief and slowly wiped her face; then looking at him, she spoke as someone would who had suddenly put on years and jumped into adulthood. "I'll . . . I'll never be able to thank you, Simon, for all you've done for me granny and me. And also me granda. But it's finished now. From now on I'll have to stand on me own two feet."

"What are you talking about? Come along! it's cold standing here. Get up."

"No, Simon, no." She pulled her arm from his grip. "I'm not going back to your house."

"What! . . . Now don't be silly; where do you think you'll go?"

"I'm . . . I'm goin' to the cottage. I was there yesterday. The woodshed and the byre are all right, they're dry."

"Don't be a fool! You can't live there."

"I can for a little while anyway; and then . . . then I'll go into service or some such."

"Well, until you go into service you're coming back. . . ."

"No! Simon."

He stared at her, amazed at the authority in her voice. She neither looked nor sounded like young Tilly. He knew that not one word, not one deprecating look, not one insinuating nod had missed her during the past few days. She had been aware of Mary's feelings toward her from the first, and they must have pierced deep for her now to be refusing the shelter of his home; and in weather like this too, for the spring had seemingly forgotten to materialize. Instinctively he pulled the collar of his coat high around his neck; and then said weakly, "But where will you sleep?"

"There's plenty of dry straw, and they left enough wood for me to make another fire." Although her voice was now low, her words implied deep hard bitterness. "The woodshed has a boiler in the corner; it used to be

150

the pot house. I'll get by, never fear. And anyway, it'll only be for a short time."

Simon hung his head, every decent instinct telling him to thrust her into the cart and take her back to his home; yet he knew that if she returned there there would be hell to pay. Mary had a deep ingrained hate of her; she had the power of looking beyond the eyes had Mary, she could sense hidden feelings, like a terrier smelling a rat. . . . But for this girl to go back there among the burned-out ruins of that cottage and to live in the woodshed. . . . Well perhaps, when he came to think of it, she'd be happier there. Aye, and perhaps she'd be safer there an' all, at least for a time, for if some of those maniacs in the village got going again God knows what would happen to her. There was one thing he would like to find out, that was who started the fire . . . deliberately started the fire. Apparently it wasn't Hal McGrath for he had proved he was nowhere near the village on that day. He had cleaned up immediately after his shift, so he had said, and gone to Cooksons' foundry in Shields to pick up some pieces of iron for his father, and Billy Fogget had sworn that he was on his cart early that morning. That he had also visited Cooksons' was verified by the gaffer who had served him.

Well, whoever had perpetrated the deed that had brought on Annie's end would let it slip out one day, he had no doubt, and until then he could wait. In a way he was glad it wasn't McGrath because that fact had prevented bloodshed.

"Ta-rah! Simon. Don't worry about me, I'll be all right."

"Wait!" He pulled at her coat with one hand while thrusting his other into the back pocket of his breeches; then pressing something into her hand, he said, "That'll tide you over."

She looked at the two sovereigns and was about to refuse them when she thought, Well, it's me granda's money. But even as she thought this she asked, "How much money is there left . . . of me granda's, I mean?"

When she saw his face redden and his tongue come over his lips before he said, "Oh, a bit," she stared at him then said softly, "There isn't any left, is there?" And now he sighed and said, "No." But he didn't add, "There should be."

"How long has it been finished?"

"Oh. Oh, I can't remember. Not long." He shook his head, and for a moment she looked perplexed.

Twice she opened her mouth to speak before she said, "Well, I thank you for them, both of them; and for me an' all. But now I can't take this." She held out the two sovereigns to him. But he thrust her hand away, saying, "Don't be a fool, Tilly. How are you going to live?"

She looked downward to where her boots were showing below her old skirt; then, her fingers closing over the coins, she said, "Thanks, Simon." And with one last look at him she slowly turned away.

But she hadn't taken two steps before his voice halted her, saying, "I'll drop in and see how you are. I'll bring you a blanket or two."

"No, Simon." She was facing him again, and as she stared at him over the distance she shook her head, saying now, "Please, please, don't come near me."

"Don't be daft, girl!"

"I'm not bein' daft. They'll be watchin', talkin', waitin'."

"Who will?" It was a silly question to ask, and he knew that she thought so too when all the answer she gave was one slow movement of her head before turning from him and walking away.

2

She had been living in the woodshed two days. The first
day she cleared it out, swept the narrow pot chimney
and got the fire to burn, brought in some dry sacks and
clean straw from the byre, raked among the burned
embers of the cottage until she found the frying pan,
the kale pot and a few other cooking utensils. In one
place her foot had slipped through some mushed wood
and disclosed red embers still burning. As she worked
the slightest unusual sound had brought her head up.
There was fear in her still, but a fear threaded now with
anger.

The first night lying on the straw on the stone floor
she had lain awake and seen herself standing in the
middle of the village yelling at each house in turn and
the occupants cowering behind their curtains. Later,
her dreams picked up her retaliation and there she was
again in the village, but behind the main street now and
facing the McGrath house, and she was screaming,
"You murdered me granny, an' in a way you've killed
the parson an' Mrs. Ross for they'll never know real
happiness again. An' you've tried to befoul me. But
you won't! You won't! Hal McGrath, nor no one else.
Let anybody venture near me again an' they'll take
what they get."

The remnants of the dream had helped to stiffen her
back when early this morning she had taken the long
walk into Jarrow, but on this particular return journey
her arms weren't aching for her purchases had been
meager. She had planned that if she could last out till

153

the fair she would go to the hirings in Newcastle and get a position in some house, no matter how lowly, any place that would take her miles away from this area.

Arriving at the ruins of the cottage, she stopped within the broken gate sensing that she wasn't alone. The outer wall, still standing, blocked her view of the yard but she knew there was someone there, and she was backing toward the road again when round by the smoke-begrimed wall she saw young Steve McGrath and she drew in a long breath before moving toward him.

"Hello, Tilly," he said. "I've fetched you a couple of blankets, and there's some bacon and odds wrapped inside."

"Oh"—she moved her head slowly—"that's kind of you, Steve. But . . . but where did you get the blankets and the rest?"

"They're not from me; Farmer Bentwood asked me to pick them up on the quiet like an' last night he slipped them out on to the road, an' I hid them in the thicket down by the burn 'cos I didn't want to come up here in the dark an' frighten you. They're a bit damp, the blankets. 'Cos they would be, lying in the thicket, wouldn't they?" He sounded apologetic.

"Ta. Thank you, Steve."

"How you farin'?"

"Oh, all right, Steve."

"I put them in the byre, I couldn't get into the woodshed."

"No, I locked it up."

"You're right, you're right an' all to do that."

He now turned from her and looked through the gaping hole that had been the scullery window and what he said was, "Wicked . . . wicked," then looking at her again he added, "He's bad, rotten. He was born rotten; he'll die rotten, putrid. Aye, putrid."

"Who?" Although she knew to whom he was referring, she still didn't know why he was connecting her brother with the fire, but when he said, "Our Hal," she moved a step nearer to him and said, "But . . . but he was gone, he was in Shields when it happened."

"Aye"—his chin moved upward, stretching his thin neck out of his coat collar—"but he had it planned, he had it all set up."

"Aw no! No!"

"Aye. Aye, Tilly, An' I think you should know just to be on the safe side, but keep it to yoursel'. I'm tellin' you in case you let your guard down against him 'cos he can be smoothed-tongued when he likes; aye, like the devil. An' like the devil he coached the other two well, our Mick and George. They watched you leave the house that mornin', then they went in and brought your granny out. And then they tore the place apart lookin' for the money, they even chopped at the beams. He had worked it all out for them. They even dug the bricks out of the side of the fireplace thinking there might be a loose one there, but they found nowt." His head drooped to the side now. "But they made sure not to leave empty-handed, they took the odds and ends, like your granny's bits of pewter an' the tea caddy, an' the big brass tongs and other bits and pieces."

She was leaning against the wall now, the bass bag at her feet, one hand held tightly across her mouth, and when he said, "He means to have you, Tilly. That's . . . that's why I'm tellin' you, just . . . just to put you on your guard. I think"—he bit on his lip and his eyelids blinked—"your best plan would be to do a bunk, clear out somewhere 'cos . . . 'cos if he made you marry him your life would be. . . ."

"Marry him!" She was standing away from the wall now actually glaring down at him as she cried, "Marry your Hal! Oh! Steve. You know what I'd do first? I'd cut me throat. Aye, I would, I swear on it, I'd cut me throat afore your Hal puts another finger on me. An' . . . an' should he come near me an' me hands are free, an' by God! I'll see they're free this time, I'll leave me mark on him. I will! Steve, I will! I've stood enough. He's . . . he's a murderer. He killed me granny and it was him that was the means of Burk Laudimer dying. As you say, he's a devil."

She stood gasping now and when he said, "I only told you to put you on your guard. You won't tell Farmer Bentwood? 'Cos . . . 'cos I feel there'd be trouble, big trouble if he knew."

She turned from him without answering and went behind the wall and, taking a large key from the pocket of her shirt, she opened the woodshed door, and when she went inside he followed her and, looking around the small warm space, he said, with not a little admiration in his voice, "Eeh! by! you've got it cozy, Tilly. I wouldn't mind livin' here meself."

When she looked at him the half-smile slipped in embarrassment from his face and he stammered, "I . . . I was only meanin' . . ."

"Yes, yes, I know." She put her hand on his shoulder. "You're a good friend, Steve. I haven't many of them an' I appreciate all you've done, and all you would do for me, but . . . but I'm not gona live in this little hole all me life. As you said, I'd best go away, I'd already made up me mind to do just that. It's gettin' a place. You see I'm well past sixteen and I'm not trained, not for anything. I realize I've had it too easy."

"Not you, not you, Tilly. You've done a man's work around here, and you looked after the old couple for years."

"That was happy work." Her fingers began picking at the front of her coat as if trying to unloosen the threads, and she repeated, "Aye, happy work. It'll never come again."

"I wish I was older."

"What?"

He looked toward the boiler in the corner of the shed. The fire below it was giving off a good heat and he bent down on his hunkers and held his hands toward the iron door enclosing the fire and he repeated, "I wish I was older."

"You'll soon be old."

"It's now I want age. If . . . if I was older I would take care of you."

"Oh! Steve." Her hand was out toward him again about to drop on to his cap when she hesitated and withdrew it. She knew, without being told, what he meant by taking care of her, and at this moment she wished he was older, as old as his brother Hal, as big as his brother Hal, as strong as him, stronger, able to stand up to him, to frighten him. But there was nothing or no one on God's earth, she imagined, able to frighten Hal McGrath, only distance from him would give her any safety and rid her of the complications that life was heaping upon her, that involved Simon and his wife, and Steve here. Yes, Steve, because she realized that his feelings for her could bring him into danger; it had already, in a way, crippled his arm for he would never be able to straighten it again. And so her voice held a sharp note as she said, "If you see Farmer Bentwood thank him for the blankets and . . . and the food."

He rose to his feet and, his face now as straight as hers, he said, "Aye. Aye, I will."

He had left the hut and taken some steps along by the wall when he turned and, looking over his shoulder, he warned, "Keep your eyes open and your door locked."

She didn't answer, she just stood and watched him go.

And now the twilight had set in and with it another long night before her. There was enough chopped small wood to keep her going. She had forced herself to eat some belly pork which she had toasted at the fire opening, and a couple of potatoes cooked in the boiler; but it had been no effort to drink two mugs of black tea—she wanted to keep on drinking.

It was as she decided the time had come to bolt the

door that she heard the muted sound of a horse's hooves coming along the bridle path. Quickly she moved outside to where the back door of the cottage had been. This gave her a clear view through the living room and out through the gap that had been the front door, and through narrowed gaze she recognized the rider as Mr. Sopwith.

While he was dismounting she moved slowly until she reached the end of the wall, but she did not go further to meet him.

For a moment he stayed his approach and looked at her kindly before saying, "How are you, Tilly?"

"All right, sir."

"I understand you are living here?"

"Yes, if you don't mind, sir, just for the time being."

"But I do mind." He passed her now and walked toward the open door of the woodshed and, glancing inside, he was surprised to note that it was both warm and tidy, and, he surmised, far cleaner than some of his cottages, though it was many years since he had been inside one. He turned to her now and said, "You can't stay here . . . I mean for your own good. How would you like to go into service?"

"Service, sir? I . . . I would like that very much, sir."

"Ah yes, well, that's the first step, you're willing. But having been brought up solitary, you don't know much about children, do you?"

"No, sir."

"Are you willing to learn?"

"Yes, sir. Oh yes, sir."

"Well, I understand the nursemaid that looks after my children has left suddenly, in tears I understand." He smiled now. "You see, my four are a little wild. I'm packing two off to school shortly, but in the meantime they all need some attention. Are you willing to take them on?" Again he smiled at her.

Four children! As he said, and rightly, she knew nothing about children. She couldn't remember playing with children because the village children rarely got out this far; sometimes on a holiday she would see them playing down by the burn, but she had always been too shy to join them. More than once she had lain hidden and watched them at play, especially the miners' children because they, too, worked down the pit, and so they usually came in a group by themselves on a Sunday in the summer and would swim like fish in the water and yell and shout and struggle with each other. They always enjoyed the water, the miners' children.

"Are you deterred?"

"Pardon, sir?"

"Have I put you off accepting the position?"

"Oh no, sir. No, sir. I'll take it and gladly, an' . . . an' do me best."

"Well, you can do no more. But I must warn you, you may have a rough time of it."

"I'm used to rough times, sir."

Her face had been straight, her voice low, and he stared at her for a moment as he thought, Yes, yes, indeed, you're used to hard times; and likely, looking as she did, there were many more ahead of her. There was something about her. It was in the eyes perhaps, they seemed to draw you. This had likely frightened the villagers and yet at the same time had the power to attract the men, like that McGrath individual in particular.

There had been McGraths in the village as long as there had been Sopwiths in the Manor, and strangely history noted that every generation of McGraths brought its own particular kind of trouble; highway robbers, sheep stealers, wife abductors.

Wife abductors. The word brought his chain of thinking to a halt for it had reminded him, that's if he needed reminding, there was that dinner tonight with the Mytons. Agnes delighted in making a cuckold of the old man, and he had the idea that Lord Billy wasn't unaware of it, which made him think that maybe he wasn't unaware of his own part in her latest escapade. That he was merely one in a long string of offside suitors he recognized, and he was sorry that he had ever started the affair, but Agnes had a quality about her. Like this girl here, only of a different appeal. Yet perhaps not all that different, for this slim girl, who still had a childish look about her, had certainly aroused the fires in the man McGrath.

"Can you come along to the house tonight, you don't want to sleep here any longer than is necessary . . . do you?"

"No, sir. I mean yes, yes, I could come tonight."

"Have you any belongings?"

"Only what I stand up in, sir, and a few pots back there." She inclined her head toward the woodshed.

"Well, you won't have need of . . . the pots." He laughed gently. "Be there within the hour. Ask for Mrs. Lucas, she is the housekeeper, I shall tell her to expect you. . . . All right?"

"All right, sir. And thank you."

He had half turned from her when, looking at her again, he smiled broadly and said, "I would reserve your thanks, my crew are little demons, they'll likely put you through it. But I give you leave to take a firm hand with them. Do whatever you think is necessary to curb their high spirits."

"Yes, sir. Yes, sir." As she watched him go, her mind was in a turmoil, one part of it thanking God she had a post, the other frightening her in a number of different ways: She was going into a big house where there were lots of servants. Would they be like the villagers? And then there were the children. Terrors he had called them. How would she manage them? Suddenly she smiled to herself, a small tentative smile, as she thought, Well, I can only follow me granny's pattern with meself: smacked me backside when I was bad, an' a bit of taffy when I was good.

The night was already settled in firmly before she reached the Manor gates. Timorously she went through them, passed the lodge from where no one called out to ask her business, then almost groped her way for half a mile up the drive until it opened out to show, standing beyond a large lawn, a big house, some windows illuminated, others like great black eyes.

She skirted the lawn, went round the side of the house and came upon a courtyard lit by a lantern swinging from a bracket. She now made her way to the far end from where the sound of muffled voices was coming. There were four doors in this wall, but she didn't stop until she was opposite the end one. This one was partly open and the voices were clearer now, and mixed with laughter. She leaned forward and knocked on the door and waited a full minute before knocking again, louder this time. The chatter ceased abruptly and presently the door was pulled open to reveal a girl of about her own age who peered at her, then said, "Oh, 'tis you from the cottage, is it?"

"Aye, yes."

"Oh well then, you'd better come in."

The girl's face was straight and she stood aside to let Tilly pass her before closing the door. They were now in a small room which she could see was used as a cloakroom of sorts for, hanging from the pegs, were rough coats and shawls, and along one wall a number of pairs of boots ranging from heavy hob-nailed ones down to slippers. The room was also lit by a lantern hanging from a bracket and Tilly almost hit her head against it as she followed the girl into the kitchen.

Just within the doorway of the long stone-flagged room she stopped and gazed at the scene before her.

Sitting around a table opposite a great open fireplace were a number of people, three men and four women, and all their heads were turned toward her. No one spoke until the girl who had shown her in said, "She's here."

"I've got eyes in me head, haven't I?" This came from a short and enormously fat woman who was sitting at the head of the table and who turned now and looked at the man who was sitting at the foot of the table, saying under her breath, "You better go and tell Mrs. Lucas, hadn't you?"

"It can wait. Anyway, she won't thank me if I break into their meal."

"Sit down, lass." It was one of the two men from the bottom end of the table speaking to her now, and this remark brought a dark look on him from the cook and the footman, and as if they had spoken their displeasure aloud he leaned forward and looked along the table toward the top end, saying, "Well, she's the master's choice, whatever she be, and it would pay some of us not to forget that."

This remark seemed to affect the whole table for those sitting round it moved uneasily on the forms; and now Jane Brackett, the cook, taking control of the situation before Robert Simes could challenge her position as head of the table, lifted her small, thick arm and, pointing to a cracket near the fire, said, "Sit yourself down; you'll be seen to in a minute."

Tilly sat down. Her heart was thumping against her ribs, her mouth was dry, she knew her eyes were stretched wide as they were apt to do when she was nervous or upset. For a moment she imagined she was back in the courtroom, so thick was the hostility in the air about her. But then there appeared a ray of warm light as a young woman, rising from the table and going to a delf rack, quickly took down a mug and returned to the table and poured out a cup of tea from the huge

162

teapot that was resting on a stand between the cook and the footman.

So taken aback by this forward action, the cook was lost for words for some moments; then she demanded, "And what do you think you're doin', Phyllis Coates?"

"Well, you can see what I'm doin', can't you, Mrs. Brackett?" The answer sounded perky and was given with a grin. "I'm pourin' out a cup of tea." She nudged the cook now with her elbow. "Live and let live. We'll wait and see how things turn out. Anyway—" she bent close to the cook's ear now and whispered something which brought from Jane Brackett the retort, "I'm not afeared of charms or any such damn nonsense." Yet there was no conviction in the words and her voice was muted.

Phyllis Coates was first housemaid at the Manor. She was thirty years old and had started in the kitchen twenty years ago as scullery maid. She was of medium height, and thin, with a pleasant face and happy disposition. She considered herself fortunate to hold the position she did, and much more so because in a year or two's time she was to marry Fred Leyburn the coachman. She had taken her cue from Fred. He had been kind to the lass, telling her to take a seat, so she would be an' all, she would lose nothing by it.

Bending down to Tilly now, she said, "Would you like a shive?"

"No; no, thank you."

"Go on, you must be hungry."

She went to the table again and amid silence took from her own plate a large crust of new bread and having put on it half the ham that was still on her plate she brought it to Tilly, saying, "There. There, get it down you," and bending further until their faces were on a level, she grinned at her and said, "People never look so bad when you've got a full belly."

If Tilly could have smiled she would have at that

moment, but a softness came into her eyes and she had the desire to cry; and she almost did when the girl's hand lightly touched her shoulder and patted it twice.

There was silence until Phyllis returned to the table; then it seemed as if everybody was bent on speaking at once. And this went on for some time until the cook, her voice high and strident now, said, "Sup up your last, Ada Tennant, else your backside will get glued to that form."

Tilly saw the girl who had let her in gulp at her mug, then quickly rise from the form and go to the sink at the far end of the kitchen where the dishes were piled high on each side of it.

"And you, Maggie Short, get along and see if Mrs. Lucas an' that lot's finished."

"Yes; yes, Cook." The girl rose hastily from the table and, wiping her mouth with the back of her hand, went up the kitchen toward the far door with the cook's voice following her: "Straighten your cap and pull your apron down else you'll hear about it if she sees you like that. And . . . and tell her that—" She now paused and, looking toward Tilly, said, "What's your name again?"

"Tilly, Tilly Trotter."

There was an audible giggle from the table, but the cook did nothing to stop it; instead, looking at the kitchen maid, she said, "Tell her that she's come, the Trotter girl."

"No need to do any such thing." Robert Simes the footman had risen to his feet now. "I'll see to this matter. Come along you." He jerked his head. It was a gesture one might have used to raise a dog from the hearth, and Tilly rose from the cracket and followed him.

He didn't wait for her as he passed through the green-baized door at the end of the kitchen and it swung noiselessly into her face. She paused a moment before pressing it open again and when she found herself in a broad corridor with doors going off at each side, she again paused, only to be jolted forward by Simes's voice, calling, "Come on! Look slippy." He hadn't turned his head while speaking to her.

He was standing now outside a door, the last but one in the corridor. She saw him knock on it, and she was standing to the side of him when a voice from inside said, "Come."

He opened the door but did not go over the threshold, and his tone now dropping to one of polite subservience, he said, "It's the girl, Mrs. Lucas, she's come."

"Oh." There was a murmur from inside the room, and presently a woman of medium height wearing a gray alpaca dress, the bodice of which seemed moulded to her thin body, stood confronting the footman, who had now taken a step back into the corridor.

Staring unblinking at the thin-lipped, sharp-nosed face of the housekeeper, Tilly experienced another tremor of apprehension as the round dark eyes swept over her. She knew, even if the atmosphere hadn't warned her, that her history had preceded her; she was already feeling that she had been thrust back into the middle of the village.

The housekeeper was now joined by the butler. Mr. Pike was a man nearing seventy. He had a long, tired face, his shoulders were slightly stooped, and when he looked at her his eyes gave nothing away—his gaze was neutral.

"Well, let's get it over. Come, girl," said the housekeeper.

"Does she want to see her tonight?"

The housekeeper turned her head to look at the butler. "My order from Her Ladyship Price was to take her up as soon as she arrived."

"I don't think the mistress will thank you for taking her up at this time of night."

"What has the mistress got to do with it when that one's about? Come on, you."

Again it was as if the command were being given to a dog.

Tilly followed the housekeeper and that part of her not filled with fear and apprehension noted that the woman didn't seem to take steps as she walked, her head didn't bob or her arms swing, it was as if her feet were attached to wheels beneath the hem of the full alpaca skirt. She was reminded of a toy she once had called Bad Weather Jack and Fine Weather Jane: according to the atmosphere they glided in and out of minature doors set in a box painted to represent a house.

She followed her up a narrow staircase on to a small landing, then up a short flight of four stairs and through yet another green-baized door; and now she was walking across what was to her the biggest room she had ever seen. She only vaguely took in that it was partly railed in and that a broad stairway led from the center down to the ground floor because the housekeeper had now turned and was gliding quickly up an even broader and longer corridor than the one below. The length of it was indicated by the three colored lamps set at intervals on tables along its walls. Everything about her seemed to be wrapped in a soft red glow: the carpet was red, the wallpaper was red; there were deep red colors reflecting from some of the pictures hanging between the doors. She was dazed by the wonder of it, even transported out of herself for a moment; that was until the housekeeper came to a stop and, her voice a muted hiss, she said, "Only speak when you're spoken to. And keep your head down until you're told to lift it. You heard what I said?" The last words were delivered in an almost inaudible whisper, and for answer Tilly nodded once. "Then when I speak to you answer 'Yes, Mrs. Lucas.'"

Her head already bent forward, Tilly looked up under her eyelids at the housekeeper and obediently said, "Yes, Mrs. Lucas."

The housekeeper glared at her. Why did the mistress want to see this girl? It wasn't her place to engage staff. She was acting like an ordinary small-house mistress, the engaging of staff was the duty of the housekeeper. There was something fishy here. Another of Madam Price's tactics, she'd be bound.

In answer to the housekeeper's knock on the door, Mabel Price opened it and, after looking from one to the other, she turned her head and said quietly, "It's the girl, madam."

"Oh, I'll see her now."

As the housekeeper went to draw Tilly forward Miss Price said, "It's quite all right, Mrs. Lucas, you won't be needed."

The women exchanged looks that only they could have translated; then Miss Price, touching Tilly's shoulder with the tip of her finger, indicated that she enter the room, almost at the same time closing the door on the housekeeper; then her fingers still on Tilly's shoulder, she pressed her forward until she was standing about a yard from the couch on which a lady was lying. She could only see the shape of her lower body underneath what looked like a silk rug because, obeying orders, she had her head down and her eyes directed toward the floor.

"Look at me, girl."

Slowly Tilly raised her head and looked at the lady; and she thought she was beautiful, sickly looking, but beautiful.

"My husband has recommended you as nursemaid for our children, but he tells me you have no previous experience. Is that so?"

"Yes, ma'am."

"Do you like children?"

There was a pause, "Yes, ma'am."

"How old are you?"

"Gone sixteen, ma'am."

"You have lived on the estate since you were very young, I understand?"

"Yes, ma'am."

"Your grandmother and grandfather died, did they not?"

"Yes, ma'am."

"And there was the unfortunate business of your cottage being burned down, at least my husband's cottage being burned down."

Another pause. "Yes, ma'am."

"Well, Trotter, I hope you realize that you are very fortunate to be given this position, having had no previous experience."

"Yes, ma'am."

"You will find that my children are very high-spirited. I . . . I expect you to control them, to a certain extent."

"Yes, ma'am."

"How long you remain in my service depends on their reaction to you, you understand?"

"Yes, ma'am."

"You may go now, and Miss Price will instruct you as to your duties."

"Yes, ma'am."

She was about to turn away when she was hissed at again. It was a different hiss from the housekeeper's, it was a high, thin, refined hiss. "Thank the mistress," it said.

She gulped; then with head down and eyes cast toward the thick gray carpet, she said, "Thank you, ma'am."

A few minutes later, after having led her not into the corridor but through a dressing-room and into what Tilly took to be a closet, for it held two hand basins on

stands with big copper watering cans to the side, while
in the corner was a wooden seat with a hole in it and on
the top a decorated porcelain lid, and underneath a
porcelain pail with beautiful paintings on it and a
square straw-bound handle dangling down the side of
it, Mabel Price looked at the new nursery maid with
deep interest. She knew all about her, her business with
the parson's wife, the murder of that man, the case in
Newcastle, the cottage being burned down because she
was a witch, and as she stared at her she wondered why
it was that the master had insisted on taking her into his
employ. One thing was certain, if the mistress had got
wind of the witch business Miss Tilly Trotter wouldn't
have got through the back door of this house. That's
why he had warned her. And how he had warned her!
Almost threatened her. "You say one word about this
girl to the mistress, Price," he had said, "and you'll be
outside those gates quicker than you've ever passed
through them before. And no pleading from the mistress will make me change my mind. You understand
me?"

Oh, she understood him all right. She understood
that at times he was no gentleman and if it hadn't been
that he was deep in the clutches of the Myton piece she
might have put two and two together. But this girl
before her was just that, a girl; she was sixteen but she
didn't look it, she didn't act it. He had been wild about
the cottage being burned down, furious in fact, and if
he had found who had done it they would certainly
have gone along the line. Likely he was just sorry for
this individual. As for her being a witch, she looked as
much like a witch as the Virgin Mary did. Funny that,
her mind linking her up with the Virgin Mary. She
supposed it was because she had already been linked up
with the church through the parson's wife. Well, anyway, by the look of her she wouldn't reign long upstairs
because that bunch would eat her alive. Time would

tell, and in her estimation it would take very little time before Tilly Trotter was trotting down the drive again. Tilly Trotter, what a name!

But why had the mistress insisted on seeing her herself? Did she think that he was up to something with her? Well, if she did, it was one thing she wouldn't confide in her. She knew that.

"Before we go upstairs you had better know where you stand"—it was strange to Tilly to realize that although this woman looked refined and appeared so when talking to her mistress, the words she used were ordinary—"the ins and outs of your position. Your wages will be five pounds a year. Should you get yourself up to anything, misbehave in any way, you can be dismissed without notice. Should you take it in your mind to leave without giving a full month's notice you'll have to refund so much for each day, threepence or threepence farthing." She shook her head at the difference. "You'll be supplied with uniform which'll only be yours as long as you're in service here. You'll be allowed time to go to church on a Sunday morning and one full day off a month. If you break anything through carelessness it'll be charged against you. You understand?"

"Yes; yes, m. . . ."

"You call me miss."

"Yes, miss."

"Come on then."

She was again in the broad corridor. They now turned into a narrower one at the end of which was a steep flight of stairs. The stairs were dark and the only guidance she had was from a narrow handrail and the sound of Mabel Price's steps on the bare boards, but when she emerged at the top she found herself on a square landing lit by two lamps. There were a number of doors going off this landing and Mabel Price, lifting up a lamp, went to the first door and, thrusting it open and holding the lamp high above her head, said, "This is the children's school and day-room."

In the moment of time she had for looking round the room Tilly saw a large rocking horse, a doll's house, and various other toys scattered about the room. She noticed that a fire had burned low in the grate which was now covered by a large black-mesh screen.

The next room she was shown was a small bedroom, the main furniture being two single iron beds. In one lay a small child curled up fast asleep. "That's John," Mabel Price said; "he's the baby." In the other bed a little girl was sitting up, her arms hugging her knees, and when Mabel Price ordered, "Lie down, Jessie Ann, and go to sleep," the girl made no movement whatever but stared at Tilly, and it was to her she spoke, saying in a voice that held laughter, "You're the new one then?"

Tilly said nothing to this, but Mabel Price, going to the child, pushed her roughly backward and pulled the covers up almost smothering her face as she said, "Get yourself to sleep. If you're not gone in five minutes I'll inform your mama."

For answer the child simply said, "Huh!"

As if she had been exposed to defeat, Mabel Price marched out of the room with no order for Tilly to follow her; but Tilly did and closed the door gently behind her.

They were in the next room now. This room was a little larger, but also sparsely furnished. The eldest boy was sitting at the foot of his bed, his long blue-striped nightshirt and his fair curly hair framing his round face giving him an angelic look. His brother was tucked well down under the bedclothes, but both boys' eyes were bright with expectancy.

Mabel Price began without any introduction. "That's Matthew there"—she pointed to the cherub—"he's ten." And this is Luke, he's eight."

She was standing by the bedside, the lamp, held over

the boy, showing only his dark hair and bright eyes. Then throwing her glance from one to the other, she added without indicating Tilly in any way, "This is the new maid. Any of your carry-on and I'm to inform your father. Those are his words, and remember them! Now you get into bed." She pointed to Matthew, but the boy, instead of obeying her, simply returned her stare and she went out as if once again she were suffering defeat.

On the landing she opened another door but did not enter. Simply pointing into it, she said, "That's the closet. You will see that they wash themselves well every morning. You'll have to stand over them, it'll be no use trusting them to do it themselves. They are called at half past seven. You start at six prompt. You clean out the schoolroom, the closet, and your own room." She now pushed open another door and, marching inside, pointed to a battered chest of drawers on which was a half burned candle in a candlestick. "Light the candle from the lamp," she said.

Quickly Tilly brought the candle forward and, holding it over the long glass funnel of the lamp, she waited until it was alight, feeling all the while that this woman would go for her because of the grease spluttering on to the burning wick below. But Mabel Price seemed to ignore this and said, "This is your room, not that you'll be in it much. But to get on with your morning's work. You light the fire in the schoolroom; then after you've cleaned and tidied it up, you set the children's breakfast out. You'll find the crockery in the cupboard there. At half past seven you awake them and see that they're washed, as I told you. Their breakfast is brought up at eight. Having seen to them starting the meal you then go down to the kitchen for your own breakfast. You have from eight till half past for your meal. Ada Tennant, the scullery maid, takes your place up here while you're downstairs. At nine o'clock Mrs. Lucas, the housekeeper, does her inspection. At quarter past

nine if the weather is fine you take the children for a
brisk walk round the garden. They begin their lessons
with Mr. Burgess, their tutor, at ten o'clock. In the
meantime you empty all the slops, and see that you
wash out the buckets well. Then you see to their clothes
and necessary mending. That's as far as I'll go now.
Have you taken that in?"

Tilly stared at the woman for almost ten seconds
before she could make herself say, "Yes, miss."

"Well, I'll know tomorrow whether you have or not.
Anyway, should you want to know anything, you come
to me. My room is the fourth one along the corridor
from the mistress's, it's the end door. I'm in charge up
here, not Mrs. Lucas, understand that?"

"Yes, miss."

"Well, you'd better get to bed, not that you'll be
allowed to go to bed at this hour every night, but
you've got a lot to get into that head of yours, so you'll
have time to think over my instructions."

Alone now, Tilly looked round the room. Even the
soft glow from the candle didn't lend any warmth to it
and the patchwork quilt on the bed did nothing to
brighten it. All the furniture it possessed was the bed,
the chest of drawers, a stool, and a rickety table with a
chipped jug and basin on it. Two hooks on the back of
the door was all the wardrobe the room afforded.

Up under the roof in the cottage she'd had clippy
rugs on the floor but these boards were bare, with not a
thread of covering to them. The knobs on her brass bed
had been polished bright, the curtains on her window,
although faded, had been crisp and clean, but the
window in this room didn't require curtains because it
was let partly into the roof.

She dropped down on to the edge of the bed. Her
mind was in a turmoil; she had met so many people
during the last hour and apart from two of them they
had all been alien to her. Yet not only to her, for there
was alienation among themselves. She had sensed it

from the moment she entered the house; each was trying to get the better of the others in some way. And those children, what was she to make of them? Well, she would soon find out in that quarter, she was sure of that. But the staff, they were another kettle of fish altogether. She'd have to go careful; if she pleased one, she'd offend the other, and she'd have to find who she wanted to please and who she didn't mind offending. Her granny used to say speak the truth and shame the devil, but she already knew that this wasn't the kind of house where it would be wise to speak the truth. . . . And the mistress of it? She didn't know what to make of her. A grand lady doubtless, but cold; somehow not alive. No, no; that wasn't what she meant. Oh, what did it matter, she had tomorrow to face. Six o'clock in the morning . . . prompt, which meant rising before that. But how would she know when it was time to get up? She should have asked her, that woman, Miss Price. Likely there would be a knocker-up. Well, she could think no more, she was tired and weary in both mind and body. . . . It must be nice to be dead, just to lie there still and have no worries.

She shook her head at herself, she mustn't start to think like that again. She'd got a job, wasn't that what she wanted? A job, and she must learn how to do it, and learn quickly or else. . . . Aye, or else.

3

She started the following day by learning how one knew when it was time to get up when her shoulder was roughly shaken and a voice said briefly, "Up!"

She came quickly out of sleep to peer at Ada Tennant and when the girl again cried, "Up!" she surprised her by answering as abruptly, "All right! All right!" and when the scullery maid backed three steps away from her and the grease of her candle spilled over before she turned toward the door, she knew a moment of victory, and again one of her granny's sayings came to her: "Give what you get. I never believed in a soft word turning away wrath."

Her mind was clear. Strangely, she remembered nearly all the instructions that Miss Price had given her last night and she went about them with agility; until she attempted to wake the children. When gently she shook Matthew's shoulder the boy's fist came out and struck her a blow on the arm. It was as if he had been waiting for her coming. She stood for a moment, her body half bent over the bed gripping the place where the boy's fist had hit her, her arm was paining because it had been no light blow; then as if she stepped out of her timid body she was amazed at her next reaction for, her hands on the boy's shoulders, she was pinning him to the bed. Bringing her face down to his, she whispered, "Don't you ever do that again because whatever you do to me I'll give you twice as much back." She paused while their eyes bored into each other in the lamplight and for a moment she imagined she was holding down

175

Hal McGrath, and then she asked him, "Do you understand me?"

It was evident to her that he was so taken aback by her reaction that for a moment she seemed to have stunned him, and not him alone for Luke, sitting up in bed, stopped rubbing his eyes and gaped at her, his mouth partly open. Then she turned to him and said, "It's time to get up."

After a moment's hesitation he pulled the bedclothes back, but when he went to put his feet on the floor his brother cried at him, "Stay where you are! There's plenty of time."

Tilly looked hard at the boy for a moment before going to the other bed. Here she finished what Luke had begun: pulling the bedclothes right to the bottom of the bed, she put her hand gently on the boy's elbow and eased him to his feet; then looking from one to the other, she said, "You'll be in the closet in five minutes."

It wasn't until she stood on the landing that she realized her legs were trembling, and she asked herself, "What made me go on like that? Well, start the way you mean to go on." It was as if her granny were at her side, directing her.

In the next room she had no trouble with Jessie Ann, but the four-year-old John seemed a chip of his ten-year-old brother and when she tried to lift him from the bed he kicked and kept saying, "Don't wanna!" and as he kept repeating this she thought, He speaks no better than a village child.

The first incident in the nursery war took place in the closet when Matthew purposely kicked over a bucket of slops. As the water spread across the floor the others screeched with glee and jumped out of the way, but Tilly stood in the midst of it, and as she looked at the excrement floating around her feet she could at that moment have been sick. But there was her grandmother again seeming to shout at her now. "'Tis no time for a weak stomach, go for him or else you'll not last long here." And so, instinctively, she reached out and gripped the boy's arm and pulled him in his slippered feet toward her. For a moment he was again too taken aback to fight; even when he attempted to she held his arms against his sides, and her grip was surprisingly strong. She had not wielded an axe or used a saw to no avail during all her young days and the strength of her hands must have got through to him for, like the little bully he was, he whined and said, "It was an accident. I tripped, I did. Didn't I, Luke, I tripped?"

Staring into his face again, Tilly said, "You didn't trip, you did it on purpose"—her voice was quiet now—"but I'm tellin' you this, you do this again an' I'll make you clean it up, every last drop." And she added, "Your father has given me the position to look after you, an' I'll do it gladly, but any more of such pranks and I'll go right to him an' let him deal with you."

The boy was truly astounded: maids didn't react like this, they cried, they whined, they pleaded, they brought extras and titbits from the kitchen to placate him.

But the boy's surprise was nothing to the surprise Tilly herself was feeling. It was as if on this day she were being reborn. Like the little lizards who shed their skins, the fearful, frightened Tilly Trotter was sliding away from her. If she could get the better of this fellow she felt she would lose her fear of people, all people. . . . No, not all people; there was one man she would always fear. But he was miles away beyond the walls of this house, wherein was encased another world. He had no hope of getting at her here, and she would see that she didn't meet up with him on her day off a month. Oh aye; aye, she would see to that.

"Go now, get your clothes on." She addressed the

177

two older boys and, looking at Jessie Ann, she said, "Take John"—she wasn't even sure of their names— "and I'll be along to dress you in a few minutes. Away now. But before you go out there, wipe your slippers on the mat."

They wiped their slippers and they went away, all of them, without a word but with backward glances. They couldn't make this one out; she had got the better of Matthew, and they had never known anyone get the better of Matthew.

When the door closed on them she looked at the filth around her feet and again her stomach heaved. But heave or not, it had to be cleared up and so, grimly, she set about the task.

She didn't realize that this particular nursery breakfast was an unusually quiet affair. There were no spoonfuls of porridge splashed over the table; the bread and butter was not stuck downward on to its surface; and so when Ada Tennant came into the room she stood for a moment gazing at the four children all quietly eating their meal. Then turning to Tilly, she was about to make some remark when she changed her mind. Her eyes widened just the slightest and what she said now and in a civil manner was, "Your breakfast's waitin'."

"Thank you."

Ada Tennant's eyes widened still further. It was likely true the rumor about her, must be. An' the way she spoke! She hadn't said "Ta" but "Thank you," just as if she was educated. And look at this lot sittin' here like lambs. But how long would it last? Then the rumor was utterly confirmed when Tilly turned in the open doorway and, looking toward the children, said, "Behave yourselves mind."

When the door closed on Tilly, Ada Tennant gazed at it. It was as if she knew the minute her back was turned they would start, and she had given them a warning.

She herself had started to work here when she was eight years old, now she was fourteen. She had seen this lot grow up, and for the past three years it had been her morning chore to attend them at breakfast, and she had dreaded it. She still did. She turned and looked at the children and, taking advantage of the new lass's authority, she said, "You heard what she said, so get on with it."

And they got on with it.

Breakfast was almost finished when Tilly entered the kitchen, and it seemed to her now that when she left the top floor she had also left her new-found courage behind. Two men were leaving by the far door; and the only ones seated at the table now were the cook and Phyllis Coates, the first housemaid. Amy Stiles, the second housemaid, was filling copper cans of hot water from a boiler attached to a second fireplace in the kitchen. Tilly hadn't noticed this last night. It was an enclosed fire with a boiler on one side and a round oven on the other, and as she turned and looked toward it the cook spoke. What she said was, "Are you tea or beer?"

"Pardon. What?"

"I said are you tea or beer?"

"I . . . I would like tea please."

"Well, get it." Cook jerked her head toward the stove.

After a moment's hesitation Tilly made her way toward the stove. At the same time Phyllis Coates rose from the table, smiled at Tilly, pointed to the dresser and said, "Bring a mug an' a plate" and when Tilly did this, she muttered under her breath, "You help yourself from the pot." She pointed to a huge brown teapot standing on the hearth near a heap of hot ashes. "But first come and fill your plate, the porridge is finished." And on this she walked along the room to the round

179

oven. Tilly followed her and watched her pull open the iron door to disclose a large dripping tin in which there were a few strips of sizzling bacon.

"Mostly fat left," Phyllis said, "but help yourself if you want any."

Tilly helped herself to one narrow slice of the bacon; then after placing her plate on the table she filled her mug with the black tea from the pot, and when she sat down at the table Phyllis Coates pushed toward her the end of a crusty loaf.

As Tilly ate the bread and bacon and drank the bitter tea she noted that there was a basin full of sugar opposite the cook; also a platter with a large lump of butter on it and a brown stone jar that evidently held some breakfast preserve. But she was grateful for the bacon and bread and the tea, and when she had finished cook was still sitting at the table but had as yet exchanged no word with her, in fact she had hardly looked in her direction.

It hadn't taken her ten minutes to eat her meal and when she rose from the table Phyllis Coates rose with her, and when cook spoke to Phyllis, saying, "You're goin' about your business early this mornin' then?" the first housemaid answered, "It'll take me, with the old dragon due in a fortnight's time. She'll have her eyes in every corner."

"Well, she won't find any mucky corners in my kitchen."

"She'll find mucky corners in heaven, that one."

This last retort was made as Phyllis Coates followed Tilly through the door and into the broad passage. She walked by Tilly's side to the end of it where it turned toward the back stairs, but once round the corner she pulled her to a stop and, her voice rapid and her tone low, she said, "Don't let Ma Brackett frighten you. She's only over the kitchen, she's got no other say in the house. The one you've got to look out for is Miss

Price." She raised her eyebrows upward. "She's the one who rules the roost here. Not the housekeeper, Mrs. Lucas; she thinks she does but it's only in name, it's Miss Price who has the say. An' watch out for Simes. That's the footman, you know. He's a crawler, he'd give his mother away for a shillin' that one. Mr. Pike, the butler, the old fella, he's all right. Amy Stiles, she's my second, she's all right an' all. Not much up top but she's all right. An' take no notice of Maggie Short. She's as ignorant as a pig that one. An' Ada Tennant, you know the scullery maid, the one who's up in the nursery now, she's got a slate loose." She tapped her head. "Outside there's three gardeners an' my Fred. That's Fred Leyburn. He's the coachman." She smiled now. "We're walkin' out. Should get married shortly."

For the first time in weeks Tilly smiled widely, and she said, "I hope you'll be happy."

"Ta, thanks. He's a good man. He's been married afore, his wife died, but he's a good man. It was him who said last night when we had a minute, 'Put her wise'—that was you—'to the set-up inside, you know, who's what an' everything.'" She drew her head back into her shoulders and surveyed Tilly for a moment. Then shaking her head, she said, "I must admit you're a different kettle of fish from Nancy . . . Nancy Dew-hurst, that's the one whose place you've taken. She was older than you by years, eighteen she was, but didn't look half as sensible; cried her eyes out every day. Of course mind, they'll likely bring you to tears an' all afore you're much older, I mean that lot in the nursery. Real hell bent little devils they are, especially Master Matthew. Oh! that one, he's got somethin' missing an' that's his horns. Well there, I must get on. You see, the mistress's mother is comin' in a fortnight's time, comes twice a year when the roads are passable. She lives near Scarborough. Oh and don't you know she's here! Everybody runs around like scalded cats for a month.

181

An' you know we're very understaffed. There used to be twice as many in the house at one time, when the wings were open. Well, when I first come years ago there were over thirty servants inside and out, now there's about half that many. But they expect the same out of us. Oh aye; yes they expect the same out of us. Anyway"—she smiled again—"if you want to know anything, I'll be around the first floor till twelve."

"Thank you. Thank you very much."

"You're welcome."

As Tilly turned away she called softly to her, "Keep your full breakfast half-hour, you'll need it afore the day's out," and for answer Tilly nodded at her, then went toward the stairs.

Again she was feeling confident, and again a strange feeling of courage was rising in her. She had a friend, in fact she had two friends, the housemaid and the coachman. Well, that wasn't bad for a start, now was it? No; no, it wasn't. She ran up the whole flight of stairs to the nursery floor.

At twenty past nine she was standing in the schoolroom and protests were coming at her from all sides. They didn't want to go out for a walk, it was cold, they wanted to stay in and play. Matthew had some beetles in a box and they were going to race them.

She let them go on with their protests for some minutes; then, holding up her hand, she said, "Very well. I shall go downstairs and tell your mother you don't want to go out. I would go to your father but I saw him leavin' for the mine some time ago."

Go and tell their mother! They looked at this new creature, and they really could see her doing just that, especially Matthew. If they upset their mother their father would be told and that would bring up the question again of being sent to boarding school. He didn't want to go away to school, he liked his life here.

182

He was wise enough to know that he would have no dominion over anyone at boarding school; in fact, he was aware that the tables would be turned and he would have to obey. He didn't like obeying. But for some strange reason he knew that he had better obey this thin, weak looking girl who had a grip like iron and who had the habit of staring you out. He turned to his brother and said, "Aw, come on," and immediately Luke and Jessie Ann repeated, "Yes, come on." But John just stood, and when she held out her hand and said to him, "Come along," he looked up at her and said, "I've w . . . wet myself."

At this the others doubled up with laughter and, as if their young brother had scored off her for them, they cried almost in one voice, "He always wets himself."

She looked down on the boy and, her voice and face stiff, she said, "You're too big to wet yourself, you should go to the closet."

Jessie Ann, her wide gray eyes full of mischief, tossed her long ringlets first from one shoulder then to the other and cried, "He'll go on wetting himself until he's put into trousers, and he won't have them until he's five. Luke wetted himself until he was five, didn't you, Luke?"

Tilly gazed at the little boy, who had every appearance of a girl, dressed in a blue corduroy velvet dress with a white frill at the neck, his thick straight brown hair hanging on to his shoulders. He looked more of a girl than did Jessie Ann. She felt like taking him up in her arms and hugging him, wet as he was underneath; but these were children who, she surmised, at the slightest show of softness in her would make her life unbearable so that she, too, would be crying every day. Well, she wasn't going to cry every day, she had finished with crying, she was going to get on with this job. So, bending down to the small boy and watched by the other three, she said, "Well, I'll change you this

183

time, John, but if you wet yourself again you'll keep your wet pants on till they dry on you. An' you won't like that, will you now?"

"N-no."

"Well then. An' should you wet yourself just afore we are goin' out into the garden then we'll leave you behind 'cos I won't be able to waste time changin' you."

Where was she getting the words from to talk to children like this? She who had had little to say except to her grandma and granda and, of course, Mrs. Ross, dear, dear Mrs. Ross. Funny—she straightened up and stood looking over the children's heads for a moment – wasn't it strange, but she felt she was acting in much the same way as Mrs. Ross would do when dealing with children; in fact she was speaking to them as Mrs. Ross had spoken to her Sunday school. She smiled to herself, and when she again looked at the children her voice was brisk and had a happy sound, and, looking at Jessie Ann, she said, "Bring me a pair of clean pantaloons from the cupboard."

"What!" Jessie Ann looked as surprised as if she had been told to jump out of the window, and so Tilly leaned toward the round fair face and in words slow and clear she said, "You heard what I said, Jessie Ann. Bring me a pair of John's pantaloons from the cupboard."

After a moment's pause Jessie Ann did just that, she brought a pair of small pantaloons and handed them to Tilly. . . .

The play area in the garden was a stretch of lawn which was bordered by the vegetable garden on one side and a stretch of woodland on the other, and when the children began to play desultorily with a ball she stood watching; until Matthew aimed it directly at her, not for her to catch she understood but with the intention of hitting her, and when she caught it she kept it in her hand for a moment, then threw it to Luke; and Luke threw it to Jessie; and Jessie, after a pause, threw it back again to Tilly; and now Tilly threw it to John, and he ran away with it and they all chased him, and she among them; and when the little boy fell and the other children tumbled on top of him and he began to cry, it was then she picked him up and held him in her arms and her hand cupping the back of his head pressed it into her shoulder as she said, "There now. There now. 'Tis all right, you're not dead," while the others stood looking at her in amazement. After a while the play went on.

When they returned to the nursery it was to find an old man sitting there. He rose from a chair before the fire and as she went to take her coat off she looked at him and said, "Good morning, sir," and he answered, "Good morning." Then poking his head forward, he added, "Your name is?"

"Trotter. Tilly Trotter, sir."

"Tilly Trotter. Trotter Tilly. Tilly Trotter." Matthew had his head back now chanting her name, and Mr. Burgess, looking at the boy, said, "Don't be silly, Matthew. It's a nice name, it's a singing name; a name you can associate with alliteration. . . . Ah, now that's a word we can use this morning, Matthew. You will find out what alliteration means and give me some examples, eh, like, Miss Tilly Trotter?" He smiled at Tilly and Tilly smiled back at him. Then she stood looking at him as he marshaled the children toward the table. Here could be a third friend. He spoke kindly, he looked kindly. Again she was reminded of Mrs. Ross. This man knew words like Mrs. Ross did. And then she started visibly as he said, "You . . . you were acquainted with Mrs. Ross?"

It was a long moment before she answered, "Yes, sir."

"They . . . they were friends of mine." As he inclined his head toward her she wanted to say, "I'm sorry, sir." And she was sorry that he had lost his friends, sorry as she was that she had lost Mrs. Ross.

"She taught you to read and write, did she not . . . Mrs. Ross?"

"Yes, sir."

As they looked at each other she knew that he knew all about her. Yet he was being civil to her, nice to her; he didn't blame her for what had happened to his friends.

"The world is yours if you can read and write."

Again she answered, "Yes, sir."

Now he turned from her, saying to the children, "Well, what are we waiting for? Let's begin! for there's no time to waste, life is short; at the longest it's short."

She noticed, with not a little surprise, that the children obeyed him, even Matthew did. They fetched their slates and pencils from a cupboard and took their places around the bare wooden table.

Unobtrusively now, she made her way out of the room and crossed the landing to her own room. Here she hung up her coat and hat and, slumping down on to the side of her bed for a moment, she thought, That's that! The worst is over, I'm set.

It was fortunate in this moment she didn't realize that her battle, the real battle of her life, had not yet even begun.

At eleven o'clock she took a tray of hot milk and biscuits to the schoolroom. But just within the doorway she stopped. The tutor was speaking and he was making the words sound like a lilt, like music. He was saying, "The boy saw that the land was green, as in the beginning, and water swept, as in the beginning, and as beautiful and mysterious, as in the beginning; and he knew that it was the seasons that made it so for without the seasons what would there be? . . . Devastation! And he asked from where do the seasons get their orders? And the answer came, from the sun. . . . Ah, now we'll talk about the sun, shall we?"

He stopped and looked toward Tilly still standing with the tray of steaming mugs in her hand, and he said, "Well now, the sun can wait; here is Miss Trotter with refreshment."

He had called her Miss Trotter. It was the first time in her life she had been called Miss Trotter. It sounded nice somehow.

She handed the children the mugs, and a large one of tea with milk and sugar in it she placed before him; then having set the plate of biscuits in the middle of the table, she withdrew.

The children hadn't spoken. Mr. Burgess, she thought, was a wonderful man, so . . . so like Mrs. Ross. The Sunday school children hadn't talked either when Mrs. Ross was speaking.

At dinnertime the meal was good, and she noted that she was given a fair share like everyone else; but no one spoke to her, except Phyllis Coates and the coachman. Somehow, it didn't seem to matter. When Mrs. Lucas had inspected the nursery floor she had hardly said two words to her, although all during her inspection she had kept muttering, "Hm! Hm!" However, in the afternoon Miss Price had been more verbal, much more verbal.

"You are not to say 'you' to the children," she said; "you'll address them in the following manner: Master Matthew, Master Luke, Master John, and Miss Jessie Ann. You understand?"

She had said she understood.

"And go down at once and tell Mrs. Lucas to fit you up with suitable uniform."

When she had carried out this order, Mrs. Lucas had not been at all pleased; she had muttered something under her breath that sounded like bitch. But then it couldn't possibly have been—a woman in Mrs. Lucas's position wouldn't call anyone in Miss Price's position a bitch.

Toward the end of the day she had one pleasant surprise. The master came up to the nursery and, after talking to the children, he called her out on to the landing, and there he said, "Well, how's it gone?"

"Very well, sir," she had answered.

"Do you think you can manage them?"

"I'm having a good try, sir."

"They haven't played any of their tricks on you yet?"

"Not as yet, sir."

"There's plenty of time." He had smiled at her. "Look out for Matthew; he's a rip, as I've already indicated."

"I'll look out for him, sir."

"That's right. Good-night, Trotter."

As he turned from her she said, "Sir," and he looked toward her again. "Yes?"

"I would just like to say thank you for . . . for givin' me the post, sir."

"'Tis nothing. 'Tis nothing." He shook his head, smiled once more at her, then went quickly from the landing; and she stood until the sound of his feet running down the stairs was smothered in the carpet of the lower floor. . . .

She had seen them to bed, she had tidied up the schoolroom, carried down the last slops from the closet, washed out the pails, then by the light of the candle she had taken in the waist of the print dress she was to wear tomorrow and moved the buttons on the bodice and on the cuffs. It was ten o'clock now and she was dying with sleep. Getting out of her dress, stockings and shoes, she left on her bodice and petticoat to sleep in and, pulling the cover back, she got into bed, thrust her feet down, then only just in time smothered a high scream as the thing jumped around her legs.

Within a split second she was standing on the floor

again. Gulping in her throat, she groped around for the candle, then made her way out on to the lighted landing and lit her candle from the lamp. Back in the room she held it in her shaking hand over the bed; and there, as startled as she was, sat a large frog.

A gurgle came into her throat and steadied the trembling of her hand. The little devil! And he was a devil. He wasn't just an imp like some young lads, he was a devil. It was in his eyes, and she was going to have trouble with him if she didn't do something about it. These were the kind of tricks which could scare the daylights out of you, and once he got away with it they would get worse. What should she do? She leaned forward and picked up the frog just as he was about to make another leap. She had handled numerous frogs, having had to save many of them from losing legs when they took refuge under pieces of wood she had been about to chop.

She turned and looked toward the door. They were both likely out there, the two older ones anyway, waiting to hear her scream.

. . . Do unto others as you'd have them do to you. Her granny was again in her head, but her saying was a little confused now with her grandfather's laughing remark to his wife's parable: Do for others before they do for you. Anyway, she would give Master Matthew tit for tat, and see how that worked.

Silently she crept out of the room and into the boys' room. They were now both tucked well down in bed, but instinctively she knew that Matthew was very much awake and had only just scrambled into his bed. Placing the candlestick on the box table to the side of the bed, she gently pulled down the bedclothes that half covered the boy's face, and as gently she lifted up the neck of his nightshirt, then with a quick movement she thrust the frog down on to his chest.

The result of her action frightened her more than

when the frog had jumped up her bare legs, for when the animal's clammy body flopped against the boy's bare flesh he let out an ear-splitting scream, and then another, before jumping out of bed and shaking madly at his nightshirt.

When the frog leaped on to her bare feet before making its escape under the bed, she took no heed but, gripping the boy's shoulders and shaking him, she cried, "Whist! whist!" and when he became quiet she bent down to his gasping mouth and said, "Tit for tat. I told you, didn't I?"

She turned her head now quickly toward the door when she heard running steps on the stairs, and she had only just pushed him back into bed when the door was burst open and Mark Sopwith appeared.

"What is it? What's wrong?"

The boy was sitting up in bed and he stammered, "Fa . . . Father, Fa . . . Father."

Mark took hold of him, then said, "What's the matter? Did you have a dream?"

The boy now glanced from his father toward Tilly and it was she who stammered now, "Ye . . . ye . . . yes. Yes, he had a dream, a night . . . nightmare."

"What is it? What's wrong? The mistress is upset."

They all looked toward Mabel Price who had burst in and was standing at the foot of the bed dressed in a blue dressing-gown with her hair hanging down her back in two plaits, and Mark said, "He's had a nightmare. Too much supper likely. It's all right. . . . Tell your mistress he's all right. I'll be down presently." His tone was curt and held a dismissal, and after looking from one to the other she left the room.

"Settle down now, you're all right." He pressed his son back into the pillows, and when the boy said again, "Father," he asked, "What is it?"

There was a long pause before Matthew muttered, "Nothing, nothing."

"There now, go to sleep." He tucked the clothes around the boy's shoulders; then nodding to Tilly, he beckoned her out of the room.

On the landing he looked at her standing in her petticoat and bodice. He hadn't realized before that she was only partly undressed. She must, he imagined, have been getting ready for bed. Although she was tall, almost as tall as himself, she looked like a very young girl, for her face had a childlike quality. He said, "Did he have a lot to eat tonight?"

"No, sir . . . and"—her head drooped—"and it wasn't a nightmare."

"No?" It was a question.

"Well, you see, sir, when I got into bed I was startled like 'cos I found . . . well, he'd put a frog in me bed, and . . . and I thought the only way to get the better of him was tit for tat. He . . . he must have been waitin' for me screamin' and . . . and I just stopped meself, but . . . but I didn't think he'd be frightened like that when I put it down his shirt."

"You put the frog down his shirt?"

"Yes, sir." Her head drooped still further. She didn't know why she was telling this man the truth, she felt that she must be mad, he could put her out of the door this minute for treating his children so, gentry's children were allowed to do things that others weren't, specially to servants. She should never have thought tit for tat, not in this household.

Mark looked at her lowered head. Her face certainly portrayed her character for she was still a child. There had been no adult vindictiveness behind her action, and perhaps it would teach Master Matthew a lesson. He needed teaching a lesson, and likely he had taken it in for he hadn't given her away. Yet he knew that his son's reticence in this matter hadn't been to save the nurse-maid but to avert his own displeasure and so bring nearer the threat of boarding school. Well, little did he know it but the threat was upon him. He said now, "I can understand your motive but . . . but you must have scared him badly."

"I'm feared I did, sir, and . . . and I'm very sorry."

"Well,"—he smiled a wry smile—"don't be too sorry. Though I wouldn't take such drastic measures again. Still, for the short time he'll have with you I think you'll manage him."

Her eyes widened and she whispered now, "You're . . . you're not dismissing me, sir?"

"No, no." He shook his head. "I'm sending him and his brother to boarding school. They don't know it yet"—and now he poked his head close to hers as he ended, "In fact their mother doesn't know it yet, so—" He tapped his lips with his forefinger, and she smiled back at him and answered, "Aye, sir, not a word."

"Well now, get away to bed and I'll go down and tell the mistress that you haven't tried to bewitch him."

It was the wrong thing to have said and they both knew it.

"Good-night, Trotter."

"Good-night, sir."

Strange girl, strange girl. The thought ran through his mind as, slowly this time, he went down the bare stairs, while Tilly, getting into bed once more, thought, He didn't mean nothing; he's a nice man, a very nice man. He put her in mind of her granda, though he wasn't so old.

4

The day the boys went to boarding school was a day of tears, lamentations, recrimination, and the revelation to Tilly of how a house is run below stairs.

At ten o'clock in the morning she had taken all the children to their mother's room. They were all crying, Jessie Ann most of all, and when their mother joined in Tilly could hardly stop her own tears from flowing. What had touched her more than anything was the young bully's attitude toward herself not an hour ago; while she was helping him into his new clothes he had drooped his head and pressed it against her waist as he muttered, "I don't want to go, Trotter; I'd . . . I'd behave if I could stay."

For the first time in their acquaintance she put her arms about him and said, "It won't be for ever, Master Matthew. There's the holidays and they're long. You'll be home for Christmas an' just think of the parties you'll have."

He had raised his head, and looking up into her face, she had seen the frightened boy behind the bully as he said, "It . . . it will all be so different, I won't know what to do; and they'll be big boys."

"You'll hold your own, Master Matthew. Never fear, you'll hold your own. And you're not going to the end of the world, just outside Newcastle. And when you come back at Christmas we'll have some carry-on, like we did last week. You said you didn't enjoy it but I know you did when we played 'Pat-a-cake, Pat-a-cake' and 'Here we go round the mulberry bush,' and"—she

193

had bent her knees until her face was level with his—"I'll let you put another frog in me bed, and I promise you I won't stick it down your nightshirt." But his answer to this had been like one from an adult, for all he had said was, "Oh! Trotter."

Now she was marshaling them out of the room and Mabel Price was saying, "There now. There now. No more tears, not from big boys, no more tears." And the master was bending over the mistress soothing her. But that she wasn't soothed was evident when her voice, raised unusually high, reached the landing, saying, "I shall never forgive you, Mark, never!"

Then she was standing with most of the staff on the steps watching Fred Leyburn driving the master and the boys away.

It was an event, and for many of the staff a happy event, that that little rip was leaving them, at least for a time; and Tilly should have been the happiest among them, but strangely she wasn't. In a way, in a very odd way, she would miss him, much more than she would Luke.

"Come along about your business, all of you!" Mrs. Lucas was floating up the steps now and her voice scattered the rest.

On her way upstairs Tilly was joined by Mr. Burgess who had just arrived. "Well," he said, "I've missed the departure, I saw the coach going out of the gate. Best thing that could happen to those two, by far the best thing."

"But you taught them well, Mr. Burgess."

"Learning isn't enough, Trotter, if it isn't associated with your fellow men and women." He inclined his head toward her and smiled. "Learning is only of any use when it helps people to live with one another, put up with one another, and in this narrow establishment what I could have taught that boy would have helped him not at all."

She was amazed to think that he thought this house a

narrow establishment and yet in a faint way she knew what he meant.

He said now in an undertone, "Have you read the book that I gave you?"

"Yes. But . . . but I don't understand it."

"You will as you read it again and again."

"One thing seems to turn against the other and it hasn't a story."

"Well, I wouldn't say that now; Voltaire is telling you of life. When I gave you the book I thought perhaps I was starting you at the top of literature instead of at the bottom, but from now on when you read lower down in the scale you will understand more for having read the top bars first, if you follow me."

No, she didn't. Anyway, not quite. But she liked listening to him and she had learned a lot from him. He had given her two books, not just loaned them to her, given them to her, but the only time she had a chance to read was by the candle at night, and then she soon ran out of light because she was allowed only two candles a week. But lately she had conceived the idea of saving the droppings and molding them and putting a string through them. She daren't look at her books during the day in case Miss Price came on them, but what she did do, and what she could do without being questioned, was look at the children's work and now and again listen to Mr. Burgess teaching them. . . .

The mistress was in great distress all day, she knew this by the activity below. She had left her day couch and returned to bed, and by eight o'clock that night the master hadn't come home. Then at supper there was revealed to her another side of the master's character, which startled and depressed her. It was when Amy Stiles said, "Doesn't take you all day to go to Newcastle and back; you'd have thought he'd have come right home knowin' the state the mistress was in."

"Which mistress?" There had been a snigger at this and Frank Summers, the head gardener, repeated,

"Aye, you've said it, which mistress. She's a whore that one; her rightful place is on the Shields waterfront."

"An' she's all airs and graces." Again Amy Stiles was talking. "How she dare come in this house and visit the mistress God above knows. She's brass-faced, that's what she is, brass-faced. They say she treats them all up at Dean House like dirt 'neath her feet. And another thing that say"—she looked round the table now—"the old fellow knows what's going on."

"How do you know that?" Phyllis Coates looked at Amy for a second.

"How do I know that? Well, because our Willy knows the still-room maid, Peggy Frost. She thinks the old boy's dotty, but wily dotty, you know. At the table he calls her, me darling, me dearest, and she's always kissing him on the head, and she's always saying funny things to make him laugh. And he laughs, a great belly laugh."

"By! By! you are well informed." Phyllis Coates was nodding her head.

"Don't be funny, but I know this. 'Tis said she's got more than one on the string an' the master might be playing second fiddle."

"'Tis said! 'Tis said!" Phyllis Coates tossed her head. "The things you hear, Amy. You know"—she now looked around the table, thumbing toward her companion—"she should be writing a book, she's got the 'magination."

There was laughter at this, but it died away when the cook said, "Well! enough. Let them up there attend to their business and we down here'll attend to ours. 'Tis Saturday and the end of the month, let's get down to it." Then as if she had said something she regretted she glanced sharply at Tilly and now added, "You finished?"

"Yes, Mrs. Brackett."

"Well, you can go."

"Why should she?"

They all looked at Phyllis Coates. "She's been here on two months, she's one of us, she should have her share accordin' to her place."

There was a long silence following this remark, then the cook muttered, "It'll be coppers only then."

"Well, coppers are not to be sneezed at." Now Phyllis Coates turned and smiled at Tilly, and as Tilly rose to leave the table she said, "Sit down."

What followed next didn't seem real to Tilly. The cook brought to the table a box holding silver and copper and, tipping it on to the board, she spread it out with her hands; then taking from the ample pocket of her white apron a notebook, she wet her finger on her tongue and licked over its pages before she began to read: "Grocer an' meat exchange brought total twenty-five shillings; fishmonger and poultry exchange, eighteen shillings and ninepence; miller, two pounds seven and fourpence." She lifted her head and looked about her. "That was with putting a penny on the stone, an' things, instead of three farthings like last month; I don't see why Mrs. Lucas should have the plums."

"I'm with you." Robert Simes nodded toward her. "Her and Mr. Pike come off very nicely at their own end, thank you very much. Oh, I know what I know. Only nine bottles to the dozen!" He tapped the side of his nose with his finger, and to this the cook said, "You needn't tell me, I'm not blind or daft, I wasn't born yesterday"; he then went on: "Now the eggs an' vegetables an' fruit that went to the market, that was good this month with the currants an' things, eight pounds two and sixpence." There were nods of approval all round the table. Wetting her pencil between her lips, the cook began to add up the sum and after a long pause she said, "Twelve pounds, thirteen and sevenpence I make it."

"Is that all?"

The cook looked at Robert Simes and she nodded, saying emphatically, "That's all!"

"Lord! old Pike used to make nearly as much as that on the wine bill at one time."

"Aye, at one time we all did well, but this house is not as it was at one time, and we all know that an' all, don't we?" The cook's double chins were flapping against the starched collar of her print dress and there were murmurs of, "Aye. Aye."

"Well now, to share it out." The cook now put her hand among the silver and coppers and, separating the coins, she said again, "Well now, three five to you, Robert." She pushed three pounds five toward the footman. "The same for meself." She extracted another three pounds five. "Two pounds for you, Phyllis, and two pounds for Fred. You can take his." She pushed four sovereigns down the table. "One for you, Amy." She handed a sovereign to the second housemaid. "Fourteen shillings for you, Maggie, although you haven't deserved it, you haven't worked for it." The girl giggled as she picked up the four half-crowns and four single shillings from the table. "Now that leaves. . . . What does it leave?"

Everybody at the table knew that the cook was aware of what it left, she had had it all worked out before she had tipped up the box, and now she said, "Nine and sevenpence, so what are we going to do with that?"

"Well, 'tis mine." Ada Tennant was bobbing her head.

"We said Trotter was in on this, didn't we?" Phyllis Coates was staring across the table at the cook now and the cook muttered, "Well it better be halved then."

"'Tisn't fair and you know it, Cook. By rights Trotter's above me and Amy here."

"That'll be the day." The cook now cast an almost vehement glance at Tilly, and as Tilly was about to say, "I don't want anything," the cook said, "Half or nothing."

When the four and ninepence ha'penny was pushed down the table toward her, Tilly hesitated in picking it

198

up, until she glanced at Phyllis Coates and Phyllis's eyebrows sent out a message by moving rapidly up and down.

When Tilly lifted up the coins she felt for a moment that they were burning her fingers, it was like stolen money. And in a way it was stolen because they were doing the master and thinking nothing of it; even Phyllis seemed to accept it as her right.

A few minutes later, after she had left the table, Phyllis caught up with her at the bottom of the attic stairs and, her voice a husky whisper, she said, "Don't you worry, you'll have your full share next month. Fred'll see to it."

"I don't want it. I mean . . . well—" She looked down on Phyllis from the first step of the stairs and although she knew it might turn her friend against her she couldn't resist saying, "It somehow feels like stealin'."

Phyllis was in no way insulted by this remark, it only proved to her how naive this lass was in the ways of a household such as this, and so she punched Tilly gently in the arm as she said, "Don't be daft. How do you think we get things together who are soon to be married? or them who've got their old age to face? 'cos take it from me, the gentry do nowt for you. Twelve pounds a year I get and they think they're giving me gold dust. And Fred gets twenty-five and his uniform. We won't be able to set up a very big establishment on that. No"—she now patted Tilly's arm—"take all you can get, lass, and ask for more. It's the only way to survive in this life. And don't let it worry you, the thought of stealin'. My God! no, 'cos they'd have the last drop of blood out of you, the gentry. An' the master's no better than the rest, although he does a good turn here and there when it pleases him; like letting people stay in a cottage. But if he's put out, you're out. As for the mistress, well she got rid of the whole laundry staff, four of them, 'cos her lawn petticoats got put in with the coloreds. That's why we only have two dailies. You mark my words, girl. Now go on and don't look so depressed. Why, it should be the happiest night of your life; you've got rid of that little bugger, haven't you? an' that's all he was, a little bugger."

Tilly lowered her head, biting on her lip to stop herself from laughing. Yes, she supposed that all Phyllis had said was true, especially about the little bugger. It sounded so funny though, coming from her, for she had never heard her swear before. She leaned toward her and said softly, "I'm glad you're my friend, Phyllis," and Phyllis, pleased and embarrassed, gave her such a push that she almost fell on to the stairs as she said, "Get away with you! Go on an' get to bed." And on this she turned and ran down the passage back to the kitchen, and Tilly went upstairs four and ninepence ha'penny richer.

It was her third Sunday off. The summer was at its height, the sky was high, and the sun was hot, so hot that it penetrated the crown of her straw hat and lay warm on her head. She was glad of the thin dress she was wearing; it was a cotton one that Phyllis had given her. She'd had to let the hem down and again take in the waist. Her waist and hips were so narrow that she had to put tucks in everything she wore.

She was making her way, as usual, toward the cottage, for the simple reason she had nowhere else to go. If she'd had even a half-day on a Saturday she could have gone into Shields and seen the market, but she couldn't gather up the courage to ask either Mrs. Lucas or Miss Price to change her day. But she was content. Life was running smoothly, she had been in service for three months, and the two remaining children she was finding were manageable; she was learning things from Mr. Burgess; she had Phyllis and Fred for friends and also Katie Drew. Yes, she could class Katie Drew as a friend for on the two previous Sundays she had visited the ruined cottage she had met Katie and her brother, Sam, somewhere along the road. In fact, she now looked forward to meeting them, she expected to meet them.

On her first Sunday off she had almost shunned going to the cottage in case she should run into Hal McGrath, but when she had met up with Sam and Katie Drew she felt safe; and on her following Sunday off they had been there again, and here they were now coming toward her. She had the desire to run and meet them, and when Katie left her brother and ran, she, too, ran, then they both stopped simultaneously and said, "Hello."

"How you getting on, Tilly?"

"Fine, Katie. Are you all right?"

"Aye. . . . Isn't it a lovely day?"

"Yes, beautiful. I'm sweatin'."

"You're not the only one. Sam here"—she nodded to Sam who had now joined them—"he's just said he'll need a scraper to get his trousers off."

Tilly looked at Sam and Sam looked at her. He had on his Sunday suit and a clean neckerchief. His face, she knew, had been scrubbed yet there remained on it the marks of the pit, especially around his eyes. His lashes seemed to be stained with coal dust and there were blue indentations on his brow, the insignia of a pitman.

"Hello there," he said.

"Hello, Sam . . . isn't it hot?"

"Can't be hot enough for me."

"You said your clothes were stickin' to you." His sister pushed him and he pretended to fall over, and when he straightened up, he said, "Aye, they are, but I like them that way. I'll think about this all day the morrow."

"Me an' all," Katie said, nodded her head, and Tilly was amazed when she thought of the morrow and the depth of the pit that this fifteen-year-old girl, who looked twenty if a day, could still smile. Yet because both of them spent most of their lives in the bowels of the earth they seemed to savor the daylight more than she did. Their enjoyment of the sun oozed from them. They walked with their faces held up toward the sky. Funny that, she thought, for she was in the habit of walking with her head down looking toward the earth.

"We've been round the cottage; someone's been sleeping in the byre."

"Well, they would find good shelter."

"Aye, there's that in it." Sam was nodding at her. "It must be hellish being on the road, not having a roof over your head. An' there's many like that the day, God help them. But it won't go on, not for ever." He looked at Tilly and, nodding slowly, he repeated, "No, it won't go on for ever. We're comin' alive to the fact that we're human beings, not animals, an'·we've got the rights of human beings. Things are movin'. The masters will have to look out for themselves afore long, you'll see. They won't always have the upper hand, it'll be wor turn some day. I mightn't live to see it, but wor turn 'll come, an' then God help 'em."

"They're not all alike, Sopwith's not bad."

"There isn't a pin to choose atween them." He leaned in front of Tilly and glared at his sister. But she laughed at him, saying, "Aw, don't get on your high horse, man, it's Sunda'. And anyway, just think where would we be the day if Sopwith hadn't taken you on and given us the cottage."

"He wouldn't have taken us on if he didn't need men, he didn't do it out of any charity. None of his kind do owt for charity; they make you pay interest in sweat, all of 'em. An' the cottage, what is it after all, two rooms."

"Aw now, our Sam"—Katie stepped in front of him now—"fair's fair. What did we have in the other place? Mud floors. There's a solid stone one in this. And the pittle isn't oozing up a through it from the middens. Now be fair."

"Listen to her!" He was laughing now as he looked at Tilly. "You haven't got to ask whose side she's on. She does as much work for him as a man, an' he pays her half as much, an' she still stands up for him. Aw . . . women!"

"Aye, women!" Katie was nodding at him, laughing with him now. "Where would you be without us? I know where you'd be, you'd still be an urge in me dad's belly."

"Well, here we are back again." They looked at Tilly and she stepped over the broken gate and led the way up the path, and as always she wanted to turn her eyes away from the burned out shell of her home. The saddening effect it had on her didn't seem to lessen, and when she rounded the side wall and came into the yard she stood still, looking toward the byre; then shaking her head, she turned abruptly about and walked back to the gate.

The brother and sister looked at each other, then followed her in silence.

On the bridle path Katie said, "What time have you got to be in the day?" and Tilly answered, "I've got another half-hour 'cos it's still light, half past six the day."

"Well, 'tis only on three. I tell you what. Would you like to come back to our house an' have a sup tea?"

Tilly smiled down on Katie into the round homely face that would never know prettiness but which had such a quality of kindness in the eyes that to her in this moment it almost appeared beautiful, and she said, "Oh yes, thank you very much, I'd like that. Aye, yes, I would."

"Well, what we waitin' for?" It was Sam who now turned from them and strode ahead; and as they followed him they both began to laugh, not knowing why, except perhaps they realized that for a few hours they were free; perhaps because it was a beautiful, warm sunny day; but most of all perhaps they realized they were young and that for a fleeting moment they were experiencing a spurt of joy, which is the natural gift of youth.

It was a two mile walk to the Drews' cottage. It lay to the north of the estate, and was reached by an angled bend that led off the coach road. The cottages were situated on the very boundary of the Sopwith estate and within half a mile of the pit. There were sixteen cottages in the two rows. The Drews' home was in the end cottage of the second row and when Tilly entered it on this hot steamy Sunday afternoon, it appeared to her like a small cramped box after the spaciousness of the Manor. Not only was it small and cramped, but it had a mixed odor which she likened to the smell that emanated from soot and soap-suds, the last soap-suds in the poss tub at the end of the day's wash, an arid, body sweating odor. The small room seemed crammed with people and she stood just within the open door as Katie introduced her, speaking first to a big woman whose bony frame seemed devoid of flesh. "Ma, this is Tilly, the lass I told you about."

The woman stopped cutting slices of bread from a big loaf on the end of a table which was surprisingly covered with a white tablecloth, and she paused for a moment and smiled at Tilly as she said, "Well, come in, lass, come in. That's if you can get in. But, as they say, never grumble about being crowded until you can't shut your door. You're welcome. Sit down. Get your backside off that cracket, our Arthur, and let the lass take the weight off her legs."

When Arthur, a grinning boy of twelve, sidled off the low stool, then stood with his back against the white-washed wall near the small open fireplace, Tilly wanted to protest that she didn't mind standing, but feeling very awkward all of a sudden she sat down on the low cracket and looked shyly around the sea of eyes surveying her. Some were looking at her from under their brows, others straight at her. She was wondering why they were all crammed into this room on this rare and lovely day when she was given the answer; it was as if she had asked for it.

Continuing cutting the bread, Mrs. Drew said, "Sunday, we're all together for Sunday tea. Rain, hail, sun or snow, 'tis one time in the week I have me troubles all around me at one go."

"Aw, Ma. Ma!" The same protest came from different quarters of the room.

"Do you like workin' up at the big house?"

"Yes; yes, thank you." Tilly nodded to Mrs. Drew, and the big woman, scooping up the slices of bread in handfuls on to a large colored flat dish, said, "Well, it's one thing, you get trained to be quick in big houses, not like this lot here." She pointed to a tall young woman and a smaller one who were taking down crockery from the hooks on an old black-wood Welsh dresser, the back of which Tilly noticed in some surprise was forming a kind of high headboard to a double iron bed along the edge of which were sitting two young boys and a youth.

"Oh, Ma. Ma!" It was the same laughing protest.

"Are those griddle cakes finished?" Mrs. Drew now looked toward a plump child who was kneeling before the fire turning pats of round pastry which were resting on an iron shelf, which in turn was resting on top of a flattened mound of hot ash.

Before the child could answer, Sam Drew, bending over his sister, said, "She's been scoffin' 'em, Ma."

The small girl, her face red from the heat of the fire, sat back on her hunkers, crying, "Oh, our Sam! our Sam! I've never touched one," slapping out at her brother as she said so. And he slapped playfully back at her; then looking at Tilly, he said, "This lot must look like a menagerie to you."

She smiled but could find no reply to this. He was right, they did look like a menagerie.

"Well, if you've got a good memory I'll start at the top and work downward. That one over there"—Sam pointed to a short, thick man sitting at the edge of the table—"that's me big brother, our Henry, twenty-four he is, an' married, lock an' chain you know."

Ignoring his brother's clenched fist, he went on, "Then there's me next." He thumbed his chest. "Then comes our Peg, that one who's slow with the crockery." He pointed to the taller of the two girls moving between the table and the delf rack. "And then Bill. He's seventeen, him sittin' on the bed, the daft-looking one."

"I'll daft you, our Sam, if you don't look out."

"I'm lookin' out, so get on with it." Sam grinned at his younger brother, then said, "And his two daft companions, there's Arthur there on the left, he's twelve, and Georgie, he's the one that looks like a donkey about to bray, he's ten."

"Oh, our Sam!" This came from different parts of the room now.

"Then there's our Katie, who's not right in the top story. . . ."

"Oh, you wait, our Sam!"

"And the best of the bunch is Jimmy there. He's a natural scarecrow, aren't you, Jimmy? A penny a day he can earn standin' in the fields."

"Oh, our Sam! Our Sam!"

"And then there's my Fanny." He bent and rubbed his fingers in the thick brown hair of the kneeling child, saying, "She's seven, aren't you, Fanny? An' she's going' down the pit next year, aren't you, Fanny?"

"Now you shut your mouth, our Sam!" It was his mother turning on him now, no laughter in her face.

"Don't joke about her goin' down the pit. She's not seein' top nor bottom of the pit except over my dead body."

"I was only funnin', Ma."

"Well, don't fun about that; the pit's got the rest of yous, but they're not gettin' her. Nor Jimmy there. There's two of you I aim to give daylight to."

"Aye, Ma; aye, you're right"—Sam's voice was very subdued now—"'tis nowt to joke about."

Mrs. Drew had stopped pouring out mugs of tea and she now looked at Tilly; but for some seconds she did not speak. When she did her voice, although low, held a deep note of bitterness as she said, "The pit took four of mine in seven years, me man included, so you can see me reason for stickin' out for two of them, can't you?"

"Yes; yes, Mrs. Drew."

"Well now, that said, let's eat."

It was, Tilly imagined, as if the tall gaunt woman had suddenly turned a knob somewhere inside her being and switched off the bitter memories, for now her voice was jovial again as she cried at her daughter, "Peg, bring the china cup, we've got company."

When Peg brought the fragile china cup and saucer to the table and handed it to her mother, Mrs. Drew took the saucer between her finger and thumb and gently placed it on the table; then looking at Tilly, she asked, "You like your tea with milk, lass?"

"Oh yes, please."

"An' you can have sugar an' all if you like." This was from the upturned face of Fanny. They all laughed and there was a chorus: "And you can have sugar if you like" in imitation of the small girl, and she, swinging her head from side to side, exclaimed, "Aw yous! you're always scoffin', yous!"

"And now we're all here we'll start. I said, we're all here"—Mrs. Drew now looked again at Tilly as she

207

placed the china cup and saucer before her—"Except there's my Alec. He's on a double shift—it's the water down there—he'll be dead beat when he does come up. Shouldn't be allowed, twenty-four hours under at one time! and he only a bit of a lad."

"He's eighteen, he's older than me an' I've done a double shift."

"Oh listen!" Sam held up his hand. "Hero Bill's done a double shift." He leaned toward his younger brother now, saying, "Aye, but it wasn't in water standin' up to your neck." Then, his tone altering, he said, "Somethin's got to be done. By God! somethin's got to be done."

"Now! now!" It was his mother's voice again. "'Tis Sunday, we've got company, no more pit talk."

Since only nine could be seated at the table, two of the younger boys, Arthur and Georgie, remained seated on the bed, and when their mother ordered them to come to the table to get their shives, thick slices of bread with a piece of cheese in the middle, she looked from one to the other as they approached and said, "You don't deserve nowt either of you; 'tis a wonder you're not in jail."

"Why, what have they been up to?" Henry, the married son, said, turning his head toward them. "What's this? What you been up to, you two now?"

When they didn't answer he looked at his mother and she, evidently trying to suppress a smile, made her voice sound harsher than ever as she said, "What have they been up to? Just tried to burn the Mytons' place down, that's all."

"What!"

There were splutters from different members at the table. Some of them choked, so much so that Katie had to be thumped on the back before their mother went on, "They were scrumpin' apples an' one of the gardeners caught them, an' being kind to them instead of taking them up to the house an' then callin' the polis, he thumped them well and roundly, bumped their heads together, kicked their backsides and set them flyin'. And what do you think they did last night as ever was?"

"Well, what did they do, I'm waitin'?" Henry asked.

Again the table was convulsed with laughter, and it was Sam who now said, "They stuffed straw up half a dozen drainpipes, you know the old trick, an' set fire to them."

"No!"

"Aye."

"At the Myton place? Oh my God! I wish I'd been there. Eeh! you young buggers!" He turned and looked toward the bed where the two boys were sitting with their heads hanging but with their shoulders shaking with laughter.

"And not content with that"—the mother nodded at her eldest son—"they went back into the orchard and helped themselves to apples, not windfalls this time but from the trees. My God! when they told me that I was sick. To try a second time! God! they're lucky they weren't caught. Anyway"—she grinned now—"three good stones of them they brought in. As they said, they could have brought a cartload 'cos everybody was too busy pullin' the burning straw out of the drainpipes."

"They'll end up in Australia those two." It was Sam now nodding toward them.

"They'll never live to reach Australia."

As Tilly watched Mrs. Drew's head move slowly back and forward there was rising in her a swirl of merriment such as she had never felt in her life before, and when Mrs. Drew ended, "Swing they will, the both of them, from the crossroads an' we'll all have a field day," the laughter burst from her throat. It surprised not only herself but all those at the table, because they had never heard anyone laugh like it. It was a high wavering sound that swelled and swelled until, holding her waist, she turned from the table and rocked herself. She laughed until she cried; she couldn't stop laughing, not even when Katie, herself doubled up with laughter, put her arm about her and begged, "Give over. Give over." Nor when Sam lifted her chin and, his own mouth wide, cried, "That's good. That's good." And he kept repeating this until he realized her face was crumpling and that the water running down it was no longer caused by merriment; and so, straightening up, he looked around the table and raised his hand, saying, "Enough is enough."

The noise in the room gradually subsided, and Tilly turned to the table again and, her head bowed, murmured, "I'm sorry."

"Sorry, lass? You've got nowt to be sorry for. We've never had such release in this room for many a long day. It's good to laugh, it's the salve for sores. Aye, it's the salve for sores. Drink your tea, lass."

Gratefully now Tilly drank her tea. Then she looked at the sea of faces about her, warm, caring faces, and she thought she had never felt such closeness as there was in this family. Most of them spent their lives underground, even the girls; but there was a happiness here that she envied, a happiness here that she longed to share. She looked across the now silent table at Mrs. Drew as she said, "It's lovely tea, lovely."

5

It was Guy Fawkes Day, and afterward Mark Sopwith always looked back on this particular day as the time when the catastrophe began.

It started badly. Eileen Sopwith was still weepy over a letter she'd had from Matthew saying he hated the school and wanted to come home; added to this, she was irritated by the fact that her husband's son, Harry, the only issue of his first marriage and now in his second year at Cambridge studying law, had decided—without asking her permission—to join them for the long Christmas vacation. She had never liked Harry, although since her marriage to his father she had seen him only during the school holidays. But even as a boy his manner had annoyed her. He had an air of aloofness that was disconcerting and when she looked at him she saw his mother in him and so was reminded that she wasn't the first woman in her husband's life.

That she was of an intensely jealous disposition Mark had found out after Matthew was born, for she begrudged his affection for the child feeling that it detracted from his love for her. Even after John was born and she had decided to become an invalid, her jealousy hadn't lessened. Her possessiveness for the children, he understood well enough, was designed to alienate their affection away from himself so that he would be more likely to turn to her, not to receive love but to give it in the form of petting and fussing.

She liked to feel his fingers going through her hair, she liked to feel him fondling her hands, even stroking the pale skin of her arms inside the elbows; but never did she allow his hands near her breasts, she was an invalid now and mustn't be distressed in that way. Had she not borne him four children? Was he not satisfied? He was forty-three years old and she thirty-eight. Good moral people should be past that kind of thing. It went with the begetting of children and Mark knew only too well she had begot all she intended to beget.

But as yet on this day it wasn't she who was the main issue.

He always breakfasted alone. The breakfast-room, he considered the cosiest room in the house. It was in this room he had tasted his first meal downstairs, but that hadn't been until he was twelve years old and had been attending boarding school for four years.

He breakfasted light, never more than one egg, one slice of bacon, and a kidney. He had never been able to stand fish for breakfast. He was sitting back in his chair wiping his mouth on a napkin but his mind was three miles away . . . no five, away in the mine where the weak spot was. He must get Rice along there this morning and look at that stretch himself. The pump was having a job to clear it of water. One of the women had nearly drowned there last week; and he didn't want that again, it gave the pit a bad name. They hadn't had an accident now for three years, and even then it had really been nothing, only two dead; not like the Jarrow lot, a hundred odd at one go. Twenty-two colliers had died at Rosier's pit last year. He wished to God he didn't need the mine, the worry of it was beginning to tell on him; his gray hairs were thickening at the temples and his face was becoming lined. Agnes had tactlessly pointed this out to him the other day.

Agnes. There was another worry; he hadn't seen her now for three weeks. They had parted with hot words. He really didn't care if he never saw her for another three weeks, or three months, or ever, but he doubted if she'd let him go that easy. She was like a leech, that girl . . . that woman, for she was no girl, she was a hungry, devouring, body-consuming woman. He had met a few women in his time, intimately so, but never one like her. The saying that you could have too much of a good thing applied to everything. There might have been a time when he would have doubted this, but not any more.

He rumpled his table napkin, threw it on the table, and as he rose to his feet the door opened and Simes said, "There's a gentleman to see you, sir."

"A gentleman! at this hour. Who is it?"

"Mr. Rosier, sir."

Mark did not repeat the name Rosier, but his brows drew darkly together and he paused for a long moment before he said, "Where've you put him?"

"In the library, sir."

"I'll be there in a minute."

"Very good, sir."

When the man had closed the door, Mark stood rubbing the cleft below his lower lip with his first two fingers. Rosier at this time in the morning! now what would he be after? Well, there were only two things that interested Rosier, his mine and his money. Which could have brought him here? He had understood he was still abroad taking his tall, stately, socially ambitious wife on a tour of America. He moved his head slightly back and forward before straightening his cravat and smoothing down the pockets of his long jacket; then he left the room, crossed the hall and entered the library.

George Daniel Rosier had been gazing at the portrait hanging over the empty fireplace and he turned abruptly when the door opened. He was a small man, his complexion was swarthy, his hair was thin with just a touch of gray here and there. His nose was long and protruding, it was the largest feature of his face. He looked a common man; three generations gone, his people had been mill workers. The stigma was still on him, and he fought it by bluster. How he had come to be chosen by a daughter of the landed gentry was a puzzle to everyone. Well, perhaps not everyone, certainly not to Agnes Rosier for she was already past the choosing age when he married her, and she was tired of refined poverty. Within a year of the marriage she had borne him a son who was now four years old. She had also almost trebled the servants in his household and nearly driven him mad, not with the fact that she wanted to entertain those in high places, but with the cost to his pocket for such entertainments.

His mine was a good one as mines went, but being the taskmaster that he was, he drove his overseers and they in turn drove the men and women under them, with the result that his mine became noted for unrest among the workers. Time and again he had threatened to bring the Irish in but had been sensible enough, as yet, to withhold his hand in that direction. But with this latest business of education rampant among the scum, he could see himself bringing a ship-load over. Yet he wanted to avoid the trouble and expense this would cost him, and that was why he was here this morning.

"Good-morning." It was Mark speaking, and to this Rosier replied briefly, "Morning."

"What is the trouble, something happened at your place?"

"No, there's nothing happened at my place, not as yet; and there's nothing happened at your place as yet; but you go on enticing my colliers away and something will happen."

"What are you talking about?" Mark's voice was stiff.

"Now! now!" Rosier turned his head to the side and looked toward the window; then jerking his chin back he glared at Mark as he said, "Three fellows you took on recently, the three my overseer dismissed."

"What about it? I took them on because I needed

214

men. Your overseer broke their bond, not them. Apparently he didn't want them on the job."

"You know as well as I do why they were dismissed. Look, Sopwith, as man to man—" Rosier's nose twitched, his lips pursed and he brought his shoulders almost up to his chin as he said, "You let these fellows get reading and writing and you know as well as I do that'll be the beginning of the end."

"I don't agree with you."

"Aw, don't be so damned naive, man."

"I'm not damned naive, and I'll thank you not to infer that I am. You've got a rule that your men don't learn to read or write, well, I have no such rule in my pit and if I need men I'll take them if they come asking for work whether they can read or write or not."

"You will, will you?"

"Yes, I will!"

"Well"—Rosier gave a broken laugh now—"by what I hear, things are not going too brightly for you. You had water below before I went away but now I understand they are up to their necks in it. You had to close one road, how many have you left open?"

"As many as you have."

"Never! never!" Now the laugh was derisive. "You only need your pump to stop and you'll have your men and horses floating out through the drift."

Mark stared at the small man. He was raging inside but endeavored not to show it; and so, keeping his voice as level as possible, he said, "Why precisely did you come here this morning?"

"I told you, just to warn you that you're a bloody fool if you let them get away with this reading and writing business. But there is one thing more. . . . Well, seeing that you're up against it and are hard pressed for money. . . . Oh! Oh! Oh!" He jerked his head with each word. "Rumors travel even as far as America. Anyway, I came with a friendly gesture and I give it to you now, if you need money I'll be willing to advance it."

"You will?"

"Yes; I said I will and I will."

"May I ask what guarantee you'd like?"

"Oh well, that could be gone into."

"No, no, no; let's get down to business straightaway. I presume you would like a share in the mine. Is that not so, say a half share?"

Rosier's eyebrows moved up, his nose stretched downward, his lips pursed again, his shoulders once more tried to cover his jawbone and with a nonchalant air he muttered, "Why yes, something along those lines."

Mark stared at the man for a moment; then turning slowly about, he went to the door and, opening it, said, "Good-morning, Rosier. When I need your help I'll call upon you, and at a respectable hour."

"Huh! Huh! Well, take it like that if you will but I'll tell you something." He was now facing Mark in the doorway. "I bet you a shilling it won't be very long before you're swallowing your words. You'll see." He bounced his head toward Mark and again he said, "You'll see."

As Rosier stamped across the hall, Robert Simes was standing waiting at the door.

Mark stood where he was until the door had closed on his visitor, and he remained there until he heard the sound of the carriage going down the gravel drive; then he turned and went back into the room and over toward the fireplace where he took his fist and beat it hard against the edge of the marble mantelpiece, saying as he did so, "Damn and blast him to hell!"

He had never liked Rosier; his father had never liked the elder Rosier, in fact his father had never recognized the man, looking upon him as an upstart. But everything George Rosier had said was right. He was up against it, he needed money badly, and if his pumps went his mine would go too.

The thought spun him around and seemingly as if his mere presence at the time would be enough to hold back the water and so avert final disaster, he hurried out of the room, calling to Simes to tell Leyburn to bring round his horse immediately, and without paying his usual morning visit to his wife, he went to a cupboard at the end of the hall, donned his cloak and hat and hurried out.

Jane Forefoot-Meadows was a lady in her own right when she married John Forefoot-Meadows. He, too, had been born and bred in the upper class, so when their only daughter Eileen said she wished to marry Mr. Mark Sopwith, if they didn't actually scowl on the affair, their frowns were evident. True, he came of an old well-known family, but he was a widower with a young son; that he was a mine owner didn't carry much weight with them, for from what they gathered it was a drift mine employing not more than fifty men and thirty women and children at the most. There were mine owners and mine owners. Moreover, Mr. Mark Sopwith lived north of Durham and that was such a long, long way off, it would mean that they would hardly ever see their dear daughter during the winter, the roads being what they were and themselves no longer young.

Jane Forefoot-Meadows was a possessive mother; it was doubtful if she would have welcomed any man for her daughter's husband, but from the beginning she had disliked Mark Sopwith and never bothered to hide her feelings from him. Whenever they met she managed to convey to him how she pitied her daughter's existence in Highfield Manor, in a house that wasn't properly staffed, and the children being brought up without capable nursemaids or tutors. But unlike her daughter, she hadn't been aghast at Mark sending his sons to boarding school; at least, so she surmised, there they would have proper grounding. Truthfully she knew she wasn't fond of any of her grandchildren, she only suffered them because her daughter had given them birth.

After John was born and her daughter took to the sofa, she'd had a talk with Doctor Fellows, in fact it had been at her instigation that Doctor Kemp had called in Doctor Fellows. It was from Doctor Fellows's guarded replies to her questions that she guessed there was nothing seriously wrong with her daughter, that she was merely using the weapon of many such women in her position. Her decline was a fence against her husband's sensual appetite, and she was with her in the erecting of such a barrier. She'd never had to erect such a barrier herself for her husband wasn't an emotional man, and she thanked God for it. In fact she often wondered how she had conceived a child at all. She would not put the term "impotent" to her husband, she just imagined him to be not inclined that way, and that suited her.

But her son-in-law was very much inclined that way if all rumors were true, and the rumor that had brought her flying to the Manor this particular day was no rumor. Oh no, it was no rumor. She had been so incensed by what she had heard that she had wanted to start out on the journey last night; only the fact that she was afraid of the dark had stopped her, but the coach had been ordered at first light this morning, and here she was now springing a surprise on the whole household, not least of all on her daughter, for when she marched into the room Eileen almost jumped from the sofa, crying, "Mama! Mama! what has brought you?"

"You may well ask. But don't excite yourself." She held up a hand. "Here Price, take my bonnet and cloak," she called, then turned her back toward the maid, and Mabel Price, as much astonished as her mistress, sprang forward, relieved the tall, dominant figure of her cloak and bonnet, then with a free hand

218

pulled a chair to the side of the sofa. Without even a word of thanks or a glance toward her, Mrs. Meadows took the seat; then stretching out her arms, she held her daughter, making a sort of soft moaning sound as she did so.

"Is there anything wrong with Papa?"

"No! no!" Jane Forefoot-Meadows straightened herself. "Not more than usual. His gout is worse of course, and he coughs louder each day, but he still goes on. No, no; nothing wrong with him."

"Then . . . then what has brought you? Are you ill?"

"Now do I look ill, my dear?" Jane Forefoot-Meadows raised her plucked eyebrows high and touched lightly each rouged cheek with her fingers.

"No, no, Mama, you look extremely well, and I am so glad to note this."

"Well, I wish I could say that you look extremely well too, my dear, for I'm afraid that the news I have to bring you"—she now turned her head and for the first time looked at Mabel Price and, her voice seeming to come out of the top of her nose, she said briefly, "Leave us."

Mabel Price hesitated only a moment before turning sulkily away and going out of the room.

"Now, my dear—" Jane Forefoot-Meadows tapped her daughter's hand which she was still holding between her own and asked softly, "How are you?"

"As usual, Mama. The slightest exertion tires me and I do miss the boys. Not that I saw much of them admittedly, but I knew they were there above me." She raised her eyes to the ceiling. "And at times I heard their laughter; it was so refreshing. Now very little sound comes from above, and Matthew hates the school. But Mark is obdurate." Her face tightened. "This is a point he will not budge on. I've begged him. Mama, I've begged him. . . ."

"Mark! Mark!" Jane Forefoot-Meadows tossed her head to the side now; then bending forward, she looked straight into her daughter's eyes as she asked, "Do you know a person by the name of Lady Agnes Myton?"

"Oh yes, Mama, she's a neighbor, she visits at times."

"She what?" Mrs. Forefoot-Meadows drew herself away from the sofa as if she were stung by this latest news, and she repeated on an even higher tone, *"She what?"*

"As I said, Mama, she's a neighbor, she visits. . . . Lord Myton took Dean House. You know Dean House, well he took it last year."

"Yes, I know Dean House and I have heard a little of Lord Myton. I've also heard a lot of his wife, and that she should dare to visit you . . . well! my dear."

Eileen Sopwith now pressed herself back into the satin pillows of the chaise-longue and, her face straight and her words coming from her almost closed lips, said, "What are you meaning to infer, Mama?"

"Well—" Mrs. Forefoot-Meadows now rose to her feet and, throwing one arm wide in a dramatic gesture, she said, "Do I have to explain further?"

"Yes, I'm afraid you do, Mama."

"Tut! Tut! The very fact that I'm here should be explanatory enough. You can't be aware, I presume, that she and Mark are having an affair. And this is no new thing; apparently it started when she was hardly settled in the house. She is his mistress and she makes no secret of it."

Eileen Sopwith was now holding her throat with her hands, and her face had gone a shade paler than its usual tint. She tried to speak but words wouldn't come, and so, looking at her mother who had again sat down, she listened to her saying in a low excited whisper, "You remember Betty Carville, Nancy Stillwell's daughter who married Sir James? Well, apparently she and Agnes Myton were at the same Ladies' Seminary and Agnes Myton was over there visiting last week and, being the trollop that she is, she regaled

Betty Carville with the story of her amours. And not satisfied with your husband, apparently she has her eyes set on someone else too, a workman of some sort. Can you believe it? a farm worker. I couldn't get the gist of all Nancy Stillwell had to tell me because I was so shocked at hearing about Mark. Nancy said that Betty said that Agnes Myton said she was having the time of her life; it was much more fun than London . . . and you know what happened in London." Mrs. Forefoot-Meadows again rose from her chair, adding as if in answer to a question, "Well . . . no, no; it is better that you don't know. Disgrace that was, utter disgrace. Myton's an imbecile else he wouldn't stand for it. Yet I understand, but I don't know how far it is true, that he went for one of her swains. Was going to run him through with a sword or shoot him or something. So when he finds out about this, if he doesn't already know—" She turned again and looked at her daughter; then, her voice dropping to a warm sympathetic tone, she rushed to the sofa and enfolding Eileen's stiff body in her arms, cried, "Oh my dear! my dear! Don't . . . don't upset yourself. . . . Now I've got it all worked out. You're coming back with me, you can't possibly stay here, and you're bringing the children. No! no! don't argue." She shook her head even though Eileen had neither moved nor spoken. "I know I'm not very fond of gamboling youngsters, but your happiness comes first. Oh my dear! my dear! that this should have come upon you. Didn't you know this was going on?" Releasing her hold, she stared at her daughter; but she, to her mother's surprise, pushed her firmly aside as she slowly swung her legs from the couch and sat on the edge of it. She then stood up and walked somewhat unsteadily toward the window and looked out.

Had she known this was going on? Hadn't she suspected something from the first? Perhaps; but her suspicions had been allayed because she had seen no change in him, no elation . . . no despondency. His manner had continued to be the same toward her, except when they quarreled over the children being sent away to school, then he had yelled at her. But to think that he and that woman . . . all these months! How long had she been resident in Dean House? Over a year. The whole countryside must be aware of it.

It was as if her mother had picked up her thought for her voice came stridently across the room, saying now, "It's the talk of the county, it has even closed doors to her. Haven't you had the slightest suspicion?"

It was now she turned on her mother and, speaking for the first time, she said, "No, Mama, I've had no suspicion. What do I know of what's going on in the world, tied to this room as I am? In fact I don't know what's going on in my own household."

"Well, that's your own fault, my dear."

They stared at each other now in silence until Eileen said with deep indignation, "Mama!"

"Oh my dear, don't look like that. And don't take on that haughty air; you and I know why you took to the couch. There are other ways you could have gained your liberty from his bed; gone visiting, or gone abroad for a time, or come to me. Yes"—her voice sank now—"yes, you could have come to me. How often have I asked you to? But no, you choose to be incarcerated, and that is the word, my dear, incarcerated in this padded tomb, and you have refused to be disturbed. You know you have. Yes, you know you have." She nodded her head vigorously. "But, my dear," she went on while walking toward her daughter with outstretched arms, "all I ever wanted in life, all I want now, is your happiness, your welfare. Come home with me. Gradually you will regain the strength you have lost while lying on that thing"—she thrust her hand disdainfully back toward the chaise-longue—"because, you know, a few more years and you wouldn't be able to use your legs at all. It happened to Sylvia Harrington. Oh yes, it did." Her head made a deep obeisance at this. "And Sarah de Court became unbalanced."

"Oh! Mama, Mama, be quiet!" Eileen stumbled past her mother and, grabbing at the side of the chaise-longue, she sat down on it with a slight plop, and when her mother, standing in front of her, demanded, "Well, what are you going to do?" she looked up at her and said pleadingly, "Oh, Mama, don't you realize this has come as a shock to me? Just . . . just give me a little time."

"All the time in the world, my dear." Mrs. Meadows bent over her, her voice and manner expressing her deep solicitude. "All the time in the world. All the time in the world." Then she added, "What time do you expect him back?"

"It . . . it could be this evening."

"I wouldn't wait till then."

Again they were staring at each other. "Is he at the mine?"

"Yes, I think so."

"Then I would send for him, my dear."

"Oh! Mama."

"Well, just ask yourself the question: Do you want to go on living in this house knowing that he is having his daily satisfaction with another woman, and also knowing, my dear, and this is what you've got to face, that you are tied here for the rest of your life, tied to this chaise-longue, which you will be as I warned you if you stay on it much longer? Now do you want that? Or do you want to come home, have your health restored, and live again? Scarborough is a wonderful place in the winter season. You know that, you used to enjoy it."

"I never did, Mama."

"Yes, you did in your early days. You only stopped enjoying it when you thought that you'd never be married; then you jumped at the first man that asked you."

"That isn't fair, Mama." Eileen's head was up. "He

223

wasn't the first man who asked me, there were others but you didn't approve."

"And rightly so; they weren't fit to be your husband."

"But you thought Mark was."

"No, we didn't, we had our misgivings, but you were so bent on it. Anyway, my dear, I must go now and refresh myself in the closet. Then I will have something to eat and we'll talk again. But if you take my advice you will send for him, and now."

Eileen watched her mother leave the room; then once again she was on her feet and walking toward the window. Here she stood gripping the curtains and looking down on to the gardens.

There was a deep bitterness inside her, but it was a bitterness born of hurt vanity rather than of lost love. She knew that she had never really loved Mark Sopwith. In the first place she had wanted him, or rather she had wanted to be a wife. But being a wife had turned out a disappointment to her. Marriage had been full of perplexities, painful perplexities that seemed to be of no concern to her husband. Never having been married before, nor been intimate with any other man, she had no one with whom to compare him, and so she couldn't say if he was a better or worse husband than the usual run of such. She only knew that, like her mother, she was possessive of what she owned, love didn't come into it. You didn't love a house or a horse, they were merely possessions, accessories to living. She reached out her hand and, lifting a silver bell from a table, she rang it, and within seconds Price had entered the room.

"Yes, Madam?" Her manner was subservient but her eyes and her whole expression were eager; she had heard bits and pieces of what had been said and she knew what was afoot, although as yet she didn't know what the outcome was going to be. The only thing she hoped was that her mistress wouldn't take any notice of

her mother and go off. Although she would likely take
her along with her, life in the Forefoot-Meadows'
household wouldn't be like it was here. She had been
there only once before and the hierarchy in the servants' hall was stiffer than what it had been above
stairs. In this household she could throw her weight
about, she had power, but what would her standing be
in Waterford Place? Something between the upper
housemaid and the footman. Oh Lord! she hoped it
wouldn't come to that.

"Tell Mr. Pike to get a message to the master at the
mine and ask him to return, he is needed here."

"Yes, yes, madam."

A few minutes later, having passed on the message to
him, Pike looked at her and said, "What's afoot? What
brought the old girl?" and her answer was, "You'll
know soon enough."

It was a full two hours later when Mark entered the
house. The message had been delivered to him when he
was well below ground and examining a road that was
almost three foot under water, and the conditions
underground were such that he couldn't leave without
trying to find a way out of a desperate situation, for if
the pumps couldn't keep the water below this level then
it would rise, and if it should branch into the main
roadway, well, that would be that.

The first intimation he had that his mother-in-law
was in the house was when he said to the butler, who
was at the door awaiting him, "What is it? What's
wrong?"

"Nothing that I know, sir, except that Mrs. Forefoot-
Meadows has arrived."

Mark screwed up his face as he peered at the old
man. They sent for him because his mother-in-law had
arrived? Had his father-in-law died? Was that what had
brought her? Of couse not, she wouldn't be here if that
were the case. She had only been gone a short while

from the house, and her departure had filled him with pleasure. And so what had brought her today? Something of import surely.

He ran up the stairs, across the gallery, along the corridor, and as he tapped on his wife's door so he thrust it open and was surprised to see her sitting in a chair by the window. It must be two years or more since she sat up like that; at least, since he had seen her in such a position.

The only other person in the room was Price and he turned his head and looked at her. Following his wordless command she left the room. He walked toward Eileen and stood looking down at her. Her face looked tight, her eyes hard. She had never had a nice-shaped mouth and now it looked a mere slit. He was the first to speak. "I understand your mama has arrived, is something wrong?"

He saw her swallow deeply before saying, "Well, it all depends on how one views the word 'wrong.' She came to bring me some news, but some people wouldn't consider her news bad, they would likely look upon it with some amusement, whereas others would be shocked by it. Myself, I'm not only shocked and astounded, I am hurt and humiliated."

Before she could say another word he realized what was coming, and his own features fell into a stiff mold and, unblinking, he looked at her and waited.

When she spoke, her words were precise and to the point, and her voice was not that of the invalid he had come to know holding a thread of soft whining, but was hard and brittle. "I understand that I am the last person in the county to know that you have a mistress," she said. "I'm not unaware that a number of men take mistresses but generally they do it discreetly, at least the gentlemen among them do. But not only is your affair with that Myton woman the talk of the county, *your slut*"—she almost spat the words out—"has made it a cause for amusement in Scarborough. What is more, she has even coupled you with workmen who also supply her needs."

His head was buzzing. He tried to speak but found he couldn't put into words the fact that he had been trying hard for months now to break the association, and that in any case it had been a hole in a corner affair at best. The description was accurate, too, because their love-making had mostly taken place in a hollow in a corner of the wood above Billings Flat. And so how could news of it have got around other than through that ravenous bitch spouting it out to her friends.

The words he now used surprised even himself as in a quiet, weary tone he said, "I'm not of such importance that Scarborough would bother to find much entertainment in my doings, be they right or wrong, and I'm assuming that my fame has reached Scarborough."

"You admit it then?" She had pulled herself to her feet and was holding on to the back of a chair now, and he turned to her, saying, "What do you expect me to do? Your mother has given you her version, and you haven't asked me for any explanation."

". . . As if there could be one."

"Oh yes. Oh yes, Eileen, there could be one." His voice had risen suddenly and there was an angry light in his eye as he poked his head toward her now and said, "How long is it since I've lain with you? How long is it since you've even let me touch you? Years. I am a man, I have bodily needs, it's got nothing to do with affection or love or care of family, they are just needs, like the need to eat or drink. If you don't eat you starve, if you don't drink you die of thirst. If a man doesn't have a woman then he also dies in his mind; one can go crazy with such a need. If I had taken one of the sluts from the kitchen would you have felt any better about it, because that is the usual pattern? I could have taken Price, your dear, dear Price. Oh yes, yes"—he tossed his head from shoulder to shoulder now—"her invitation has been in her eyes since you took to that couch. What would you have thought of that, eh?"

"How dare you say such a thing! *Price!*"

"Oh! Eileen, for God's sake don't be so naive! But you're not naive; no, not really, you are blind, you have made yourself blind like you made yourself an invalid. Oh you haven't hoodwinked me all the way, that couch has been an escape. I knew it, your mother knew it, so don't blame me entirely for what I did and for what—" He only just stopped himself from adding, "I intend to go on doing." And he would go on doing so, but not with Agnes Myton.

He turned abruptly from her now and walked the length of the room and back. She was still standing staring at him when he asked, "Well, what do you intend to do?"

It was a full minute before she answered him. "I'm going home with my mother," she said.

Well, he hadn't been surprised at that either. He knew that that was what the old girl would have advised her daughter to do. However, after a month or so at Waterford Place, she would, if he knew anything about her, be glad to come back, no matter what the conditions. But then she surprised him, in fact shocked him, by saying, "And I have no intention of returning here, ever. I shall take the children with me of course."

"You'll what!"

"You heard what I said, Mark. I shall take the children with me."

"You will not."

"Oh yes, I shall; Mark. If you don't let me have them without fuss then I shall take them legally. I shall take the matter to court."

He screwed up his eyes into narrow slits. He didn't know this woman. He stared at her, the while she returned his look with her gray eyes that had taken on a slaty deepness, and as he stared the probing of his mind revealed to him, like a door being thrust open, that she was using his indiscretion as a form of escape and that once away from this house and him she would no longer remain an invalid. He saw that the determination that had kept her riveted to her couch would now be turned into energy to bring her back to an ordinary way of living. For a moment he saw himself through her eyes like some primitive jailer, guarding a captive chained to a wall yet ignorant of why he was holding a prisoner at all. He also knew in this moment that he could let her go without the slightest compunction; but it was a different kettle of fish altogether as regards the children. Yet what could he do if the children were here alone. Of course they wouldn't be alone, there was Trotter upstairs. But there would be no mistress to guide Trotter, or any of the others.

She astounded him still further with her coolness when, her voice breaking into his thoughts, she said, "If you don't put any obstacle in my way I shall make it possible for the children to visit you at times. Should you cause an obstruction now, then my papa will place the matter in the hands of our family solicitor, Mr. Weldon, and it will have to be settled legally."

My God! He put his hand to his head and turned from her, and again he walked the length of the room. He couldn't believe it. This was his delicate sickly wife talking. What a pity, he thought now with a wry humor, that he hadn't openly shown his infidelity immediately after she had refused him her bed. Oh, he gibed at himself, let him be fair, she herself had never refused him her bed, she had got dear old Doctor Kemp to pave that part for her. Still, if she had known from the beginning she'd a rival it might, who knew, have assisted in a cure.

But what did it matter, he was tired. He was tired of so many things, the mine, his home that was only half run, his stables that were now almost empty of thoroughbreds, of Lady Agnes, oh yes, of Lady Agnes, and

of Eileen. Yes, he turned and looked at her, he had
been tired of Eileen for a long time. Let her go. But the
children. . . . Well—he bowed his head now—what
could he do? Life was a burden, you either shouldered
it or you threw off your pack, took up your gun, went
into the woods and, placing the muzzle against the
throb in your temple, you just moved your first finger,
then peace; nothing, nothing, just peace. He turned
slowly and walked out of the room.

6

Tilly wanted to cry, not only because of the uncertainty
of the future but because she was going to lose Jessie
Ann and John, for since Matthew and Luke had been at
school life in the nursery had become a kind of holiday.
And then there was Mr. Burgess. What was to become
of him? He had assured her not to worry, there were
always children who needed coaching and he had an
abode. His three-roomed, long attic cottage was a
palace, he had told her.

She had seen his palace, and she didn't think much of
it, at least the contents. There was hardly any furniture
in it, a chair, a small table, a dresser, and in the
bedroom a single rough bed, but what it lacked in
furniture it made up with books, for there were books
of all kinds, shapes, and sizes on rough home-made
shelves around the walls. The only comfort she could
see in the place was the open fireplace; there wasn't an
ornament or picture in the cottage, nor yet a bit of
decent china. Yes, he had his abode, but he couldn't
have saved any money because after he was paid once a
month he always trudged into Newcastle and bought

more books. She considered him worse off in a way than any of the staff, or even the miners. Oh, much worse off.

The whole house was in an upheaval. She had been packing the children's clothes all day. All the servants were in a state, not knowing what was going to happen. The only good thing, from their point of view, about this whole situation was that they were getting rid of Price, because she was going with the mistress.

Tilly hadn't really had time to consider her own fate, she only knew that once the children had left the house she wouldn't be needed and that Mrs. Lucas would then make short work of her. Mrs. Lucas didn't like her no more than did the cook. In a way, they were like the villagers; every time they looked at her there was suspicion in their eyes.

Jessie Ann, who was standing by her side, now said, "Don't put my fuzzy-wuzzy in the trunk, Trotter, I like my fuzzy-wuzzy." She lifted out the negro doll with the corkscrew hair and held it tightly in her arms; then looking up at Tilly, she said, "Why won't you come with me, Trotter?"

"Well, Miss Jessie Ann, because . . . because it's a long way and . . . and anyway, you'll have another nursemaid waiting at that end."

"Don't wan' n'other." It was John speaking, and Tilly looked tenderly down on him. In spite of Mr. Burgess's efforts he still spoke, she thought, like a village child. Mr. Burgess said it was an impediment which time would erase.

As she bent down to pick him up, she straightened his dress, saying almost tearfully, "You'll go into knickerbockers now."

"Don' w-wan bockers."

Jessie Ann laughed and Tilly smiled and she held the boy pressed close to her for a moment, and as she did so Phyllis Coates slid quietly round the nursery door, hissing, "Tilly!"

"Aye, what is it?"

"There's . . . there's a lad at the back door, he says he wants to see you. He's a pit lad by the look of him. Cook sent him packing, or she tried to, but he stood his ground and said he wanted to see you private for a minute. It might have got around about the business, you know"—she jerked her chin—"he might think you're goin' away with the bairns."

"What's his name? What's he look like? Is . . . is he a man? You said a lad, but did you mean a man?"

"No, no, he's not a man, a lad about fifteen or so."

Tilly let out a long drawn breath. For a moment she had thought that Hal McGrath had dared to come to the house. She wouldn't put anything past him. Last night she had lain in bed wondering where she would go from here. In any case it would be in a direction away from the village, for once he got wind that she was no longer protected by the house she hadn't a doubt but that he would come after her again. But from the description that Phyllis was giving her the visitor could be no other than Steve. Why should he come here though?

"Tell him . . . tell him I'm not free, not till after the morrow when they go," she said.

"Look"—Phyllis took the child from her arms—"go on, slip down the back way, you needn't go through the kitchen. Go through the still-room and out that door; you can whistle him down the yard."

When she hesitated, Phyllis pushed her, saying, "Go on, they can't do much more to you, you'll be out on your heels the morrow, anyway."

Yes, Phyllis was right, an escapade like this could at any other time have brought on the sack, but she was already for the sack, so what matter.

When she reached a corner of the yard she saw Steve standing looking over the half-door of a horse box, and she did whistle him. He turned sharply, then came toward her at a run. His face was bright, his eyes laughing. He began straightaway, saying, "I had to see you, I've some good news. Our Hal's gone for a sailor."

Her eyes widened and her mouth opened into a gape before she repeated, "Gone for a sailor?"

"Aye; him and wor Mick an' all. George was with them. They were on the quay in Newcastle. They got into a fight, George said, with three other fellows, proper sailors, 'cos they were scoffing them. Our Hal and Mick said they couldn't paddle canoes and the sailors jumped them. Our George run for it an' hid behind a warehouse an' he saw two fellows come off a big ship an' talk to the sailors; then together they hoisted our Hal and Mick up the gangway, an' the last our George saw of them was when these fellows seemed to be dropping them down a hatchway.

Steve now bowed his head and, putting his hand around his waist, he began to laugh; then looking up at Tilly, he said, "I've laughed more since yesterday than I've done in me life, I think, 'cos our George was afraid to come in and tell me ma and da what had happened to their shining pair. You see an hour or so after they were took on board the ship up anchor an' went off, and when George asked some fella on the quay where it was bound for he said some place like the Indies. . . . Aw! Tilly"—he caught hold of her arm—"can you imagine what they'll be like when they wake up? Our Hal's always hated the water, he wouldn't go swimmin' in the burn with the other lads. The great big 'I am' hated the water." He now threw his head back and when his laugh rang out, Tilly, her own face creased with smiles, cried at him, "Ssh! Ssh! you'll have the kitchen lot out on us." Then pulling him around the corner and through an archway from where a narrow path led to the middens, she looked at him and whispered, "Oh, Steve, 'tis the best news I've heard in me life I think. I was worried sick. You see, I'll likely be out of a job the morrow."

"Why?" His voice was sharp. "They sackin' you?"

"No, no. Well, not sackin' me, but the mistress is leavin' to go to her mother's house. There's been trouble atween her and the master and she's taking the children with her."

"Aw"—he shook his head—"nobody's allowed to have good news, are they, not without bad followin'?"

"Oh, I don't mind now, well, not so much. But I liked it back there"—she jerked her head toward the high wall—"yet the thought of meeting up with your Hal again was terrifyin' me."

"Well, you're safe now for a year, perhaps two of three. Me da said if the ship was bound for the Indies it could be for trading an' they mightn't see these shores again for years. Eeh! he did go on, nearly went mad. Me ma didn't, she just said, 'Bloody fools.' And you know, Tilly, from the stories I've heard 'bout ships an' sailors he'll get his deserts all right." Without pausing a moment, he looked up at her and, the smile sliding from his face, he said, "'Twas my birthday yesterday, I was sixteen, Tilly."

"Oh you were, Steve? Oh I'm so glad. May it return again and again."

"Thank you, Tilly. I wish I'd been eighteen."

"You will be soon enough."

"Do you like me, Tilly?"

"Like you? Of course I do, Steve. You know I do, you're my friend." She stressed the word, then said quickly, "I'll . . . I'll have to be goin', one of the maids is standin' in for me, there'll be trouble if she's caught."

"Oh aye, aye. But wait a minute."

As she moved away he put his arm out to her and checked her, saying, "Where will you go? I want to know."

"I haven't really thought. I could go back to the woodshed at the cottage, but I think I might go and see Mrs. Drew. She's a nice woman. You know, you saw Katie that day an' her brother Sam. Mrs. Drew will tell

me what to do, and they'll take me in for a night, I'm
sure, until I find me feet."

"Can I come and see you there?"

There was a pause before she said, "Why yes, Steve,
of course. Now I really must be goin'. Thank you.
Thank you for your news, Steve. Oh aye, aye, thank
you."

"It's all right, Tilly. I . . . I don't mind what I do, for
you." His voice trailed away.

She walked backward from him for a number of steps
before, smiling and nodding at him, she said, "Will you
be able to find your way out?"

"Aye, I found it in, I'll find it out."

On this she turned and ran back through the archway
and into the yard; but once having passed into the
still-room she paused for a moment and closed her
eyes. It was a good job, she thought, Steve was only
sixteen, else she'd be having trouble with him. No, no;
that was the wrong word to use about Steve, she owed
Steve a lot, not trouble. Well, she said to herself, you
know what I mean. Then as quietly as possible she
scurried out of the room, along the passage and then
came to a dead stop for there, with their backs to her,
were the housekeeper and the butler, and the housekeeper's voice not unduly low was saying, "Tomorrow
I'll come into me own, then I'll sort them out, all of
them. There'll be changes here, and I'm starting with
cook. I'm going to put a stop to her fiddling on the side
right away. In future I'll be in that kitchen to meet the
tradesmen from the top to the bottom of them. In any
case there won't be so many pickings after this with six
less."

"Six less?" It was a quiet inquiry from the butler, and
she said "Yes, six. The mistress and the children and
Madam Price; then there's the old man, Burgess, and
that weird witch of a girl who gets on me nerves every
time I look at her. That's one I'll be glad to see the back

of, and once the mistress is out of this house she'll be the first to take her bundle, you'll see."

And Tilly saw. At twelve o'clock the next day only half an hour after the coach had left taking the mistress, her mother and the children away, she was walking down the back drive with her bundle.

Only Phyllis had wished her good-bye and God-speed; the rest of the staff paid no attention to her, they were too taken up with the war that was going on between the housekeeper and the cook. They all really knew that because of Mrs. Lucas's seniority she would win, nevertheless they were interested in the battle even though they all stood to lose by the inevitable outcome.

Tilly had not heard one of them say, not even Phyllis, that they were sorry the mistress was going, nor to ask what the master was going to do now he would be left on his own. Strangely, she hadn't seen the master since this business had flared up three days ago, and to her knowledge he hadn't seen the children. He certainly hadn't come up to the nursery, unless he had done so while she was dead asleep. She was sorry for him. Of course, he hadn't acted right by his wife, but then, as they had said around the table time and time again, the mistress was no use to him in the way a wife should be, so perhaps he wasn't entirely to blame. She still liked him, she still thought he was a kind man. Anyway, he'd been kind to her.

When she reached the lower gates she stood outside the disused lodge and looked at the gaping windows. Nobody had lived in there for years they said. It was almost overgrown with grass, as were the gates that were never closed now. This part of the estate had been sadly neglected. She wished she could have a little house like that. It would be lovely, like living in the cottage again.

She stood looking at it for a moment while she

thought, If Mrs. Drew can't take me in I'll come back and sleep there the night. The master wouldn't mind I'm sure. And the thought directed her steps through the tall grass and weeds to the window. Through it, the room appeared dark and she couldn't see anything. She pushed her way now along the wall and round to the back of the lodge, and there to her surprise she found a pathway had been made leading from the back door away into the long grass and the thicket of the wood beyond. So somebody came here.

She was passing the narrow scullery window next to the back door when she heard the rustle of footsteps coming through the dried grass, and she turned and almost dived into a thicket behind her.

The footsteps seemed to come to a stop just near her head. Then her mouth slowly opened and she stifled an exclamation as she saw a hand come down through the grass, turn over a small stone and take something from under it. She next heard a key grating in the lock of the back door and before she had time hardly to close her mouth the key grated again; then the hand came through the grass and placed it under the stone once more.

When the footsteps died away she laid her face down among the stems and let out one long-drawn breath after another. Then she asked herself why she was afraid of anyone seeing her round by the lodge. Well, she told herself, they would put two and two together and think she was going to stay there and the next thing that would happen would be Mrs. Lucas bearing down upon her.

She now put out her hand and unearthed the key and, looking at it, she asked herself who it was had gone in and out of there so quickly, and why? Getting up, she turned and looked in the direction of the wood. Whoever it was had come from the house, and this wasn't their first trip not by a long chalk. She nodded to herself.

She went quickly to the door and inserted the key; then she was standing in what had been the scullery and the reason for the secret visit was immediately apparent. On a bench within an arm's length of her stood a skip holding at least three dozen eggs, and next to it lay a whole sucking pig that must have been recently slaughtered; on the floor below the bench were two other skips, one full of plums and the other holding large luscious bunches of grapes.

Eeh! the things that went on. All this pinched from the small stock. She shook her head. The Manor didn't have a home farm, but there were a hundred or so hens in the lower meadows and three sties full of pigs. Mr. Pilby, besides helping in the garden, looked after the livestock, but Mr. Summers was the chief one outside and he looked after the greenhouses. Her head was still shaking as she thought, They're all at it inside and out. Yet both Mr. Summers and Mr. Pilby were as mean as muck; she'd had personal experience of this. One day when she was out with the children and she'd pulled an apple off a tree, Mr. Summers had gone for her. And to think they were doing this all the time. They were robbing the master. Did they think of it that way?

She could have understood it if they were slipping something to somebody outside who was out of work or who never saw a grape or an apple for that matter, but to sell it in piles like this. A feeling of anger rising in her, she turned abruptly away and, after locking the door, she replaced the key and went round the lodge and into the road.

One thing was clear. If Mrs. Drew couldn't take her in she couldn't go back to that place and sleep, she'd have to make her way to the shed behind the cottage. . . . But what if there was a tramp in it?

Now not only did her head shake but her whole body gave an impatient jerk; she'd have to meet that trouble when she came to it. Let her get to Mrs. Drew's first. . . .

Biddy Drew hailed her with warmth but with some surprise, saying, "What brings you at this time of the day, lass?"

"I've . . . I've lost me job, Mrs. Drew."

"They sacked you?"

"Wasn't like that, no. The mistress . . . well, there's been trouble and she's gone back to her mother an' taken the bairns with her and so I'm not needed any more."

"Huh! I said it all along, 'tisn't only the poor that have their troubles. Well, come along in, lass, that's if you can get in. As you see I'm up to me eyes in soap-suds; twice a week I have to be at it. I pick me day 'cos I like to get them dried outside; if not, you have them hangin' round the room for evermore. Look, push that lot off there"—she pointed to a large mound of pit clothes lying on the form—"and sit yourself down. I'll put the kettle on; I'm in need of a drink meself, me tongue's hangin' out."

Tilly didn't sit down but she placed her bundle on the form and said, "Can I help you?"

"Help me?" Biddy turned and looked at her; then smiling widely, she said, "Aye, well, you might. But you'll have to take your hat and coat off first, wouldn't you, lass? Then we'll have that sup tea an' a bit crack, an' then we'll get goin'."

Tilly took off her hat and coat and hung them on the nail on the back of the door leading into the other room and as she did so, she said, "Where's everybody the day?"

"Oh, Peg, Katie and Sam are down below"—Biddy nodded her head toward the floor—"Bill and Arthur were on back shift, they're asleep in there." She nodded now toward the other room and when Tilly drew her lips together and said quietly, "Oh," Biddy said, "You needn't whisper, lass, the militia could go marching through here an' it wouldn't disturb either of them once they got their heads down. Fanny and Jimmy are in the fields at Richardson's farm, cleanin' up." The smile sliding from her face, she said, "It's hard work for a bairn of seven, but she's in the air and light and that's something."

As they sat down on the bench, mugs of steaming weak tea in their hands, there came a high cry from behind the fireplace wall, and when Tilly turned sharply and looked behind her, Biddy laughed and said, "Oh that's Annie Waters. She's as deaf as a stone; some of them must have got into bed without washin' and she's hauling them out. Seven she's got an' all men. They're all down below an' they're a mucky lot. Pit dust or not, they're still mucky." She smiled tolerantly, then said, "Well, lass, come on, let us have your news."

Tilly gave her the news, and when she had finished, Biddy, inclining her head toward her, said quietly, "Well, he's no better or no worse than any of the rest of them. The gentry were ever like that. As me mother used to say, if one doesn't satisfy a man, ten won't. But on the other hand there's some women, lass, worse than men, and when you get a woman inclined that way, well, nothin' 'll stop her except that she should be taken to bed every year with a bairn. But about your Lady Myton, well, that lady is makin' a name for hersel', I can tell you that. It isn't the first time I've heard about her. And she's a right madam, but in the high and mighty way you know, servants are scum 'neath her feet. There's gentry and gentry, lass, and some of them would use you like cattle. The McCanns at the far end of the row"—she jerked her head toward the door—"their Peggy was sent home from her place outside Newcastle. The lasses in that house used to be sent from the kitchen upstairs to a special room and there the dirty old bugger had his way with them. And one of the stable lads was always blamed for it. By the way"—she leaned forward and asked Tilly a personal question now and Tilly, the color flooding to her face, lowered her eyes as she said, "Yes, me granny told me, Mrs. Drew, after I started when I was thirteen."

"Aw well, you know all about it then. But nevertheless, lass, take care, keep your eyes open and your skirt down an' you'll be all right."

"Yes, Mrs. Drew."

Biddy finished the last of her tea; then getting to her feet, she said, "Of course there's black and white in all classes, lass; 'tisn't only the gentry for there's the keeker up at the pit, Dave Rice, he'd have you on your back afore you could say give over if he had his way. I meself have had to fight him off afore this. Dirty old bugger! The last time he had a go at me I threatened to put me pick shaft where it had never been afore if he didn't leave over."

"You were down the mine, Mrs. Drew?" Tilly's eyes widened.

"Fifteen years, lass, fifteen years." She turned her head away now and looked toward the open doorway leading into the mud road and, her voice dropping, she said, "'Twasn't bad as I got older, but I was but a bit of a bairn when I first went down. God! I was scared to death, crawling, crawling, crawling, day after day, me knees and me hands bleedin'. I didn't know what it was all about." She turned and looked at Tilly. "A child can't take it in, you know; that's why I'm not for lettin' my Fanny or Jimmy go down. The others have had to in order that we should eat, but we're not doin' so bad now an' they're all with me in this to keep the last two clear of that bloody black hole." Her voice ended on a bitter note; then her tone changing quickly again, she said, "Well, let's for the wash-tub, lass. If you're goin' to help, take this lot there and put them through the mangle. It's out in the back under the lean-to, you know where. Then hang them on the line."

"Yes, Mrs. Drew." As Tilly went to pick up the tin bath of wet clothes she paused for a moment and said,

"About tonight, Mrs. Drew, do you think . . . do you think I could stay here until I get fixed up the morrow some place?"

"Where else, lass? Where else? It might be on the mat in front of the fire, or you might have to stand up against the wall." She laughed, then said, "Go on, go on, you'll always have a place to rest your head here."

Warmed, and almost on the point of tears, which kindness always evoked in her, she went out through the back door to the lean-to where an iron mangle stood, its wooden rollers worn thin in the middle. It was of a type similar to the one that she had used in the cottage and so it was no hardship to wring out the clothes; but when it came to pegging them out, which meant her going into the lane which was bordered by the middens, her stomach almost heaved with the smell. But then she chided herself, for what did the smell matter when she had been received with such kindness.

As she went between the mangle and the clothes line it came to her that instead of going into Shields the morrow to look for a place she could perhaps get a job in the mine beside Katie and stay in this family, this family that seemed bound together with love and warmth. Oh, she would like that. Oh, she would. She'd do anything if she could only stay with this family.

7

It was Katie who said, "You go down the pit? Don't be daft! you'd never last five minutes down there, not you."

That was three days ago; since then she had tramped daily around Shields only to find that all respectable posts required a reference, and sometimes not only one but three. She had thought of going back and asking the master for one, but then that would mean facing the staff in the house again. She had thought, too, of Simon; he would have spoken up highly for her, she was sure, but she couldn't bring herself to go to the farm because likely or not she'd meet his wife.

Days could pass now when she never thought of Simon, but the moment his name came into her mind the pain came into her heart. Still, she was able to tell herself now that time would erase this feeling. It would have to, because she didn't see herself as going on alone all her days, she needed someone, someone to love and to love her. Yet the real need in her was not so much for someone to love her but to be kind to her; she treasured kindness.

So it was as she lay in bed facing Katie who had young Fanny curled into her back, that she again put her suggestion to her. This time, her voice a whispered hiss, Katie said, "You haven't any idea, lass, what it's like down there. I'm used to it but I'd give my eye teeth if I could get a job up top. And yet at the same time I tell meself I should thank God I've got work, that we've

243

all got work, 'cos what else is there for us around here? But you down there? No, Tilly; I can't see you down there, ever. An' our Sam won't hear of it either. . . . You'll get work, work that'll suit you like what you've been doin'."

"I won't, Katie; as I've told you, I've got no references, an' all I was offered today was a job in a pub on the waterfront. I was told about this place from the woman who gets people jobs. You have to pay sixpence and after I gave it to her she gave me two addresses, and as I said, one was the pub. It was awful. There were women in there, Katie . . . oh, you wouldn't believe it!"

"Oh, I believe it all right"—Katie's voice sounded practical—"I believe it 'cos I've seen it. You haven't to go any further than the Cock and Bull on the coach road. Stand out there on a Saturday night in the summer and you'll see some things that you've never seen afore, especially when they start throwing them out. What was the other job?"

"It . . . it was a kind of boarding-house, and she said I'd . . . I'd have to live in. I nearly thought about taking it until she said she didn't mind me not havin' references—it was something about the place. I got out as quickly as I could, an' she came after me to the door."

"You were lucky"—Katie started to shake with laughter—"you might have landed up in bed with a Swede."

"Oh, Katie!"

They pushed at each other, and Fanny cried, "Stop kickin', our Katie," and a male voice from the other end of the room said, "Shut up yous over there, I want to get to sleep."

"Shut up yoursel'!" hissed Katie. "You shouldn't be listenin'."

"I wasn't an' I want none of your old lip, else I'll come an' pull you out of bed."

"We wouldn't have far to fall, would we?" Katie was laughing again, and Tilly chuckled with her because their bed was merely a straw-filled mattress on the floor, and this made out of hessian bags. But still it was warm, and when half an hour ago she had dropped into it, it had seemed as soft as a down couch to her for her legs were aching and her feet were blistered with walking.

When Katie put her arms around her she shyly did the same, and soon, their heads together, they went to sleep.

At four o'clock in the morning Biddy gently shook Katie. She was lying on her back and she muttered a protest, but then, blinking the dead sleep from her eyes she quietly stepped over Tilly and, pulling on her over clothes that were lying on the floor by the side of the shaky-down, she stumbled into the kitchen and blinked in the lamplight.

Peg, who slept with her mother in the kitchen, was already dressed and gulping at some hot porridge, as was Sam. No one spoke; not even when the three of them went out of the door and Biddy closed it behind them: sleep was still on them, the morning was bitter, there was a day's grind ahead, what was there to say?

Three mornings later there was an addition to their number. Tilly was with them and, breaking the rule, Biddy patted her on the shoulder and said, "God be with you, lass"; then added to herself as she closed the door on the blackness and the bitter frost, "You'll need Him."

Tilly's heart was thumping against her ribs as she followed Katie around the end of a row of bogies, then almost brushed against the flank of a horse that was being led toward a huddle of buildings set at the side of a wide slope which disappeared into the ground.

The scene was lit by swaying candle lamps, the candles held in place inside rude tin boxes.

"Keep close if you don't want to be trampled by the cuddies," Katie said, pulling Tilly toward her as they went between a group of horses hardly discernible as they stood in deep shadow.

"Come on, this way, and mind what I told you, don't be afraid to answer him back, and if he asks if you're willin' to be bonded say, Why aye . . . what else?"

Tilly made no answer, but, as Katie had bidden her she kept close to her side. And then they were standing at the window of a wooden hut and a man was peering at them. Tilly couldn't distinguish his face because he was standing against the light, she only saw that he was short and thin. But that didn't make him uncommon, all the men who went down mines seemed to be short and thin. It was his voice that made him different, it was deep and rollicking and he seemed to sing his words. "Aye, well, here you are, Katie Drew, and half a day gone!"

"Stop your carry on, Mr. Rice, it's too early in the mornin'. I've brought her." She nodded toward Tilly.

"Aye, I'm not blind, I didn't think she was your shadda. Well now, lass, I suppose she's told you all there is to know. You know somethin'?" He leaned toward her from the window. "She thinks she knows more about this bloody hole in the ground than I do. You willin' to be bonded, lass?"

"Yes . . . aye."

"Well, if that's the case you know what you're in for, and I'm tellin' you something, you're lucky. If Katie here hadn't spoke for you you'd never have been set on; there's a queue from here to Jarrow for a job like this."

"Stop your kiddin', Mr. Rice; you know damn fine anybody's got to be on their last legs afore they go down that bloody hole." She jerked her head to the side. "Anyway, I'll take her in."

"Aye, you will after she signs. Come in here a minute."

Katie pushed Tilly before her and into the hut and to the front of a high desk on which there were two ledgers. Dave Rice, opening one of them, said, "Give us your full name, then you can write your cross."

Tilly slanted her eyes toward Katie and a small tremor of Katie's head sent a warning to her, so what she said was, "Tilly Trotter."

"Married?" There was a grin on his face now as he poked it toward her.

"No," she said.

"Then it's Tilly Trotter, spinster." After writing her name in the ledger he put the date to the side of it; then stabbing the pen on to the paper, he said, "Put it there"; and she put her cross by the side of her name.

His face straight now, he said, "You know the rates, twelve shillings a fortnight. But that depends, of course, on how much they bring out. You'll be workin' marrer with Katie and Florrie Connor, isn't it?" He turned and glanced at Katie and she said, "You know as well as I do."

"Cheeky monkey you!" He grinned at Katie now. "It's about time you had your arse smacked. I'll have to see about it."

"That'll be the day. Come on." She tugged at Tilly's arm, and they were hardly out of earshot of the hut when she said, "Mean bugger that. You watch out for 'im, if you're not along of me. Now hold your hand a minute." She pulled Tilly to a stop and, lifting her lantern, she peered at her through its flickering light, saying, "Now I've warned you, you're gona get a gliff when you get along inbye, 'cos I'm gona tell you something here and now, Miss Nursery Maid from the big house"—she punched her gently in the shoulder— "in a couple of days' time you'll realize that the cleanest things, in all ways, down here are the horses. An' at bait time keep your eyes straight ahead an' don't take no notice of what you see on the thill."

"The what?"

247

"The thill, the floor, you know at the coal seam, it's called that, the thill. As I said, keep your eyes straight ahead 'cos things go on round corners that'll likely make your hair rise on your scalp. I suppose it's true what our Sam said last night, you should have kept on lookin' for a decent position. Still here you are, you've signed up an' you can't get out of it unless you go and die like Florrie Thompson, whose job you've got. But it wasn't the coal that killed her, it was the consumption. . . . Aw! come on, here's the squad." She half turned to where the group of men, women, and children were making their way toward the incline and she added, "I thought we'd get to the face afore they came, I wanted to show you things quiet like. Not that it's ever quiet down here, but with the crew around us . . . aw, come on, come on, put a move on."

Bewildered, her innards seeming to have broken loose in the casing of her stomach, she scurried now to keep up with Katie's trotting steps. She was afraid as she'd never been afraid before. This was a different kind of fear. The fear associated with Hal McGrath had come and gone from time to time but this particular fear she felt was going to be permanent. She was walking into a world that didn't belong to any kind of life she had yet imagined. She was going along what appeared to be a tunnel with iron rails down the middle, and she went to step in between them for easier walking when Katie with a bawl that nearly took her head off cried, "Do you want to be run over afore you start? Don't be so bloody gormless, lass, that's the rolley way. Look." She pointed ahead to where a young lad was coming toward them leading a horse, and as they came nearer, Tilly could see the three bogies full of coal rattling behind the horse.

It seemed that she had been walking and stumbling for an interminable time when the tunnel widened out into a bay, which in comparison to the tunnel was well lit by lanterns hanging on nails stuck into two square supporting pillars which were holding up the roof. The rolley line now met up with others coming out of different roads, and on these there were more horses dragging more tubs.

For a moment she stood transfixed at the sight of a man squatting in the corner doing his business. His moleskin trousers were dangling over his knees and the rest of his body was bare.

"What cheer, Katie!"

"What cheer, Danny!"

Katie didn't look toward the squatting man as she answered him but she nevertheless appeared unaffected by his pose.

"This way." Katie was tugging again at Tilly's arm, and now they were going down one of the side roads. It was impossible to imagine they were going any deeper into the mine, but this was made more evident to her when the road on which they were now stumbling along began to go steeply downward. Moreover, it was much narrower than the main one and the roof seemed much lower, for after bumping her head against a spar of wood that was being held in place by two pit props all the sympathy she got from Katie in answer to her exclamation of pain was, "You'll larn."

That she was learning was evident when on the sound of a horse's hooves and the rattle of the wagons she pressed herself into an aperture seemingly scraped out of the wall between the pit props until the horse and bogies had passed.

She noticed that the leader of the horse was but a small boy, and that the horse was not a horse like those in the first part of the mine, this was a small Galloway pony. She had often wondered why when these ponies were let out in the fields they kicked their heels and seemed to go mad for a while, but now she could tell why. Oh yes, she could tell why.

When a few minutes later she let out a stifled scream as a rat the size of a small cat ran almost over her feet

Katie stopped for a moment and after laughing said quietly, "Don't be feared of them 'cos you'll have to get used to them. In fact there's one along here we call Charlie, an' he's a cheeky little bugger is Charlie."

Tilly gulped in her throat but said nothing, although she thought it was strange how Katie kept swearing down here, yet she hadn't heard her swear at home. . . . Would she become like Katie?

"We're nearly there. . . . Look! watch out for that sump." She pulled Tilly to the side of the roadway. "It looks just a little puddle but it'll take you past your knees if you go in. They'll be filling it in shortly. Never walk on smooth coal dust, take my tip, or you'll find yourself swimmin'. An' you just might one of these days, if that doesn't hold—" She jerked her thumb toward the low roof. "Seam up there's flooded out and it drips through." She raised her lantern and pointed to where the water was oozing through a fissure in the roof, then added reassuringly, "Don't worry, it'll hold the day. And for a good few more I hope."

Once again the road opened out and immediately they stepped into a hive of activity. If Tilly hadn't known different she would have imagined that the small figures darting here and there were a number of children playing, except that their voices were raucous and that most of their words were profane. They looked like imps for only the whites of their eyes and the gray of their open mouths and tongues showed any color.

As she stood, her eyes staring, there arose in her a feeling which mounted; amazement mingled with compassion and expressed itself in horror. Then her mouth widened and her chin dropped as she saw come crawling from a side road a small creature. She couldn't at first make out whether it was a girl or a boy, but it looked no bigger than Master John. It was a boy and he was in harness, but the harness was strapped around his waist and extended between his legs and it wasn't made of leather but of chain, and the chain was attached to a shallow skip loaded to a point with coal.

She watched as a man unbuckled the harness and slowly the child rose from his hands and knees and stood swaying for a moment, then rubbed his black knuckle into his eyes as if he were arising from sleep.

She was unaware that she had been gripping Katie's arm, and Katie, recognizing her feelings, shouted above the hubbub, "Oh, he's older than he looks; that's Billy Snaith, he's ten. Hello there, Billy."

There was a pause of seconds before the child answered wearily, "Hello, Katie."

"Tired?"

"Aye, I'm jiggered. What's it like up top?"

"Cold but dry."

His reply, if he made any, was lost when a raucous voice shouted above the melee, "Come on the lot of yous if you want to go! Well, alreet, if you want to stay I don't mind puttin' you on another shift."

The answer to this was murmurs and growls from the incoming shift. But what was amazing Tilly more than anything was the apparent acceptance of this way of life, and also the humor threading it. Yet there was no sign of humor in the line of straggling children making their way to the outside world.

"That's the low drift lot." Katie nodded toward the departing children. "The road in there's too low for a Galloway to get in."

"Why don't they make it bigger?"

In the inquiry there was a note in Tilly's voice that could have touched on anger, and Katie laughed as she said, "Don't ask me. I suppose they would if they could; it's got something to do with the seams." She nodded up toward the uneven stone roof. "It means cutting through that an' some of it won't be cut through, an' there are places where it would be dangerous to try 'cos there's the water to contend with. Look at that pump there." She pointed across the space. "Goin' hell for leather all the time twenty-four hours a day. It's like tryin' to drain the Tyne. Anyway, we're lucky we can walk in to our place, an' believe me I do think meself lucky"—she was nodding at Tilly now — "'cos I was three years on that shift where Billy is, and by! it was a long 'un. The day I was moved to the fourth road"—she pointed ahead of her—"I wouldn't have called the Queen me aunt. Yet I cried all that first night—relief I think it was."

Tilly made no response to this; her mind was in a whirl with the overlying pattern of horror.

They were in a small group now, people in front and people behind, but there was no talking until they came on a single bogey, one boy pulling in front, a second almost horizontal adding his puny efforts as he pushed at the iron contraption laden with coal. And then someone shouted, "Better get a move on, Robbie, else you'll catch it."

The boy in front paused, turned his head slowly and looked at the man; then seeming to draw his shoulders up over his head he moved on again.

"Don't linger." Katie was pulling at Tilly's arm, impatience in her voice now; then she whispered, "If you stopped every time you say that you wouldn't last long down here, now I'm tellin' you so if you mean to work, an' you'll have to 'cos you've bonded yourself, you'll have to buck up." It was as if her warning was final.

They now arrived at what Tilly took to be a dead end, for it looked like a long blank wall except that there were men hacking at it. They had hardly reached them when one of the men turned and shouted, "You've taken your time; we'll be up to our bloody necks in it if you don't get crackin'!"

This was answered by a mouthful of cursing from a woman among the group and there was a ripple of laughter accompanied by bustle, and Katie whispered,

"That's big Meggie. She keeps them in their place, caution she is in more ways than one. Keep on the right side of her." The last was a whisper almost in Tilly's ear, "Now here's what you do. Your bait? Where's your bait? . . . Oh my God!" She reached out and snatched Tilly's bait from a shelf of rock and on a laugh she said, "You're green all right, that wouldn't last two minutes there. That's what I'd give it, two minutes before Charlie'd be at it. Look, you see the knot in the string, you hang it up here, like this." She demonstrated by hanging the small parcel of food from a nail in a beam and allowing it to dangle downward. "There! He hasn't learned to walk the tight-rope yet but some day I bet he does; he's a clever 'un is Charlie."

"Why . . . why don't you kill them, I mean him, the rat?"

"Oh, we kill 'em, but not Charlie. The blokes are superstitious about Charlie. As long as Charlie shows his face they guess they're all right. They say he can smell fire damp better than any of their new fangled ideas, an' I believe that's true, like I believe safety lamps is dangerous. Our lads won't use them, they stuck out against them. There was war on at first but they stuck out an' we've hardly lost any men in the last twenty years, well, not to speak of, not compared with others. There's been hundreds killed in mines along here. Me ma remembers Heaton Colliery. Seventy-five killed in a flood there. . . . Look"—she broke off—"don't stand there like a stook, do what I'm at, take that shovel an' fill that skip, like this." She thrust her shovel into a heap of coal and she had filled the skip within a few minutes.

Tilly took the shovel and began to fill the skip. Shoveling was no hardship, her muscles were attuned to the saw; what was troubling her was the coal dust in her throat that seemed to be choking her, the coal dust in her eyes that was blurring her limited vision in the dim light, and the noise, the bustle; and then . . . the lifting up of the skip on to the shoulders of the children. Some fell to their knees with the weight of them before they got adjusted, and the children didn't go down the road she and the others had come up because this had the rolley lines laid on it; they went by a narrow by-pass disappearing into blackness as if walking into the mouth of hell. Before she had been at the work an hour she was associating the whole place with hell and its horrors.

When time had passed to which she couldn't put a name, a halt was called and, dropping her shovel, she went and leaned against the wall and slowly slid down to the floor; and there Katie joined her. She had brought a can with her and, taking the lid off it, she handed it to Tilly, saying, "Here, wash your throat, an' spit the first mouthful out."

Tilly gulped at the tepid water and it tasted like wine, and had swallowed half of it before she aimed to spit it out.

"You've done well for a starter."

Tilly made no answer.

"You'll get used to it after a bit. You're achin' now I know, but in a day or so you won't know that you've got any arms or legs, or back, 'cos they'll all work together; it's only your throat that'll trouble you."

A man came and sat down at the other side of Tilly. He was naked except for a pair of ragged drawers. "How's it goin', lass?" he asked.

Tilly did not know how to answer him; the answer she couldn't give him was "All right"; it was Katie who replied for her, saying, "She's a bit winded, Micky; but as I was tellin' her, in a week or so's time it'll only be the dust that'll worry her. I'm right, aren't I, Micky?"

"Aye, lass, aye, you're right. 'Tis the dust that's the trouble. Gets you, the dust." He took a swill from his can; then wiping his cleaned washed lips with the back of his black hand, he added, "And finally in the end. Aye, 'tis as you say, Katie, the dust. Anyway, it mightn't trouble you for very much longer. Do you know what I was hearin' when I was in Shields t'other Sunday? A fellow was spoutin' and he was sayin' that there's one or two blokes up in London Town trying to get a bill out to stop bairns and lasses being down here, an' in factories an' all, that is until a certain age. But he's tryin' to potch women and children in mines altogether."

"Is that true, Micky?"

"Aye, I heard it from this fellow's own lips, lass. And what's more, I saw him gettin' run in. He had a big crowd round him, Sunday strollers you know, and the polis took him for breakin' the peace."

Katie was silent for a moment before she said, "I was gona say bloody lot of silly Holy Joes up there tryin' to take the bread out of wor mouths, but I don't know, it could be the best thing that could happen, that's if they give us other jobs."

"Aye, that's it, lass, if they give you other jobs, but where are the jobs for lasses and women, only service, or the fields. You've got your pick, but whichever you choose you're under a bloody master, aren't you? Well, there's one thing, lass"—he now gripped Tilly's knee tightly—"you haven't got to get dressed up for this lark, have you? Wear nowt if you like. Aye, wear nowt. What about it, eh, Katie?" He leaned over Tilly and peered at Katie and she pushed him, saying with a laugh, "Go on you! you're a Micky drippin'."

"Well, here we go!" He pulled himself to his feet; then looking round at the squatting figures, he said, "Where's big Meggie . . . as if I didn't know? That lass should be in a bull pen."

A voice from the other side of the roadway shouted, "What d'ya think her secret is, Micky? Twenty-two years old an' never been dropped yet; she should have had 'em by the litter with her carry-on."

There was muffled laughter as the various figures rose from the ground and the process of shoveling started all over again. Push in the shovel, lift, throw. Push in the shovel, lift, throw. When the rhythm stopped a small back was waiting to be laden with your efforts.

Push in the shovel, lift, throw. Push in the shovel, lift, throw. Dear God in Heaven! she could never stand this. That place in Shields serving in the bar appeared like paradise to her now; even the boarding-house job seemed attractive. She'd have to tell Katie when they got out of here . . . when they got out of here. Would this work ever stop?

Some time during the day it stopped for half an hour, then again for a break to sit down by the wall and drink from the can.

Three o'clock in the afternoon and a final halt was called. She had lost count of time. She couldn't hear what Katie was saying. Later, she couldn't recall the walk from the face to outbye. She only knew she was aware that some of the children didn't accompany them. It was later Katie told her that a few of them were on twelve hour shifts; two hours overtime she said, whether they liked it or not; they had to clear the face for the next shift.

At one part of the road when coming out she had been aware of walking through water and of some of the men stopping and discussing it saying that the landing box must be overflowing.

And she recalled standing at the mouth of the mine amid the sweating horses and blackened men and looking upward toward the bright sky. The sun was shining, two larks were competing with each other in a chorus of sound, and as she gazed upward the wind lifted her hair from her brow. And she could have stood like this, she felt, for ever but Katie, practical to the last, said, "You can sniff it all the way home. Come on, lass."

And when she arrived home Biddy did for her what

she had never done for her own children. In the narrow confines of the scullery she eased her into the tin bath and gently she washed the grime from her, hair and all. Then after helping her to dry herself she slipped over her head a stiff calico nightdress and led her to the shaky-down, and there she let her sleep for four hours before awakening her and giving her a meal. It was a bowl of mutton broth and dumplings and she brought it to the bed in a basin placed on a tin tray, and while Tilly sat up and then sleepily ate it, Katie lay snoring solidly by her side. And when she had finished the meal Biddy took the bowl from her, saying quietly, "Away you go, put your head down, lass; your first day's over. It'll never seem so bad again."

8

The days turned into weeks and the weeks into months, and Tilly learned what it was to work in water up to her knees. She learned not to pass out when she saw a man injured by a fall of stone or coal, or saw one trapped in the brokens where he had been pulling the pillars in order to drop a roof. She learned how to make her own candles with cotton wicks and ox tallow because this worked out cheaper than paying the viewer to supply you with them. And she learned to trust Charlie. This happened on the day one of the men, seeing the rat standing on his hind legs sniffing before scurrying away up the road, cried to them, "Run for it!"

The brattice, a wooden partition which aided the currents of air to flow, had in some way blocked the flow and a small child detailed to watch at the air door had fallen asleep. This time the build-up of gas was slight, but nevertheless it could have caused an explosion if touched off by a candle lamp. There was jollification the following day when Charlie returned, and pieces of bait were put on the shelf for him. Charlie, the men swore, was a better gas detector than any canary.

Tilly also learned that most people look alike when covered in coal dust, for twice in as many months she had passed close to the master and he hadn't even given her a second glance. She had wondered that if he noticed her name on the books whether he might seek her out and speak to her. But then, she supposed, he never saw the names of his workers; this was left to the viewer.

One thing she knew for certain and that was she hated every day she went down into the depths of the earth, and that if there were the slightest chance of other work she would jump at it, even working in the fields. But there were queues for those jobs and the field managers picked their own gangs. Anyway, during the winter there was no work for them.

Another thing worrying her was Sam. She could read the signs all too clearly. He had laughed at Steve's first visit to the house to ask how she was, but when the lad put in an appearance on both the following two Sundays he hadn't laughed or chipped her as the others had done. She had wanted to say, "Steve is like a brother to me, no more, no less," but that would have left the road open for him, so she said nothing and let them assume what they liked about her and Steve.

Then something happened that made Sam show his hand. It was on a Sunday at the end of her fourth week down the mine. The family had gathered as usual, the children had been out playing in the road, and it was young Jimmy who rushed in gabbling, "Tilly! Tilly! there's a gent on a horse askin' for you."

Tilly had risen to her feet. There were two people she knew who rode horses, one was the master, the other was Simon, and she knew it wouldn't be the master who'd come looking for her. She felt her face turn scarlet and, looking round the now silent company, she sidled from the form as she said, "I'll . . . I'll be back in a minute."

"Do you know who it is?" It was Biddy asking the question, and she looked at her and said, "Yes, I think so, Mrs. Drew. It'll likely be Si . . . Farmer Bentwood. He's . . . he's the friend I told you about who looked after me granny and granda."

"Oh, aye, lass, aye. Well, ask him in. He'll have to squeeze, but ask him in."

She did not say "Yes" or "No" to this but simply thanked Mrs. Drew. She didn't want Simon to see this overcrowded room, he wouldn't understand her living in such conditions; nor would he understand the warmth and happiness they engendered.

He was standing by his horse's head in the muddy road. Several doors were open along the row and heads were peering out. She was embarrassed by the situation, she knew what they would be thinking: why was a lass like her being visited by a man on a horse and dressed as he was? for he could be taken for a gentleman.

"Hello, Tilly."

"Hello, Simon."

"I . . . I didn't know where you had gone until . . . until the other day."

"Oh, I've been here some weeks now."

"My God!" The words came from under his breath as he looked up and down the row; then he said, "Look, we can't stand here, come for a walk."

She looked behind her toward the half open door before muttering, "I'll get me hat and coat."

Back in the room she passed through them and

addressed herself to Biddy as she said, "I'm . . . I'm just going for a short walk, I . . . I won't be long, I'm gettin' me hat and coat."

There was silence again as she returned pulling on her coat and it was Sam who spoke now, saying, "Why can't you ask your visitor in?"

She glanced at him as she said, "He . . . he hasn't got much time."

Out in the road again, walking by Simon's side, her eyes cast downward, she realized that she hadn't walked like this for some time now, it was as if she were ashamed. For the last few weeks she had held her head high; perhaps it was because she wanted to look at the sky and drink in the air.

"Why didn't you come to me after you left the Manor?" He was muttering his words for they were still in the row.

And she answered low, "You should know the answer to that."

They had passed the end of the row and were in the open country before he spoke again. "I could have at least seen that you were decently housed."

She turned on him now, her voice high. "I am decently housed. I'm happier with them"—she jerked her head backward—"than ever I've been in me life with anybody . . . well, except me granda and grandma. But they were old; back there, the Drews, well, they're all youngish, and the place might look awful but they're clean, an' they're good, an' it might surprise you, Simon, but they're happy."

He pulled the horse to a standstill and looked at her. "And you, you're happy, working down the pit, because that's what they tell me you're doing?"

She swallowed and looked to the side now as she said, "No, I can't say I'm happy workin' down the pit, but . . . but I have them to come back to."

"Look"—he bent toward her—"I'll give you the

money; you can get a decent room in Shields until you find a place to go into service or some such, but . . . but I can't bear the thought of you down there"—he now thumbed angrily toward the ground—"and the things that I hear go on. They act like beasts."

"No, they don't. Well, perhaps a few of them do"—her voice was raised again—"but you can't judge them all alike. As for acting like beasts, there's plenty of them up top, and you should know that. I've just escaped one because he's gone to sea."

"I know, I know." His tone was quiet now. "Yet Tilly"—he shook his head slowly—"I somehow feel responsible for you. . . ."

"Well, you needn't, I'm responsible for meself and workin' for me livin'"; I'm on me own feet, and what's more I'm not hounded any longer. Even over there" – she pointed in the direction of the Manor—"they would have burned me alive, aye, and I'm not kiddin'. Take us back a few years and they would have had me burned alive. They were as bad as the villagers, except for a couple of them, and the tutor."

He stared at her in silence for a moment, then said, "Does he know that you are working in his mine . . . Sopwith?"

"I don't know, and it wouldn't matter if he did. But I do know this: if he had offered to keep me on in a job below stairs I would have refused it, an' I was badly in need for a roof over me head at the time. Such was the feeling against me that I'm tellin' you I would have refused it because they, all of them"—again she thumbed in the direction of the Manor—"they're a lot of thieves an' scroungers an' not fit to wipe any one of the Drews' boots. Diddling him, the master, at all turns. You've never seen anything like it."

"Diddling?" He raised his eyebrows and smiled weakly at her. "Well, everybody knows that goes on."

"Aye, it might, a bit here and there, but not to the

extent that lot takes it to. You know nothing, Simon. If your men were robbing you like the staff rob Mr. Sopwith you'd go broke within weeks, I'm tellin' you."

"Well, that's his look out. He's got a housekeeper, hasn't he?"

"Huh! housekeeper. Anyway, that's over and done with, I'm here and I'm gona remain here till something better turns up. But whatever it is I'm stayin' along with the Drews as long as they'll have me."

"So I needn't have worried?"

She looked him full in the face now, saying quietly, "No, you needn't have worried, Simon."

Again there was a long pause; and when he eventually spoke his voice was soft and full of meaning as he said, "I'll always worry over you, Tilly. No matter what comes my way in life, nor no matter how I change, my feelings for you will remain the same as they've always been."

She stared into his face for some seconds before saying quietly, "Good, like they were when I was a little girl."

Her eyes were unblinking and he closed his own for a moment and bit on his lip before looking at her again and murmuring, "Just as you say, Tilly, like they were when you were a little girl."

His gaze was hot on her belying his words and she turned her head to the side, saying slowly now, "I may be starting courtin' soon."

When he made no answer she looked at him again. "Sam, he's the eldest, he wants me; he's a good fellow."

"And you? You want him?"

She forced herself to look straight into his eyes as she answered, "Yes, because I can't see I'll do any better and I'll have a house of me own and. . . ."

"Huh! a house of your own," he broke in, his voice almost a shout now as he cried, "Don't be silly, a house of your own! I wouldn't use any one of those along that row for sties."

"No, perhaps you wouldn't." Her voice was almost as loud as his; but then, taking a deep breath and her tone changing, she said, "But then you're very fortunate, Simon. You've always been very fortunate; in fact, you don't know you're born. Now I've got to go back, Mrs. Drew likes us all there at teatime on Sunday . . . in the sty."

"I'm . . . I'm sorry." His head was turned to the side now and she answered, "Yes, so am I. . . . Good-bye, Simon." Her voice was soft, but he didn't answer and she turned away. Pulling her coat closer around her neck, she bent her head and ran back to the row.

Simon stood and watched her until the door closed on her, and then, turning toward the horse, he put his two hands on the saddle and bent his head toward them as he muttered to himself, "Well, I tried, so what has to be will be. Let things take their course."

9

Mark Sopwith was experiencing a deep loneliness which was making him feel as if he were hollow right through. The house appeared empty, and even when there was a movement in it it seemed to be at a slower pace. Mrs. Lucas had assured him that he had no need to worry about the household, she would see that it ran as smoothly as before.

It was Pike who presented him with the monthly accounts. These, he noticed, were reduced hardly at all, yet there were six people less to feed. But he let it pass, at least for the present; there were more serious problems on his mind. This morning he was to make a thorough inspection of the mine with his agent. The day before yesterday they had repaired the clack-valve in the pump on the fourth level and the water there was now much lower. They had also had a new bucket attached, a heavier type which helped with the down-stroke in the cylinder. Yet things were still not right; there was more seepage coming in from the upper level, and this was likely being fed by a spring near the burn having diverted itself. Springs were hell to locate; they caused more trouble than the river because you knew where the river was.

Then his private affairs: he'd had one polite note from Eileen saying that the children were well and happy and that when they broke up for the Christmas holidays, weather permitting, she'd allow them to come and stay overnight.

His teeth had clenched hard on that line—she would allow them to come and stay overnight. Was this to be the pattern of the future, his children for one night? No, he wasn't going to stand for that. All right, let her have a legal separation, then he'd put in a legal claim, and in that way he'd have his children for so many months, well, at least weeks in the year.

He had breakfasted at the same time as usual but this morning he did not rise from the table immediately he had finished, but remained seated staring toward the bright glowing fire to the right of him; and as he did so he asked himself again if this was to be the pattern of his life. He couldn't marry again unless she divorced him. And if he took a mistress it would mean seeing her only at intervals, whereas what he needed at this moment was a companion more than a mistress, a loving companion, someone to sit opposite him, smile at him, listen to him, touch his hand—he didn't want to roll with her . . . All right, if that too should happen to be in the picture it would be a bonus, but he just wanted a woman near him, close, warm. He had friends, or rather he'd had friends before this affair had flared into the open. Since Eileen left he had seen Albert Cragg just once, and then Bernice hadn't shown her face. Only Albert had called, and he had the nerve to convey diplomatically to him that Bernice, having been a friend of Eileen's . . . well, he understood, didn't he? . . . Yes, yes, he understood.

John Tolman had called too, but also unaccompanied by Joan. Only Olive and Stanley Fieldman had visited together, when Stan in his hearty way had thumped him on the back as he said, "You'll ride the waves, laddie. Never fear, you'll ride the waves." That was the only reference he had made to the scandal of which he had become the chief figure. But what about Agnes? Olive Fieldman hadn't been as reticent as her husband and he gathered from what she said that Agnes's escapades had become so notorious that every decent door was now closed to her. But as Olive had pointed out, it didn't seem to worry her in the least; she was a most remarkable person.

Yes, Agnes was indeed a most remarkable person. She wasn't really a woman at all, merely a ravenous collection of primeval instincts, with a ruthless disregard for everything and everyone who didn't suit her purpose. It didn't seem to trouble her in the least that she was blatantly violating the standards of the society in which she moved.

He rose and went to the fire and, holding his hands out to the flame, he asked of it, "What am I going to do?" and the answer came tersely, "Get down to business. Robinson will be waiting for you."

It could have been about eleven o'clock. Tilly had just loaded a full skip on to Betty Pringle's back. Betty was eleven years old, her body was thin and her shoulders permanently stooped, and her face, when it was washed, gave one the impression of age, even when she laughed, for her eyes never smiled.

Betty never complained, even when the skip was piled so high that the coal stuck in her neck she said nothing. Her father had been killed in this mine three years ago and she and her twelve-year-old brother were the only means of support for her mother, who was ailing with "the sickness."

At first Tilly had barely filled the child's skip, but this had brought the barrow man storming up the roadway saying he would report them both to the keeker and they would have their money docked if the skips weren't filled properly, for it was taking him twice as long to get his corves filled and therefore he was behind in taking his loads outbye. And so from then Tilly filled the skips to the required measure, and spat out the coal dust not only to clear her throat but as a significant reply to what she thought of the barrow man.

Indeed Tilly was learning, and fast.

Today the work was excruciating. Straightening her back, she went hurriedly toward the shelf where Katie kept the tin box holding the candles. To get to the shelf she had to splash through water that came up to her calves. She didn't mind; it was warm and for a moment it washed the grit from out of her clogs.

Tempers were on edge along the whole face; the hewers were swearing at the putters, the putters were swearing at the women and children because they couldn't keep pace with transporting the coal from the face to the middle landing; everything about them was sodden wet; everybody was working in water. It was into this atmosphere that one of the putters came running back from the middle road with the news that Alf, the horseman, had just told him that the boss, the master, the check weighman, and the agent were all on their way up to number four face.

"Well, let the buggers come," was the general comment. "Oh aye, especially him. Let him see the real conditions in his bloody mine. Another foot and we can't go on. Aye, let him come. Let them all come."

Half an hour later they came, in single file: the check weighman first, then Mark, followed by the agent; and they were all wearing high knee-boots.

They stopped almost opposite to where Tilly and Katie were working. No one had stopped work and no one spoke. The voiceless silence was eerie, there was only the tapping of the picks and the grating of the shovels. Then the check weighman said, "It's risen in the last hour." He stuck a rod in the ground, then added, "Four inches."

"Well, it can't be all coming from number three drift; you've seen to that, haven't you? the pump's working?" Mark had turned to the check weighman and he answered, "Aye, sir, we've seen to that. But it's up above I fear the trouble is." He pointed toward the roof. " 'Tis as if there were a leak in the river and it was finding its outlet here 'cos we're touching on river level at this point."

It was as the agent spoke for the first time, saying, "And that's quite possible. Yet we checked the fissures juat a short while ago," that a strange noise alerted everybody. The men at the face stayed their picks in mid-air, and when a big rat that was perched on a shelf suddenly leaped forward and scampered down the road away into the dimness, a weird cry rang around the enclosed space. It galvanized everybody. Men, women, and children, tumbling and yelling, made for the road, and the check weighman's voice above everyone else's now seemed to verge on a scream as he cried, "Run! Run, sir!" But even as the man thrust out his arm to grab Mark, a wave of water swept them all forward like matchwood.

Tilly heard herself yell as she lost her footing and sprawled into the water. She could swim a little, having taught herself in the burn, but now the motions of her flaying arms were impeded by bodies and clutching hands, and faces with wide open mouths confronting her one minute then spun away from her the next. The whole terrifying nightmare scene was lit by a lantern here and there on shelves where the water had not yet reached.

She was swallowing the filthy water in great gulps, she knew she was dying and it was no use struggling, but she struggled. Her hand went out sideways and found a rung of a ladder and she clung on to it realizing it was the ladder leading up to some old workings where they had been dropping the roof only last week, and that if she could get in there she'd be safe.

As she attempted to pull herself upward a hand came out and grabbed her shoulder, the nails digging into her flesh, and as she was dragged upward the water, having billowed her skirt, left her knees bare and they scraped against the rough stone, but her agonized crying out was mixed with relief when she felt her feet touch solid ground although still under the water.

There was no light now and in the pitch blackness she kept tight hold of the hand. As she gasped for breath a whimper came from the side of her, and she put out her other hand and touched a small head that was just above the water and, gasping, she said, "Who is it?"

"Betty. Me, Betty Pringle."

"Oh, Betty; thank God you're safe, at least for the present. And . . . and who are you?" She brought her hand now from Betty to touch her rescuer, and when she felt the sodden cloth of a coat she realized that he must be one of the three men, the weighman, the agent . . . or the master. She wouldn't know until he spoke, but he didn't speak. And now she stammered, "This . . . this is the old workin'. They . . . they were dropping the roof, but it'll likely be dry further in."

The hand was still holding hers but the man said nothing, and she thought, He's stunned; whichever one of them it is he's stunned.

"Hang on to me." Her words were meant for both the man and Betty. The man still held her hand and after feeling the child grab at her skirt she moved forward, and the man came behind her.

The lay of the ground told her they were moving upward, but they hadn't gone more than a dozen steps when the earth below them shook, and the roof above them shook. It seemed to Tilly in this moment that the whole world was rocking; and then she was screaming again, as was Betty.

She didn't know whether it was the man who threw her forward or whether it was the upheaving of the earth, but she seemed to fly through space before her head hit something and a blankness descended on her.

When she came around the earth was steady again but her mouth was filled with dust. There was no water here. Slowly she raised herself upward, but when she tried to stand she was impeded by something across her legs. Her groping fingers told her that these were two pit props, and when she felt the rocks on top of them she realized that they might have saved her from broken shins.

She tried to call out but the words stuck in her throat. She listened. There was no sound, only the sound within her, the terror that was rushing up to her throat to find release.

When at last she found her voice it was small, she could hardly hear it herself, and she said, "Is anybody there?"

There was no answer. She pulled herself clear of the props and began to crawl around on her hands and knees. She was muttering to herself now: "There's been a fall, it's a fall, the mouth of the old workings must have caved in. 'Twas the water; it couldn't stand up against the water. . . . Is anybody there? Betty! Betty!" Her voice was getting stronger, and now she was yelling. "Mister! Mister!" She had been climbing over mangled stones and props but now suddenly she could move no further forward because the stones and the props had become a steep wall.

"Oh my God! Oh my God! they must be under there, the man and Betty." She started calling again, "Mister! Mister! Betty! She stood up now, groping at the stones, and like someone demented she started to pull at them and throw them behind her.

When her foot touched something soft she dropped on to her knees and, groping blindly, she moved her hands over it, then almost shouted in her relief. It was the man. Like her, he too had been knocked out. But then her fingers tracing his body, her relief sank into dismay; he was lying on his back with his legs above him, and these had been caught. Her fingers moved down over one trouser to where his knee should be, but all she could feel here was a great block of stone. His other leg was hanging downward and only the foot was caught above the ankle, fastened tight by a pit prop which in turn was weighed down by the wall of stone.

Now her hands were running over his face, then she was undoing his jacket, then his waistcoat. When her fingers touched his shirt her hands became still for her touch told her what the material was made of, fine flannel, a material so thin it was almost like silk. The children had had shirts like this. Oh my God! the master. When her fingers went through his vest and on to his flesh her head turned to the side as if listening, and when the beat of his heart came to her hand it seemed to pass up her arm and shock her into vitalized life, for now, lifting Mark's head, she cried, "Sir! Sir! wake up." When she got no response she edged herself forward so that she was half sitting, half leaning among the debris, and in this position and supporting his head against her thigh, she now started patting his face, like a mother trying to restore a child to life and gabbling all the while, "Come on. Come on. Please, please, wake up. Oh! sir, do wake up, please."

For the moment she had forgotten about Betty; then

her head turning from one side to the other in the darkness she called, "Betty! Are you there, Betty? Can you hear me, Betty?" And as she called once again the head resting against her moved and Mark let out a long agonized groan.

"That's it, sir, wake up. Wake up."

"What! What!"

She kept patting his face. "Come on, wake up. Wake up properly. Oh! please wake up."

"What is it? What happened?"

"There was a fall, sir. You . . . you pulled me out of the water and . . . and we came into the drift and there was a fall."

"A fall?"

"Yes, sir."

"I can't move."

"No, sir, your feet are caught, but . . . but it'll be all right, they'll come, they always come and get people out, they won't be long."

"Who . . . who are you? I . . . I know you, don't I?"

"I'm Trotter, sir. I . . . I used to be the children's nurse."

"Ah, Trotter. Trotter." His voice faded away and once again she was patting his face, saying, "Come on. Oh! come on, sir, wake up properly. Please wake up. Look, they'll get us out, they have special men for gettin' people out. Sam is one of them, Katie's brother. Aw come on, come on, sir. Can you hear me, sir?"

When he groaned she said, "That's it, that's it, keep awake. That's what they say you've got to do, keep awake. You haven't got to move about, just keep awake."

"I can't move."

"No, but you soon will. Are you hurtin', sir?"

"Hurting? No, I'm not hurting, Trotter. I . . . I just don't feel anything. Yes, yes, I do, my neck is stiff, I'm lying . . . rather twisted."

When she shifted amid the tumbled stones, jagged edges here and there pierced her flesh; then she eased his head up between her small breasts and asked softly, "Is that better?"

"Yes; yes, thank you." Again his voice from a whisper faded away; and there was silence about her once more, and it was as terrifying as the blackness. This was like no blackness she had ever experienced before. No matter how long a road in the mine there had always been a glimmer of light somewhere; but this blackness was encasing her like a shroud. She could be in her grave, buried alive. . . .

Her body trembled violently and she coughed, jerking his head on her breast, and he moaned and said, "Oo . . . h! Oo . . . h! How long ago did it happen? I . . . I seem to have been asleep."

"Not long, sir; about half an hour I should say."

"Is that all?"

There was a surprised note in his voice. Then his words spaced, he said, "I . . . wish . . . I . . . could . . . move."

She made no answer, and again slowly he asked, "Do you think you might be able to move the stones from my feet, Trotter?"

Some seconds passed before she muttered, "I . . . I'd better not, sir; the . . . the way you're lying I could bring the rest down on top of you."

"Yes, yes, of course."

"They won't be long, sir, they won't be long."

"The . . . the little girl?"

She didn't answer, and he muttered, "Oh! dear, dear. Oh! dear."

She sat now quite still saying no word. She didn't know whether he had fallen asleep again but it didn't seem to matter, her body was cramped, she felt weary, sort of bad, ill. Her mind was now picturing light. She saw herself walking over the open land back from

Jarrow to the cottage, and she realized that time passed differently when it was spent in light. You didn't really think of time in the daylight not unless you had to get somewhere in a hurry. There were so many things that showed up in the light and took up time, like the sky and the grass and cows in a field, and the burn. She liked the burn. Some says when it was running low and the water just dribbled over the stones it appeared to be talking, chatting. And then there were the larks. They made you forget time. You put your head back and tried to follow their flight, but even when you couldn't see them any more you could hear them. . . .

The scream that ran through her head seemed to be mixed up with the lark song and she pulled herself upward crying loudly, "What is it? What is it?" She felt his arms flaying and realized that she must have slipped while she dozed, for her groping hands now found his head resting against a stone. Now she was to the side of him, her arms about his shoulders pushing him upward, and when his scream turned to a shuddering moan she felt his face pressed tight into her shoulder and she stammered, "Are . . . are . . . are you in pain?"

His mouth was moving against her neck; she felt his tongue come out and he gulped several times before he said, "Yes."

" 'Tis bad?"

"Yes." The word seemed to have required effort and she could feel the air leaving his chest and his shoulders hunching.

She said in an apology now, "I . . . I must have dozed an' you slipped. Look." She put out one hand now and felt the twisted surface of the stones to the side of them, and coming to a crevice she put her hand in and pulled gently, then a little harder, and when she felt the stone was tightly fixed she said again, "Look, if you could put your hand in here and hang on for a few minutes, I . . . I could rake some stones and props from along there and build up under you so as you could rest. It's . . . it's the way you are lying that's hurtin' you. Can you do it?"

He twisted his body around and her hand guided his into the small cleft, and now he muttered, "Yes, yes; go ahead."

Like a mole now she scrambled here and there and pulled the loose debris toward him. Once she lost her direction and when, feeling the wall again, her hands didn't find him she yelled, "Where are you?"

"I'm . . . I'm here." His voice came from just to the side of her, not an arm's length away, and she gasped as if in relief and stumbled toward him, dragging two broken props.

As she gradually built up the mound she kept easing him upward, saying, "Is that better?" and when he didn't give her any answer she knew that the angle of the stones was still not right.

Not until she had built up the support until it had almost reached her waist did he say, "Yes, that's better, thank you, thank you."

"Is . . . is the pain any easier?"

"Yes, yes, it's bearable now. It's . . . it's mostly down my right side; I don't feel much at all in the left leg."

"Well, your right is just caught a little bit just around the ankle."

"It's . . . it's likely cramp."

"Yes, yes, it could be cramp, sir."

She slumped down exhausted by the side of the pile, and presently he said, "Where are you, Trotter?"

"I'm here, sir."

"Would . . . would you give me your hand, Trotter?"

"Yes, sir." She put her hand out gropingly toward him, but when she felt his fingers entwine with hers she could feel her change of color even in the darkness. Just a short while ago she had been holding him, his face had been pressed into her neck, and his head had lain between her breasts, but that contact was different from this. He had asked to hold her hand.

"Hands are comforting things, don't you think, Trotter?"

"We'd . . . we'd come badly off without them, sir." She felt she had said something funny and she smiled in the darkness, and as if he had seen her smile he answered, "Indeed we would, Trotter. Indeed we would. How old are you, Trotter?"

"Coming up eighteen, sir."

"I never knew you were in the mine. In fact if I had known this was your intention I would have endeavored to put you off."

"I . . . I needed work, sir."

"Yes, I can understand that, but this is the lowest type of work for a woman, and I shouldn't think you're suited to it."

"They tell me I'm quite good at it, sir."

"How long have you been here?"

"Since three days after I left the Manor, sir."

He didn't speak for some minutes and then he said, "I should have seen to you but . . . but as you know the house was in an upheaval."

"Yes, sir. Oh, I understand, sir."

"Why didn't you go to the farm to your friend Bentwood? He was a friend, wasn't he?"

"Yes, sir."

"You stayed there after the fire, didn't you?"

"Only for a short time, sir. I . . . I left the day me grandma was buried. I went back to the cottage. That's . . . that's when you found me there and kindly offered me the post."

"But . . . but why couldn't you stay on the farm? I am sure he could have found you something to do. I thought about that at the time. Why didn't you?"

When she didn't answer he said, "I'm . . . I'm sorry, I appear to be probing into something."

Her fingers were now gripped so tightly that she wanted to cry out, and when the darkness was filled with a long shuddering groan she got to her knees; then putting out her other arm, she placed it around his shoulders and held him to her, saying, "There, there. There, there."

"Oh-my-God!" He released the grip on her hand and she put it up to his face. It was running with sweat. Tears in her eyes now and in her voice, she said, "If only I could do something for you."

It was a long moment before he answered, "You are doing something for me, Trotter, you're here. There . . . there, it's gone, I don't feel anything at all now. It just comes in spasms. I . . . I suppose I'm not used to pain. When I come to think of it, I've never been ill in my life. Toothache yes. I . . . I once had two teeth pulled and I remember I raised Cain . . . What is it? What is it? Oh, please, don't cry. Now, now, don't cry like that. Look—' his hand was on her cheek now and his voice was soft as he said, "What am I going to do if you fail me? I shouldn't have thought you were the kind to have vapors, Trotter?"

"N . . . no, sir; I'll never have the vapors."

"Good; I really didn't think you would. Sit by me and rest. You know I . . . I don't think we should be talking, they say it uses up the oxygen. But . . . but the air seems quite clear. What do you think?"

She sniffed and said, "Yes. Yes, sir, it does since the dust's settled. Would there be any way fresh air could get in, sir?"

He thought a moment before he answered, "No, I don't think so, Trotter, not from inside anyway. If this fall is not too thick and it hasn't affected the main roadway there's a chance there might be a crevice among the stones. Yet—" his voice sank almost to a whisper as he ended, "I think that's too long a shot to hope for."

The grip of his fingers slackened once more and she realized he had fallen asleep again, but now she made no effort to rouse him because she, too, was feeling tired and she told herself she'd have a doze for a little while, it would do her good, and also pass the time until she heard them knocking, because that's what they did, the rescuers, they knocked on the stones and you answered.

How many times had he said he was dry during these last hours, or was it days? It must be days. Her head was muzzy, she wanted to sleep. It was some time ago that he had said, "The air's going, Trotter, start knocking again."

She had knocked for a short time, but she had no strength in her arms now, they didn't seem to belong to her, she just wanted to sleep. But when she fell asleep she was always awakened by his groaning. He didn't cry out loudly any more, he just groaned, and when it went on too long she forced herself to kneel and hold him.

She was holding him now and he was gasping for breath. She no longer said, "Does it hurt?" or "They'll come soon, sir," and when his words came slow and soft, as if pressed down by the atmosphere, saying, "I . . . I think the end is almost near, Trotter," she did not contradict him, for she knew within herself the end was almost near. But somehow she wasn't afraid, she would be warm if she was dead. She felt sure of that, warm all the time. Not like now, burning one minute and cold the next, but just warm and comfortable.

"It's all right. Sit down, you're tired. Just give me your hand."

She slumped down again while keeping hold of his hand.

"Do you believe in God, Trotter?"

"I don't know, sir. Sometimes yes and sometimes not. My . . . my granny did, and granda too."

"They were a nice couple."

"Yes, yes, they were."

"Trotter."

"Yes?" She was aware that she wasn't adding "sir" so much now when she answered him, but what did it matter?

"I'm going to tell you something. I . . . I was lonely this morning. Or was it yesterday, or some other time? But I remember I was lonely, and now I don't feel lonely any more. Strange, but I don't."

"That's good," she said wearily. She wished he would stop talking so she wouldn't have to answer. She felt a bit sick, more than a bit sick, she was feeling bad, real bad.

As if he had heard her wish he said no more, and after a time she forced herself to kneel up and to put her ear toward his mouth to see if he were still breathing. And when she slumped down again it was to ponder on the thought that the reverence she seemed to have had for him while in the Manor was gone. He could have been the check weighman or the agent or Sam. . . . Sam had wanted to marry her, he had told her so, and contrary to what she had said to Simon her reply had been no, and a definite no, even though she had said it in a nice way telling him that she didn't want to marry anybody yet, but that she liked him. And in answer to a further question he had put to her, she had said, no, she hadn't anybody in her eye. Sam would be very sorry about her going. Would Simon? Yes, oh yes, Simon would be sorry. And he'd blame himself. Anyway, why bother to think. Her teeth were chattering again. Why was she cold? It wasn't cold in here, anything but. She moved slightly to make her position easier on the stones because the way he was holding her hand her arm was being pressed against the jagged end of a prop. Then a most strange thing happened: the wall of rock just below where the master's feet must be pinned opened and out stepped her granny and granda, and they came and sat one each side of her and she felt a happiness that she hadn't experienced before. And it didn't matter that they didn't speak or answer her questions, they were there.

It was three and a half days before the rescuers got through to them, and the way hadn't been made through the fall of stone. This would have been impossible because the fall had blocked the main road too. They came through the side of the drift, just a foot to the side of where the last prop had been pulled from the roof.

When they found them they knew it was impossible to remove Mark Sopwith without amputating both feet, in fact one leg below the knee. As for the girl, she was still breathing when they brought her out but they thought there was little chance that she would live. They carried her through the crowd lining the bank; sightseers had come from as far away as Newcastle and Gateshead because it wasn't every day that the owner of a mine got a taste of what his men often got. Such was the feeling.

It was as they placed Tilly in a covered cart that Biddy pushed her way forward and demanded, "Where are you takin' her?"

"The hospital, the workhouse hospital in Shields."

She turned and looked at Sam; then they both stood and watched the tail board being put into place.

"Has she got a chance?" It was Katie now speaking to one of the men, and his answer was, "Hard to say, lass, but I doubt it. The only good thing that can be said for her is she's whole, unlike the boss who's lost his feet."

"My God!" The murmur carried the news around the crowd.

When half an hour later they moved the closely

wrapped form of Mark into the daylight an open landau was waiting with planks laid from door to door, and a mattress on top of these; and so with one man at each horse's head and another two supporting the temporary platform on which Mark now lay, they slowly drove him home.

PART THREE

The Workings of the Witch

1

For one full week he existed in a nightmare in which he imagined that he had no feet. As a child he had been subject to bad dreams; an unknown fear would overtake him and when he went to scream no sound came and he would wake up sweating, the bed clothes in a heap about him.

As he grew older the intervals between the nightmares lengthened but the intensity remained, and in some way his mind had taught him to recognize the experience of the nightmare when in the midst of it and he would wake himself up, saying, "It's only a dream. It's only a dream."

But now the nightmare had been with him solidly for seven days and when he was in the midst of it he would yell at himself, "It's only a dream. It's only a dream," but unlike his awakening in years past he now recognized the nightmare as real, and not being able to bear the thought he forced himself to descend into the fantasy of the dream again. When on the seventh day he could no longer dream he made himself look down the bed toward the hump of the wire cage that covered the place where his feet should be and, even now clinging to his dream, he told himself they must be there because they were paining.

As he gazed down the coverlet a strange face intruded itself in front of the cage and a strange voice said, "Ah! we're awake. There now, you feel better this morning?"

He looked up at the bulbous bosom covered in a white starched apron and at the round face above it topped by the frilled white cap, but he made no reply, and the voice went on, "Now we'll have some soup, won't we?"

A minute later he almost screamed aloud as the nurse, her arms underneath his oxters, attempted to prop him up against his pillows. What he did was to take his hands and with all the strength he could gather push violently at her; and as she reeled away the set smile slipped from her face and, indignantly, she said, "Now! now! I was only trying to make you comfortable."

"Well, don't do it like a dray horse." His voice sounded strange to his ears—it was hoarse, cracked.

"Doctor Kemp is on his way up," she said stiffly.

His answer was to turn an almost ferocious glance on her. There was a wild anger inside of him, he wanted to claw, smash, rend. He looked down at his hands where his fingers like talons were grabbing up fistfuls of the silk counterpane.

The door opened and Simes stood aside and ushered Doctor Kemp into the room.

The doctor was a small man. He looked robust, jolly and well fed, and his voice matched his appearance in heartiness. "Well! well! now this is better, we are really awake at last. Well done! nurse. You've got him looking bright and. . . ."

"Shut up!"

Bot the doctor and the nurse stared at him in amazement and when he added, "Get out!" while flicking a finger in the direction of the nurse, Doctor Kemp put in, "Now! now! what's all this about?"

"Oh my God!" Mark now lay back on the pillow, grabbed the front of his head with outstretched hand and cried, "Don't ask such bloody silly questions." And glaring again at the nurse, he said, "Did you hear me? Get out." And on a wave of indignation the nurse went out.

"That isn't very kind." Doctor Kemp's face was

straight. "Nurse Bailey has looked after you very well this last week."

Had he been conforming to pattern Mark should have said, "I'm sorry," but what he did say was, "Tell me about this?" stabbing his finger toward the bottom of the bed.

"Ah well, it had to be done."

"Why? In the name of God, why? Couldn't they have removed the stones?"

"Yes, they could"—Doctor Kemp's voice was as loud as Mark's now—"but you would have been dead by the time they got you out, along with those attempting to move the fall from the inside. I did what I had to do."

"You did it then?"

"Yes, yes, I amputated, and only just in time. They were going rotten on you, man. You'll be lucky even now, let me tell you, if you get off without gangrene setting in."

"Thank you, thank you, that's good to know."

"Well, you're alive, you should be grateful."

"What! you've taken off my feet and you tell me I should be grateful!" The spittle ran down his chin as he finished, and he wiped it roughly off with the side of his hand.

"Life is life after all. It could have been worse."

"Could it? Really! tell me how."

"Yes, I'll tell you how." The doctor was standing close to him now, his plump body pressed against the side of the high bed. "You could have been blinded, as one of your men was three years ago; you could have been caught up to the hips with no hope of ever getting out of that bed again; but as it is you'll be able to get about on a wooden leg and with the help of crutches."

Mark closed his eyes, then sank deeper into the pillows. Of a sudden his anger seemed to be seeping away with his strength; he felt tired. It seemed a long moment before he spoke again, and then he said, "Eileen, I suppose she was told?"

"Yes."

"But she hasn't been?"

"No. But your mother-in-law came. She stayed two days, but you didn't recognize her or anyone else at that time. I told her I would keep her informed, which I have done."

"And Eileen didn't come?" The words were soft, almost as if spoken to himself, but the doctor answered, "She's a sick woman, you must take that into account."

Mark turned his head slowly and looked at Doctor Kemp, and he said, with almost a sneer on his face, "I wish I were as well as she is at this moment. As for being sick, you know how sick she is, don't you, doctor?"

"She has the usual woman's complaints." The doctor had turned from the bed now and was going through his bag which he had placed on a table, and he said, "I must have the nurse in, and if I may offer you advice I would say be civil to her because you're likely to be together for some weeks yet."

Mark said nothing to this; instead, he asked, "Were many killed?"

"No, no; only a girl."

"A girl?" The word brought him up in the bed supporting himself on his stiffened arms and he turned toward the doctor and said, "She died then, Trotter? Aw no! No!"

"No, it wasn't the girl Trotter, it was a small child, Pringle. Her father died almost in the same area three years ago, you remember?"

Yes, yes, he remembered. And so it was the small girl who had died, a child he had pulled out of the water. It was all coming back now like pictures shown by a magic lantern. Trotter, she had held him and comforted him. During all that time he had not seen her face but he could see her plainly in his mind's eye.

"The girl, Trotter, what happened to her? Was she all right?"

286

"No, she wasn't all right, and she still isn't. She got pneumonia."

"Where is she now?"

"The hospital, the House hospital in Shields."

He lay back on his pillows again. The workhouse hospital. He knew what that was like. And she had pneumonia. Pneumonia needed care. She had come through that dreadful ordeal in the black hole only to die under the rough care that one would receive in the workhouse hospital.

"Nurse." Doctor Kemp was calling, and when the nurse entered the room the atmosphere became chilly indeed.

It was when the examination was over, the bandages changed, and Nurse Bailey was handing the dish of blood-stained wrappings through the half opened doorway to Amy Stiles that Mark said in an undertone, "I would prefer a man to look after me."

"You have a man at nights, Simes is with you then, but you require a nurse. And I have great faith in Nurse Bailey, so be a good fellow and be civil to her."

Just before the doctor left, Mark said, "The mine, how is it?" and Doctor Kemp busied himself with his bag for some seconds before he answered. "There's plenty of time to go into that," he said; "you get your strength back and then you can deal with those matters. Now be a good fellow." He nodded toward him as if to a small boy, then went out, followed by the nurse, and Mark, lying back exhausted, said half aloud, "Well, that's the end of that then. The end of so many things." Then presently he added, "Pity I didn't let Rosier carry half the weight after all."

2

When Tilly saw the tall figure of Biddy Drew marching up the narrow ward she half rose from the stool by the side of her bed before sinking back on to it again, but when Biddy stood over her her hands were extended out to greet her.

"Aw, Mrs. Drew, it's good to see you."

"An' you, lass, an' you."

Their joined hands wagged up and down for a moment. Then straightening herself, Biddy looked about the ward, sniffed hard, and shook her head before she exclaimed, "My God! lass, Katie said it was bad, the smell's worse than our middens."

"You get used to it."

When Biddy went to sit down on the side of the bed Tilly hissed quietly, "You're not allowed to sit on the bed, Mrs. Drew, they . . . they don't like it."

"Well, like it or not, lass, I'm gettin' off me legs for a minute"; and so saying, she sat down.

Tilly, smiling weakly at her, moved her head as she said, "Oh, 'tis good to see you."

"I would have come afore this but I've been hard pushed. Still, Katie an' Sam have kept me posted as to how you're going on. By! you were thin afore, lass, but you'd make a good clothes' prop now."

"Yes, I would, wouldn't I. . . . How are things?"

"Not much better, lass, I'm sorry to say, except that Sam's been set on in a candle factory. But what he's gettin' there won't keep him in shoe leather. 'Tis a bad time of the year for work for anybody, the winter." She now leaned forward and gripped Tilly's wrist as she said, "I want to thank you, lass, for lettin' us have what was in your bundle. It saw us through a couple of weeks, it was a godsend. And I'll repay you sometime, I will, I promise you I will."

"You've repaid me already, Mrs. Drew; you gave me a home when I needed one badly."

"Aye, well, that's what I've come about the day. When are you coming back to it?"

"Well, they told me I can only stay in the ward another two or three days and then I've got to go into the House."

"You're goin' into no house, except me own. The House indeed!" She tossed her head. "I've heard about the House, an' my God! this is bad enough."

"Most of them are old people."

"I can see that, lass."

"Anyway, I suppose I should be grateful they pulled me around. By the way, how did you get here? Did you walk all that way?"

"Well, I set out to walk, lass, but I was lucky, there was a cart passin' takin' stuff into the market. It was from the Manor. One of the gardeners was driving it and he gave me a lift. All talk he was about the goin's on there."

"Did . . . did he say how the master was?"

"Oh aye, he talked about little else. Turned out a real tartar, he was saying, going a bit off his head he thinks."

"The master going off his head? No!"

"Well, that's what he said. Anyway, he's making himself felt, feet or no."

At this Tilly bowed her head and bit on her lip, she couldn't bear to think of him without feet. She had lain at nights thinking about what he must have gone through when they cut them off and her thoughts had made her vomit.

"Sacked the nurse he did last week." Biddy was laughing now. "Threw something at her, the gardener said. There's war on in the house because everything's upside down. He has the footman looking after him and by all accounts he's not having a pleasant time of it either. Swears like a trooper, he says, and was never known to swear afore. Well, it seems that he's rousing them, and by what you told me afore, lass, it'll do some of them good. . . . Have you had anybody else to see you?"

"Yes; Steve came. You know the boy, Steve McGrath. And . . . and Simon, Mr. Bentwood you know, the farmer, he's been every week." She turned her head away and after a moment Biddy said quietly, "And what does he propose to do for you, lass?"

She looked quickly up at the older woman and she saw that there was nothing that Biddy didn't guess at; then lowering her eyes again, she said, "He . . . he wants to get me a room, or . . . or some place in Shields."

"And what then?"

"What do you mean, Mrs. Drew, what then?"

"You know what I mean, lass. Some farmers are still rich enough to afford a kept woman on the side, is that what you intend to be?"

"Oh no! No!" Tilly shook her head. "I wouldn't, Mrs. Drew."

"I know you wouldn't, lass. Well, what you've got to do is, as soon as the doctor passes you clear of this ward, an' you say that's in a day or so, well then you've got to make your way back home. You can get the carrier cart from the market, that's if you can't get word to any of us to come an' fetch you. It'll take you beyond the village, not a mile from our door. Do you think you'll be able to manage that?"

"Oh yes, Mrs. Drew, yes. And thank you. The journey can't come soon enough for me."

They looked hard at each other, then gripped hands.

Three days later Tilly made the journey from the workhouse back to the pit row. She caught the carrier cart from the market place, but when she alighted at the turnpike road she felt that her legs wouldn't carry her as far as the house.

It was three o'clock in the afternoon and there was a slight flurry of snow falling. Before she was half-way there she'd had to stop several times and rest with her back against a tree or a stone wall or a gate leading into a field; and when eventually she arrived frozen and looking on the point of collapse, Biddy dragged off her outer clothes and her boots and chafed her frozen limbs all the while ordering those about her to put a hot brick in the bed, to put on the bone soup that was to be their evening meal to heat, and Tilly took all the ministrations without uttering a word.

Within half an hour she was tucked up warmly on the shaky-down. And there she lay for the next few days. The day following her getting up, she was sitting before the fire when a knock came on the door, and when Biddy opened it there stood a young woman warmly dressed who said, "I'm from the Manor, I'm Phyllis Coates, the master sent me an' . . . an' Mr. Leyburn." She jerked her head to the side, indicating a man standing by the side of a coach. "Could I have a word please with Tilly, Tilly Trotter?"

"Come in." Biddy's voice was quiet. She was asking herself why she hadn't heard the coach coming up to the door. But then there was a thin hard-caked layer of snow on the ground. She looked toward the coachman before shutting the door; then she walked slowly toward the fire where the visitor was bending over Tilly.

"Hello, Tilly. How are you?"

"Oh, fine, fine, Phyllis. 'Tis nice to see you. It was good of you to call."

"Well, I haven't come on me own." She turned to where Biddy was pushing a wooden chair toward her and said, "Ta . . . thanks"; then sitting down, she began rapidly, " 'Tisn't me at all that should be here, 'tis Mrs. Lucas, but . . . but she couldn't come. She made an excuse, the snow, but the master had given orders that she was to come and ask you to go and visit him."

"Visit him?" The repeated words were a mere whisper.

"Yes"—Phyllis nodded—"that was the order that came down from upstairs. It wasn't given to Simes, it was given to Pike and he told Mrs. Lucas. But you don't look up to goin' for a drive, I'll say that straightaway."

"I'm . . . I'm all right, Phyllis, just a bit wobbly on me legs."

Tilly now watched Phyllis glance around the room, and her glance which took in Fanny, Jimmy, and Arthur, who were sitting close to one side of the dull fire, showed that she found the stark poverty distasteful.

"The master's kept in touch about your condition through Doctor Kemp, and . . . and he ordered Mrs. Lucas to send you stuff from the kitchen. Of course you know I'm upstairs most of the time, and she said she did, but I've got me doubts . . . did she?"

"No, Phyllis, no, I've received nothing from the Manor."

"Eeh! the old bitch." Phyllis now turned and glanced at Biddy, saying, "It's the housekeeper, she always had it in for Tilly here. But now she won't be able to do much 'cos the master wants to see her. Do you think she's fit to travel?"

Biddy seemed to consider for a moment. She looked

down into Tilly's upturned face; then, as if making a decision, she said, "We'll wrap you up, lass; you'll be riding all the way, you can't come to much harm. Come on, get on your feet."

Tilly got on her feet, and Biddy bundled her into her coat and hat, and over her shoulders she placed her own shawl. A minute later when Tilly went to follow Phyllis out of the door she turned and, putting out her hand, she placed it on Biddy's chest, and Biddy, putting her own hand over it, said below her breath, "Take whatever comes, lass, grab it with both hands; he's not just takin' the trouble to send for you to say it's a cold day."

Tilly was not a little puzzled by Biddy's advice. Hadn't she warned her against accepting a room from Simon? Of course she couldn't mean the master was offering her anything like that, that was silly, but why had she said take what comes and grab it with both hands? Perhaps she was referring to money. But she hadn't done anything to be rewarded with money. Anyway, she'd know when she saw him, she'd know why he wanted to see her when she got there. . . .

As she was helped up the steps and through the lobby into the big hall there arose from some place within her, that was almost forgotten, a thread of laughter, merry laughter, sardonic laughter. She had been almost thrown out of the back door last year and here she was arriving in a coach. And being shown in through the front door! But her reception, she noted immediately, was anything but pleasant, because Mr. Pike, who had always been civil to her, looked at her now with a face lacking even the slightest warmth. As for Mrs. Lucas, who was standing at the bottom of the stairs, well, as Katie would have said, vinegar was sweet.

That there was little semblance left of the Tilly Trotter who had once worked in this house was evident when she came to a stop in the middle of the hall and, slowly pulling the shawl from around her shoulders, handed it to Mr. Pike.

That the man was amazed by her brazen gesture she was well aware, and the thread of laughter widened in her as she stared at him for a moment ignoring the fact that Mrs. Lucas was waiting and that Phyllis was looking at her open-mouthed. Yet as she looked at the butler, whose existence in comparison with those people living in the rows was one of high luxury, she found herself thinking the most odd thought. He wasn't alive. None of them here were alive, for they really knew nothing about life, not life as it was lived by those who groveled in the bowels of the earth. That occupation made you savor life, life on the surface of the earth. Even if you only had skimmed milk and a crust and a few taties for your diet, you relished life in a way that these people knew nothing about.

Although her legs were wobbling beneath her long faded skirt, there came into her a strength that made her walk steadily toward Mrs. Lucas and say, "I understand the master wishes to see me?"

Mrs. Lucas opened her mouth, then closed it again, turned and floated up the staircase without having to resort to holding the banister, as Tilly found she herself had to do before she was half-way to the landing.

Then they were crossing the gallery and going down the wide west corridor. Presently Mrs. Lucas paused, cast one glance in Tilly's direction before knocking on a door, then opened it and stood aside while Tilly passed her. She had not announced her in one way or the other but she stood long enough to hear her master, who was sitting in the long basket-chair in front of a blazing fire, exclaim loudly, "Hello, Trotter. Well! hello."

It was, as she said to them all in the kitchen a few minutes later, as if he were greeting an equal. She had never heard the likes of it, and it didn't portend good. Mark her words, it didn't portend good.

"Sit down. Sit down. Take off your coat. Simes, take Trotter's coat and hat. Sit down. Sit down."

Just as she knew that she herself had changed during the past year, so she now recognized that the master had also changed, but within a shorter time, for his voice and manner now were different from those she had recognized in the dark; but then she told herself, he must have been changing since the time the mistress left him. In any case, there was one thing certain, he had changed.

After she was seated in the big chair opposite to him, he looked at her for a full minute before turning to the footman and saying, "Leave us. Oh and by the way, tell Mrs. Lucas to have tea sent up, a good tea, sandwiches, cake. . . ."

"Yes, sir."

When the door had closed on the footman, Mark leaned forward and asked quietly, "How are you, Trotter?"

"Quite well, sir."

"Well, you don't look quite well. You were thin before, you're like a rake now."

She laughed gently, then said, "So I'm told, sir. Mrs. Drew says she'll never be short of a clothes prop."

He smiled widely, then said, "You're staying with the Drews?"

"Yes, sir."

"A bit crowded, isn't it?"

"Yes, 'tis a bit crowded. But they're good people; I'm happy there."

She drew in a long breath then looked toward the fire, and she remained silent waiting for him to speak again. When he did it was to ask her a question. "Did you ever think we'd see daylight, Trotter?"

"No, sir."

"Nor me either." And now his voice became a mutter as he ended, "And I've wished more than once since that I hadn't."

"Aw no, sir, no! don't say that."

He turned his face toward her now and, his mouth smiling, he said, "Can you remember all that transpired down there, Trotter?"

"Now I can, but at first when . . . when I was in the hospital I couldn't call anything to mind except the blackness."

"Yes, I think that was the hardest to bear, the blackness. You know the mine's finished, Trotter, flooded out?"

"So they tell me, sir."

"And you know something else, Trotter?"

"No, sir."

"I'm not sorry." Again he looked toward the fire when he went on speaking: "I must have been only half conscious most of the time but I remember you vividly. You talked to me like a mother." His eyes came toward her again. "You held me when I was yelling my head off, and God! how I yelled. That pain. Anyway, there's one thing certain, Trotter, I'll never own a mine again."

"Oh. When the water goes down, sir, you could start it up."

"Not me, Trotter, not me. I knew nothing about mines until I spent those days, and it was days, wasn't it? . . . three and a half days we were together down there. Well, that gave me a lifetime of experience of what men go through. No"—he shook his head slowly—"I'm finished with mining. Let somebody else have it on their conscience but not me. I'm not strong enough to stand that kind of thing, I've got a weak stomach." He laughed; then his face falling into lines that made him look almost like an old man, he sat staring at her, and she was so troubled by the sadness in his countenance that she wanted to extend her hand toward him, just as she had done in the darkness. But that would never do. No, that would never do.

"I sent for you, Trotter, for one or two reasons. First, because I wanted to see you and thank you for bringing me through that awful time."

"Oh, sir, I didn't do. . . ."

"Be quiet. Be quiet. I know what you did. But the other thing was, I wondered if you would be well enough to come to us over the holidays. I'm hoping to have the children here to see me. It might only be for two or three days but if you could. . . ."

"Oh, sir, yes; oh yes, sir, I would love that." She moved forward on her chair and bent toward him eagerly as she said, "Nothing would give me more pleasure, sir."

"Good, good; that'll make me happy too. I'm longing to see them."

"I can understand that, sir."

"Of course we've got to take the weather into account, but I think we'll have a thaw and the roads will be clear. Ah"—he turned toward the door—"here comes tea."

Simes was entering the room carrying a large silver tray on which was set a silver tea service. He was followed by Amy Stiles. She was carrying a four-tiered cake stand on which there were plates of bread and butter, sandwiches and cakes. She set the stand down to the side of the table which was placed against the basket chair. She did not raise her eyes and look at Tilly, nor did Simes look at her, not even when the master said, "That'll do; Trotter will see to me," did they look in her direction.

When the door had closed on them, Mark, leaning toward her, said, "Pretend you're back in the nursery and about to feed the five thousand."

She smiled as she rose hastily to her feet, and after she had poured out the tea into the thin china cups she laid a napkin across the shawl that covered his legs, then handed him a small plate with one hand and extended the large plate of bread and butter toward him with the other. But he shook his head and said, "I rarely eat at teatime," and taking the bread plate from her, he poked his head toward her as he said softly, "Tuck in."

She wanted to act polite as her granny would have wished, but her stomach told her that politeness was stupid in this case, and so she tucked in. She had four pieces of bread and butter, she had three sandwiches and two pieces of cake, and as she ate she tried to do it delicately, not as her appetite bade her and gulp. She had never tasted food like this for months, and not even while she had worked in this house, for then the bread in the kitchen had been cut in collops. At one stage she became embarrassed that he didn't talk while she was eating but sat looking at her, and then he said, "I hope you got all the things I sent you when in hospital?"

She swallowed deeply, staring at him, her mouth slightly agape; then the color suffused her thin cheeks and she was about to say, "Yes, thank you," when he asked pointedly, "You got the packages?"

She gulped again before she now said hesitantly, "Yes . . . thank you."

"You didn't get them?"

She bowed her head, then turned and looked toward the window as she said, "No, sir, I didn't get anything from you."

"Bloody lot of thieves!"

It was strange to hear him swear, but in this moment he sounded very much like Sam when he was railing against the check weighman or the pit masters as a whole.

"Things go astray in a hospital, sir."

"If my orders had been carried out, Trotter, these things would not have gone astray. I ordered special food to be sent four times, it was supposed to have been delivered to you."

She watched him grind his teeth, then droop his head

toward his chest as he said, "Things are not right in this house. This is what happens when there's no mistress to take charge."

As she stared at him she could have said, "Things were happening like this when the mistress was here, sir," but she doubted if he would have believed it.

"Well"—his head bobbed on his shoulder now—"someone will pay for this, you mark my words."

"Please, please, sir, I . . . I don't want to cause trouble. You see I've got to face this. They didn't like me when I was here, except Mr. Leyburn and Phyllis, Phyllis Coates. The rumors from the village had followed me, about . . . about me being a witch, and things like that. They resented me, and at the same time, although it's hard to believe, sir, they were a bit afraid of me, and . . . and once or twice I played on that with Ada Tennant—she's the scullery maid you know." She smiled now and for the first time she asked him a direct question, "Do I look like a witch, sir?"

She saw his shoulders move, and then he began to chuckle before surprising her with his next remark. "Yes, yes, you do, Trotter, you look very much like a witch, but a kind witch, a benevolent witch."

"Oh, sir!"

"You charmed my children anyway into some semblance of order, especially when the rip went. Well now, to get back to the question of the children. I would like you to get the rooms prepared upstairs. I asked Mrs. Lucas this morning if anything had been done up there of late and she had to admit that there hadn't. She put it down to the fact that they had all been very busy and concerned about me." He pulled a slight face. "I can smell an excuse a mile off. Yet"—he sighed now—"I've got to admit we're very understaffed; for the size of this house we're very understaffed. You know, Trotter, in my father's time you couldn't move for maids and menservants, you were tripping over them. Ah well, those days are gone. Now"—he leaned back in the chair—"when do you think you'll be fit to start?"

"Oh, any time, sir."

"Well, I wouldn't say any time; by the look of you I think you are in need of a few more days' rest. Would you like to to come here and take it? Your room is still vacant, I imagine, upstairs."

"Oh no, sir, no, sir." The words came at a rush. "No; I'd better not come before I'm needed."

He made no immediate answer, but stared at her for a long moment before saying, "Someone of your disposition, Trotter, will always be needed. . . . Well, say three days' time?"

"Yes, sir."

"In the meantime, by the look of you I think you need feeding up. Ring that bell there, will you?" He pointed to a thick twisted rope with tassels which was hanging to the side of the fireplace, and as she pulled it twice, which was the signal that he needed attention, she imagined she heard the clanging of the bell in the kitchen and the reluctant scurrying toward the stairs.

When Simes came into the room, Mark turned to him and said, "I had chicken for lunch, I hardly touched it; tell cook to pack it up. And also the remains of the pressed tongue and a couple of jars of preserves. And tell Pike that I need a bottle of burgundy. When was the last baking done?"

"I . . . I wouldn't know, sir."

"You're below stairs and you don't know when the cook was baking! Couldn't you smell it, man?"

"I . . . I think yesterday, sir."

"Then tell her to send up a couple of loaves and cakes too, and bacon, a couple of pounds of it . . . the best end."

"Yes, s . . . ir." The words were spaced now, and when Simes was almost out of the door his master stopped him with, "Wait! I want them packed in a hamper and brought up here. I wish to inspect them, you understand?"

Again the man said, "Yes, sir." But now the words were clipped and a slight agitation showed in his manner.

Tilly was sitting now on the edge of her chair. She was embarrassed; he was meaning all this food for her to take away with her. She should refuse it. But no, she wouldn't. She could see it all spread out on that bare wooden table; she could see the gleam in the eyes of the youngsters, especially when they saw the cakes. But mingled with her embarrassment was a certain bewilderment, she was puzzled by his manner. All the time she had been in this house before she had never heard him speak to the servants as he was doing today. But then she had never heard him talk as he was talking now. As she had thought earlier, he was a different man from the master she had respected, and an altogether different man from the one she had come to know down in the darkness. There was a roughness about him, and a hardly suppressed anger.

Her eyes resting on the foot of the chair where the cover, instead of being supported by the toes of two feet, dropped smoothly over the edge, she thought sadly that it was because of his feet he was fighting inside of himself, because of his feet he was taking it out of the staff, likely because there was nobody else to take it out on. None of his own people were with him. That was sad. Why didn't the mistress come back? She was no woman to leave him like this alone. Granted she was poorly, but her presence would have been a comfort to him.

"What are you thinking, Trotter? You're miles away."

Caught off her guard, she turned her eyes quickly from the foot of the chair and said, "Oh, something that me granny used to say."

"What was it?"

What did her granny say? Her granny had so many sayings. "Well, she used to say, when one door shuts another one opens."

"And you think one has opened for you?"

She smiled brightly now, knowing she could say in truth, "Yes, sir. This time last week the future looked pretty black, no work, nothing, and now I'm to have my old job back, well, just for a short while. But . . . but I'm very grateful. And yes, as me granny would have said, the door has opened for me, sir."

His face was straight and his eyes looked blank as he said now, "The people in the rows are all out of work, what are they doing?"

"Travelin' the road, sir, looking for jobs. Sam, he was one of your hewers, perhaps you won't remember him, but he was the one that Mr. Rosier sacked because he was learning to read."

"Oh yes, yes, I remember him all right."

"Well, he's got work in a candle factory. It's nothin' compared to the mine but . . . but it's something. The fear among them is of being turned out on to the road and. . . ." Her eyes widened, her mouth fell into a slight gape—she had forgotten for a moment to whom the cottages belonged. When she closed her mouth and gulped he reminded her of the very words. He gave a slightly mirthless laugh as he said, "You forgot for the moment, Trotter, didn't you, you were talking to the landlord?"

Her head was down and she said, "Yes, yes, I did, sir."

"Well, you can tell them they're safe for a time, until the place is sold. In any case, whoever takes over might start the mine up again." He made a jerking movement now and brought himself up straight in the chair and, leaning well forward toward her, he said, "Don't pass that on, Trotter, I mean about anybody taking the place over."

"No, sir, I won't."

"You give them the assurance that they're not going to be turned out but . . . but the fact that I may eventually sell the place, well that slipped out, you understand?"

"Oh yes, sir; yes, sir; I'll say nothing about that."

"Ah! at last." He turned and looked to where Simes was entering the room carrying a weighty hamper, and he said to him, "Place it down there," pointing to the floor between the basket chair and Tilly's feet; then without looking at the man, he said, "Tell Leyburn to have the coach around in . . . well, what shall we say?" He looked toward the window. "It's getting dark, say fifteen minutes' time. Then you return and take this hamper downstairs and place it in the coach." He paused now, then looking up quickly into Simes's face, he said, "You heard what I said, Simes, didn't you? Place . . . it . . . in . . . the . . . coach."

The man's face was red, his manner definitely troubled.

The door closed again. "Well, now," he said, "take what's left on that stand, Trotter, and put it in the hamper."

"Oh, sir, there's enough."

"Do as I tell you, girl."

She did as he told her, and then she closed the lid and, rising from her knees, she looked down at him as she said softly, "Thank you, sir. I'm grateful, so grateful."

When he held out his hand she placed hers in it, and as he shook it gently he said, "If I remember, we prepared to die like this, didn't we, Trotter?"

There was a lump in her throat. "Yes, sir; we did that."

"You're a good girl, Trotter."

"Oh, sir." She shook her head, holding back the tears; then turning quickly, she picked up her hat and coat and after she had placed the hat squarely on her head and buttoned up the coat to the neck she sat down once again on the edge of the chair waiting, and he, quiet now, sat looking at her.

She was so young, so thin, so poorly clad, but there was something about her face that was ageless; it was a kind of knowledge in the back of her eyes. It was the eyes that gave off the witch impression, he supposed. They were deep brown yet clear like pebbles that had been constantly washed by the sea, no impurity in them. She could have been his daughter born between Harry and Matthew. She intensified the longing he had to see his children, to hold Jessie Ann in his arms again. The anger that had subsided during this last hour or so rose for a moment and he cried inside, "Damn! Blast her to hell! She's cruel, cruel." Why hadn't she come back? Any woman worth her salt knowing the predicament he was in would have returned, if only to lie on her chaise-longue again. He had the dreadful feeling he was going to cry. He blinked and turned a thankful glance as the door opened and Simes came in once more.

Tilly was on her feet now. "Good-bye, sir," she said, "and thank you so much. I'll . . . I'll be here on Monday."

"Good, good. Thank you, Trotter. I'll have the coach sent for you."

She wanted to say, "There's no need, sir, I can walk"; instead, she remained silent and inclined her head by way of acknowledging his kindness. Then she went out, followed by Simes carrying the hamper.

There was no one in the hall; Biddy's shawl was lying across the back of a carved hall chair standing between the windows. She picked it up and placed it around her shoulders. There was no butler to open the door, and she noted that Simes had to place the heavy hamper on the floor before he undid the latch of the front door. Then so hard did he push it back that it hit the wall with a resounding bang.

Fred Leyburn was standing on the gravel drive

awaiting her approach. He had taken the hamper from Simes and placed it inside the coach, and now he held out his hand and assisted her up the step, and as he did so, he murmured, "Be careful, madam," and when from under her lashes she looked at him, he winked broadly at her, which made her almost fall on to the seat. She had a most inordinate desire to laugh, yet she knew it wouldn't remain ordinary laughter but would be the kind of laughter that finished up with her crying.

A door had opened just a little bit; she somehow sensed it could swing wide, and if it did, as Mrs. Drew had advised, she was going to take whatever came through it and grab it with both hands.

3

"It's a bloody conspiracy."

"Don't you dare use that language in my presence, Mark Sopwith!"

"Well, it is. If you could travel the road why couldn't the children?"

"Because as I told you both Luke and Jessie Ann have developed whooping cough."

"Well, in that case I say again, Matthew and John would be well out of it."

"Doctor Fellows advised strongly against it. Anyway, you have Harry coming for the holidays, you won't be alone."

"Harry is a grown-up man, I want my children around me. . . . She's done this on purpose, hasn't she, just to spite me?"

"Don't be so childish, Mark. Really! you have become impossible. She was very concerned for you."

"Huh! she's shown it. If she was concerned she would have been back here."

"She's in no state to see to an invalid."

"She wouldn't be expected to see to me, and well you know it; but she should be here."

"What! and countenance your mistress?"

"Hell's flames, woman!" He tossed his head from one side to the other; then grabbing a book from the table he flung it across the room, bawling, "I've no mistress! It was finished long before she got wind of it."

Jane Forefoot-Meadows stood with her hand gripping the black velvet bow pinned to the top of her plum velvet dress. That she was shocked and not a little frightened was evident, and she stood speechless staring at her son-in-law while he, his head bowed, muttered now, "I'm sorry, I'm sorry, only I'm so damned lonely here, mother-in-law." He lifted his head now and looked at her and asked quietly, "Have you any idea what my life is like? The contrast is too much to take at once, a house buzzing with children's voices and a complaint every time I open the door about one or other of them being up to their tricks, then an almost empty house; well, empty of every person that mattered to me. That was bad enough but I was able to get out, go to work, ride, move"—his voice was rising again—"but now!" He turned his hand palm upward and held it out toward the bottom of the long chair. "I tell you, Mother-in-law, sometimes I feel I'll go mad."

"Doesn't anyone visit you?" Her voice was soft now, her tone sympathetic.

"One or two, the men; but they always come alone, they never bring their wives. Sometimes I want to laugh, but most times"—his head drooped—"I just curse."

"I've noticed that in the short time I've been with you. Yes, I've noticed that." Her voice was astringent again. "You never used to use such language."

He looked up at her, and with a twisted smile on his face he said, "Yes, I did, but not in front of you or the children." And now he put out his hand. "Forgive me. I . . . I appreciate what you've done in coming yourself, I do really."

She came and sat beside him and asked, "When is Harry coming?"

"The day after tomorrow I think. He was here the first two or three days after they found me but I didn't know much about it. It was no use him staying; he couldn't do anything and he had accepted an invitation at the end of term to go to France with a friend of his. But by his last letter he should be here two or three days before Christmas."

"That'll be nice; you won't be alone."

"No, I won't be alone."

They sat in silence for a few minutes, and then she said, "Doctor Fellows is looking into the business of—" She stopped embarrassed, and he prompted, "Yes? Tell me. About the feet?" She wetted her lips and inclined her head, then said, "Yes. But he thinks it might be six months or more; what I mean is, they can't do very much until the wounds are . . . well, healed."

"Yes, I understand."

"There is a man in Scarborough who has been fitted with a complete leg"—she was nodding at him now, warming to her theme—"and no one would ever believe it, you can't tell which is the real and which is the artificial one. Of course, in your case it will be slightly more difficult because. . . ."

"Yes, yes, Mother-in-law," he interrupted her, closing his eyes tightly.

"Oh. Oh well, I was only trying to tell you."

"I know. I know." He nodded slowly.

There came a tap on the door and after he had called, "Come in," the opening door revealed Tilly, but she stopped when she saw Mrs. Forefoot-Meadows.

307

"Come along in. Come along in, Trotter," Mark called to her. "I've disappointing news for you. Mrs. Forefoot-Meadows has just come to tell me that Jessie Ann and Luke have caught the whooping cough, and so, of course, none of them will be able to travel."

"Oh!" Her face registered her disappointment. "Oh, I am sorry."

"This is Trotter, Mother-in-law." He turned to Jane Forefoot-Meadows. "You may remember, she was the children's nurse."

If Jane Forefoot-Meadows did remember she showed no recognition, she merely inclined her head and said, "Oh yes."

"She is also the young woman who was incarcerated with me down below; she was the one who kept me sane during those three and a half eternities we spent together." He turned and smiled at Tilly, but Tilly did not answer his smile; she was looking at Mrs. Forefoot-Meadows and Mrs. Forefoot-Meadows at her.

Again Mrs. Forefoot-Meadows said, "Oh yes," and on this Tilly turned and took her leave. But she had not reached the door when Mark, twisting his body around in the chair, called to her, "I'll send for you later, Trotter; stay put until I call you."

She inclined her head and went out, then stood on the landing looking first one way then the other. Nothing was straightforward, nothing turned out as you expected. The door wasn't opening after all. She let out a long shuddering breath and went toward the stairs that led to the nursery floor.

It was almost twenty-four hours later when Mark sent for her. Except for the time it took her to go down the stairs and empty the slops, she had remained in the nursery quarters. Her meals had been brought up to her, though reluctantly it would seem from the attitude of the bearer, whether it was Ada Tennant or Maggie Short, neither of the girls had a word to say to her, they even scurried from her presence as if they were indeed expecting a curse to be put upon them.

It was Simes who summoned her to the floor below. Both his manner and his voice were offensive. He had thrust open the schoolroom door as if expecting to find her at a disadvantage in some way; then jerking his head at her in much the same way as Mrs. Lucas did, he said, "You're wanted down below," and stood staring at her as she rose from the schoolroom table and closed the book she was reading. He watched her as she went to the rack and replaced the book on the shelf. This was another thing that made her different and feared, she could read, not only headlines from a newspaper but apparently books like those in the library down below.

She did not turn immediately from the bookshelf, she knew he was standing watching her, but when she did confront him, her back straight, her voice firm and, she imagined, in a good imitation of Mrs. Ross, she said, "Very well, thank you." The thank you was a dismissal, and it must have brought his lips tight together for he went out banging the door after him.

Her back no longer straight, she leaned over the table and looked down at her hands pressed flat on it and asked of them why they should all hate her so, she had done nothing to bring it about. But there was one thing certain, she would never be able to do anything to make them change their attitude toward her.

When she entered Mark's room he was again sitting in the long basket-chair opposite the blazing fire, and he smiled at her; but it was a thin smile expressing weariness, and when she stood at the foot of the chair and looked at him, he said slowly, "Come and sit down," indicating with a lift of his hand a chair by his side.

When she was seated he said, "Yesterday you looked almost as disappointed as I was."

"I was, sir, very disappointed."

"My mother-in-law has promised me faithfully that,

weather permitting, she'll bring at least one of them on her next trip this way."

"That'll be nice."

He laid his head back against the cushion now and his voice was merely a mutter as he said, "But that won't be for some time; the roads will get worse before they're better."

She nodded. "She's a very brave lady to have made the journey, her being so—" She stopped, she had almost said "old"; and now he turned his face toward her and smiled widely as he said, "You nearly said old, didn't you? My! my! Trotter, you must not even think of that term with regard to my mother-in-law, else all her paint and powder will be wasted. But nevertheless, I've got to agree with you, for her age, which I won't mention, it was very brave of her to make the journey and without her maid. Yes, without her maid. And now about you."

She moved uneasily on the chair.

"What will you do if you go back to . . . the Drews?"

"Look for some work, sir. That's all I can do."

"What will you say if I offer you a post here?"

Her eyes widened for a moment and then, her lids drooping, she moved her head slowly as she answered, "'Twould be no use, sir; they wouldn't accept me, them down below, the staff."

"Because of the witch business?"

"I suppose so, sir. There's something about me they don't like." She lifted her hand in a gesture that implied she couldn't understand the reason.

"Bloody ignorant fools!" he said; then added, "But what if I was to say to you you'd have a position of authority over them, as Price had. Oh, I knew all about Price's authority, she even dominated Mrs. Lucas, didn't she? Well, let me put it to you like this. Simes sees to my wants. Now between you and me"—his voice fell to a whisper and he leaned his head toward her—"I don't care for Simes; he's a subservient individual. You know what subservient means, Trotter?"

She paused thinking. Mr. Burgess had used that word, she had heard him explain its meaning to the children. She couldn't remember the word he had put in its place but she knew the meaning of it. She was smiling as she said, "A crawler, sir."

As his laugh rang out, her smile widened into what could only be described as a grin, and for a moment she felt utterly happy—she had said something to make him laugh. Now if she could only remember some of the things that were said in the Drews' kitchen and caused roars. But he was talking about her position. . . . Her position. She became astounded as she listened to him.

"I had a nurse at the beginning. I didn't like her either. She talked and acted like a sergeant-major and she treated me as if I were still in binders and of the same age mentally. And I cannot talk to Simes—you can't talk to somebody you don't like—but I can talk to you, Trotter. It's strange this. I asked myself last night why it was I could talk to you, but I couldn't find the answer, for after all you haven't much to say. Now, have you?"

"Well, 'tisn't my place, sir."

"No, Trotter, it isn't your place." He sighed. "Haven't we gone through this before? I remember faintly discussing place with you down there. Perhaps I'm mistaken. Anyway, what would you say if I asked you to forget your place and speak first for a change. Tell me what you think, about anything"—he spread his arms wide—"this, that or the other, just so the time will pass."

She stared at him for a moment before she said, "Have you thought about engaging Mr. Burgess again?"

"Burgess? Now why would I want to engage Burgess? I think I'm past the learning stage. I know my letters, at least I think I do." He made a slight face at

311

her, and she smiled as she answered, "'Twas for conversation, sir; Mr. Burgess talks well. I used to like to listen to him talking to the children, he made the simplest things sound . . . well, interestin' like. I could have listened to him for hours. He gave me books to read and. . . ."

"Burgess gave you books to read? . . . And you read them?"

"Some of them, sir. Others were beyond me. The first one . . . well, I can't understand it yet."

"What was the title?"

The title. She thought a moment, then said, "*Can . . . did . . . de.*"

"*Candide.* My God! he never gave you that. Voltaire's *Candide?* Oh, really!"

"Well, he said it was a great adventure and when I told him I couldn't understand it, he said he didn't expect me to, not yet, only if I'd read it once a month for twenty years."

Again Mark put his head back and laughed, saying now, "The old fool."

"I liked him." Her voice had a flat note to it. "He was very kind to me and I learned things from him."

"I'm sorry Trotter." His voice was flat too now. "That remark was meant in a most kindly way. Burgess, I'm sure, is a very wise man. . . . So you'd like me to engage him merely to talk?"

"Well, not only to talk, sir; perhaps he could look after you. He's not all that old; well, what I mean is not too old to work; he can't be seventy."

Mark stared at her. Not too old to work, he can't be seventy. Strange, but he felt he was learning from this girl as she must have learned from old Burgess. "You might have hit on something there, Trotter," he said, "I'll think about it. But now back to you. How about you taking on the position of nurse-cum-matron-cum-dictator of the first floor?"

312

She half rose from the chair but his hand on her knee pressed her down again and when she began "They wouldn't have it, sir, they'd. . . ." he interrupted, "To hell with them, Trotter! Am I master here or not?"

"Oh yes, sir."

"Well, if I say you're in charge of me and of this room and of all that goes on above the kitchen level, then that's how things will be. So what do you say?"

"Oh! sir, I . . . I can't say anything. It's just too big, too much."

"Too big, you say? Well, do you think you're big enough to tackle it, and them?" He flung his hand outward toward the door.

Their glances held, she felt her back straightening, her chin tucking in. The door had opened. Was she going through it? Automatically she placed one hand on top of the other, palm upward in her lap, very much as she had seen Mrs. Lucas do when she was going to lay down the law, and now her face unsmiling but her eyes bright, she said, "I'll be grateful to accept the post, sir."

"Done! Done, Trotter. Well, if nothing else we'll have some excitement in the house during the next few days. What do you say?"

His words almost took the stiffness from her back and lifted her hands from her lap. Yes, indeed there would be excitement. They would lead her a hell of a life; they'd make things unbearable for her. . . . But only if she let them. Yes, only if she let them. And with the master behind her, well, she couldn't fail. Or could she? Could she bear the hostility that would rise up from the kitchen quarters and the servants' hall like black suffocating vapor from a midden bog?

When his hand suddenly came on hers she started visibly, and then her eyelids blinked rapidly as he went on, "When a girl who was entrapped in darkness had the courage not to show her fear but to give her attention to someone who was in dire need of it at the time and to go on doing it for days, well, I would think she would have enough courage to face a few mean-minded people. What do you say?"

She swallowed deeply before answering. "Aye, sir; you would think so."

They now smiled at each other. Then briskly, he said, "You'll have to have a uniform and decent clothes. You'll go into Shields tomorrow or wherever Mrs. Lucas deals and fit yourself out. And by the way, go now and tell her I wish to see her. . . . You afraid?"

"No, sir." She rose to her feet, paused for a moment to look down on him, then walked from the room, her brisk step denying the tremor inside her.

As he watched the door close behind her he lay back and his body slumped into the pillows and he closed his eyes. The days wouldn't be so long from now on; part of the loneliness would lift. Her very presence took him out of himself, and what was more, he was going to enjoy the war that was impending.

Of a sudden a deep, almost shameful sadness enveloped him. His mental state must be very low if the only thing he could find of interest was friction within his staff. As if in denial, he reached out and picked up a book from the table and began to read, and as he did so he thought wryly that his choice of literature would meet with the approval of Mr. Burgess.

4

"I'm not standing for it, it's gone too far. My God! when you come to think of it, I knew from the first time I clapped eyes on her there was something weird about her. She's a witch I tell you, she's a witch."

"Don't be silly, Cook. . . ."

"And don't you tell me I'm silly, Phyllis Coates. You admitted it yourself last night there was something very strange the way she's got around the master."

"Aye, I did, but that isn't to say she's a witch."

"Well, then, you explain to me how a slip of a lass who was brought up livin' from hand to mouth in a cottage on this very estate an' spent most of her days digging or sawing wood, how other has she got the power to entertain a man like the master, an' not only him but now Master Harry? You tell me, Phyllis Coates. Why if she were an educated person you might be able to understand it, but she's an ignorant little slut who's never been further than Shields in her life. Now you explain to me where she gets her powers from."

"She's not ignorant, Cook, she can read and write better"—her voice dropped—"than Mrs. Lucas, so Fred says."

"Aye, and what was the cost of her readin' and writin', ruination of the parson's wife an' him an' all. And don't forget about the farmer, him on our very door so to speak, and the fiasco on his weddin' night all through her. And now Master Harry walking with her in the grounds."

"Someone talking about me?"

The cook, Phyllis, and Maggie Short who was standing stoning raisins at the table, all started and turned toward the kitchen door leading into the yard.

During the period between the death of his mother and the remarriage of his father, Harry Sopwith had been in the habit of running wild about the place, but all this had been put a stop to with the advent of Eileen. And now this was the second time in four days he had come into the house through the kitchen. He was changed was Master Harry, they all said so, free and easy, sort of gay. It was as if he were pleased to find his stepmother gone from the house.

He said again, "Did I hear my name mentioned, taken in vain?" He was looking from one to the other; then, his eyes coming to rest on the cook, he said, "Well, Cook?"

Looking back into the long, tanned face of the young man, cook saw this as an opportunity to make her stand and for her grievances to be expressed in the proper quarters, and so she said, "Aye, you did hear your name mentioned, Master Harry, but not taken in vain." Then remembering how she had mentioned his name, she side-stepped the issue by saying, "We were glad to see you back an' so happy like in spite of the tragedy that has befallen the house, and—" now her fat head wagged on her fat neck and, her lips forming a tight rosebud, she spat out, "And I say tragedy in more ways than one."

"Yes?" He inclined his head toward her.

"Aye, Master Harry. I might as well come clean 'cos things have got to such a pitch we can't go on like this, none of us can." She looked from one to the other. "'Tis that Tilly Trotter, Master Harry."

"Trotter? What's she got to do with tragedy except that she was in it, very much up to the neck so to speak?"

"'Tisn't that tragedy I'm referrin' to, 'tis the trouble she's caused since she's come into the house. It was a peaceful house afore she stepped into it. It began the day she came to look after the children, but then we came back to normal like once she was gone. But now she's back an' life's unbearable, Master Harry."

The tolerant smile slipped from the young man's face and he asked, "In what way, Cook?"

"Well—" She looked from Phyllis Coates to Maggie Short as if for support, then said lamely, " 'Tisn't right, she shouldn't be in the position she's got, not over us. From Mr. Pike downward we all say the same, 'tisn't right. She's even topping Mrs. Lucas."

"In what way? Explain yourself."

"Well"—she tossed her head—"she sends down orders through Maggie Short there"—she jerked her head in the direction of the kitchen maid—"or Ada Tennant who's in the scullery." Her head moved in the other direction now. "She even gives orders to Mr. Pike for them outside. Well, it's not to be tolerated, Master Harry, oh no! We've got our heads together an' I'll tell you this much"—she paused now—"we . . . we want it put to the master"—again she paused—"either she goes or we all go. There, that's how we feel, from top to bottom that's how we feel."

"Oh, those are strong words, Cook."

At this point Mrs. Lucas came through the green-baized door and the cook turned eagerly toward her, almost shouting down the length of the room now. "I've been tellin' Master Harry about that 'un up there." Her head jerked toward the ceiling. "I've told him if the master doesn't get rid of her he'll have to get rid of us, it's one or t'other, isn't it, Mrs. Lucas?"

The housekeeper came to a stop at the top of the table and, looking at the cook, she said, "It is my place, Cook, to say what the staff have decided or not decided, but"—she now turned her head slowly and looked at Harry—"I must say this, Master Harry, things are not right in the house and there's got to be changes or else . . . well, there'll be trouble. You can't run an establishment with resentment like what is filling this house at the present moment."

"Why haven't you put this to my father if you feel so strongly about it, Mrs. Lucas?"

"I . . . I intend to; it's got to be settled."

"Settled?" He bent his head slightly toward her. "Which means I understand from the cook that if Trotter doesn't go you will all go?"

Mrs. Lucas's tight frame gave a slight shudder that brought her head wagging and she said, "Well, yes, something along those lines because I . . . I am at the end of my tether. I'm the housekeeper but I'm not given my position. It . . . it was bad enough when Miss Price was here, but . . . but she was a lady compared with the person upstairs."

Harry's eyes narrowed as he looked at Mrs. Lucas and his voice was quiet and very like his father's as he said, "I have been here four days now, Mrs. Lucas, and most of the time Trotter seems to have been tending my father, seeing to his needs and the business of the rooms. The only time, to my knowledge, that I've known her even come downstairs was when she took the air in the garden yesterday, and except for the twice I've been out riding I've been in the house most of the time. I don't see what you're getting at."

Mrs. Lucas looked at the cook and the cook looked at Mrs. Lucas, then they looked at Maggie Short, but when the eyes turned on Phyllis Coates she had her head bowed and her eyes cast toward the floor, and Harry looked from one to the other and he broke the silence by saying, "I'll inform my father of the situation."

"Thank you, Master Harry." Mrs. Lucas's voice sounded prim.

Harry now walked up the kitchen past Maggie Short and Phyllis Coates, who both dipped their knees, and through the green-baized door into the hall and up the stairs.

Why did they hate the girl? There was nothing about her to dislike that he could see; in fact, he had never seen his father so light-hearted even when he had been able to get about. Yet his father had changed, he was a different man, nervy, he talked louder than he used to, and he was impatient most of the time. Well, that was all to be expected. My God! it must be dreadful to have no feet.

Tilly was in the dressing-room when she heard Harry enter the bedroom and she remained there busying herself with sorting the linen and choosing a shirt and cravat which the master would wear on the morrow. She liked the feel of all his clothes, especially his underwear; as she had discovered down below, the fine wool felt almost like silk.

Their voices came to her muted, then rising and falling, and she did not pay much attention until she heard Mark say, "I'm sorry about Parliament, it will be beyond me"; then Harry's answer, "That's all right, I was never keen on it anyway. But I'll be grateful for another year up there. You can bring it down to a hundred, I can manage on that."

"No, we'll keep it to a hundred and fifty."

"Is there no hope at all of the mine being reopened?"

"None whatever I should say, well, not without a lot of money being spent on it. And you know that's an impossibility for me now, it will take me all my time to support Eileen and the children from my investments, and these, as you know, fluctuate. Should they go down . . . well, I'm afraid this place will sink with them."

"How many have you employed here now, Father?"

"Oh, about a dozen inside and out. It's nothing I suppose, but they all need feeding and clothing and by some of the bills Mrs. Lucas presented me with last week they must be eating their heads off down there. Still, what can you do? I don't suppose it could be run on less." There was a long pause; then as Tilly went to close a drawer her hands became still as she heard Master Harry say, "Where's Trotter, next door?"

"No, I thought she went upstairs. Yes, she went up there. Listen."

She, too, listened to the faint footsteps going across the nursery floor and wondered for a moment who it could be. Then Harry's voice brought her head jerking toward the half-open door as he said, "How do you find her?"

"What do you mean?"

"I mean, how do you find Trotter? Is she quarrelsome, throwing her weight about, anything like that?"

"Don't be silly. What are you getting at? She's the best thing that's come into my life since this happened. Oh"—there followed a laugh now—"you've been hearing the witch story."

"Witch story?"

"Yes, some of them think she's a witch. Can you believe it? Ignorance, you know, Harry, can be really terrifying, for if there was anyone less like a witch than that girl it would be hard to find."

"No, I hadn't heard the witch story. So they think she's a witch, do they? Good heavens! Likely that's what it's all about."

"What what's all about?"

"They want rid of her downstairs."

"They want what!"

"Mrs. Lucas and the cook, I think they're going to present you with an ultimatum, either she goes or they do."

In the silence that followed Tilly's imagination couldn't conjure up any picture of the reaction these words had on the master until she heard his voice filling the room like a bawl now: "My God! an ultimatum? Either they or she? The bloody craven upstarts!"

"Now, now, don't excite yourself."

"Excite myself? God! I wish I were on my feet. I'd give them ultimatum. Anyway, I can do it from here."

"Now! now! now! Father. Now please don't get so excited, you'll only make yourself ill."

"Shut up! Shut up! I'm not an invalid. I'm handicapped but that's all. Anyway, you can tell them to come up and present their ultimatum."

"What do you intend to do?"

"Take them at their word. They go, every damn one of them who won't take orders from Trotter . . . they go."

"But you can't do that, Father, you can't leave the house without a staff."

"I can leave the house without a staff of that kind; and perhaps you don't know it but there are people roundabout here crying out for work."

"But they won't be trained to this kind of work."

"Look, Harry, Trotter wasn't trained. She was an ordinary girl, she had one advantage, she could read and write, but you know something, she's better than any of those damn nurses I had. And as for Simes, well she could wipe her feet on Simes. What's more, she's intelligent. I've thought these last few days, given the chance she could do something, that girl. Old Burgess set her off reading. No, no, it was the parson's wife. But he took her deep into it, Voltaire as ever was. Can you believe it, Voltaire? She admits she doesn't understand it but she will one day I'm sure. But as for that ignorant lot, ultimatum! Well, let them bring their ultimatum. You tell Lucas I want to see her."

"I would . . . I would rest on it, Father, if I were you. The Christmas holidays are on us and it would only make things very unpleasant."

"But aren't they already unpleasant?"

"Well, think it over. Let them come to you."

"Get me a drink will you, Harry? The decanter's in the cupboard in the dressing-room."

Tilly opened her mouth wide, then closed it and turned swiftly to stand with her back to the drawer, her hands outstretched at each side of it. And that was how Harry saw her when he entered the room. When she swiftly put her fingers to her lips he gave a slight nod, went to the cupboard, took out the tray with the decanter and a glass on it, and returned to the bedroom.

A few minutes later, excusing himself, he went into the dressing-room and closed the door; but finding the room empty, he went out into the corridor before making his way to the nursery floor; and as if she had been waiting for him Tilly faced him as he entered the schoolroom.

Smiling at her, he said, "They say listeners never hear any good of themselves, but that wasn't true in this case, was it, Trotter?"

"I'm . . . I'm sorry, Master Harry, I'd no intention of listening but . . . but when you mentioned my name, well, I couldn't get out of the room."

"I understand. Well, anyway, you now know about the ultimatum."

"It's better that I go, Master Harry."

"Oh no, no, Trotter, I don't think so. I . . . well, I agree with my father, there's changes needed in the house, and outside too. Just before I met you in the garden yesterday I had come across both Pilby and Summers fast asleep in the greenhouse. I know it is winter and the ground is too hard to dig but from what I could see during my walk, there were a thousand and one things they could have been doing; the gardens are very neglected. Yes, I think there are changes needed both inside and outside the house, but it is making the change that is going to be awkward. My father thinks he could re-staff from the men and women who are out of work at the mine."

"Aye, yes, he could do that." Her eyes widened and an eager note came into her voice. "I don't want to see

322

anybody pushed out of a job, Master Harry, but I can tell you this much, he could do that and save himself a deal of money into the bargain, because most of them would just work for their food and shelter."

"Oh"—his face stiffened—"that would never be allowed, we're not starting a new slave trade."

"I . . . I wasn't meaning to annoy, Master Harry, but what I say is true. With all the master's workmen and their families, the main concern is food. Yet"—her voice sank—"after saying all that I feel it would be better if I went."

"My father wouldn't hear of it. But don't worry, something will work out. It's strange how such trifles are overcome."

. . . Such trifles.

At half past three the following afternoon Tilly was hurrying back from a visit to the Drews.

Early that morning the master had given her half a sovereign to buy herself a present for Christmas, and she had taken it to Biddy, and Biddy had held her in her arms, and Katie had fallen on her neck, and the youngsters had cried, and she had cried with them.

She had not stayed more than fifteen minutes because she was eager to get back to her duties, and in spite of the bitter winds the whole Drew family had insisted on seeing her to the end of the row, and their cries of "Merry Christmas, Tilly!" as she ran along the road into the deepening gloom had warmed her.

She was taking the short cut behind the lodge at the back gates of the estate when she stumbled into Frank Summers, a small basket of eggs in one hand and a rough parcel from which protruded a side of bacon in the other. They both stopped and stared at each other. It was she who spoke first. "I . . . I advise you to take those back, Mr. Summers," she said.

There was a pause before he answered; then, "Mind your own bloody business you!" he growled, "else I'll give it to you where it hurts most, right atween your eyes. I've had enough of you. The lot of us have. You! You young scut!"

He put down the basket and parcel in front of the door and began to advance on her, and she cried at him, "Don't you dare! Don't you dare lay a finger on me! If you do you'll know about it. Now I'm warnin' you."

But even as she spoke she backed from him and rounded the corner of the Lodge toward the drive, the while he slowly advanced on her, muttering, "You dirty sneaking young runt you! Puttin' Master Harry on to us yesterda'!"

"I did no such thing."

"Who else then?"

"Perhaps he's finding things out for himself." She was still moving slowly backward.

"You're a menace. You know that? You're a menace."

"An' you an' the rest of you are a lot of thieves. You've been robbin' the master for years. You've been stuffin' things in there"—she flung out her arm now—"all summer. You're as bad as them in the house, chargin' the master double for everything with their share-outs once a month. You should be ashamed of yourself, the lot of yous."

"Shut your mouth, you sneaking little witch! The bits we take nobody would miss."

"Bits!" She was yelling back at him now. "Dozens of eggs at one go; and pigs . . . I know, I've seen you at it afore. And they're picked up for the market, aren't they? And the fruit from the greenhouses. For two pins I'd go back right there and tell the master everything."

"You do, me dear, you do, an' you take it from me you won't be able to see out of your eyes or walk for weeks. This is one you haven't got frightened, witch or no witch. . . . Look, I'm not afeared to grab you."

As his hands came on her she screamed and tore at his face with her fingers. But it was all over in a moment because she seemed to be torn from him and thrust into the long grass, and as she saw a whip descend across his shoulders she held her hand tightly over her mouth.

When she scrambled to her feet Summers was standing bent against the wall of the lodge holding his hand to his neck.

"Go on! Get away and pack up whatever belongs to you and get off this land as from today!"

"You . . . you didn't employ me." Summers was walking backward now, still holding his neck. "'Tis only the master can sack me!" and Harry followed him, saying, "Well, I'm acting for the master, and—" He now looked toward the parcel and the basket lying at the lodge door and ended, "Give me the key of the lodge."

"I haven't got it."

Harry turned his head and looked toward Tilly. She did not speak but bent down and groped in the grass. After a moment she found the stone and took from under it the key and handed it to him.

Opening the door of the lodge, Harry went inside. On the bench in the scullery there were three empty fruit skips and, leaning against the wall under the bench, was a sack filled up to its gaping top with potatoes.

Turning to Tilly, he said, "Bring those packages in, Trotter"; and when she entered the scullery, he said, "Put them on the bench there and take up the empty ones."

She did this and went outside again where Summers was standing some distance away scowling darkly. When Harry said to him, "Get back to your quarters and stay there until I come," the man moved his head slowly and ground his teeth before turning away.

Harry now looked at Tilly, saying quietly, "Throw

those skips into the grass. Whoever is going to pick that stuff up"—he nodded toward the window—"will come before dark surely. . . . Can you lead a horse?"

"I . . . I haven't done so yet, Master Harry."

"Well, come." He led the way on to the drive, saying, "He's gentle. Just take the lead, walk by his side, and take him to Leyburn. No, on second thoughts, I'll tie him up along the drive."

"But . . . but what if there's more than one of them, Master Harry?"

"Don't worry; I'm not going to do anything brave, I'm just going to see who picks the stuff up. But I don't think it'll be any of the miners or those really in need, not if, as you say, this has been going on for a long time."

She lowered her head as she muttered now, "I've . . . I've wanted to speak about it but I knew it would only cause trouble."

"You say inside is as bad too?"

"Worse, if anything, Master Harry. The bills could be lessened by half, I know that."

"Are they all in it?"

"Aye, yes."

"Good Lord!" He jerked his head. "How does it work?"

"They dish it out according to their positions."

"And you? How did you come off when you looked after the children?"

Her head was bent again. "They allotted me coppers, I didn't want it but . . . but they had enough against me so I took it to keep the peace."

"Well, well, we live and learn. I know there's always bound to be rake-offs, but I thought it would only be the butler with the wine, you know, or the housekeeper getting a little percentage back from the tradesmen. But you think everything has been doubled?"

She didn't answer for a while, but then moved her head in an uncertain movement, saying now, "Well, I don't know what the bills were but it seemed a lot of money to me that was doled out from Cook's book.''

"Cook's book?" There was a high inquiry in his voice now.

"Well, she was over the kitchen staff and . . . and. . . . Oh, I feel terrible, Master Harry, saying all this.''

"Well, you're only confirming what I already overheard from the road. And apart from that, I think I came just in time because that man was vicious, he could have done you an injury; and apparently''—now he poked his head toward her—"he isn't afraid of witches.''

She didn't smile, she was sick to the pit of her stomach. Mr. Pike, Simes, Mrs. Lucas, the cook, Maggie Short, Ada Tennant, Amy Stiles, Phyllis Coates—Oh aye—Phyllis. What would happen to Phyllis? And Fred, Fred Leyburn. And then the outside men. She didn't care what happened to Summers, nor yet to Pilby, but Mr. Hillman . . . well, he had his cottage, and his wife wasn't in the best of health either. She had at one time been one of the laundry maids but she'd had to give it up when the daily ones came in. . . . It was Christmas and they'd all be out of work. She'd be putting them out of work. Oh no, she couldn't take the blame for that.

"Go along now; but don't say anything to my father.''

She turned away and went up the drive and into the house by the side door, and when she reached her room on the nursery floor she lit the candle and sat down for a moment on the side of the bed. She was still in her outdoor clothes, but she was cold right to the heart of her. What was it about her that seemed to invite trouble? Was she so different from other girls? No, not that she could see. The only difference was that she could read and write a bit; but as yet her writing wasn't up to much. These two accomplishments were the only

difference that divided her from the rest of youth
because she was sure her feelings were just like those of
other girls of her age: Katie, for instance, although she
was younger; Maggie Short in the kitchen. There now
came a doubt in her mind. Did they lie awake at night
thinking of love? Not by anybody. Oh no not by
anybody, just by one person. But no matter what they
thought, people didn't react to them like they reacted
to herself. And it wasn't only women who were against
her, it was men too. They either loved her or hated her,
there was no in between, no friendliness. That's what
she wanted. If she couldn't have love, then friendliness
was the next best thing, and at this moment that
seemed as remote from her as the nightly desire and
dream that Simon Bentwood was laying his head on
her breast.

She rose from the bed and took off her coat and hat
before putting on her bibbed apron and her white linen
cuffs; smoothed her hair back, then adjusted her
starched cap on top of it and, ready, she went down to
the next floor.

5

The Christmas holidays came and went, as did New
Year, and there was no jollification in the house. The
staff were perturbed; since the dismissal of Summers
they had been waiting daily for a call to the master's
room; but no such call had come. It was as if the master
was ignoring the whole affair, and soon there were
heard murmurs among them that Frank Summers
deserved all he got, doing a bit on the side like that.
And apparently not just a bit, by what John Hillman let

out, because both Pilby and Hillman had been in on it. Nobody else had known about it, not even Leyburn because his work mostly kept him to the yard. But that the master was annoyed about something was evident in the fact that this year there had been no Christmas gifts sent down to the servants' hall, and no message to Mr. Pike to take a bottle or two from the cellar. But that hadn't stopped him, of course. Then again, they thought this omission could have been because there was no mistress in the house and it was usually the mistress who remembered these kinds of things.

So with time passing and Mr. Harry now gone, their anxiety disappeared, although the perplexity still remained, and there was resurrected the feeling against —that one, because again, hadn't she been the cause of trouble? If she hadn't sneaked on Frank Summers he'd still be here, wouldn't he? So what was going to be done about her? Nobody was safe as long as she stayed.

Then out of the blue the call came down to the kitchen. The master had summoned Mr. Pike, and Pike came back downstairs on legs that were feeling decidedly weak, and he, summoning Mrs. Lucas, the cook, and Simes, announced, "The master wants to see you all."

On this Mrs. Lucas demanded, "Why wasn't I informed if the master wanted to see any member of the female staff?"

And to this Pike replied wearily, "What you forget, woman, is that I am really in charge of the house, but I've let you take the lead for years, it's saved trouble. And now let me tell you, I think we're all in for trouble."

Tilly opened the door to them and she could have been an automatic hinge on it for all the notice any of them took of her for their eyes went directly to the basket-chair and the man sitting upright in it.

They stood in line at the foot of the chair and Mark looked at them: the tall, thin, weary-looking Pike, the narrow-faced Simes, Mrs. Lucas looking like a small tightly stuffed model of a human being, and the woman Brackett, the cook, looking as if she had sampled every dish she had ever cooked in her life. Strange, he had only seen her twice in as many years but she seemed to have doubled her size. His eyes slid from her to Trotter who was going into the dressing-room, and when the door closed on her he turned his attention to the group before him, and it was to them as a group that he spoke.

"I have been waiting," he said, "for you coming to see me, because I understand that you have a proposition to put before me. Is that so, Mr. Pike?" His voice was quiet, his tone even, and there was about his manner a casual air that deceived them all; yet not quite in Mr. Pike's case, and he, knowing he should be spokesman, was finding difficulty in answering his master, and he blinked and he shuffled his feet on the carpet, rubbed his hands together as if he were washing them, then said, "Well, sir, it's . . . it's . . ."

"Yes, go on."

Mr. Pike now switched his eyes to the side and to where Mrs. Lucas, who was looking at him, as also was Jane Brackett, and the cook's irritation made evident by the sudden movement of her hips told the housekeeper that if she wasn't careful Jane Brackett would get in before her, and so she, looking at her master, said, "He finds it difficult, sir, as . . . as we all do, to speak . . . to speak about this matter."

"What matter?"

"Well—" Mrs. Lucas proved she had a body inside her uniform because it stretched and her neck craned around to the dressing room door, and now her voice dropping a number of tones, it came over just above a whisper as she said, "Trotter, sir."

"Trotter!" Mark's voice sounded high with surprise. "What about Trotter?"

"Well, sir. . . ."

330

It appeared that the housekeeper was in the same difficulty as the butler, and this being evident Jane Brackett could see the whole interview coming to nothing, or at least going against them, so it was she who broke in. "Begging your pardon, master, it isn't my place I know, 'tis Mr. Pike's or Mrs. Lucas here to put it to you, but . . . but it's got to be said and we all think alike, sir, from the top to the bottom." She now looked at Mr. Pike standing at one side of Mrs. Lucas and at Simes on her other side, then continued, "Trotter is a bad influence like. There's been no peace in the house since she's come, and what's more . . . well, as Mrs. Lucas here will tell you"—the rolls of fat on her neck indicated the housekeeper as she jerked her head—"nobody's got their place any more. You see, master, as you know, you don't have to be told I'm sure of that, you have your place on a staff and it gets your bile when someone like the likes of her start throwing their weight about and giving orders."

"Trotter throwing her weight about? That surprises me, Cook. She has always appeared very diffident to me, rather shy."

"Oh! master"—she was nodding at him—"people can be taken in. We know what we know, don't we?" She looked from one to the other again. "It . . . it was the same when she was on the nursery floor, nothing went right in the house, she seemed to brew trouble, and . . . and now it's worse."

"Really!" He hitched himself slightly up in the chair; then leaning forward and his manner definitely expressing sympathy and his voice low, he said, "And what do you suggest I should do?"

Jane Brackett felt exuberant. There now, why hadn't they done this before? And she dared to move so much out of her place as to take a step nearer the foot of the chair and, her voice low now, she said, "Get rid of her, master."

"Get rid of her?"

"Yes, master."

"But what if I can't." He didn't say won't, but as if appealing to her he used the word "can't," which emboldened her now to say, "Well then, master, I'm afraid you're in for trouble. Well, what I mean is, begging your pardon, we said it afore Christmas but we let the holidays go by, but you see . . . well"—she attempted to straighten her front shoulders—"it's either her or us. You'll lose your staff, master, if you don't get rid of her, and . . . and we've proved ourselves, we've been with you for years, Mr. Pike here the longest, since a lad he's been in your family, and I've served you well for the last ten years, master, and. . . ."

"Yes, yes, you have, Cook, yes, indeed, you have served me well for the last ten years." He was now leaning back against the pillows. "But you haven't served me as well as you've served yourself, Cook, have you?"

Her face changed color. She didn't speak, no one spoke, nor moved, and now he lifted his eyes from one to the other before he said, "You've all served yourselves well, haven't you? How much have you made out of *your* little book, Mrs. Lucas?"

"S . . . sir!"

"And you, I understand, Cook, have a special book for your fiddling. Summers wasn't in it, *you* ran your racket, didn't you?" His voice hadn't risen but his manner had changed and the words that he was speaking were dropping like pointed icicles on their heads. "Now your proposition is that I get rid of Trotter or you go. Well now, for your information I am keeping Trotter, so what does that tell you?"

Still no one spoke.

"You, Simes, and you, Mrs. Lucas, and you, Brackett, will take a week's notice as from today. I will allow you a month's pay in lieu of further notice. As for you, Pike, I'm going to give you a choice, you served not only my father but also my grandfather, but although it is an understood thing that the butler has his perks, it is also understood that they don't amount to robbery. Now you may go with the rest or you may stay. You needn't answer now, you can fight that out when you get downstairs. In the meantime, there remain four other members of the indoor staff: those who wish to stay you will send up to me; after they have been you will bid Leyburn, Pilby, and Hillman to come to me. That is all."

"'Tisn't right."

"What isn't right, Simes?"

"To . . . to be thrown out like this."

"But you don't care for your position, Simes."

"I've . . . I've never said. . . ."

"No, you've never said but your attitude when you thought I was at your mercy was at times nothing short of callous. You can leave me now, all of you; and I think, Simes, you had better help Mrs. Lucas out, she needs your assistance."

Pike and Simes with Mrs. Lucas between them made for the door, but Jane Brackett remained staring at him, her mouth open to speak; but no words came, and she didn't move until Mark's voice, at the pitch of a shout now, cried, "Leave me, woman!"

She left, wobbling, he thought, like a fat bull at a cattle show.

It was some minutes before Tilly made her appearance in the room. Her face was ashen white, her head was bowed, and so he cried at her, "Don't let your conscience on this matter bring you low, Trotter, you didn't start this business. Now by what Harry worked out for me, the household expenses can be cut by half, and that's something to be considered at this time, that is providing you're successful in arranging what we talked about yesterday. . . . Lift your head."

She lifted her head, then said, "They'll be out of work, sir, I can't help feeling sorry. . . ."

"Did they feel sorry for you? They would have had

you thrown out and never turned a hair. That woman, that cook, she's vicious. My God! to think one has been served by such as her." He turned his head to the side. "You just don't know what goes on in your own house. Anyway, remember what you once said to me." He smiled slowly. "It seems so far away now, like a dream, but I remember you saying, when one door shuts another one opens. Well, this afternoon take the coach and carry out what was decided on yesterday. . . . Well! come on, look pleased, girl."

"I am pleased, sir." Her voice was soft, but she could have added, "I'm afraid too because the cook, Mrs. Lucas, and Simes now have joined the villagers."

The Drews' kitchen smelled of wet clothes, sweat and the fumes that come from banked-down coal dust. There was no blazing fire today, the free coal was finished and the only way to keep some sort of a fire going was to rake the pit heap.

The kitchen was crowded, all the family were indoors with the exception of Sam.

They had greeted her, each in his own particular way, the older boys with jerks of their heads and a smile which expressed their liking, but the girls, Katie and Peg and Fanny, crowded around her and their welcome was none the less warm because she had come empty-handed. And this fact was brought into the open by Jimmy suddenly saying, "You brought nowt the day, Tilly?"

There was the sound of a crack as Biddy's hand contacted her son's ear, and when he cried, "Oh, ma!" she yelled at him, "And I'll oh ma you if you don't keep your mouth shut. That's the only thing about you that grows, your mouth." While the others laughed, Tilly put her hand out and drew Jimmy toward her side and, smiling down at him, she said, "I haven't come empty-handed."

She was aware of the eyes all on her now and of some slanting from her toward the door and the coach outside. They still couldn't get used to her coming to visit them in a coach and she was aware that the older ones were trying not to imagine there was something fishy behind the privilege afforded her.

Now they were waiting, and she savored their waiting; then putting her hands out impulsively and grabbing Biddy, she pulled her down to a chair, saying, "You'd better sit down before you fall down when you hear me news."

Like a troop advancing to a central point, they all came slowly toward her, but she continued to share her glance between Biddy and Katie who was standing at her mother's side, and slowly she said, "Can you cook, Mrs. Biddy Drew?"

Biddy closed her eyes for a moment and turned her head to the side; then looking at Tilly again, she said, "Yes, ma'am; given the ingredients, I'm not a bad hand at cooking."

"Good. You're engaged. Miss Drew"—she now looked at Katie—"would you care to assist your mother in the kitchen? I'm aware that you are no hand at cookin' but there's hope for you, you could learn."

"Eeh! Tilly, what you gettin' at?"

"Aye"—Biddy's face was straight now—"what you gettin' at, lass? Come on, don't keep us in the dark."

Tilly straightened her shoulders and looked around them with tenderness, and she said quietly, "You've all got jobs if you want them."

"All of us?" Biddy pulled herself to her feet.

"Aye, and not only you but one or two of the men down the row, the Waters and Mr. McCann, but they'll only be on part time. . . ."

"Eeh! My God! jobs. You mean it, Tilly?"

"Where's this to be, Tilly, I mean the jobs for the men, Tilly?"

"Listen. Listen, and . . . and it mightn't suit all of you, at least not the older ones, but . . . well—" She now said, "Can I sit down?"

"Out of the way!" Biddy swept two of the boys from the front of the form, and Tilly, sitting down, began from the beginning, filling in the parts that Biddy or Katie knew nothing about which was the hate that had been directed toward her in the house, and also the fiddling that had grown out of all proportion both in the house and in the grounds, and then she ended, "It wasn't really me, it was the master who thought of you."

"I'll believe that when they give me wings." It was Alec speaking and she turned to him and said, "It's right, Alec."

"With a little push from you." Katie accompanied this by digging Tilly in the side playfully with her fist.

She went on talking while they gazed at her openmouthed, and she ended, "Ada Tennant's staying, she's the scullery maid, and Phyllis Coates, the first housemaid, she's staying, but Amy Stiles . . . well, I think she wanted to stay but she was frightened of the cook and so she's going. So you, Peg, would be under Phyllis. As for the men . . . well now, there's a point here. The master, I think, is up against it in more ways than one as the mine's finished, an' as I see it he's still got to support the mistress and children, although they're staying with her mother, so in all cases the wages won't be anything like you got in the pit. But what you will get is your food, good food, the men an' all, and that's something."

Biddy now dropped her head back on her shoulders and looked up toward the ceiling and what she said was "Something? It's everything, lass. Oh, thanks be to God in Heaven!" and her head coming slowly down, she added, "And to you, Tilly Trotter. It was a lucky day for us when our Katie stumbled across you."

Katie smiled and again punched Tilly, and she,

turning and looking at Alec who was the eldest there, said, "Well now, Alec, there's you and Arthur and young Jimmy here"—she pressed the boy to her side— "what would you feel like working outside, I mean digging and clearing and seeing to the vegetables and things like that? There's little livestock, only hens and pigs, but there's piles of land that used to be cultivated for vegetables and now it's all overgrown, and . . . and as I put it to the master, not only is there enough space to grow stuff to feed the whole household but, just like they've been doing on the side, it could go to market and help to pay your wages."

"Lass"—Biddy gripped hold of Tilly's arm—"as long as we can eat through this winter we'll work like Trojans, because what more is needed if you have food, heat and shelter?"

"Will Sam see it that way, Mrs. Drew?"

"Oh aye, lass, Sam 'll see it that way, I can promise you. And so will the Waters and McCann and any other that could get work for their food."

"But their jobs mightn't last all that long. Over the winter months perhaps. And yet I don't know." She looked over their heads toward the smoldering fire and said, "All that land there, a couple of horses and a plow."

"And it used to be under plow. There used to be a farm at this end of the estate an' all at one time, so I'm told."

"Oh, speaking of farms, that reminds me. Not that the farmer was here, but the young lad, Steve, he came on Sunday expecting you to be here and was asking how you were."

"You'll have to look out for him, Tilly." It was Alec laughing and nodding toward her now, and she looked at him solemnly as she said, "He's just a friend, a childhood friend"; and under the warning glance from his mother, Alec said, "Aye. Aye."

Biddy now, to the surprise of her entire family,

turned her body sharply around and, dropping her head on to the table, began to cry. Such was the amazement of all her brood that no one moved for a moment. They had never seen their mother cry, not one of them could remember ever seeing her shedding a tear, not even when their father died. They had heard her making strange noises in the bed that night, but they hadn't actually seen her cry.

"Aw, Ma! Ma!" The protest came from all of them and she lifted her head and said, "'Tis all right, you cry when you're happy, and aw, lass"—she turned to Tilly—"the sight of you this day and what you've brought us . . . well, I'll never be able to thank you, lass."

Tilly herself felt the rising of tears in her throat now. It was wonderful to be liked, to be loved, and she felt that Mrs. Drew loved her like she did each one of her children. She rose to her feet now, saying, "I'll have to be getting back."

It was as she went to the door that Katie said softly, "If that lad calls again what shall I tell him?"

"Oh"—Tilly turned to her—"just say I'm all right and thank him for calling."

"He was askin' did he think he could call up at the house now that you're settled there in a good position, and I said I didn't know but when I saw you I would ask you."

"Come on. Come on, our Katie, let Tilly get away. It wouldn't do for him to go up there. You don't want him up there, Tilly, do you?"

Tilly looked at Biddy and said, "Well, it could be awkward."

"Aye, I'm sure it would. Well, I'll deal with him kindly when he next comes."

"Thanks. Ta-rah." She spread her smile over them, and they all answered, "Ta-rah! Tilly. Ta-rah."

Biddy stopped them all from following her into the road, but as Tilly went toward the coach and Fred

Leyburn, who was standing flapping his arms about himself to keep himself warm, Biddy followed her, and at the step she whispered, "You'll let me know when, lass?"

Smiling now, Tilly said, "Oh dear, I forgot. On Saturday afternoon; they'll be gone by then."

"Well and good, lass."

Biddy stood back. The wind, taking her apron, threatened to lift it over her head, and she pressed it down with her hands and remained standing so until the coach rolled away past the end of the muddy row.

PART FOUR

And the Bewitched

1

The early months of 1840 were to Tilly like time spent in a new world. All her long life she was to look back upon them as a form of awakening, for it was during these months that she learned to take on responsibility. She learned the sweet taste of deference, but above all she learned what it was to be a constant companion to a man, a gentleman. There was also bred in her a new fear, or rather the resurrection of the old one, for most of the work that the Drew boys and Mr. Waters and Mr. McCann had done outside in the way of planting had on two occasions been completely trampled to ground level.

It was after the second devastation that the master had ordered the setting of man-traps. As Sam had said to her, he hated the very name of man-traps and the men who laid them, and also he hated the men who ordered their laying; yet after seeing their efforts reduced to nothing he had been forced to consider another side to the business, and in anger he himself had helped to set them up and put a notice on both lodge gates to the effect that the grounds were trapped.

The destruction in the garden had definitely been the work of a number of men, and Tilly didn't know if they came from the village or from Jarrow, which was Jane Brackett's home. But she had a suspicion, as they all had, that the raids had been planned in Jarrow, for the cook had been known to say that if it was the last thing she did she'd bring "that 'un" down, and not only her but the lot of them.

But today was bright, a high wind was scudding the clouds; it had been blowing for days as if in answer to Tilly's prayers to harden the roads, because if the master was to be disappointed this time he wouldn't be able to contain himself. There were times of late when his frustration had burst forth in temper and he had stormed at Mr. Burgess and everybody who came near him, including herself; not that she minded, nor did Mr. Burgess. Mr. Burgess was wonderful with him. His half-daily visits when he helped to bathe him and talk to him had brought a new interest into his life.

For herself she had discovered something afresh about Mr. Burgess. He liked to gossip, and that he brought the news of births, deaths and scandals to the master's ears she was well aware, particularly, she thought, about the scandals because often when she was entering the room Burgess would change the conversation and in a way that wouldn't have deceived a child.

The house, she had felt for weeks, was growing happy. It was cleaner than she had ever seen it. And even at this early time of the year the gardens were looking different. Paths had been weeded, hedges cut, ground that hadn't seen the light of day for years had been cleared. John Hillman was working for his money these days, but he was seeing that all those under him did the same, and the result was pleasing, so much so that Mark had talked of getting a wheel-chair to take him around the grounds, for he couldn't see himself ever being able to stand on false feet which would enable him to use crutches.

So on this bright morning Tilly, excitement and not a little apprehension filling her, was making a tour of the house to see that everything was in order for the arrival of Mrs. Forefoot-Meadows and the children. She was as excited about the children coming as was the master.

All the furniture in the dining-room was glowing, the

344

epergne in the center of the table sprayed out daffodils, and the silver on the long mahogany sideboard gleamed; and in the drawing-room the fire was blazing in the grate, the lace drapes at the long windows had all been washed, the heavy velvet curtains and pelmets had been taken down and brushed, even the tops of the oil paintings surrounding the walls had been dusted. Tilly was satisfied there wasn't a speck of dirt anywhere.

In the hall a big blue vase of ferns banked the great newel post at the bottom of the stairs; the red stair-carpet that was worn in parts had been taken up and relaid and the effect, Tilly thought, was almost like new.

On through the house she went. The nursery floor was in readiness, the room that she had once occupied was now given over to Katie, whose work it would be to tend to the children during their three days' stay in the house. Her own room now was at the other side of the dressing-room, and she still couldn't get used to the difference. A feather bed, a huge wardrobe with full-length mirrors for doors, a wash hand-stand with her own bowl and jug and a slop bucket so pretty that she hated to pour dirty water into it.

She stood now in front of the mirror. It wasn't often she had time to stand and appraise herself, but when she did she was always surprised at the reflection. She was eighteen but she looked older. Perhaps it was her uniform, a beautiful uniform, gray alpaca. The waist clung to her like a skin. The skirt wasn't very full; they had wanted to put another panel in it but she had said no. That would, she had thought, be aping the ladies, and she felt she had stepped out of her place enough without her dress causing comment. She was wearing drawers now for the first time in her life, and also boned stays. She didn't mind the drawers but the stays she found cumbersome; yet she wore them because there were what was called suspenders hanging from the bottom and these kept up her white cotton stockings better than garters.

Her cap was different too; this one didn't cover all her hair but sat on the top of it, as she laughingly thought to herself, like a starched crown.

She moved closer to the mirror and touched the skin of her face. Her complexion wasn't bad. She knew she was being mealy-mouthed, but she couldn't say, it's lovely, 'cos as her granny would have said, never believe what the mirror tells you 'cos you only see what you want to see.

She now fastened the top button of her dress, smoothed her hands down over her hips, then went out into the corridor, turned into the dressing-room and there paused for a moment to see that everything was in order, then went in to the bedroom.

Mr. Burgess was sitting by the cane chair and his head was back and he was laughing, and the master was laughing too. His face was flushed, his eyes were bright, and he was looking different this morning, younger. He had taken pains to brush his unruly hair flat across the top of his head. He was wearing a white silk shirt with a ruffle. He had also, she noticed, forced himself to put on trousers, which she considered was a big step forward, for he mostly spent his days in his nightshirt and dressing gown. However, the small cage this morning was across the bottom of the chair with a rug covering it, but his dress and the way he was sitting gave the impression of wholeness.

"Well, Trotter, done your rounds?"

"Yes, sir."

"Everything in order?"

"As far as I can see, yes, sir."

"And the meals? As much as I enjoy roast beef, roast lamb, meat puddings and such I don't think they will satisfy my mother-in-law's palate. Have you seen the cook?"

"Yes, sir; we discussed the meals last night."

"And what did you hatch up?"

"Well, sir, Mrs. Drew thought of starting with white soup, and then a bit of boiled salmon with sauce, and the main course to be roast chicken with carrots and mashed turnips and other vegetables; then she was making a choice of puddings, cabinet pudding or rhubarb tart and special custard with eggs, I mean made with eggs"—she laughed—"and fruit—she could have a choice—and then there's cheeses."

Mark turned now and looked at Mr. Burgess, saying, "What do you think of that, Burgess?"

"It sounds very appetizing, sir, very appetizing indeed, in fact it's causing my juices to rise." As he spoke he got to his feet and now looked at Tilly, saying, "I'm sure Mrs. Forefoot-Meadows will be pleased.'

She did not answer, except that her eyes smiled at him.

Mr. Burgess now turned to Mark, saying, "I will leave you now, sir, if I may, but I shall be here in the morning and share your pleasure in seeing the children once again."

"Thank you, Burgess, I'm sure they'll be delighted to see you. And if I'm not mistaken they will wish they were back under your care."

"I would wish that too, sir, but—" he shrugged his shoulders and spread out his hands. "C'est la vie, telle quelle . . . telle quelle."

"Yes, indeed indeed."

Mr. Burgess went out and Mark, turning to Tilly, said, "I don't think I've felt so excited about anything since the night Harry was born. And isn't it a bit of luck that he'll be here the day after tomorrow. He'll have one day among them anyway." He turned his head away and looked toward the window, saying now with deep bitterness, "Three days! Damnable!"

Sensing his changing mood, she went quickly toward the chair and, straightening the cover that had slipped slightly from the cage, she said brightly, "They'll likely make so much narration, sir, that you'll be glad to see the back of them."

His head came around to her sharply and his voice seemed to be censoring the stupidity of her remark when he said, "Yes, as glad as I would be to see the back of you, Trotter."

She stood silent now looking at him as she often did when she thought it was better not to give any answer to his remarks.

"If Mr. Burgess had remained a little longer he would have said that that remark of yours was stupid, trite. Do you understand that?"

"All I understand is, sir, that I was aiming to lighten your despair with regard to the children."

His expression altered as he stared at her: there had been spirit in the answer that wouldn't have been there a few months ago. He didn't object to it, in fact he liked it for he was catching a glimpse of the emerging woman that lay beneath the yes, sir, no, sir, attitude of hers. His voice quiet now, he asked, "If you had four children taken away from you what would you do, Trotter?"

He watched her think a moment before answering, "As . . . as I've never had children I cannot tell to what depth my feelings would go. I can just judge on the reactions of Mrs. Drew to her family. But I'm not as strong as Mrs. Drew so I think I might go mad. Then again, sir, it's a question that is difficult to answer because if I had four children why should they be taken away?" She felt the blood rushing to her face and her eyes widened as she stared at him; and now his voice ominously quiet, he said, "Go on, finish."

When she didn't speak he supplied the meaning to her words, saying, "You were about to tell me that you would never do anything that would bring about losing your children, was that it?"

She remained mute.

"Well, my answer to that, Trotter, is, you have a long way to go yet and a lot to learn about human nature, and also a great deal to learn about the penalties for sin. Some sentences are out of all proportion to the crime . . . What's that?" He turned quickly and, raising himself on his hands to look over the broad sill of the window, his whole expression changing, he cried, "It's the coach! It's them. Go on down. Go on down."

She turned from him now and ran out of the room and across the landing and down the stairs. Pike was already waiting; both doors were thrown wide open and there, on the drive, the coach had come to a standstill.

It was her place, she knew, to stand at the top of the steps and welcome Mrs. Forefoot-Meadows in, as she had seen Mrs. Lucas do, but she so much forgot herself she ran down the steps and it seemed that before she reached the bottom they were around her shouting, "Hello! Trotter. Hello! Trotter." Even Matthew was smiling.

"Enough! Enough! Behave yourselves." The voice of their grandmother did not immediately quell their boisterous enthusiasm, but they left Tilly and raced up the steps and into the house; and Tilly, looking at Mrs. Forefoot-Meadows, said, "I hope you had a good journey, madam?"

The surprise of being greeted by this girl seemed to have struck Jane Forefoot-Meadows dumb because she looked from her and up the steps to where Pike was standing; then turning from her without even the acknowledgment of a nod, she swept up to the terrace and passed Pike, saying as she did so, "What's this? What's this?"

"I hope you had a pleasant jour. . . ."

"Never mind about the journey, where's Mrs. Lucas?"

"She's no longer here, madam."

"No longer here!" As she unloosened her cape she looked about her, saying, "And Simes?"

349

"He's no longer in the master's service either, madam."

"What's going on here?" At the bottom of the stairs she stopped and again she looked around the hall. The difference in the house was already striking her, yet she couldn't put an actual finger on it.

When a moment or so later she entered Mark's room she put both hands up to her ears, crying, "Stop it! Stop that noise this instant!" and again the laughter and chatter subsided.

Going toward the chair now, where Mark had Jessie Ann cradled in one arm and John in the other, while the two older boys sat halfway down on either side, she did not ask after her son-in-law's health but said, "What's this I've come across? No housekeeper, no footman, and that girl!"

"It's a long story, Mother-in-law, a long, long story, and you'll hear about it all in good time; but first, get off your feet."

"I've been off my feet for hours, my bones are stiff. . . . Stop making that racket, John, and speak correctly. Haven't I told you?"

"Y . . . yes, Gramama."

Mark looked at his small son who no longer seemed so small; not one of his children seemed small now, they had all grown in their different ways. But John's speech was worse than when he had been at home, he was actually stammering now.

"Leave your father alone and get away all of you up to the nursery, and get out of your traveling clothes and don't come downstairs until I give you leave. Away with you now."

Mark bit on his lip as Jessie Ann and John slid from his arms; then Jessie Ann, looking toward the cage, said, "Are your feet still sore, Papa?"

Mark did not take his glance from her and he continued to smile at her as he said, "Yes; yes, they're still sore, my dear."

"Perhaps you want your toenails cut, mine stick in me and Willy Nilly digs the scissors in and cuts them off. It hurts. . . ."

"Who's Willy Nilly?"

It was his mother-in-law who answered now, saying, "Williams, their nurse. Go on, children, do as you're bid."

And they went scrambling and laughing out of the room, and the noise was like music in his ears, it was as if they had never been away. Yet they had been away and the change in all of them was evident, at least in their growth.

"Well now, what's this? The house is all topsy-turvy."

"No, Mother-in-law, the house is no longer topsy-turvy. The house, I am pleased to say, is being run as it should have been for years."

Her plucked eyebrows moved upward, the wrinkles around her eyes stretched themselves, and she said one word, "Indeed!"

"Yes, indeed. Sit yourself down and I'll give you all my news. I'm sure you'd like to hear it before you give me yours."

Flinging off her dust-coat, she sat down and she made no comment whatever until Mark had finished outlining the story of the changeover, and then she said, "Pit folk in the house?"

"Yes, as I said; and outside too and doing splendidly."

"It can't work."

"But it does." His voice was high. "And I'm going to tell you something more, at one-third of the cost."

"A third!" She pulled her bony chin into the sagging flesh of her neck that formed a ridge around the high collar of her dress.

"Yes, a third; and from what I gather the whole house is cleaner, and from what I see"—he pointed to the window—"the grounds have been unearthed in all quarters. Then there is the food. The bills have gone down in a remarkable way, for everybody, I understand, eats well, including myself."

"That girl, do you know she was at the bottom of the steps when I got out of the carriage, leaving Pike at the door?"

"Perhaps she wanted to greet you."

"Don't be ridiculous, Mark; she doesn't know her place."

His face and voice lost its pleasantness now as he said sharply, "She knows her place all right. She's running this house, and what's more she's seeing to me."

She almost made to rise; then her mouth opened and closed again on his words: "She's a better nurse than that big battleship who tended me. . . ."

"It isn't right, it isn't decent, she's. . . ."

"Oh, the decencies are seen to by Burgess."

"Burgess . . . you mean the tutor?"

"Yes, the tutor. He comes in every day and sees to the main decencies, so have no fear, my dear Mother-in-law, the proprieties are being observed."

"I don't like it." She rose to her feet. "Neither will Eileen."

"God in Heaven!" It was as if he had been startled by the remark so quickly did he bounce up from the back of the chair. "What's Eileen got to do with it, I ask you?"

"She is still your wife."

"Then if she's my wife she should be here. What do you think I've felt like all these bloody months being left. . . ."

"I will not have you swearing in my presence, Mark."

"I'll swear where I bloody well like, Mother-in-law, and if it doesn't suit you, you know what you can do. But don't you come here talking about morality or improprieties that would shock my wife, for I won't

352

have it. Her place is here with my children. Three days she has allowed me! My God! if I take it into my head I'll keep them for good and let her fight it out."

"Don't agitate yourself so, Mark, and don't talk nonsense. The children's place is with their mother."

"And her place is here!"

"You should have thought about that some long time ago. Anyway, I have things to discuss with you, but the time is not now, I am tired after my journey. You don't seem to appreciate, Mark, the trial that journey is to me."

He drew in a number of deep breaths before lowering his head, when he muttered, "I do, I do; and I appreciate the effort you make." Then lifting his head, his voice still quiet, he said, "But can you appreciate what it is like for me to be tied to this chair, to this room? I've asked myself more and more of late, is it worth going on."

"Don't talk nonsense! I won't stay and listen to such weak prattle; I shall join you later."

As she stormed out he couldn't but marvel at her spirit; no one knew her right age but she couldn't be far from seventy. Had she passed some of it on to her daughter things might have been different. He lay back in his chair and looked toward the cage covering the stumps of his legs. If only he had been left with even one foot. He pulled himself up straight on the chair; he must make an effort and try this wooden leg business.

For two days the house had been alive with scampering feet and laughter. No longer were the children kept to the nursery floor; even Jane Forefoot-Meadows found it impossible to confine them, for as soon as her back was turned they were down in their father's room or out in the grounds, or following Tilly around the house. They had at first viewed with surprise the change in the staff, particularly in the kitchen. They had accepted

Katie in the nursery, but who was this little girl no older than Jessie Ann and not as big who was working in the kitchen? And there was no fat woman cooking there now but a tall woman with a big bony face.

During their first encounter Matthew had inquired imperiously of Biddy, "What is your name?" and she had answered, "Biddy, master. What is yours?"

And without hesitation he had said, "Matthew."

"Well, how are you, Master Matthew?"

"I am very well, thank you." The conversation wasn't going as he imagined it should, and he had turned and looked at his brothers and Jessie Ann, and they had all burst out laughing, and it was Jessie Ann who said, "What are you making for our tea, Mrs. Biddy?"

And Biddy had delighted her by bending down and whispering, "Fairy cakes, miss, with cream on their wings."

As Biddy put it to Tilly later, the house was alive with life, and at seven o'clock on the evening of the second day when the life was filling the nursery with laughter it brought Mark's head around toward the dressing-room door, calling, "What's going on up there, Trotter?"

Tilly came into the bedroom and, pushing the table and his half-eaten supper away, she said, "I think they're havin' a bit carry-on."

"Carry-on!" He was still looking upward. "It must be something to cause those gales of laughter. Go on up and see what it is."

She smiled at him, saying, "They'll want to come down if I go up, sir."

"And what harm is there in that?" he demanded, poking his face toward her. "Their grandmother is at her supper and she's likely to be there for another hour if I know her. Go on up."

She only just stopped herself from actually running

out of the room because she realized that was a habit she must get out of; but once on the landing she ran along the corridor and up the stairs and burst into the nursery, there to see Katie sitting on the mat before the nursery fire holding Jessie Ann while they both rocked with laughter. Luke was sitting at the nursery table, his arms spread out over it, his head between them, and Matthew was standing in front of John saying, "Say the other one. Say the other one."

"What is it?" Tilly looked from one to the other but they just spluttered, until Katie, getting to her feet now and drying her eyes, said, " 'Twas Master John, Tilly, he . . . he was saying a piece of poetry."

"It's all about us." Jessie Ann came toward her, yelling, "It has our names in it, Trotter, even Papa's."

"And is it that funny?"

It was Matthew who answered, "Yes; yes, it is, Trotter. Go on, John, say it again for Trotter. Go on."

And John, his face one huge grin, took up his stance with feet planted slightly apart, hands joined behind his back, and began, stammering almost with each word:

"Ma . . . Matthew, Mark, Luke and J . . . John,
Hold the c . . . cuddy till I get on.
If it k . . . kicks pull it . . . its tail
If it p . . . piddles hold the p . . . pail."

Again they were doubled up, John as well now. He was on his knees and trying to stand on his head while the other children rolled in agonies of laughter, and Katie, her hand across her mouth, looked at Tilly and muttered, "They didn't learn it here, believe me. One of the gardeners at their granny's. An' that isn't all. The fellow must be from these parts 'cos they know 'When I was a laddie' "—she nodded—"you know, 'When I was a laddie and lived with me granny.' "

"Never!" Tilly was biting down hard on her lip now.

And then she muttered in an aside, "But that isn't as bad as Matthew, Mark. I had me ears boxed once for singing it." She now turned from Katie, saying, "Quiet! Now quiet! Listen." They were all standing around her now, and she looked from one to the other. "I'll take you downstairs to your papa if you promise to leave the minute I bid you, because your grandmama will come up immediately her supper is done. Promise?"

"Yes, Trotter. Yes, Trotter."

As they made for the door she cried at them, "Put your dressing-gowns on," and they all scampered out of the schoolroom and into their rooms leaving Tilly and Katie looking at each other, both with their hands over their mouths now; then Tilly said, "He . . . the master, he heard the laughter."

"Can you hear as plain as that down there?"

"Yes, when the noise is so loud."

"We'll have to be careful. . . . It's lovely havin' bairns in the house, isn't it?"

"Yes, Katie, lovely. But I'll tell you something, they're different bairns to those I met at first. Eeh! they were demons, especially that Matthew."

"Aye"—the smile slid from Katie's face—"he's a bit bossy is Master Matthew, wants his own way, wants to rule the roost."

"That's nothing; you haven't had a frog put in your bed or bowls of porridge splashed all over the table."

"Is that what you had?"

"Oh yes, and more."

The children came back into the room now, crying in loud whispers, "Come on. Come on, Trotter."

Taking John's and Jessie's hands, she ran them out of the room, but stopped at the top of the stairs, warning them, "Now, go quietly, tiptoe, because if your grandmother hears you she'll be up like a shot."

They nodded at her; then in exaggerated steps went quietly down the stairs, along the corridor and into their father's room; but there they almost threw themselves on him, chattering and laughing, until Mark quietened them, saying in mock sternness, "I haven't sent for you to have fun but to inquire what was making the noise and disturbing my supper."

They pushed at each other now, sniggering and giggling; then Luke said, "It was John, Papa, he was saying a funny rhyme; but it's about us."

Oh dear me! Tilly groaned to herself. That's one thing she should have done, she should have told them not to repeat that one.

Again Matthew was taking charge. Pulling his young brother to the side of the basket-chair, he said, "Perform for Papa. Perform for Papa. Go on."

And John performed for Papa; but there was no great burst of laughter at the end because they were all looking at their father's face. His eyes were wide, his nose was twitching, his lips were slightly pursed. Was he vexed? He looked over their heads toward Tilly and he said one word, "Katie?"

"No, no, sir; they didn't learn it here." Oh dear, he wasn't going to laugh.

When his face began to crumple, the children scrambled toward him, but he put his hand up in a warning gesture, crying now, "Laugh if you dare. One sound out of you and up the stairs you fly, because don't forget, the dining-room is below here, and who is in the dining-room?"

"Grandmama." They all said the word together.

"Yes, Grandmama."

He looked at his small son whose face was bright with the fact that he had entertained them, but what had really made that coarse rhyme funny was the child's stammer. It had worsened considerably during his absence from the house.

"He knows a song, Papa, about Grandmama."

"About Grandmama?"

357

"Yes, Papa." They all started to giggle now; then Luke said, "We all know it, Papa, but John sings it the best. Go on, John. Sing 'When I was a laddie.'"

John seemed only too eager to please and, taking up his stance again, he began to sing now and he hardly stammered at all as, his face one big smile, he gaily went into the song:

"When I was a laddie I lived with me granny,
  And many a hammering she give m . . . me,
  But now I'm a m . . . man I can hammer me
    granny,
  And it serves her right for hammering me."

He finished the last line with a rush and when Mark, unable to contain himself, lay back against the cushions, his hand tight against his mouth and his eyes now gleaming with tears of laughter, they fell upon him, all the while smothering their own laughter.

Pressing them from him, Mark said, "Who's . . . who's been teaching you these rhymes . . . your nurse?"

"No, Papa; it's Brigwell, one of the gardeners."

"Old Brigwell?"

"Yes, Papa." They all nodded at him.

"Oh, may he be forgiven! But he won't be should your grandmama hear of any of these rhymes."

"Oh, we don't let her hear," said Luke. "We sing altogether, in the stables. Don't we, Matthew?"

Mark looked at the boy whose fair head was no longer covered in curls. He couldn't believe he was almost twelve years old, yet he looked older, and when Matthew said, "Shall we all sing it for you, Papa? It sounds very jolly when we sing it," he moved his lips one over the other before saying, "Yes, yes; I should like to hear you sing it all together. But—" He raised his hand and wagged his finger before pointing it toward the carpet, saying, "Don't forget who's below."

Scrambling now, they all stood in line at the foot of the basket-chair, with Tilly who was already there, and it looked as if she, too, was about to perform. And she could have joined them, so happy did she feel inside, for she had never seen the master so light-hearted for months, in fact never at all, for his face now was looking like that of a young man; and so when they started her lips too moved in unison with theirs.

"When I was a laddie I lived with me granny,
    And many a hammering she give me,
    But now I'm a man. . . ."

It was at this point that the door opened quietly and only Mark saw the visitor, and as the children were singing the words "I can hammer me granny" he raised his hand slightly as if to warn them, but they were oblivious of the intruder, because the sound being made by their combined voices, although muted, was taking up all their attention. They finished the last line, "And serve her right for hammering me."

"What . . . is . . . this! What did I hear?"

The children turned really startled, and it was Jessie Ann who piped, "Just singing a little song for Papa, Grandmama."

"I heard what you were singing: hitting your granny" —it would appear that she couldn't allow her tongue to use the word hammering—"And it serves her right for hitting you. Where on earth have you learned such a thing?" She was towering over them, and now her glance lifted to Tilly. "You have taught them this?"

"No, ma'am."

"Then it's that person up above. Mark, you must. . . ."

"Hold your hand! Hold your hand! Good-night, children. Good-night. Come and say good-night to me."

They now scrambled to the couch and each placed his

lips against his cheek before being hustled out of the room by Tilly.

"That girl . . . !"

"That girl's got nothing to do with this issue, Mother-in-law. No one here taught the children the rhymes."

"Vulgarity!"

"Yes, indeed, vulgarity. But they didn't learn it here."

"I don't believe you. . . ."

"Believe me or not." His tone was sharp. "You'll have to go back to your own home to find out the person who brings a little merriment into their existence, and you'll find it in your valued old retainer, none other than Brigwell."

"Brigwell! I don't believe it."

"Believe it or not, Brigwell taught them that little ditty. And more. You don't know the half of it."

"Brigwell has been in our family . . . well as"—she tossed her head—"as long as I have."

"Yes, and likely he found it very dull."

"Mark!"

"What do you know what goes on in people's minds, what they do in their spare time? You've lived behind a moat in your pseudo-castle since you were a girl."

He stopped abruptly and they stared at each other; then she said, with deep indignation in her tone, "I am beginning to see another side to Eileen's existence in this house for you talk like a. . . ."

"Like a what?"

"A man who has stepped down from his class."

After a moment longer, and while continuing to stare at her, he laid his head back against the cushions and let out a mirthless laugh; then almost childishly he made use of her words by saying, "Oh, if only I could step down from anywhere at this moment, what I would not give."

"I can well understand that, but your manner certainly doesn't beg sympathy."

"Who is begging sympathy?" He was again glaring at her.

"Oh, Mark!" She tossed her head now, the artificial coils in her hair bouncing as if they would jump away from her scalp; and then her whole manner changing, she said, "I had hoped to have a quiet talk with you tonight about . . . about a private matter, but I can see you're not in the mood, so I will leave it until tomorrow."

"I won't be in any better mood tomorrow, Mother-in-law, so sit yourself down and get started on your private conversation."

He sounded weary and his tone took the edge off the bluntness of his words, and after a moment she seated herself in the chair to the side of the fire and opposite him; then arranging the three over-skirts of her gaberdine dress, she placed her two long narrow feet together, joined her hands in her lap, then said, " 'Tis difficult to know where to begin when touching on your private life."

He did not help by word or sign, but waited.

"Eileen wishes me to assure you that, as sorry as she is for your predicament, there is no possibility of her returning here. That being so, she wishes to be fair to you and offers you a legal separation, and you could settle on her a sum, a moderate sum. . . ."

There was another pause while she waited now for some response to her words, but when none came her hands moved from her lap and, as if she had just put on her gown, she adjusted the row of small silk bows leading from the neck to the waist; and there her fingers became still as she said, "She thinks it would be to your advantage."

Again Mark made no answer. But during the last few minutes while he had been listening to his mother-in-law his body had stiffened, and he had the impression that his toes were pushing past the cage and against the shawl covering it. His feet began to pain him and the pain now spread up his legs until it reached his waist, and there it took the form of a wire band constricting him.

"Now please, Mark, don't be angry. She is thinking of your interests too."

"Be damned, she is! Legal separation! Do you know something? She's a fool. A legal separation would be a judicial separation and in such a case I could claim custody of the children."

"No!"

"Oh yes, Mother-in-law, yes. . . . My god! a moderate sum, when I'm having to beggar myself to pay her what I do. It's a wonder she hasn't thought of divorce; but perhaps she has and has found out that a woman can't divorce her husband for infidelity only. Now Mother-in-law—" He pulled himself further down the chair and leaned toward her until he was almost within an arm's length of her as he cried, "You can go back and tell my dear wife that if she's not careful I shall yell it out aloud in court that she never allowed me her bed after John was born, and that the invalid business was a put-up game; very much so, because my children informed me only this morning that Mama goes out walking now; Mama goes out driving now; Mama went to the theater last week. And too, Mr. Swinburne took Mama all around the picture gallery; and Mr. Swinburne took Matthew and Luke and Mama to a musical afternoon. . . . Mama has suddenly got the use of her legs, hasn't she, Mother-in-law? Oh—" Slowly he eased himself back on to his cushions; then looking at the blanched face of his mother-in-law, he said, "You go back and tell your daughter I'll strike a bargain with her. If she returns my children to me without any fuss I'll increase her personal allowance, but if she doesn't I can, as I've said, apply for a judicial separation, in which case the law will give me custody of my own children."

Jane Forefoot-Meadows was on her feet now, her

face diffused with a natural color. She cried at him, "She will never let you have the children! Make up your mind to that."

"She mightn't have any choice. Anyway, I have them now, Mother-in-law"—his voice was ominously quiet—"possession is nine points of the law. What if I decide to keep them with me?"

"She'll fight you. She'll bring up your constant infidelities which amounted to cruelty. Yes, cruelty! That's what she can charge you with. Just you wait and see."

Speechless now, he watched her flounce around and sail out of the room, and as the door banged to behind her he gripped hold of each side of the chair and actually shook it in a spasm of anger while with his head down on his chest he brought out, "Damn and blast you and her to hell's flames!"

The next morning there was an argument between Mark and Jane Forefoot-Meadows with regard to the counting of time. She had arrived on the Monday afternoon and she said she was going to leave on the Thursday morning.

To this he had replied coolly, "The children were to stay with me three days and they either stay with me three full days, returning on the Friday morning, or they do not return to Waterford Place at all."

That he was utterly in earnest Jane Forefoot-Meadows realized. Nevertheless she did not comply with this demand without protest, and in no small voice.

Katie was downstairs collecting the children's lunch, and Tilly, hearing the noise from above combating even Mrs. Forefoot-Meadow's voice from the master's bedroom, hurried up to the nursery floor and when she pushed open the schoolroom door it was to find Matthew and Luke rolling on the floor, their battle being egged on with cries from Jessie Ann and John.

Having separated them, she held them apart. Luke appeared to be on the verge of tears but Matthew's face was merely dark with anger.

"Now what is this all about?" Tilly demanded. "Fancy wasting your time fighting. What's come over both of you? What I should do is knock your heads together. Don't you know that your father can hear you down below?"

"We . . . we can hear Grand . . . Grandmama yelling," John stammered.

Tilly turned a warm affectionate glance on the small boy and he laughed back at her; then loosening her hold on the two boys, she said, "There now, make it up. But why on earth are you fighting anyway?"

"It was 'cos of you, Trotter," Jessie Ann put in pertly.

"Me?" She looked from one to the other of the boys, and while Matthew stared back at her, Luke hung his head and Jessie Ann went on, "Luke said he was going to marry you when he grows up and Matthew said he wasn't 'cos he's going to marry you himself."

She should have laughed, she should have pulled them into her arms and said, "You silly billies," but as she looked at them the old fear erupted in her. Men, they either loved her or hated her, but whichever line they took it led to trouble, now even trouble among children.

She was saved from making any comment to the boys by Katie entering the room carrying a laden tray, and as she lowered it on to the table she turned quickly to Tilly, saying, "Anything wrong, lass?"

"No, no; they were just having a bit of carry-on and I came up to see what it was all about."

"They were fighting," put in the ever informative Jessie Ann. "Matthew and Luke, they were fighting about who's going to marry Trotter."

Katie was on the point of bursting out laughing when the look on Tilly's face prevented her; but being Katie she had to see the funny side of it, and so, pulling the cloth from over the covered dishes, she said, "Eeh! well, I think they'll have to take their turn 'cos there's three of our lads are after her an' all."

"Don't say that!" When the side of Matthew's hand came sharply across Katie's arm she winced and cried, "Here now! None of that," and Tilly, grabbing Matthew by the shoulder, shook him as she demanded of him, "Say you're sorry to Drew."

"I shan't."

She straightened up. "Oh then, well you shan't, but don't you come fussing around me or expect me to tell your father what a fine fellow you are." She turned on her heel now and marched out of the room, but she had just reached the top of the nursery stairs when Matthew caught up with her and, grabbing her apron, he pulled her to a stop. His face was scarlet, his lips were trembling, his round gray eyes were bright, and when he muttered, "I'm . . . I'm sorry, Trotter," she, too, felt a moisture in her eyes. It was something for the great Master Matthew to say he was sorry; he had certainly changed. When she put her arm around his shoulder she found herself suddenly hugged to him, and she stroked his hair, saying, "There, there now."

When he looked up to her the moisture had deepened in his eyes and was lingering on his fair lashes, and his voice sounded tight as he said, "I don't want to go back with Grandmama, Trotter; none of us do."

"But you'll have to."

"But why can't we stay here? You could look after us, and Drew, and I wouldn't mind going to school from here as long as I could come back. Can't . . . can't you persuade father to keep us?"

"It . . . it doesn't seem to lie with your father, Matthew, it's your mother who has to be persuaded to come back. You understand?"

He moved his head slowly and lowered his eyes as he said, "Yes, yes, of course." Then his head jerking upward, he blinked at her as he now brought out rapidly, "I . . . I meant what I said, I won't let Luke marry you, I'll . . . I'll marry you when I grow up. I . . . I know it isn't the right thing for a gentleman to marry a menial but it's different with you because you can read and write. You'll let me marry you, won't you, Trotter?"

"But I'm nearly twice your age, Master Matthew."

"Oh, I know that and I don't mind, because you'd be able to look after me better, being older. And anyway, you're not really twice, only six years, and if I know you'll marry me it would be something to look forward to because the holidays are very boring at grandma-ma's."

"Well; just as you say then, Master Matthew."

"Oh, thank you, Trotter, thank you. You know what, Trotter?" His voice sank to a whisper. "A boy at school told me he had once kissed a girl right on the mouth, but I didn't believe him because I know that you cannot kiss anyone on the mouth until you are married. Can you, Trotter?"

"Er"—she gulped in her throat—"no. That's right, Master Matthew, that's right." He now smiled at her and she gulped again before saying, "Go along and get your dinner and . . . and tell Drew that you're sorry."

"Yes, Trotter, yes." He backed two steps from her, then turned and ran into the schoolroom, while she stood at the top of the stairs not knowing whether to laugh or cry. You can't kiss anyone on the mouth until you are married. Who'd have thought that went on in Matthew's head, him of all people, the terror, the little upstart that he was, or had been. Growing changed people; it was changing herself, and with the change came wants, just starting in that eleven-year-old-boy, but galloping in herself now.

She hurried down the staircase and to her duties.

2

The children had been gone a week and Master Harry had left yesterday, not for the University but for France again. From what Tilly had overheard in conversation between him and his father, his friend who was half French had a sister and for most holidays, the sister and her parents returned to a castle in France, a chateau they called it. The master had explained that to her last night; he had talked about his son in snatches all the evening. "He wasn't always gay like this, you know, Trotter," he had said; "he was a very solemn child and a more solemn youth. I am glad he has these friends in France because it has shown me another side of him. He is quite the man of the world, don't you think, Trotter?"

"Yes, sir, he's a very nice young gentleman, Master Harry, very likable."

"Yes, indeed, very likable. I wonder if he'll marry this French girl. Her name is Yvette. Nice name for a daughter-in-law, Yvette. . . . Do you miss the children, Trotter?"

"Oh yes, sir, yes, sir, very much. The house is so quiet without them."

"Yes, it is. Everyone seems to have deserted us at once, even Burgess."

"His cold was very heavy, sir. I think it was wise of him to stay in bed for a few days, colds can be catchin'."

"He lives entirely alone, doesn't he?"

"Yes, sir."

"That must be very trying. I'd hate that, to live entirely alone."

"I . . . I don't think he minds so much, sir, he . . . he kind of loses himself in books." She smiled now. "He has hardly anything in his house but books, just the bare necessities and books."

"You have been there?"

"Yes, sir, I . . . I have been a number of times, but . . . but I went on my half-day on Sunday."

"How does he manage to cook for himself?"

"Oh, his wants are very few, I think; he . . . he mainly lives on porridge and milk most times, and a little mutton now and again."

"Really! Does he have a meal when he's here?"

"Well"—she turned her head slightly to the side—"he sometimes has a snack in the kitchen, sir."

"In future, Trotter, see that he has a good meal on each of his visits. And I think it would be a kindness if you slipped along and took him something hot now that he's unwell, or send one of them from downstairs."

"I would very much like to take him something, sir. It . . . it wouldn't take me long, I could be there and back within the hour."

"Well, do that, do that. And you needn't hurry; you've hardly been out of doors for days." He paused before he ended, "Do you find it tiresome to be tied to this room and me?"

"Tire-some!" Her lips lingered over the word; then she shook her head and her smile widened as she said, "Oh, no, sir, no; there's nothing I would like to do better. It has been like a —" She looked to the side, then lowered her head, and he said, "Been like a what?"

"A kind of new life to me, like the things Mr. Burgess used to talk about, bringing one alive."

"Looking after me has been like that to you?"

"Yes, sir."

He stared at her for a long moment before he said quietly, "You don't ask much from life, do you, Trotter?"

"Only peace, sir."

"Peace!" The word was high, and he repeated it, even louder now and on a laugh, "Peace! At your age, girl? 'Tisn't peace you want at your age, it's excitement, laughter, joy."

She returned his stare. He seemed to be forgetting her position, and not only hers but also that of the very young who had at one time worked for him. There had been very little excitement, laughter and joy for those who had had to tear a living out of the earth, whether above or below it. What she had meant to convey to him by saying she wanted peace was the peace wherein she could work without fear, without having to fight against the waves of resentment.

"Why are you looking so stiff-faced? Have I said something to annoy you?"

Again she didn't answer him, at least not immediately, because masters or mistresses didn't trouble whom they annoyed. In her class, servants were there to suffer annoyance. He was in a way placing her in an awkward situation. As the saying went, she was neither fish, fowl, nor good raw meat. At times she didn't know where she stood with him, as servant, or nurse, or confidante, especially when he talked to her about the children and his son, Harry, and even his mother-in-law; although one person he never mentioned was his wife.

She said flatly now, "What I meant, sir, was all I desired was to work in peace, and . . . and out of that could come a bit of laughter now and again, but as for excitement and joy, well —" Her voice sank low in her throat as she ended, "It doesn't come to everybody, sir."

His eyes held hers now as he asked, "Don't you want it to come to you, Trotter?"

And she dared to answer, "What one wants and what one gets are two different things, sir. I . . . I haven't as yet seen much excitement and joy among the people I know, except on fair days when some of them get drunk. All they seem to do most of the time is work and. . . ."

She was startled by the movement that he made. Swinging out his arm, he almost knocked over the jug of fruit juice standing on the table with a glass beside it. Only her own quick movement stopped it from tumbling to the floor, and after she had steadied it she stood back from the long chair and looked at him in astonishment, for his look was almost ferocious as he cried, "What is in your mind, Trotter, and in the minds of most of your class is that you are the only people who suffer indignities, the only people that joy doesn't touch, the only people who haven't any chance of excitement, these you make yourself believe are prerogatives of the upper class. Now am I right?"

She dared to answer him but in a very small voice, "Well, aren't they, sir?"

"No, they are not, Trotter; money, position, titles, none of these bring happiness. Excitement perhaps when one has the money to run an estate and shoot, or money enough to seek big game, that kind of excitement, but joy, real happiness, is no more the prerogative of the rich than it is of the poor, it is something that is within you. Yes, yes, of course"—he jerked his head up and down as if answering some remark of hers now—"I know what you're thinking: you don't go hungry when you've got money, you can be sick in comfort, like me"—he now spread his arms wide—"my money and position enables me to have someone like you to wait on me hand and foot—foot! that's saying something—whereas if I were a poor man I wouldn't be able to enjoy these privileges. Granted, granted, but if I were a poor man, Trotter, I wouldn't be weighed down with responsibilities, I wouldn't be afraid of public censure, I wouldn't have to conform to patterns that are against the grain; I wouldn't have to keep up a way of life I can't afford, I wouldn't have a thousand and one things that irk me; and if I were poor I wouldn't have to lie here, Trotter, thinking about ways and means of how I'm going to carry on now that the mine is no longer working."

He turned his head away and pressed his lips tightly together, and, her voice soft and contrite, she said, "I'm sorry, sir. I'm sorry I've upset you."

"You haven't upset me"—he was looking at her again—"I'm just trying to explain something to you."

"I . . . I know, sir, and I understand."

"You do?"

"Yes, sir. I . . . I haven't the words to explain how I understand but . . . but I do."

He let out a long breath and slumped against his cushions, then smiled ruefully, saying, "Well, if that's the case we're getting some place, and at the beginning of this conversation, if I remember rightly, you were about to go some place."

She answered his smile now by saying, "Yes, sir, to Mr. Burgess."

"Well, get yourself away before the sun goes down. Enjoy your walk, and give him my best respects. Tell him I miss his conversation and"—he brought his head forward toward her—"his tidbits."

"I'll do that, sir, and I . . . I won't be long."

"Take your time, but get back before dark."

"Oh yes, sir, I'll be back before dark."

When the door closed on her he screwed his eyes up tight as if trying to blot out the mental picture of her, then muttered to himself, "Oh! Trotter. Tilly Trotter. Tilly Trotter."

Mr. Burgess was delighted to see her.

"What have I done to deserve such kindness, I'll never be able to eat all that." He pointed to the cold

chicken, the meat pie, the bread, cheese, and slab of
butter, among other things, on the table, and she
answered, "Well, if you don't you'll never be able to
get out of that chair. And just look at your fire, it's
almost dead. I thought you said there was a boy
brought your kindlin' and coal in?"

"I . . . I did, he does, but he hasn't been for the last
two days, he mustn't be well himself, it's these bitter
winds. Do you know there was frost on the window
pane this morning and here we are at the end of April?
I long for the summer."

"You'll never see it if you don't look after yourself."
She bustled about the room and he smiled at her as he
said, "You'd make a marvelous mother, Trotter; you're
just like a hen, be it a little tall."

"Oh, Mr. Burgess!" She flapped her hand at him. "I
don't take that as a compliment."

"Well, you should because the master thinks you're a
wonderful hen."

"Mr. Burgess!" Her tone was indignant even while
she suppressed a smile, then she added, "I don't feel
like a hen."

"No, my dear, I'm sure you don't; you're more like a
peacock. Given the right clothes you could outdo any
peacock."

"Tut! tut!" She turned away from him. "I think your
cold's addled your head. Anyway, hens, peacocks and
the rest of the farmyard, if you don't make yourself eat
I'll ask the master if I can send one of the girls over to
see to you, and you won't like that, will you?"

He aroused himself in the chair, saying, "No, Trotter, I wouldn't like that. I can't abide people fussing
around me and moving my"—he paused—"things."

Seeing that the main things in the room were books,
and that these were scattered everywhere, she could
imagine his reaction if anyone were to attempt to tidy
him up; but she was genuinely concerned for him, and

so for the next half-hour she brought in a stack of wood and coal, she emptied slops, she filled cans with fresh water from the well, and when she had finished she washed her hands in the tin dish standing on a small table at the end of the room, and as she dried them she looked toward the window and said, "It looks as if it could rain and the twilight's setting in, so I'll have to be off, but you'll promise me, won't you"—she went up the room and stood in front of him—"that you'll eat everything that is in that cupboard?" She pointed toward the old press from which she'd had to take books to make way for the food. "And if I can't get over tomorrow I'll be here the next day."

Mr. Burgess didn't speak, but he held out his hand to her, and when she took it he said quietly, "You bring happiness to so many people, Trotter."

Her face had no answering softness in it when she replied, "And trouble an' all, it would seem, Mr. Burgess."

"Don't you worry about the trouble, my dear; people bring trouble on themselves, it's their thinking that creates the trouble. You go on as you are and one day you'll come into your own. Yes, you will." He moved his head slowly up and down. "I have a strong premonition about many things and I've always had one about you, one day you'll come into your own."

His words, said with such deep sincerity, brought a lump to her throat and she turned from him and, getting into her coat, she buttoned it up to the neck, then put on her hat which was the same straw one that she had worn for years. Finally, picking up the basket, she said, "Now take care, won't you?" and he answered, "Yes, my dear, I'll take care. And thank the master for me and tell him I'll soon be on duty again."

"He'll be glad to hear that, he misses you."

"And I him. Yes, I him. I find him a very interesting man."

373

They stared at each other for a moment longer; then again she said, "Good-bye, Mr. Burgess," and he answered, "Good-bye, my dear," and she went out.

The air had turned even colder and it caught at her breath, and the twilight, threatening to be short to-night, made her hurry her step.

Mr. Burgess's cottage was situated up a narrow lane at the end of which were two roads, one that would eventually take you into Shields, the other into Jarrow. Along one side of the Shields road was a high bank which led on to common land. At the far side was some woodland running along the top of what was almost a small gorge. Once through the wood you came on the estate. She had come from the house by this route and she was returning the same way.

Inside the wood it was dim, even dark in parts, but this didn't frighten her. No darkness frightened her now since she had experienced the total blackness of the mine; even night-time seemed light to her now.

She was emerging from the wood and was passing the last big tree close to the edge of the gorge when her heart seemed to leap into her throat and bring her breathing to choking point as a man stepped from the side of the tree and blocked her path. For a full minute neither of them moved, but they stared at each other; and as she looked into the face of Hal McGrath a scream tore up through her but found no escape past the constriction in her throat.

"Aye, well, so here we are, eh?"

Her lips fell apart. She took a step to the side, and slowly he did the same.

"Didn't expect to see me the day, did you, *Mistress* Trotter, 'cos a mistress I hear you are now up at the big house? Done well for yourself, haven't you?"

Still no words came.

"Been easy in yer mind lately, haven't you, since I was well outa the way? An' things've been happenin'

374

up there, haven't they? By! from what I hear they have that. You know what they're sayin' back in the village? They're sayin' that no ordinary lass could have brought about what you've brought about. Got rid of the whole caboodle you did, and put your own crew in, an' now your sail's full of wind you're away. . . . Well, haven't you anythin' to say to me after all this time? No, not a word?"

He pulled his head back from her now as if to survey her better, then went on, "You've changed, thickened out a bit. You needed that, but I don't know whether I'm gona like the woman better than the lass. Anyway, we'll see, eh?". . . . On these last words his hands came out like the snapping wires of a hawser and when they gripped her arms she found her voice and she screamed at him, "You leave go of me, Hal McGrath. It's no girl you're dealin' with now. Leave go of me!" Being unable to use her arms she used her feet; but her skirt impeded the blows and only caused him to laugh. Then he swung her around as if she had been a paper bag and, pulling her clear of the dim wood, he thrust her against the bole of the tree, and holding her there, he growled, "That's better. I can see what I'm doin' here, eh? I can see what I'm doin'."

When she again used her feet he leaned his body at an angle toward her. Then his jovial manner changing and his face close to hers, he hissed at her through his clenched teeth, "God Almighty! but I've dreamed of this night after night, day after day. Me belly wrenched with sickness, me arms nearly torn out of their sockets, sea-boots in me arse, I still dreamed of this minute, and now it's come an' I'm going to have me payment, an' there's nobody on God's earth gona stop me. Do you hear that, Tilly Trotter?" He brought her shoulders from the tree now and with a quick jerk banged her head back against it. Then as she gasped and cried out, he said, "That's only the beginning 'cos I've never known a minute's luck or peace since me thoughts settled on you. I thought it was the money at first, but it wasn't, that was only part." Now to her horror he gripped her throat with one hand and like an iron band he held it to the tree, and as her hands tore at his face and her feet kicked at his shins he did not seem to notice. With his other hand he ripped her coat from her back, with one twisting pull he tore the front of it open and the buttons flew like bullets from the cloth; and now his hand was on the bodice of her print dress, and when the cotton was rent his fist was inside her body shirt tearing it from her bare flesh.

It was when his fingers dug into her breast that the scream tore through her body but found no escape; and then gathering her last remaining strength she did what she had done once before, she brought up her knee with as much viciousness as she was able to his groin. Instantly his grip sprang from her throat and he was standing away from her bent forward, his two hands clutching at the bottom of his belly.

Filled with terror as she was, she hadn't the strength to run for a moment, and in the gasping pause she took in the fact that he was standing on the very edge of the steep bank. She also knew that in another moment or two he would recover and then God help her, for if she did run he would catch her. How she forced herself to put her hands on him she never knew but she ran at him and the impetus nearly took her over the side at the same time as it toppled him backward, his arms now wide and the curses flowing from his mouth, and in the instant she turned to run she heard him scream. It was a high, thin scream, not like something that would come from his throat at all. She remained still, turned about again and looked down. His body was at a strange angle. He was on his back, he had fallen among an outcrop of rock and his middle seemed heaved up. For a moment she saw him in a position similar to that in which the master had lain. When he made no movement she put her hand to her mouth and whimpered, "Oh no! God, don't say that."

The next minute, holding her tattered clothes about her, she scrambled down the steep bank; then her approach to him slow, her step cautious in case the whole thing were a trick, she paused within an arm's length of him. His eyes were closed. Then slowly they opened and he groaned. When she saw him try to move she turned quickly away, but his voice stopped her as he growled, "Me back. I'm stuck. Give me a hand."

When she shook her head he closed his eyes again; and now his words slower and with what she detected might be panic in them, he muttered, "Then get somebody. Don't leave me here, you bitch, with the night comin' on. D'ya hear? D'ya hear?"

She knew his eyes were following her as she climbed the bank. Once on top she began to run.

It was almost dark when she reached the house. She had seen no one at all.

Letting herself in through the still-room door, she came into the corridor, and there halted. There was the muted sound of laughter coming from the servants' hall. It was around the time of the day they stopped to partake of a drink of beer or tea, and a bite.

On tiptoe now, she stumbled up the back stairway, and like an intruder she slunk through the green baize door and across the gallery. And it was as she made her way past Mark's bedroom to go to her own room that his voice came loudly from the room, saying, "Out there, is that you, Trotter?" Then louder, "Trotter!"

She now leaned against the wall to the side of the door, and when his voice came again, demanding, "Who is it out there?" she knew there was nothing for it but she must put in an appearance or else he would undoubtedly ring the bell to the kitchen.

When she opened the door and moved slowly into

the room he drew himself up on the chair, exclaiming, "God above! What . . . what has happened to you?"

"Hal McGrath. He was waiting for me outside the wood."

"Good God! look at you. What has he done? Come . . . come here. Sit down. Sit down!"

His hand going out now and gripping her wrist, he muttered, "What happened?" then added, "Never mind. First of all, go and take a glass of brandy." And when she shook her head he commanded, "Go along, girl! It will stop that trembling."

In the dressing-room a minute later, after pouring herself out a small amount of the brandy she sipped on it, choked and started to cough; and it was some time before she could control it and go back into the bedroom.

His impatience showing in his voice now, he said, "Well! Come, tell me." And she told him all there was to tell, but when she finished, "He's . . . he's hurt his back, he . . . he can't move. Somebody will have to be told," he interrupted quickly, saying, "Somebody will have to be told? Have some sense, girl. The best thing that can happen is that he be left there and let's hope the night will finish him off because that man is a danger to you. Go now and change your things. And listen. Don't mention this to anybody, not a soul. Do you hear? . . . Did anyone see you come in in this state?"

"No, sir."

"Good. Now look; go into my closet and clean up as much as you can because if any of the staff see you in that predicament they might blame me. What's more, never try to tiptoe past my door, my ear has become attuned to your step, even on the carpets." His voice had now taken on a light note, doubtless to cheer her, but she couldn't move her face into a smile. . . .

Having washed, she put on an overall she kept to

cover her uniform when cleaning the closet out. She took this precaution just in case she should see someone when making the short distance between this and her own room. And again she was fortunate. So, as no one but the master knew what had happened to her, why should she be worrying now in case Hal McGrath should die out there. She wanted him dead, didn't she? Yes, oh yes; but she didn't want his death on her conscience. If only she could tell someone. Who? Biddy? But the master had warned her to keep silent . . . yet, oh dear God, she didn't know what to do.

She got the answer when a tap came on the door and Katie came quietly into the room, saying, "Tilly, that lad's come again, Steve. He wants to see you. He was here just after you left. You all right? You look peaky."

"I . . . I feel a bit bilious."

"Well, it must have been the duck 'cos my stomach felt a bit squeezy after me dinner. It takes some getting used to, rich food, after hard tack for years." She smiled broadly, then said in a whisper, "Are you comin' down?"

Tilly nodded, adding, "I'll be there in a minute tell him."

"Aye. Aye, all right, Tilly."

A few minutes later she went down the corridor but not on tiptoe. In the kitchen she looked about her and Biddy, jerking her head toward the yard, said, "He wouldn't come in, he just said he wanted to have a word with you."

They exchanged glances and she went out.

The yard was lit by the candle lantern hanging from a bracket and its light seemed to have drained all the color from Steve's thin face and he began straightaway without his usual greeting of "Hello, Tilly."

"He's back, our Hal," he said. "He came in last night. There he was this mornin' when I came off me shift. I could have died. He knew I'd come and tell you, an' he threatened to do me in. Me ma kept me in the house all mornin'. She took the ladder away from the attic so I couldn't get down, and then when she did let me out he'd been gone for hours. I . . . I came as quick as I could, Tilly, I. . . ."

She put her hand on his arm and said, "I know, Steve. I've . . . I've met him."

"You what! And you're still whole? Eeh! Tilly, the things he said he would do to you. And he was solid and sober when he said them, that made it worse. Eeh! Tilly"—he shook his head—"what did he say? How did you get . . . ?"

She now pulled him away from the light of the lantern and into the darkness of the high wall that bordered the gardens, and her voice a whisper now, she told him briefly what had happened. After she finished he didn't speak for some time; then he said, "You think his back's gone?"

"Well, he couldn't move, Steve. And . . . and he might die, and I don't want him on me conscience."

"You're daft, Tilly, you're daft. You don't know what you're sayin'. I'll tell you somethin' and it's the truth. It's either you or him. He's not right in the head, not where you're concerned he's not; an' he never will be as long as he breathes. He'll do for you either way. If in some way he were to marry you he'd still do for you, he'd beat the daylights out of you. You've got into him somehow. I don't understand it, I only know that you come atween him an' his wits, so the best thing to do is . . . is leave him there."

"No, no, Steve. Neither of us could stand it if we left him there to die. I hope he dies, but . . . but not that way, not without something being done, so go and see if he's managed to get up. If not, well, you know what to do, tell your da, and they'll come and fetch him."

When he shook his head slowly she said, "Please, Steve, please, for my sake."

"I won't be doing it for your sake, Tilly, don't you see—it's like signing your death warrant, an' me own an' all, for he'll cripple me altogether one of these days. He's not going back to sea an' he'll hound you, you won't know a minute's peace. Aw Christ! Why was he born?" He became quiet for a moment, then said, "Go on in." He pushed at her roughly. "Go on in, you're shiverin'. It'll be all right. Go on in."

"You'll go? Promise me you'll go, Steve."

"Aye, all right, I'll go."

"Thanks, Steve, thanks."

He made no answer and she watched the dark blur of him turn away into the night.

3

It was the following afternoon when the news reached the Manor, Sam brought it. He had been into Shields to the corn chandler's. All the news of the town and the villages about sifted through the corn chandler's and, like chaff wafted on the wind, it spread. Of course a dead man found in a gully wasn't all that exciting, not for Shields anyway, sailors were always being found up alleyways bashed and stark naked. The waterfront had its own excitements where killings were concerned. But this fellow had just come off a boat in the Tyne the day before yesterday, and he had been found early on this morning lying in a gully, a knife through his ribs. The general opinion was that the poor bugger would have been best off had he stayed at sea. But that was life.

Had he been in a fight? Nobody knew, only that he was lying on his face. It looked as if he had fallen down a steep bank and on to his own knife because his initials, they said, were on the handle of the knife.

But why would he have his knife out if he wasn't fighting? Well, as far as could be gathered there was no sign on his body that he had been in a fight, black eyes or bruises, nothing like that, just a few scratches on his face where apparently the brambles had caught him.

Sam gave the news to Katie and Katie took it into her mother, and Biddy stared at her open-mouthed until Katie said, "What is it, Ma, are you sick?" and Biddy answered, "No, it's just come as a bit of surprise, that's all, because he was the fellow who used to torment Tilly, an' for him to die like that and near the grounds an' all."

"Aye, he was, and she for one'll be pleased at the news. I'll go and tell her."

She met Tilly in the corridor, outside the master's room.

Staring at Katie, Tilly opened her mouth twice before she could whisper, "Dead? He's dead?"

"Aye; as I said. Fell on his knife, so Sam says! Dead as a door nail, so you'll have no more trouble from him. What's the matter? Eeh! you're not gona pass out, are you? Some folks do with relief—it's like shock," she was speaking in a soft hiss.

"I've . . . I've got to go and see to the . . . the master."

"Aye. Aye, Tilly, but I thought you'd like to know."

"Yes; thanks. Thanks, Katie, ta."

Tilly turned away and went back into the room where Mark was waiting for her. His eyes narrowing, he looked at her as he said sharply, "Well, what is it? You've . . . you've had news?"

She went and stood by his side, and now she wrung her hands as she gabbled, "They've . . . they've found him, but believe me . . . believe me, sir, not as I left him. When I left him he was lying on his back over the outcrop. News has come that he was on his face with"—she gulped in her throat and wetted her lips before she brought out in a thin whisper, "with a knife atween his ribs."

"A knife?"

"Aye, yes, sir."

"A knife." He chewed on his lip a moment. Then he said, "Somebody must have been there after you, somebody who hated him even more than you did."

"Yes, sir."

"Have you any idea?"

She lowered her eyes. "His . . . his brother, he came last night. I asked him to go and find him because . . . because I couldn't have his death on me conscience and . . . and I thought he might die in the night. He, Steve . . . he promised to go and . . . and. . . ."

"Well, it seems evident that he did go and all I can say is he's done you a very good turn."

"But if they were to find out he'd . . . he'd swing."

"Very likely"—his voice was cool sounding—"but we shall see what transpires. And, Trotter." He reached out and gripped her hand and, pulling her nearer to him, he looked up into her face as he said, "You're rid of him. That's one fear less in your life. And it's been your chief fear, hasn't it?"

"Yes, sir. But now I'm afeared for Steve."

"Well, why should they suspect him? Only you and I know about this matter, so who's to accuse the brother of killing him? Now come." He shook her hand. "You won't be implicated in any way."

"I . . . I don't know so much, sir. Steve said that Hal had threatened to beat him up if he came and warned me. And anyway, the mother locked Steve up in the attic, and when he went out, Hal McGrath, they would know he was goin' lookin' for me."

"Well, let them say what they like; you've never been away from my side for a week and I'd swear to this on all the Bibles in Christendom. Forget that you visited Mr. Burgess, forget that you've ever left me for a moment. Your friends downstairs will forget it too if it comes to the push." His voice trailed away and his eyes held hers, and when with a break in her voice she said, "I'd die if anything should happen to Steve through me." His grip tightened on her fingers and, his words coming from deep in his throat, he said, "And I should die, Tilly Trotter, if anything should happen to you."

As they stared at each other her mind started to gallop. *Oh, no! No! No! Not that door.* She didn't want that kind of door to open. But yet, hadn't she known it had been pushing ajar for a long time now?

No one came to the Manor inquiring for Miss Matilda Trotter to ask her questions about her movements on a certain day because at the inquest it was brought out that the man, after leaving his ship, had spent most of the evening in a tavern on the waterfront and had left there at a very late hour. His parents admitted that he had arrived home in the early hours of the morning and yes, he was under the influence of drink. But although they insisted that he had slept the drink off before he left the house the next day, the coroner took little account of this. But what he did take into account was that there had been no sign of a struggle. There were bruises on the man's back where he must have hit the boulders as he fell before rolling on to his face and his knife. Why he should have a knife in his hand would remain a mystery; but the knife was his own and his parents had confirmed this. A verdict of accidental death was returned.

On the day of the inquest the village waited. What would the McGraths do? They wouldn't take this lying down, would they? Would Big McGrath go to the Manor and haul that Trotter piece out? because if she hadn't actually done it she had certainly put her curse on Hal. And that last night of his life he had come through the village shouting her name. The whole village had heard him.

But Big McGrath did nothing because his wife said, "No! no more," because if he opened his mouth against that one now he would lose another son.

McGrath had gaped at his wife as if she had lost her senses when she said simply, "Stevie did it. Anyway, Hal would have swung in any case because he meant to do for that accursed bitch."

"I don't believe it," Big McGrath had said, "not Stevie; he wouldn't have the guts."

"He had the guts, although he nearly threw them up in the gorge in the middle of the night—that's where I found him."

"But why . . . why his brother?" He spoke now as if he had been unaware of the animosity between his sons.

"Two reasons," said his wife. "Hal has knocked him from dog to devil since he was a bairn. The other, he's caught, like Hal himsel' was, in the traps of that witch. An' that, I would say, was the main reason."

"God Almighty! and we're to sit here and do nowt?"

"Aye," she said. "But God and the devil have a way of fighting things out. Bide your time. Bide your time and join your prayers to all the others who have suffered at her hands an' her day will come. You'll see, her day will come. God speed it and grant I'll be there."

4

Summer came and it brought the children for a full week. The house once again rang with laughter and the big event at that time was the master racing them along the broad drive in his new acquisition, an iron-rimmed wheel-chair. The only fly in the ointment of that particular week for Mark, and definitely for Tilly, was the presence of Mrs. Forefoot-Meadows, accompanied this time by her maid, Miss Phillips, who could have been twin to Miss Mabel Price.

After they departed the house once again fell into its familiar pattern, and the master became morose and seemingly more demanding as the days went on. There were times when nothing was right. These came generally after his failure to adjust to the wooden stump and false foot for his left leg. The apparatus was leather-capped, as was the smaller artificial foot to adjust to the right ankle. Yet he had more success with the leg that extended to the knee than with the foot attached to his ankle; the bones here were so sensitive that the slightest pressure caused the water to spring to his eyes and his nails to dig into whatever he was holding at the time, which more often than not was Tilly's arm.

Always he apologized for this; and one time he unbuttoned the cuff of her sleeve and, pushing it up, he looked at the blue marks his nails had caused. For a moment she imagined he was going to put his lips to them, and so she had pulled her arm away, saying, "'Tis nothing, sir. 'Tis nothing."

There was no fear in her life now. The village could

have been on another planet. It was so long ago since she had passed through it, she had even forgotten what it looked like. And those about her bore her no resentment, much the reverse. She was given respect and her wishes were adhered to in every possible way. Yet she was not happy, for deep inside her she knew that sooner or later a question would be put to her, and if she said "No," what then? And should she say "Yes". . . . But she couldn't say "Yes." She couldn't give herself to somebody she didn't love. Yet she had a feeling for him, a strong feeling but different from that she still carried for Simon.

At times when she couldn't imagine herself living any kind of life but that which she was living now she would ask herself why not, because this present way of living would lead nowhere. She knew what happened to serving girls who gave in to masters. Oh yes, she knew that well enough. Yet she no longer felt a serving girl, and that was strange. Well, not so strange, she told herself, because it wasn't every servant girl who could discuss books. And then again he wasn't like an ordinary master. There were times when she felt she knew him better than any wife would know her husband, certainly better than his own wife did, for she knew she had spent more time with him in one month than his wife had spent with him in years, at least in the years after she had taken to her couch. So what was going to come of it? She didn't know. Then one night the opportunity was given to her to find out.

It was two days before Christmas, 1840. The house was warm and there was a gaiety prevailing in it, even without the children being present. Bunches of holly were hanging here and there. There was a mistletoe bough hanging in the hall where a huge fire was blazing in the iron basket on the great open hearth. The drawing-room was ablaze with light. All the lamps were lit in the house because the master was expecting company. Mr. John Tolman and his lady, Mr. Stanley

Fieldman and his lady, and Mr. Albert Cragg and his lady were coming to dinner.

Mark was dressed in a new blue velvet dinner-jacket and a cream silk shirt and cravat. Mr. Burgess had trimmed his hair to just above the top of his collar. A few minutes before he was ready to be carried downstairs by Fred Leyburn and John Hillman he said to Tilly, "Well! and how do I look? The caterpillar emerging from the chrysalis. But a very late emergence, therefore a very old butterfly."

She smiled widely at him, saying, "You look very handsome, sir."

"Thank you, Trotter. And you, you look very . . . very charming. Gray suits you, but . . . but I would take that apron off."

She looked down at the small dainty lawn apron hemmed by a tiny frill that had taken her hours to sew, and she said, "You don't like it, sir?"

"It's all right in its place but not for tonight. You are acting in the role of housekeeper, aren't you?"

"Yes, sir."

"Do you know what is expected of you?"

"Yes, sir. I'm to take the ladies into . . . madam's room"—she had paused before uttering the word madam—"and assist them off with their cloaks, and . . . and wait in the dressing-room in case they call me. And to be on hand during the evening should . . . they need to come upstairs."

"You have been well primed. Who told you of this procedure? I just meant you to help them off with their cloaks when they came up. . . ."

"I understand it's what Mrs. Lucas used to do, sir."

"Oh, I see. Well, I shall leave that part to you. Now tell Leyburn that I am ready. . . ."

Ten minutes later he was ensconced in the wheelchair in the drawing-room, and when the butler came in to tend the fire, he said, "Everything in order, Pike?"

"Yes, sir. I think the table is as you wish it, and cook

has carried out your orders as regards the main course. The turkey is a fine bird, sir, together with the braised tongue."

"Good. Good."

"And Miss Trotter wrote out a menu for the cook to cover the rest of the meal: Soup for the first course, sir, then crimped cod and oyster sauce, followed by pork cutlets in tomato sauce; then, as I said, the turkey and tongue, sir. This will be followed by cheesecake and nesselrode pudding, and, of course, the cheeses; we have a very fine ripe Stilton, sir."

"Sounds excellent, Pike, excellent." Mark had turned the chair toward the fire; he could not let the old man see that he was amused. Now that he knew Trotter was in favor, Pike never missed an opportunity to sing her praises, if unobtrusively. And it was quite some time ago, off his own bat, that Pike had appended the miss to Trotter. It was what Trotter had once referred to as crawling, yet there were times when he felt sorry for the man, for he had aged visibly since most of the old staff were dismissed and he had elected to stay on, and his legs seemed hardly able to carry him. What would happen to him should he retire him now he didn't know, for he had known no other home but this house since he was a boy. Oh! why concern himself about such things at this moment. Tonight he was entertaining friends for the first time in more than two years, and there would be women at his table.

It was odd when he came to think about it but it wasn't he who had suggested the get-together; it was Cragg on his last visit who had said, "Isn't it about time you had some company?" and he had gladly fallen in with the suggestion.

When he heard the carriages draw up outside he wheeled himself into the hall, there to welcome his guests. "Delighted to see you, delighted to see you. Hello, Joan. Hello, my dear Olive. Why Bernice, such a long time since we last met."

"Wonderful to see you, Mark."

"You're looking so well, Mark."

"My dear Mark, how lovely to be here again."

"Will you come this way, madam?"

After a moment the ladies turned and followed the tall, slim, gray-clad figure. Their silken skirts making sounds like the ebbing waves on a beach, they swept up the staircase, across the gallery and into the wide corridor where Tilly, after opening the door leading into what was once Eileen's sitting-room, stood aside and allowed them to enter.

The room was softly lit by the light from two pink-shaded oil lamps and a glowing fire, and it showed up the gold embroidery on the chaise-longue, and the deep rose velvet upholstery of the Louis-Seize. Added light was given by the candelabra arranged at each end of the long dressing-table, and between them lay the powder boxes and toilet water ready to hand.

One after the other she helped the three women off with their cloaks, and one after the other she hung the velvet and fur-trimmed garments in the wardrobe, conscious all the while that the women were eyeing her, one of them through the long cheval mirror, another from where she sat in front of the dressing-table; the third, a very stout madam, stood looking at her without any pretext whatsoever.

Tilly wetted her lips, swallowed her spittle, then said, "If the ladies should require me I shall be in the adjoining room."

Had she said the right thing or the wrong thing, for now all three of them were looking at her directly? And then she did the unforgivable, she forgot her place to such an extent that she didn't bend her knee. Of late, she had been out of the habit of doing so, and when she did remember it was too late, she was already entering the dressing-room.

Closing the door behind her, she stood with her back to it and let out a long drawn breath, then closed her eyes tightly, and as she stood thus the muted voices came to her, words indistinguishable at first, but then snatches here and there.

"I told you, didn't I?"

"It was evident, Albert said."

"Nonsense!"

"You were right, Bernice."

"Nonsense!"

"Not after Myton; he would never stoop. Educating her? . . . Nonsense!"

"Stanley says it's impossible to educate the peasantry."

"Queer stories."

"Odd looking altogether . . . shapeless."

One of them laughed, a high laugh; then a voice said, "Well, what are we here for?" and another answered, in a quite ordinary tone, "What indeed! Let us go down."

"Girl!"

She paused a moment, then turned and opened the door. The three women were standing close together, that is as close as their billowing skirts would allow, and it was the stout one who, with a lazy gesture, waved her hand toward the door. Following the silent command, Tilly opened it and stood aside, and they all three floated past her, leaving behind them a beautiful smell of perfume.

After closing this door, too, she stood with her back to it. And now she asked herself why she should feel so angry, was it because they had been talking about her? Yet when she tried to recall the disjointed sentences she found she was unable to do so. But the impression remained strong and disturbing: they *had* been talking about her, and she imagined that if she were not the main reason, she was certainly part of the reason why they were here tonight.

"Aw, don't be daft." She pulled herself from the door and went to sit down on a chair, but stopped herself as she thought, No, it wouldn't be right, not in this room; and so, going out, she went into the master's room and there, sitting down, she asked herself why it was one instinctively disliked some people. Those three, for instance, she felt she hated them. It was the way they had looked at her, as if she were of no more account than an animal. Less, for the class was known to care for their horses and their hounds. Biddy was saying the other day that there were good gentry and bad. In some of their houses you were in luck, in others you were like muck. Biddy came out with some funny sayings. Which reminded her, she'd better get downstairs.

A few minutes later she was in the kitchen.

Here there was bustle and excitement: Mr. Pike and Phyllis were serving in the dining-room, but waiting on them were Peg and Katie, and running back and forward in the kitchen was Ada Tennant and young Fanny, while supervising them all was Biddy.

"How's it going?" She was standing by Biddy's side.

"All right from this end, lass. Everything was done to a turn. But my God! that puddin', it has me worried. I only hope it tastes as good as all the stuff that's gone into it. The cheesecake's all right and the rest, but oh"—she glanced at Tilly—"this is more up my street, not fancy puddings," and she continued stacking the small sausages around the base of the bird. Lastly, she poured a glazed sauce over its breastbone, and standing back, she looked at it with her head on one side as she said, "We could get through that quite nicely worsels, eh Tilly?" Then, "There now, Peg; put the cover on, and in you go with it. Steady! Don't spill the juice. And you, Katie, get the vegetables in."

She now went up the kitchen and took from the round oven the silver vegetable dishes, saying, "They're not that hot, you can handle them. There you are." She placed four on a tray that was large enough to cause

Katie to have to spread her arms wide in order to carry it.

Returning to the table, she said, "Once the main course is in I always think it's easy going after that."

"You'll be glad to get off your legs."

"Aye, I will. It's been a long day, but an important one." She nodded at Tilly. "You see, I've never cooked a dinner like this for the gentry afore, not for a proper do. It's different sending bits and pieces upstairs. Everything had to be right for this, hadn't it?"

"And you got it right. I knew you would."

"You look tired, lass. Anything wrong?"

"No, nothing."

"What are they like, the ladies?"

It suddenly sprang to Tilly's mind to answer, "Bitches!" but instead, she said, "If they hadn't their fine clothes on they'd look like ordinary women."

At this Biddy put her head back and laughed, then slanting her eyes toward Tilly, she said, "You're learnin', lass. Aye you're learnin'. Put me in mind of what me granda used to say, so me mother told me, when she used to come back from her place at the castle and talked about the ladies and gentlemen there. He used to say, 'Aye; aye, lass; but just remember they've got to gan to the closet like ye and me.'"

Tilly pressed her lips together, then said, "How right you are."

After a moment Biddy asked, "Where's your apron, I thought you were goin' to wear it, the one that you made?"

"The master didn't like it; he . . . he told me to take it off."

Biddy was looking squarely at her now. "Why?"

"I don't know. I . . . I suppose he just didn't like it."

Biddy turned from her and, reaching out, gently lifted up the elaborate iced pudding reposing on a shallow cut-glass dish, the base of which was surrounded by colored crystalized flowers, and she gently shook her head but made no further remark, and Tilly, divining her thoughts, turned away. . . .

The dinner lasted about an hour and a half. Snatches of talk and laughter seeped into the hall, but later, after the company had retired to the drawing-room the laughter and talk became louder, the scent of cigar smoke filled the house, and the air seemed filled with jollity. Definitely so in the servants' hall, where they were all tucking into the remains of the feast.

Tilly had had a tray brought upstairs so that she could be on hand if the ladies should require her. She had forgotten to show them the way to the closet, but none of them seemed to have been in need of it so far. It was eleven o'clock and she'd been up from six that morning and now, right or wrong, she was sitting in the armchair, her head nodding, when she heard the chatter outside on the landing.

She was on her feet when the door opened and the three women came into the room. Passing her as if she were nonexistent, they flopped down here and there on the chairs. Then one laughing said, "I need the closet," and another answered, "Me, too; but I'll have to wait until I get home and get out of me stays."

"Do you think you'll last, Bernice?"

"Well, if I don't . . . pop goes the weasel!"

Standing at the far end of the room, beside the door leading into the dressing-room, Tilly could hardly believe her ears. They were coarse these women, yet they were ladies, in fact two of them were daughters of men with titles. They had acted like great dames a few hours ago, now, full of wine and food, they were talking no better than those they employed; in fact, there were some ordinary folk who didn't discuss such things, personal things.

"Me cloak, girl!"

She walked swiftly across the room and, taking a cloak down from the wardrobe, she tentatively held it out to the woman. "That isn't mine. Don't be stupid, girl! The brown velvet."

She brought the brown velvet and helped the owner into it. Then taking another cloak from the wardrobe, she stood with it in her hand looking toward the two women, and one of them said, quite civilly, "That's mine." Then they were all ready to go and, laughing and chatting, they went from the room without a glance in her direction. And yet, strangely, she knew they were as aware of her as she was of them. Snatches of their conversation came to her as she followed them down the corridor.

"Did you see his face when Albert mentioned Agnes's new bull?"

"'Twas naughty of Albert, and Mark was mad."

"What d'you think of the other?"

"Don't really know. Could be."

"I thought I'd have the vapors when Stanley grumbled about his feet and the gout."

"'Twasn't intentional, 'twasn't."

"God! I want the closet."

Tilly didn't know if she were supposed to follow them downstairs and help to see them out, but she didn't go. Mr. Pike was there, that would suffice. The bull they were referring to was likely Lady Myton's new lover, and this must have displeased the master. They were as she had dubbed them at first, bitches, three bitches.

The door could hardly have closed on them when the master ordered to be carried upstairs, and when she saw his face she knew he was in a temper.

The men carried him past her and into the closet; afterward they sat him in a chair beside the bed. When they had gone he called to her in the dressing-room, his voice imperious, "Trotter! Trotter!"

"Yes, sir?" She stood in front of him and when he looked up at her without speaking she said, "Have you had a good evening, sir?"

"No, Trotter," he replied, "I have not, as you say,

had a good evening." He spaced the words. "How many friends can you expect to have in life, can you tell me?"

"No, sir."

"If you have two, you are damned lucky, but I don't think I have one, not a true friend. A man who was a true friend would control his wife, at least her tongue, when in company. Trotter, those three ladies came tonight to find out something. Have you any idea what it was?"

She stared unblinking at him as she said, "No, sir," knowing now that she could truthfully have said, "Yes, sir."

"That's just as well. Here, pull this shirt off me." He tore at his cravat, and when she had stripped him down to the waist he said as he always did now, "I can manage." She had already laid his nightshirt on the bed. There was no nightcap beside it, for he was strange in that he didn't like nightcaps. And yet most gentlemen wore nightcaps, so she understood. Perhaps it was because he had never powdered his hair or worn a wig. But then lots of gentlemen didn't wear wigs today or powdered. Even so, she would have thought they all wore nightcaps.

"Get yourself to bed, you must be tired."

"Yes, sir. Good-night, sir."

"Good-night, Trotter. By the way"—he paused—"it was an excellent meal, I've never tasted better. Tell cook that."

"I will, sir. She'll be very pleased."

In her room, she sat for a while in the chair by the side of the bed. She was feeling sad inside, sad for herself, but more sad for him: he hadn't enjoyed the evening, yet everybody else in the house had. Of course, she couldn't speak for the guests.

She rose slowly and undressed and got into bed.

She did not know how long she had been asleep but the crash woke her, bringing her sitting upright and wide awake all in a moment. The noise had come from the room beyond the closet and the dressing-room. Had . . . had he fallen? Had he tried to get out of bed and knocked something over?

She was out of the door, along the corridor and into the bedroom before she had even given herself the answer to the question, and there before her, showing up faintly in the glow of the night candle in the red glass bowl, was the overturned side table, the water carafe not broken but half empty now as it lay on its side, and a glass that had snapped clean in two. Also spread about the floor were a number of books and as far away as the fire, lying on the rug, was the square brass traveling clock.

"What is it? What is it?" She had gone around to the other side of the bed. He was lying back now on his pillows, his face twisted. "I . . . I had an accident, the table toppled."

"Don't worry. Don't worry, I'll soon clear it up."

He roused himself, saying, "The glass, mind your feet."

"Yes, yes, all right. Just lie still."

She lit the candles; then taking one, she hurried through the dressing-room and into the closet. As she was picking up the pail and cloth there was a tap on the door. When she opened it, there stood Katie and Ada Tennant. For some time now they had been sleeping up on the nursery floor, while Biddy, Peg, and Fanny went to the back lodge which was now their home.

"What . . . what's happened? We heard the crash."

"It's all right. He . . . the master upset the table, the side table."

"Is there anything I can do, Tilly?"

"No, no, Katie. Get back to bed." She now looked at Ada Tennant who was hanging on to Katie's arm. She seemed frightened. She was a silly girl, vacant in some way, and her mind, what little she had, was open to all impressions. And so she reassured her now, saying,

"It's all right, Ada, nothing's happened. Go on back to bed."

As Ada nodded her plump face at her, the thought came to her that in a few years time she would look like Mrs. Brackett, because like her, she was always eating.

When the girls had gone she closed the door, then went swiftly through the dressing-room and into the bedroom. He was lying as she had left him, his head back, his eyes closed.

After picking up the debris from the floor and sopping up the water from the carpet, she took the pail and the broken glass into the closet and left it there. She would deal with that in the morning. All she had to do now was to fill the carafe again and give him a clean glass.

He was sitting propped up against the pillows when she returned to the bedroom and, going to him, she said, "Is . . . is there anything more I can do for you, sir?"

His eyes were wide open and he continued to stare at her, and then he said slowly, "Yes, Trotter; sit down here beside me." He patted the side of the bed.

"But, sir."

"Trotter, please."

Her hand went instinctively now to the front of her nightdress. She hadn't even got her dressing-gown on. She said softly, "Will you excuse me a moment, sir, while I get me dressing-gown?"

"No, Trotter, I wouldn't excuse you a moment. Just sit down as you are."

Slowly she obeyed him.

"Give me your hand."

She gave him her hand, and when he took it he turned it over until her palm was upright. Then he placed his other hand on top of it and, his voice now like a low rumble in his throat, he said, "During these past months I've been very lonely, Trotter, but never so much as tonight . . . downstairs."

Her surprise overcame her feeling of apprehension for a moment and she managed to bring out, "They . . . they are your friends, sir."

"No, Trotter, no; I have no friends. I am going to tell you something, Trotter. Those men who were here tonight all have mistresses. Two are kept in Newcastle and one in Durham. One of those gentlemen has lost count of the number of mistresses he has had. And their wives know of these kept women, yet they live an apparently normal life. But me, I had one affair, not my first I admit, but the only one during the time of my second marriage, and what happens? I lose my wife and my children, and because my wife leaves me I am shunned. Had she chosen to stay, my escapade would merely have been a talking and a laughing point among my so-called friends. Can you understand it, Trotter?"

She made no answer. She couldn't. She knew what he had said was true, but the unfairness of it provided her with no words of consolation.

"I sound full of self-pity, don't I?"

"No, sir."

"Well, what do I sound like to you?"

This she could answer without taking time to consider. "Somebody lonely, sir."

"Somebody lonely." He repeated her words. "How right you are, Trotter. Somebody lonely. But it does nothing to help a man's ego to admit that he's lonely. You know what an ego is?"

"No, sir."

"Well, it is . . . it's his pride, it's that thing inside of him which tells him he's a great I am. Both big and small men are born with it. Strange"—he gave a huh! of a laugh here—"but the smaller the man the bigger the ego. You see, the small man's got to fight to prove himself. But here am I, neither big nor small, and my ego has dropped to rock bottom. It must have, to make me act as I have done tonight in order to bring you to me."

He turned now and looked at the righted table and he said, "I upset that lot purposely because I wanted you here near me." He did not turn his head now and look at her, but feeling her hand stiffen in his, he said, "Don't . . . don't be afraid of me, Trotter."

"I'm not, sir."

"You're not?"

"No, sir."

"Then why did you shrink from me?"

"I didn't shrink; I . . . I was only surprised, sir."

"And shocked?"

"No, sir, not shocked."

"You know what I'm asking of you, Trotter?"

She looked down to where their clasped hands lay on the padded eiderdown and she moved her head once as she said, "Yes, sir."

"And —" His voice scarcely a whisper now, he asked, "are you willing?"

Her head was still down as she answered him bluntly, "No, sir."

When his fingers withdrew from hers she raised her eyes and looked at him and said, "I'm . . . I'm sorry, sir. I . . . I would do anything for you, anything but . . . but. . . ."

"Lie with me?"

Again her head was down.

"You . . . you don't like me?"

"Oh yes; yes, sir." She instinctively put out her hands toward his now; then withdrew it as she went on, "Oh yes, sir, I like you. I like you very much, sir."

"But not enough to comfort me?"

"It wouldn't be right, sir. And . . . and it would alter things."

"In what way?"

"It . . . it wouldn't be the same, me going around the house, I —" She turned and looked across the dimly lighted room now and it was some seconds before she could find words to express her feelings, and then she said, "I . . . I wouldn't be able to keep my head up."

Again he made a small sound like a laugh in his throat, then said, "That is what is known as working-class morality."

"What, sir?"

"It doesn't matter, Trotter. But tell me, have . . . have you ever loved anyone?" He watched her chest expand underneath the cotton nightdress, he saw her neck jerk as she swallowed deeply, and when he insisted, "Have you?" she said "Yes."

"And he? Does he love you?"

"I . . . I think he does in a way, sir."

"In a way? What do you mean in a way?"

"Well, it would be no use, sir, 'twouldn't be right."

"Oh! Trotter. Trotter!" The sound of his laughter was more defined now and he shook his head as he said, "You're unfortunate, Trotter. It would appear that you only arouse the love of married men. I suppose he is married?"

"Yes, sir."

"Is it the farmer?"

When she actually started, he said, "Oh, don't be upset; I'm sure your secret must be suspected by a number of people for it isn't every bridegroom that leaves his bride on his wedding night to go to the assistance of a beautiful young girl. Nor does a man take her into his house in spite of his wife's protests. By the way I'm just guessing at the last. When I found you living in the outhouse I thought something was amiss in the farmer's household for you to have returned to the ruins of the cottage. . . . So, Trotter, you're in love with a man who can never mean anything to you. What are you going to do? Spend your life fighting against frustration until you're a wizened old maid?"

"No, sir." Her voice was clear now. "I shall marry. Some day I shall marry and have a family."

He peered at her now through the lamplight and her

answer seemed to deflate him still further, for he lay back on his pillows and sighed.

"I'm sorry, sir." Her voice conveyed her feelings.

"It's all right, Trotter, it's all right. But stay. Would . . . would you do something for me? It's not going to hurt you in any way. But it'll bring . . . well, it'll bring to life a sort of fancy I've had of late."

"Anything I can, sir."

"Well then, lay yourself on top of this bed with your head on the pillow facing me."

"Sir!" She was on her feet now, her hands joined together at her waist, and he said, "It is nothing much to ask. I won't hurt you in any way, I'll be under the clothes and you'll be on top of them. I just want to see you lying there."

He watched her head slowly droop until her chin was on her chest. He watched her turn slowly and walk around the foot of the bed and to the other side. He watched her pull her nightdress up slightly and her bare knee touch the coverlet. Then after resting on her elbow, she lay straight down. He watched her stretch out her hand and push her nightdress well down over her knees. And now they were lying, their faces opposite to each other.

When he lifted his hand and gently touched her cheek, Tilly closed her eyes and told herself loudly in her head not to cry, because if she cried it would be the undoing of her, for pity for him would swamp her and she would no longer lie on top of the bedclothes.

"You're very beautiful, Trotter. You know that?"

She made no answer.

"I'm going to tell you something. I dislike your name very much, I hate it every time I've got to say it, it's a harsh name, Trotter. Your name is Tilly and Tilly sounds so nice, gay, warm. A Tilly, I feel, could be no other than nice. I think of you as Tilly."

"Oh, sir."

His fingers now were moving around her eye sockets as he said, "You've got the strangest eyes, Trotter, they're so clear and deep. That's why people take you for a witch."

Again she said, "Oh, sir."

"And you know, I don't think they're far wrong. I was thinking the other day it's a good job that you hadn't been born into the class because you would have played havoc there. There would have been no peace for any man who set eyes on you."

She had to speak or cry, and so she said, "That isn't right, sir. Some people . . . some men dislike me wholeheartedly."

"It's only because they want you."

"No, sir. No, sir. 'Tis something in me. Women dislike me too. That's the hardest to bear, women dislikin' me."

After a moment his hand left her face and he lay looking at her. Her eyes were shaded now, and he let his own travel down her shape underneath the cheap nightdress.

Then of a sudden they both turned their heads and looked up toward the ceiling as the sound of a door closing came to them, and when she rose quickly to her elbow she looked at him and he at her, and now he said, "All right, my dear, and thank you."

She slipped from the bed and made for the dressing-room door, but as she turned and looked backward she saw he was lying on his side staring toward her. Swiftly she went into the room now, then through into the closet, and there, sitting down, she bent forward and dropped her face into her hands. Her whole body was shivering while her mind was chattering at her. Another minute or so and I would have. The pity of it, the pity of it. And him the master. 'Tisn't right. If only I could. But no, no, 'twouldn't be right. And as I said, I couldn't hold me head up. And he knows about Simon.

Well, if he's twigged, how many more? His wife? Oh
yes, his wife. But what's going to happen now? How
can I go on knowing what he wants, and he's so nice, so
kind? I do like him. Yes, I do, I do.

She got to her feet now, her mind saying harshly,
"Get to bed for God's sake! get to bed."

She had to go out of the closet door to get to her
room, and she had just stepped into the passage when
she came face to face with Ada Tennant. Ada was
holding a candlestick; she held it above her head and
peered at Tilly. She had a coat on over her nightdress
and Tilly, remembering her position, said sternly,
"Where have you been?"

"Just down to kitchen, I was hungry. Me belly
grumbles in the night. I've just had a shive."

Ada now turned her gaze on Tilly. Tilly wasn't
wearing any thing over her nightdress and she dared to
say, "You've been with the master? You've had to see
to the master all this time? and Tilly said rapidly, "No,
no, of course not. I've just been to the closet."

"Oh. Oh aye. Thought I heard him talkin' as I passed
goin' down. Must have been dreamin'." She now
turned away and went toward the end of the corridor
and the stairs leading to the attic, and Tilly went into
her room where, almost throwing herself into bed, she
lay stiffly staring up into the darkness. It only needed
Ada Tennant to put two and two together, and as
simple as she was, she wasn't past doing that, and it
would be all over the place that she was serving the
master in more ways than one. Swinging herself about,
she turned on to her stomach and tried to squash the
thought that had sprung into her mind: she wished she
could serve him in more ways than one, and except for
the fact that she might be landed with a bairn she would,
yes, she would, because where would this feeling for
Simon ever get her?

Gone now was the idea that if she followed such a
course she wouldn't be able to hold her head up again.

5

Routine can become tedious, but often it signifies a time of peace. From the night of the bed incident a new relationship came to life between Mark and Tilly. No reference was made to the incident, nor did his manner toward her alter in any way. But on her part, she had found difficulty for days afterward in being her natural self. Soon, however, she took the cue from him and life went on smoothly, too smoothly.

Then one morning the smoothness was ruffled. Like the surface of the sea before a storm, all had been calm, but following the slight ruffle came a wind, and it churned up the waves so fiercely that at one point Tilly thought she would drown.

She was entering the kitchen when Peg came hurrying toward her, saying, "Steve, the lad, is at the back door askin' for you, Tilly."

Endeavoring to hide her impatience, she said, "Thanks, Peg. I'll see to him," and went down to the kitchen, past Biddy who turned her bent back from the stove, raised her eyebrows and shook her head but said nothing.

Steve had grown within the last year or so. He was now almost eighteen but he looked older; it was his solemn countenance that went a long way toward putting at least two years on him. He greeted her as usual: "Hello, Tilly."

"Hello, Steve," she said. "How are you?"

He did not answer her question but asked, "Can I talk to you like, away from here?"

405

She turned for a moment and looked back into the kitchen, then said, "Well, I'm on duty; but I can give you five minutes or so."

She was surprised when he closed his eyes for a moment as he tossed his head upward; then he was walking by her side and through the archway, and into the shelter of the high stone wall which had been bordered at one time by a rough hedge, but now the land was all cleared and showed a neat path and low-trimmed box hedges.

She was again surprised by his manner when he stopped abruptly and said, "I've come to ask you something."

She didn't say, "Well, what is it?" she just waited a while, looking into his face; and so he went on, "I feel I've got to speak out and get me say in afore he gets over his pretended sorrow and comes lookin' for you."

"What are you talking about?"

"You know what I'm talkin' about."

"I don't, Steve." She shook her head impatiently.

"Well, first of all I don't care what they say about you and . . . and him. . . ." He pointed in the direction of the top of the wall and the house beyond.

"What do you mean?" Her chin came into her neck now as she felt her body stretching upward.

"Aw"—he lowered his head and shook it—"you know what I mean."

"I don't know what you mean, Steve McGrath."

"Well, you should do if you've got your wits about you. Ask yourself, which lass of your standin' is taken into a big house like that and put in charge and runnin' it like a mistress? They say you don't get chances like that for doin' nowt."

"Well, I got my chance for doing nowt." Her voice was loud, and, realizing this, she turned her head first to one side, then to the other, and pressed her fingers over her lips for a moment.

"You mean there's nothin'?" His tone was contrite now.

"I don't see why I should bother even to answer you."

"Aw, I'm sorry." He looked to the side, then kicked at a pebble on the path. "It's the village; they seem to have nobody to talk about but you. It's funny."

"I don't think it's funny."

"You know what I mean. Well, anyway"—he now drew himself up and said, "I'll come to the point, I've been beatin' about the bush for as long as I can remember. I . . . I want to marry you, Tilly. I . . . I want to know if I can start courtin' you? I'll soon be on the face workin' an' I'll earn enough to keep us. . . ."

She was looking at the ground. She, however, did not kick at a pebble but remained perfectly still for a moment with one lifted palm outwards before her face. It was this action which had stopped him talking.

There was a long silence before he said softly, "I'll wait as long as you like."

"It's no use, Steve. I . . . I don't think of you in that way."

"'Cos I'm a year younger?"

"No, it's got nothing to do with that, I . . . I just think of you . . . well, as a brother."

"I don't want you to think of me as a brother, I never have."

"I know."

"You know?"

"Well, of course, I know, and . . . and I've tried to put you off. You can't say I haven't."

"You won't put me off, Tilly, not until you go and marry somebody else."

"Steve"—she put her hand gently on his arm now —"please don't wait for me 'cos it can never be, not . . . not with you. As much as I like you, it can't be, Steve."

He lowered his head now as he said, "Things happen; you might be glad of me one day."

"I'll . . . I'll always be glad of you, of your friendship, Steve, but . . . but not as anything else."

She watched his face crumple as if he were going to cry, and what he said now startled her.

"I killed our Hal for you, Tilly."

"Don't say that!" The hoarse whisper came from deep in her throat, and she repeated again, "Don't say it. I told you to go and help him . . . oh my God! Anyway, if you did it you didn't do it for me, you did it because you hated him."

His head came up with a jerk as he said, "I hated him because of what he did to you, and what I did to him I did for you. What's more, they know that I did it, at least me ma does. But she won't give me away because she'd lose another one, an' me pay packet an' all."

The bitter irony of his words saddened her, and for a moment she wanted to put her arms about him and hold him and tell him how grateful she was for what he had done because inside she was grateful, but she knew what the result of that would be, so she said, "Oh, Steve, I'm sorry. I'm sorry, and I would do anything for you, but . . . but that. Try to look upon me as a friend, Steve. There's good lasses about. Katie, you know, she's always talkin' about you, she likes you a lot, she's a nice lass. . . ."

"Aw. Shut up Tilly! It's like tellin' a thirsty bloke to chew sand."

There was silence again between them until she said, "I've got to go, Steve, I'm . . . I'm sorry."

"I'll wait."

"Please, please, Steve, don't, it's useless."

"Aye well, I can't feel worse off than I am now, but I thought I'd get the first one in afore the farmer comes gallopin' over."

She stared at him, her brows meeting. "What do you mean, the farmer comes galloping over? I've never seen Si . . . Mr. Bentwood for months. And what makes you think he'll come galloping over here?" Her voice was stiff, as was her face now.

. "Well, he's a widower now, isn't he?"

"What!"

He stared at her. "You didn't know that she, his wife, was dead?"

Her mouth opened to let in a long draft of air and she shook her head slowly before saying, "When?"

"Four . . . no, six weeks gone. And you didn't know?"

"Well, why should I?" She was finding it difficult to speak now. "We get no one . . . no one from the village here."

"But surely somebody in the house?"

She looked away to the side as she thought, Yes, surely somebody in the house. The master, he was bound to know that the farmer's wife had died. Yet why should he? Then there was Mr. Burgess, he knew all the gossip of the countryside, he surely would have spoken of it. Her gaze flicked from side to side as if searching for an answer; then she said, "I've . . . I've got to go. Good-bye, Steve. I'm . . . I'm sorry."

"Tilly."

She refused to answer the plea in his voice and, turning hurriedly away, went through the arch and over the courtyard and into the kitchen; and there met Phyllis who was coming through the green-baize door and who in a loud whisper said, "I . . . I was just comin' for you; there's company."

"Company? Who?"

"Mr. Rosier has just been shown up."

His feelings were such that Mark would have welcomed the company of any man that morning, with the exception of the one who now stood before him.

"Well, how do I find you?"

"You find me very well." Mark did not look toward

Mr. Burgess and say, "Give the gentleman a seat," but Mr. Burgess, of his own accord, proffered the visitor a chair before he himself left the room.

"I should have called before but I have been busy."

It was now more than a year since the mine disaster, and so whatever had prompted Rosier's presence here today wasn't out of compassion or sympathy. . . . But why ask the road he knew?

"How are things?"

"As you see"—Mark waved his hand in an arc which encompassed the room—"most comfortable. Everything I need."

"Yes, yes." Rosier now patted his knee; then jerking his small body up from the chair, he flicked his coat tails to the side before saying, "I was never much use at small talk—don't believe in it anyway—I think you know why I'm here today."

Mark remained quiet, just staring at the man.

"It's like this, Sopwith, there's not a damn thing been done to your pit since the water took over. Now if you leave it like that much longer it will be too late to save anything."

"I wasn't aware that I'd given the impression I wanted to save anything."

"Don't be a fool, man." Rosier screwed his buttocks hard on the chair now, and both his face and his voice showed impatience as he said, "And don't let's spar. And I'm not going to talk light because you're no invalid. Let's speak man to man, you're in a hell of a mess."

"I beg your pardon!"

"You heard what I said all right, you're in a hell of a mess. You haven't got the money to put that place in order and, as it is, nobody but a fool would take it on."

"I would never have classed you in that category, Rosier."

"Ah, don't fiddle-faddle, you know what I mean. The place needs money spent on it, even when it's

410

pumped dry, and that'll take the devil of a lot of doing. But you know, you've always been behind the times. Now you've got to admit that. Why, you're one of the few pits that's been running solely on horses for years. You thought you could go it alone. All pits are joining up their wagonways, some going straight to the ports. Look what's happening across the river. Seghill has become dissatisfied with the Cramlington wagonway and is building its own line to Howdon."

"Go on. Go on."

"Aye, I'm going on. Now, as I proposed to you when I last spoke about sharing, the wagonway between us would have been of great benefit, we could have joined up with the main line going to the river. . . ."

"Great benefit to whom?"

"Now don't take that lord almighty tack, Sopwith. If you had taken my offer on a fifty-fifty basis we would have both benefited, now your place is hardly worth the ground it stands on."

"Then why are you here?"

"Because I'm a man who takes risks, a gambler at heart, I suppose."

"And you're willing to gamble on something that's not worth the ground it stands on? Oh, who do you think you're talking to, Rosier? Now—" He put his hand up to check a further flow from the visitor, saying, "Wait! That mine has been in our family for generations, before rolley ways or wagonways were thought of, when the ponies and horses carried the coal on their backs, and it's going to remain in our family. Dry or wet, working or still, it's going to remain there. Have I made myself clear?"

Rosier was on his feet now wagging his bullet head from side to side. "You're a bloody fool, Sopwith," he said. "That's what you are. You're sinking. All about you you're sinking, your house, your land. It might as well have been flooded with the pit for all the use it's going to be to you when you haven't got the money to

411

keep it going. I can promise you twenty-five per cent of what I'll get out of that hole in a couple of years' time, enough to keep you safe here for the rest of your days."

Mark reached out and grabbed at the bell rope to the side of the fireplace; then his hand releasing that, he picked up the bell on the side table and rang it violently.

Before Pike's stiff legs were half-way up the stairs, Mr. Burgess had entered the room.

"Kindly show this gentleman out, Burgess."

Mr. Burgess lowered his head and stood aside for the visitor to leave, but Rosier remained standing staring at Mark, and what he said now was, "Your days are done; you and your kind's time has passed. Things are happening out there. Iron is coming into its own; steam is giving horses a kick in the arse, you'll see. You'll see. You and your horses carrying the coal out on your wooden tracks! God! you're as dead as last century."

When he turned he almost knocked Mr. Burgess over; in fact, if it hadn't been for the support of the door the man would have fallen.

Pike was at the top of the stairs to meet the visitor, but he, too, was thrust aside.

Tilly held her breath for a moment as she watched Mr. Pike support himself against the balustrade; then she hurried toward the bedroom.

Mr. Burgess was leaning over the chair as she entered the room and he was saying, "Are you all right, sir?" and for answer Mark said, "No, I'm not all right, Burgess; who could be all right after that?"

Burgess straightened up and, his voice quiet now, he said, "Pigs are supposed to be intelligent, sir, and one can believe this, but on no account will they ever be capable of fitting into civilized society."

"Oh, Burgess!" Mark put his head down for a moment; then looking up at Tilly, he said, "Bring me a glass of something, not milk or soup."

She smiled at him before hurrying to the dressing room.

A few minutes later, after he had sipped at the glass of brandy she had brought him, he looked from her to Mr. Burgess and said quietly, "He's right you know, he's right in one way, I belong to the last century."

"Nonsense!"

He smiled at Burgess; then said to Tilly, "I don't suppose we'll have another visit from him, but leave word, Trotter, that he is not to be admitted to this house again, on any account."

"Yes, sir."

She left the room, went downstairs, and gave the order to Mr. Pike, who said, "Well, that's good news, for nothing would please me better than to show that gentleman the door before he got over the step."

Returning upstairs again, she went immediately into the dressing-room and there she waited until she heard Burgess take his leave. There was something she wanted to ask the master, at least there were two things she wanted to ask him; the first one was if she could have this afternoon off. When she thought of what this might lead to she put her hand to her breast as if to still the quickened beating of her heart. She knew why Simon hadn't come to see her since his wife had died, for the simple reason it wouldn't be proper and no matter how forthright he might appear she knew he cared about people's opinion of him. But there was nothing to stop her visiting him to offer her condolences. Oh, she tossed her head at the thought—she was acting like a hypocrite, thinking like a hypocrite. She was glad she was dead. She was, she was. No. No. She mustn't think like that. Well, what other way could she think? Simon was now free and she loved Simon . . . and he loved her. She had known this for years, even perhaps before he knew it.

She went into the room now and, standing a little

413

distance from Mark, she said, "Could I ask a favor of you, sir?"

"Yes, Trotter, anything. You know that I will grant you anything within my power."

"May . . . may I have this afternoon off, sir?"

When he put his head back and laughed she smiled widely. After the rumpus of that meeting it was good to hear him laugh. "Of course, Trotter, you may have the afternoon off. I think we should arrange that you have more afternoons off, you spend too much time in the house and"—he paused—"and in this room."

"Oh, I don't mind that, sir."

"I'm glad you don't, Trotter. Are you thinking of going into Shields or taking a trip into Newcastle?"

"No, sir, neither."

"Oh." He waited, his face full of inquiry, and now she put her second question to him. "Did you know, sir, that Farmer Bentwood's wife had died?"

His eyes held hers, but even before that her face had flushed with the question she had put to him, for she was remembering the confession of her feelings on a certain night some months ago.

"Yes, yes, I knew, Trotter."

She could now feel her face stretching in amazement. When she found her voice she wanted to demand, "And why didn't you tell me?" but the thought came to her, How did he know? Someone must have told him. Such a thing wouldn't be of any interest to the viewer or the agent who sometimes called about the mine; perhaps it was Mr. Tolman or Mr. Cragg. And then she knew who had brought the news, Mr. Burgess. Her voice was quiet when she said, "Does . . . did anyone else know, sir, that she had died?"

"Yes, Trotter, Burgess."

"Oh."

"You may wonder why he didn't mention it to you?"

"Yes, sir."

"Well, it's because I told him not to."

Her face again stretched; then he was going on, "I had my reasons, Trotter, very good reasons. If Farmer Bentwood wants you he'll come for you, that's how I see it. If I loved someone and I knew they were available I would make it my business to go to them and tell them how I felt."

"It . . . it wouldn't have been right, sir, if . . . she's only been gone a short while."

"Almost six weeks, Trotter."

His eyes had never left her face. "As for not being right, that's damn nonsense. I needn't ask if he's written to you because, had he, you wouldn't be showing so much surprise and agitation now."

When she bowed her head, he said, "Wouldn't it be better if you were to wait . . . in fact, I think it would be better if you were to postpone your visit. Give him time to—" When he stopped abruptly she raised her head and looked at him, and he shrugged his shoulders.

They looked at each other for a moment in silence, then she said, "May I still have the afternoon off, sir?"

"Yes, Trotter."

"Thank you, sir. I . . . I shall see to your lunch first."

As she turned away, he lifted himself up from the chair by his arms as if to follow her or speak; then dropping back, he turned his head and looked over the wide sill and out of the window, and he thought, If she goes, what then? . . . Dear God! Let's hope Burgess is right.

"I am going on an errand," she said to Biddy.

"You'll be blown away, lass."

"Doesn't matter, the sun's shining."

"Won't be for long." Katie had come in through the back door on a gale of wind and, thrusting her thick buttocks out, she pressed the door closed, saying,

"Phew! that was a narrow escape. A slate came off the roof and almost slid past me nose. Boy! one of those could cut you in two. . . . Where you goin', Tilly?"

"I'm just going on an errand."

"Oh." Katie knew when to stop asking quesions, but she added, "Well, if I were you I'd put a scarf round me hat else you'll be leap-frogging across the fields after it."

"Stop your chattin'," her mother said to her now. "Get about your business and let Tilly get away. . . . Make the best of your walk, lass; you don't get out enough."

"I will." She nodded at Biddy, then went out and with the wind at her back she had to stop herself from running.

She was well away from the house when her desire to run was frustrated by the wind now being in her face, and she had to battle against it, holding her hat on with one hand and keeping the front of her skirt down with the other.

She took the road along the bridle path and past the cottage. Here, she stopped for a moment, her back to the wind, and gazed at the charred walls. The tangled grass had grown up almost to the ground floor window-sill. It seemed a long lifetime away since she had lived there, so much had happened to her, yet she hadn't moved more than two miles away from it. She cut through Billings Flat; then to avoid the village she climbed the steep bank, went through the rock strewn field and so on to the fell proper. Coming to a low stone wall, she sat on top of it and as she threw her legs over she scattered a few sheep sheltering on the other side. As they ran from her she laughed out loud. It was good to be out in the air and the wind. She had the desire to run again, but now she was approaching the farmland and she might meet up with Randy Simmons or Bill Young or Ally Taylor.

She saw none of the hands until she reached the farmyard proper, and it was Randy Simmons she saw first. He was coming out of the byre directing a heifer by prodding its rump with a sharp stick, and he became still as he stared at her while the animal galloped away to the end of the yard. And he didn't move until Bill Young shouted, "Where's this 'un off to?" Then he, too, stopped after he had brought the animal to a halt, and from each end of the yard they looked at her.

Turning her back to the wind, she was now facing Bill Young and she called, "Is . . . is Mr. Bentwood about?"

Pushing the animal forward now, Bill Young came up to her and stared at her for a moment before saying, "Well, no, no, he's not, Tilly."

"Tell you where you'll find him."

She turned now in the direction of Randy Simmons and waited for him to speak again, and after a moment of staring at her, he thumbed over his shoulder, saying, "Workin' in the bottom field in barn down there."

"Thank you." She turned away from them. She was facing the wind again and she heard Bill Young's voice raised and Randy Simmon's answer him, but she couldn't make out what they said.

She went up the road and through a gate into a field. Once inside, she had to skirt it as it had been freshly plowed up. Then she was in a grass meadow, and down in the dip at the very end of it lay the barn.

She was running now, letting the wind carry her right to the very doors. They were closed but not locked. She pushed against one and it gave way almost a foot, and then it stuck. As she went to squeeze through the narrow aperture her hat caught against the edge of the closed door and pushed it over her eyes. When she pushed it back she was through the door but could go no further for to her amazement she was standing within a few inches of the flanks of a horse, and when it lifted its back leg and struck the rough stone floor she gasped and pressed herself against the inside of the door, then moved along it.

Why had he brought his horse in here? Was he using it as a stable now? Had he got more horses? She blinked in the dimness and peered about her. Then her eyes became wide and fixed, her whole body frozen. She had stepped into her dream of Simon and herself loving, but now the dream was a waking nightmare. She was looking at him. He was naked except for a pair of white linings, and these hung loose. His body was twisted round and he was supporting himself on one knee. As he grabbed for his coat and pulled it in front of him the woman on the straw raised herself on her elbow. She was completely naked. She had been laughing, but now her face took on a look of haughty surprise. Yet she made no move to cover herself. But when she exclaimed in a high tone that could have indicated that a servant had come into a room unannounced, "Really! that girl," there erupted from Tilly a long drawn out moan; and now she was squeezing through the door again, and once more her hat was tilted over her eyes. Again she was running and when the wind lifted her skirt up almost around her waist, she paid no attention to it.

She was going through the meadow gate, and when of habit she turned to close it she saw him standing outside the barn she didn't stop to close the gate, nor did she skirt the field, but she ran straight across the furrows, then tumbled over the wall and ran and ran, and didn't stop until she reached the dimness of Billings Flat. There, leaning for support against a tree, she put her arms around it, unheeding now when her hat fell to the ground, and she moaned aloud making unintelligible sounds, for her mind, as yet, was not presenting her with words which would translate her feelings, for it was filled with a picture, a number of pictures. She saw herself standing before the master and he saying, "Wait until he comes for you. . . ." He had known. He had known what was going on. And with the same woman, too, who had ruined his life. And the picture of Randy Simmons telling her where she would find his master and the jumbled words when Bill Young must have gone for him, knowing what she would find. And what had she found?

The picture expanded. It covered the tree trunk; it spread over the copse, up the bank, getting wider and wider, the two forms filling it! the man like a baby with his mouth to the breast, the contorted limbs, and then the woman sitting up shameless.

Nowhere in the picture did she see Simon's face clearly, because in this moment she knew she never wanted to see his face again.

Easing herself from the tree, she picked up her hat, then leaned her back against the bole. Why wasn't she crying? Her whole being inside was torn to ribbons so why wasn't she crying? She wasn't crying because she mustn't cry. She had to go back and face them all. Mrs. Drew would be kind, and Katie and Peg. She mustn't have kindness at this moment, she couldn't bear kindness. Ever since her granny had gone she had longed for kindness; kindness had meant everything to her; but kindness now would break her. What she wanted now was somebody to fight with, to argue with. That was strange, because she had never wanted to fight in her life, nor argue, but she had the desire now to strike at someone and, as if that person was herself, the fool that was in her, the romantic silly fool, a girl, even a child, she took her doubled fist and drove it into her chest, and such was the force of the blow, it brought her shoulders hunching forward.

After a moment she put on her hat, straightened her coat, wiped her wet soil-covered boots by twisting her feet this way and that on the grass, rubbed the mud from the bottom of her skirt; then, her walk slow now, she made her way back to the house.

"You haven't been long, lass," said Biddy, looking at her closely. "Would you like a cup of tea?"

"No, thanks."

"The wind's chewed you, you looked peaked."

"Yes, it's strong. I'll just go up."

"I'll send you a tray up, lass."

The words had followed her down the kitchen, and without turning, she said, "Thanks. Ta," and went through the hall and up the main staircase, across the gallery, down the landing, and into her room.

She went to flop down on the bed but stopped herself. It was as if a voice, very like her granny's, said, "Don't sit down; you're not strong enough to stand it," so she took off her things, tidied her hair, put on her uniform, and was about to leave the room and go about her duties when Katie knocked on the door and, not waiting for an invitation to enter, opened it, bent down and picked the tray up from the carpet; then coming further in, she placed it on the little table under the window, saying, "I buttered the scones. Me ma's just made them fresh. Look"—she turned her head to the side—"is owt wrong with you, Tilly?"

"No."

"Aw, you can't kid me. Can't you tell me?"

"No, no, Katie. Perhaps some other time."

"Is it that Steve lad?"

"Steve? Oh no! No!"

"All right, I'll leave you, but by the way, he, the master, he rang." She jerked her head backward. "An' Mr. Pike was down in the cellar and Phyllis was across in the stables, so me ma sent me up. Oh Lord! he scared the daylights out of me, Tilly. Eeh! I think you're wonderful the way you manage him. The way he looks at you, you feel like a plate of glass."

"What did he want?"

"Oh, he just wanted some letters taken out to catch the coach. . . . Sure you're all right?"

"Yes, Katie, thanks."

"I'll be seein' you then."

"Yes, aye, Katie."

She remained standing while she drank the tea, but she didn't eat any of Biddy's scones; then taking in a long shuddering breath, she went out and along the corridor and into his room, prepared for the questioning. But the wind was taken completely out of her sails when, after staring at her for some seconds, he made no mention of her having been out, or of the purpose of her errand, but, as if she had just a moment before left the room, he said, "I think I'll go down into the drawing-room tonight, Trotter. You know, at one time I used to play the piano. There's nothing wrong with my hands, is there?" He held them both out and turned them back to front a number of times. "I don't see why I shouldn't have a hobby, do you?"

"No, sir."

"Then tell Leyburn that he'll be needed. And also I think I'll dine downstairs tonight. Yes, yes, I will. It'll be a change. See to it, will you, Trotter?"

"Yes, sir."

She stood outside the door for a moment, her lips held tightly between the thumb and the joint of her first finger. He knew, he knew what she would find. . . . Yet how could he have known? And why hadn't he said something? Why? because it was likely too delicate a matter for him to bring up. The woman who had been his mistress now finding her amusement with his tenant. Oh, she was sick, sick. She wished she was miles away. Nothing good ever came her way; nor would it as long as she remained here. She wished it was bedtime for now she wanted to cry. Oh, how she wanted to cry.

It was as if he was doing it on purpose, it was well past ten and he was still downstairs. They had brought him down at five o'clock and he had played the piano, and

every now and again some of them had crept into the
hall and listened outside the drawing-room door; and
they all said he played "Lovely."

He dined at seven o'clock. Afterward he again went
into the drawing-room but now he played at patience.

Not until half-past ten did he give the order to be
taken upstairs and then straight into the closet where he
stayed for almost another half-hour.

When he appeared in the bedroom he was changed
and ready for bed.

The house was quiet now; the lights were out except
for those night lights in the gallery and in the corridor.

The bedclothes were turned back, his night table was
set, the fire banked down; and she was now standing
some distance from the bed, as she always did, saying,
"Have you got everything you require, sir?" and to this
he didn't answer as usual, "Yes, thank you, Trotter,"
but said, "No, no, I haven't; and I'm very tired. And
I've made this night last out as long as twenty." And
when her eyes widened slightly, he said, "As soon as
you came in that door this afternoon you expected to be
met by a battery of questions, and what would have
been the result? Well, from the look on your face I
judged that most surely you would have broken down;
and then the whole household would have been aware
of your private business. Well now, they're all in
bed . . . we hope. Anyway"—he jerked his head
upward—"there's only the two maids upstairs, and they
should be asleep by now, so come—" He held out his
hand and, his voice dropping to a gentle softness, he
said, "Sit down here near me and tell me what happened."

She couldn't move, she could hardly breathe, the
avalanche was rising in her, but she mustn't, she
mustn't cry; they likely weren't asleep up there, they
would hear her.

"Come."

She was moving toward him now and the touch of his hand drained the last strength from her.

"Did you see him?"

Her head was hanging; she was looking down on to the brown velvet of his dressing-gown and to where her hand lay in his on top of his knees.

"Tell me. What happened? What did he say?"

Still she couldn't speak.

It seemed a long while before he said, "He told you he was having an affair with Lady Myton, didn't he?"

When she moved her head from side to side, he said, "Then what happened? You must have found something out?" There was an impatient note in his voice now.

She lifted her face to his. She was gulping in her throat now, the lump there was choking her.

When the tears seemed to spring from every pore in her body and the constriction in her throat was like a knife tearing at her gullet, his arms came about her and he pulled her toward him and smothered her crying in his shoulder, saying, "There, there, my dear. There, there! no one is worth such tears. Ssh! Ssh! Ssh! Come"—his voice was a whisper—"you don't want to waken the whole house, and after my long, long night of keeping them all at bay."

Long after her paroxysm had passed he held her to him; then when at last she raised her head he took a large white handkerchief and gently wiped her face, and she said, "Oh, sir, I'm . . . I'm sorry."

"Don't be sorry for crying; you wouldn't be a woman if you didn't cry. My father had a saying about ladies who cried, he said tears were from a woman's weak kidney."

She did not respond to this with a smile and he, making a little movement with his head, said, "And this is no time to joke. I will ask you just one more question, perhaps two. First, did you talk to him?"

"No."

He drew back from her now, saying, "Then why?"

"Because—" She now drew in a shuddering breath, lowered her gaze for a moment, then lifted her head and looking at him, straight in the face, she said, "I was directed to . . . to the barn. I saw him there."

"Oh my God!" He turned his head to the side and said quietly, "Both of them?"

"Yes, sir."

"Why did you go to the barn?"

"I . . . I was directed there."

"Who directed you?"

"One of his men, a man called Randy Simmons."

"Cruel swine! Well now, it's over." He put his finger under her chin and pushed her head upward. "You remember what you said about being able to hold your head up? Well, you go on doing just that. But I'll ask you another question and then we won't mention the subject again. . . . If he were to come tomorrow and beg your forgiveness would you take him?"

She looked at him steadily for a moment before she said, "No, sir, not after today, I . . . I couldn't."

After a short silence, he said, "Odd, isn't it; we both have suffered through the one lady. You can see she has practically ruined my life, but that needn't be so in your case, in fact it could be the making of you. Put it behind you, Tilly. You're worthy of something better than the farmer. I've always known that. Go now, go to bed and sleep, and start a new life tomorrow."

She rose from where she had been kneeling by the side of his chair and, drawing in a deep breath, she stood straight, before saying, "Good-night, sir."

"Good-night, my dear."

As she went out of the door he knew he had missed an opportunity; he could have kept her with him tonight. But he didn't want it that way. There was time enough now.

6

When eventually he took Tilly she came to him like a mother to a sick child.

It should happen that about three weeks later a tragedy enveloped Mark and spread over the whole house. It came in the form of two letters. Both Mr. Burgess and Tilly were in the room at the time he opened them. The first he slit open with a paper knife; he was always meticulous about the way he opened his mail. He often looked at the postmark and the stamp before opening a letter. Now, taking the letter from the envelope, he leaned back in his chair and began to read, and the first line brought him sitting upright. His brows gathered into a deep line above his nose and his lips fell apart for the words he had just read were:

It is with great sorrow that I write this, I being Harry's chaplain since first he came to the University. His death will be a loss to many.

He seemed to have stopped breathing, and such was the expression on his face that both Tilly and Mr. Burgess stood still and stared at him. Then he was tearing at the other long envelope with his fingers, and when he pulled out the single sheet of paper his hand was already crushing the bottom of it.

My dear Sir,
It is with the deepest regret that I have to inform you that your son, Harry, was knocked down and

425

*killed instantaneously yesterday morning by a run-
away dray horse in Petty Cury. This news must
come as a great and grievous shock to you, as
indeed it has to all of us here at the college. Believe
me, sir, you have our deepest sympathy.*

*A coroner's inquest has already been held, at
which a verdict of accidental death was returned,
and I shall now await your instructions as to the
disposal of your son's mortal remains and of his
personal effects.*

*I send you these most unhappy tidings by the
mail coach. If you will reply likewise, I shall
personally ensure that your wishes are carried out
to the letter and as swiftly as possible.*

*Again may I offer you and your family my
deepest sympathy in your great and grievous be-
reavement.*

> *I am, my dear sir,*
> *Yours very truly,*
> *W. R. Pritchard*
> *Dean.*

He lay back and looked at the two faces before him.
His mouth opened and closed several times; then he
moved his head slowly from side to side and when he
did speak it was a drawn out whispered syllable.
"N . . . o!"

"You have had distressing news, sir?" Mr. Burgess
was bending over him and for answer Mark lifted the
sheet of paper from his knees and handed it to him.

When Mr. Burgess had read it he looked at Tilly and
she whispered, "What is it?"

"Master Harry."

"Oh no!"

He now handed the letter to her, and when she had
read it she gripped the front of her bodice with one
hand and, her lips quivering, she stared at Mark. His
head was up and tightly pressed against the back of the

chair, his eyes directed toward the ceiling. He was so still that for a moment she thought he'd had a seizure; but as she made to go to him his head snapped forward, his shoulders with it, and his knees came up, and now he was gripping them with his hands.

Silently they stood one on each side of him until he made a jerking movement with his head and muttered, "Leave me." And on this they went from the room.

It was a week later when the coffin arrived. It lay in state in the library for a day before being taken to the cemetery.

The funeral was a quiet affair. Mark sitting alone in the first carriage followed the hearse. Behind him came another carriage holding his mother-in-law, together with Matthew and Luke; following this were various carriages bearing male members of different families. The only mourners on foot were the male members of the staff, and these were made up mostly of the Drew family.

Both Mark and Mrs. Forefoot-Meadows sat in their carriages and watched the coffin being lowered into the ground. Mark, being alone, could cry and he cried as he had never cried in his life before. And in this moment he felt alone as he had never felt alone in his life before. He already knew the feeling of loneliness, but this was a different sort of aloneness: his first-born had gone, just apparently when they were beginning to know each other. After his second marriage the boy had been unfriendly, only returning to his old self when Eileen had gone from the house. The last time they had spoken together the boy, or the young man, the young man that he had become, had spoken to him of his affection for the sister of his friend, which explained his frequent visits to France, and he had confessed that he thought his affection was being returned. So now another young heart would also be pining.

When he returned from the cemetery the mourners,

realizing his predicament, didn't censure the fact that he wasn't present at the meal laid for them in the dining-room and presided over by Mrs. Forefoot-Meadows.

After receiving the usual condolences Mark had ordered that he be taken straight upstairs, and once there he told both Tilly and Mr. Burgess that he did not wish to be disturbed, and that he would ring when he needed them. He even refused to see his mother-in-law until the following morning which, needless to say, annoyed Mrs. Forefoot-Meadows.

When they did meet they seemed, at least for a time, as if they had nothing to say to each other. Mark sat stiffly in his chair, his eyes directed toward the window, while Jane Forefoot-Meadows sat as stiffly in hers as if waiting for him to open the conversation, and when he did it was abruptly. Turning his head toward her, he almost growled, "My son is dead, my first-born, and she hadn't even the decency to come to his funeral. What was she afraid of, I'd have her chained up?"

"She is not well. The journey would have been too much, and. . . ."

"From all I hear she's still well enough to take jaunts. You may have your informants here who take the news back to Scarborough; well, it's amazing how my friends are desirous of bringing the news from Scarborough to here."

"There is life in Scarborough, things to do, entertainments. There was nothing such here."

"God in Heaven!" He threw his head up. "The times I've tried to get her off that couch and into a coach and go to the city, to a concert or a play, but no, she was always indisposed, too ill. Hell's flames! when I think of the game she played, how she deceived me. . . ."

"Oh, Mark! Mark! think. I shouldn't bring that word into the conversation if I were you."

"Look, Mother-in-law—" He now bent toward her and, his voice quiet, he said, "There are various forms of defection and the worst of them isn't having a mistress."

"Perhaps we don't see eye to eye on this matter, nor do I think did Eileen. And while we're on the subject of news going backward and forward I am not going to beat about the bush with what I am about to say, and that is, you should get rid of that girl."

"What girl? Trotter?"

"Which other girl is there who looks after you?"

"Will you give me one good reason why I should get rid of Trotter?"

"I could give you several but the main one is your name is being coupled with her."

"Oh! my name is being coupled with her? Will you go on and describe in which way?"

"Don't be silly, Mark; you don't need me to put it into words."

"Oh yes, I do, Mother-in-law. Oh yes, I do. Trotter acts in the capacity of my nurse, also as housekeeper, and she does both very well. . . ."

"You should have a male nurse, you know that."

"I have one, Burgess; but I also like to have a woman about me to attend to the niceties of life, my life such as it is. Now the main capacity you are referring to is the part of mistress. Well, there, I must disappoint you for as yet she hasn't taken up that position."

When he broke off and they stared at each other, Jane Forefoot-Meadows realized from the look of him that he was speaking the truth; but then he added, "I hate to receive any favor that I haven't really earned, so please tell my wife that I will do my best to see that Trotter complies with the main duty in future."

"I . . . I was only putting you on your guard."

"Thank you for your concern."

"People will talk, the girl is young and . . . and. . . ."

"Yes, Mother-in-law, what were you going to say, beautiful?"

"No, I wasn't."

"Then what?"

"Oh, it doesn't matter. Only personally, I don't like the girl; there . . . there is something about her. And what's more, she doesn't know her place."

"Has she been rude to you?"

"No, she hasn't, she scarcely opens her mouth."

"Is that to be held against her?"

"There is a way to be silent and a way not to be silent. The look of the girl. Anyway, I would advise you, Mark, and I do this in all sincerity, I would advise you to get rid of her."

"And in all sincerity, Mother-in-law, I must tell you, and you can also convey the message to my wife, that I have no intention of getting rid of Trotter, ever. If she leaves this house it will be of her own wish because she has been of more help and comfort to me than anyone in my life before. Now you tell that word for word to my wife. And also tell her I shall never forgive her to my dying day for not being present with me at this time. I knew well enough that she was never fond of Harry, in fact she disliked him, but out of respect and as a matter of courtesy she should have been at my side today. In the eyes of the whole country I am being treated like a leper; not one of them will believe that she has left me simply because of the Myton affair. I am sure they think I was a monster to her. What else would have kept her away at this time?"

It was some moments before Jane Forefoot-Meadows spoke again, and then, her voice small, she said, "She sent her condolences; you had her letter."

"Oh yes, I had her condolences, I had her letter, a letter that was so formal she must have copied it from a book headed: Appropriate letters to be sent to the relations of the deceased. There is such a book, I have read it and laughed over it."

There followed another silence before she spoke.

"You must remember that she brought the boys from school out of respect."

When he closed his eyes and made no answer, she went on, "Speaking of the boys; there is a little matter I think I must bring up. Matthew has had to be moved to another school."

"Why?" His inquiry was sharp.

"Because he apparently didn't like the school he was at, and he misbehaved. This . . . this other establishment is very expensive and . . . and. . . ."

"You want me to foot the bill?"

"Well, Eileen would be grateful if you. . . ."

"Tell Eileen from me she is getting all I am able to give her. If she can't afford to keep the children, send them back home; they'll live much cheaper here, schools included."

She stared at him, her eyes hard now, before she said, "You should have sold the mine when you had the chance."

"What do you know about the mine and me getting the chance? Oh. Oh, your informant of all my doings. I wonder who it is."

"It is public knowledge that Mr. Rosier is willing to buy."

"And, Mother-in-law, let it be public knowledge to the effect that my mine will lie there and rot, which it is doing now admittedly, before I sell it to Rosier or any of his kin."

"You're being foolish. What good is it as it stands now? You haven't the money to. . . ."

"No, I haven't the money to set it going again, but I am bloody well sure it's not going to be set in working order by Rosier. I hate the fellow and all he stands for."

"You are a very trying man, you know that?"

Mark looked at his mother-in-law. She had now risen to her feet. He was about to make some tart retort, but checked it as he thought yet again that she was an old woman and she had made this long journey to be at his side at this particular time, yet he knew deep in his heart that were the journey twice as long and twice as hard she would have tackled it rather than let her daughter come back to him. The possessive mother had her daughter to herself once again. What he did say was, "Thank you for coming, Mother-in-law."

And to this she answered, "It was as little as I could do"; and when she added, "I am very sorry for you, Mark," he was surprised at the sincerity of her tone. Then quite astonished when she added, "Would . . . would it be any help to you if I left the boys for another week or so? You could send them back in the care of Leyburn. I . . . I would explain to Eileen."

He stared at her for a full minute before saying, "That's very kind of you, but . . . but no, take them back with you, there . . . there would be no pleasure, no joy for them here at the moment." He couldn't add that he didn't want to see his sons at this particular time. He couldn't really understand the feeling himself but their boisterousness, which they wouldn't be able to subdue for as yet death had no real meaning for them, and even their voices, muted as they would be coming from above, would rub salt into the wound that was gaping wide at this moment.

"I understand but I thought it might help you."

"I am very grateful and will always be grateful for your suggestion."

"Well now, I . . . I must be away. Phillips has packed. I shall send her for the boys, they will likely be in the nursery. You will, of course, wish to see them?"

"Oh yes, yes, of course."

"Good-bye, Mark."

"Good-bye, Mother-in-law. And again please accept my thanks for coming."

She inclined her head toward him and walked out.

432

After a moment, during which he lay back in the chair and closed his eyes tightly, while at the same time gnawing on his lip, he leaned forward and pulled the bell rope. . . .

Five minutes later Tilly showed the boys into the room, then left them. They stood one each side of Mark's chair and he, looking from one face to the other, smiled at them. Matthew, he noticed, had since he had last seen him changed the more. He was taller and his fair hair seemed to have darkened somewhat, but it was his eyes that showed the biggest change. Where they had looked merry and mischievous, devilish in fact at times, there was now in their depths a look that puzzled him; in an older person he would have named it misery, not untinged with fear, but Matthew was a spirited boy, so the look must have another explanation. Luke, for instance, had hardly changed at all, his round dark eyes were bright, and his mouth still had the appearance of constantly hovering on a smile. But as different as they looked, they were both of one mind, and this they confirmed within a few minutes. After greeting them he went on to say that he hoped they would have a good return journey, and he thanked them for coming. But before he had finished speaking Matthew put in, "Papa."

"Yes, Matthew?"

"I . . . I should like to ask you something. We . . . we would both like to ask you something, wouldn't we, Luke?" And to this Luke nodded and said firmly, "Yes, Papa."

"What is it you would like to ask me?"

"We . . . we would like to return home."

Again Mark closed his eyes, and now he lowered his head as he said, "I'm afraid that doesn't rest with me entirely, Matthew; it is for your mama to decide. If you could persuade her to return and. . . ."

"She . . . she won't listen to us, Papa. If . . . if you

433

could talk to her, write, and I promise you if you let us come back I wouldn't cause any trouble, I mean not to the servants, I'd be good, we'd both be good, wouldn't we, Luke?"

Again Luke nodded and said, "Yes, Papa, we would be good."

Mark swallowed deeply and as he tried to find words to answer his sons, Matthew started again: "We've . . . we've talked it over with Trotter. Trotter would like us to come back and . . . and we promised her, too, we wouldn't get up to any tricks. And . . . and I'll go to school from here, Papa. I could go into Newcastle."

Mark now put his hand gently on Matthew's shoulder and he said, "I'm sorry, my dear boy, very sorry. There is nothing I would like better than to have you all back home, but as I said, it . . . it depends on your mama. If you can persuade her, all well and good. You see, to run a house like this is difficult at any time, but when there are children, four in fact, well it needs. . . ."

Oh dear, dear, the boy was going to cry, the tough devil-may-care Matthew. He mustn't, he mustn't; he just couldn't bear it if the child cried. "Now, now! We are not little boys any more, are we?" He put his hands on both their shoulders and he forced himself to smile as he said, "I'll make it my business to see that you spend all your next holiday here, and in the meantime I shall write to your mama and talk things over with her."

He watched Matthew blink rapidly and swallow deeply before saying, "Thank you, Papa."

And Luke, now smiling, said, "Oh, thank you, Papa. And Jessie Ann and John would love to be back too." And bending forward, he whispered almost in Mark's ear, "They are like suet dumplings."

"Suet dumplings?" Mark raised his eyebrows in inquiry and Luke, his smile broader now, nodded, saying, "All of them at Grandmama's, Grandpapa, Phillips, all the servants, suet dumplings. That's what

Brigwell calls them. Sometimes he says they are stodgy pud."

Mark looked into the bright face and thought, He'll get by, he'll ride the storms out; but what about Matthew? Matthew wouldn't sit and ride the storm out, he would fight it, even when full of fear he would fight it.

"Go now," he said, "and be good boys; and we'll meet very shortly."

"Good-bye, Papa."

"Good-bye, Papa. You will write to Mama, won't you?"

"Yes, Matthew, I'll write to your mama. Good-bye, my dears."

When the door closed on the children he turned his chair toward the broad window sill and, leaning forward, rested his arm along it and laid his head down in the crook of it.

After eight hours during which he hadn't rung, Tilly ventured to tap on the door. When she opened it she saw him sitting in the dark by the window gazing out into the starlit night. He didn't turn at her approach and when, her voice soft, she said, "I have brought you a hot drink, sir," his head made the slightest movement of dissent. The room being lit only by the reflection from the landing through the open doorway, she now put the tray down and lit the candle in the night-light; then after closing the door, she returned to his side, and there she put her hand gently on his shoulder.

The touch brought him around to her and, looking up into her face in the dim light, he said, "Why? Can you understand it, Trotter? Why him of all people, on the verge of life, to be killed by a dray horse?"

She was unable to answer his why, and after a moment he said, "We were just getting to know each other. I now feel buried under a load of guilt because I neglected him for years. There were the others. He must have felt it because . . . well, you saw how he was, bright, jolly, that was because they were no longer here. Nor was she."

All Tilly could do was to go hurriedly into the dressing-room, pour out a glass of brandy, bring it back to the tray, then pour it into the hot milk. He was partial to brandy and hot milk. When she handed him the glass in the silver holder he said, "Thanks, Trotter," then added, "Go to bed; it's been a long day."

She hesitated now, saying, "I'm . . . I'm not tired; I'll stay with you a while, sir."

"Not tonight, Trotter. Thank you all the same. Good-night."

"Good-night, sir. . . ."

The days moved into weeks and the master showed no further inclination to be taken downstairs. He seemed to have lost interest in most things. Mr. Burgess told him of a new author he had come across by the name of William Makepeace Thackeray who had written a book called *The Yellowplush Correspondence*. It was very good reading and would the master like to pursue it? The master thanked him and said "Yes, yes, sometime, Burgess."

The master's lethargy was worrying the whole household. Biddy demanded what was the use of cooking for him, it was a waste of good food; not that anything that was returned from the first floor was ever wasted. But then, as she pointed out, workers, like hens, could do on roughage, but she didn't see the point of stuffing them with food made from butter, eggs and cream.

On the evening of the day she said to Tilly, "Can't you think of anything, lass, that will bring him out of himself?" they were sitting, as they sometimes did last thing at night, in the kitchen. The house was quiet, the others had all gone to their beds. The fires were banked down. The lamps turned low, with the exception of the main one in the kitchen. And now Biddy rose and, going to it, lifted up the tall glass funnel, turned the flame down low, nipped at the black edge of the wick with her finger and thumb, rubbed her fingers on the seat of her dark serge skirt, then said, "Well?" and to this Tilly answered briefly, "Yes?"

"Well then, what you going to do about it?"

"What do you think I should do?"

Biddy replaced the glass shade before saying, " 'Tisn't for me to guide you. I haven't got your mind, or heart. *You* know how *you* feel . . . and the whole house knows how *he* feels. Whichever way you look at it it's a big step. But, it could be in the right direction for you in the long run."

"Lots of folks think it's already happened, Mrs. Forefoot-Meadows most of all. She wanted to get rid of me."

"Well, that being the case, if you were to live up to the name you haven't earned, that would potch her, for he'd never let you go. And that, lass"—she turned now and looked straight at Tilly—"is what you've got to face up to, there'd be no other man for you, no respectable marriage."

They stared at each other for a moment, then Tilly rose slowly to her feet and without saying anything further went from the kitchen.

Up in her room she washed herself down in warm water from head to foot, using the scented soap from the master's closet. She put on, for the first time, a new nightdress. It was made of a piece of fine lawn that she had come across when looking through one of the boxes up in the loft. There were a lot of boxes up there holding old gowns, and one had lengths of material in it, and she had felt no compunction in taking the smallest piece of lawn which measured about four yards. It had provided occupation for her hands over the months and the final herring-boning of the front had pleased her mightily.

She now smoothed it down over her knees. Then

looking at her hands, she held them out under the lamp. They had grown soft, there were now no dark lines under her nails; the rim of flesh bordering the nails was no longer broken. The backs of her hands were almost as white as the fronts. She now put her hand up to her head. She washed her hair every week, and every night, that is if she wasn't too tired, she brushed it well before plaiting it.

She now pulled the plaits to the front of her shoulders. They reached to below her breasts and felt silky to the touch. She was clean and smelled sweet. Her body was ready but she had her mind to deal with. What she was aiming to do was likely to alter her whole life, as Biddy had hinted. What if she had a bairn? Well, what if she had a bairn? She wouldn't be the first. And if it were his, and it would be no other's, he wasn't a man to throw off his responsibilities.

But before that eventuality came about, if it did, did she really want to do this just in order to give him comfort? Or was there any other reason? Yes, there was another reason, but her mind would not allow her to dwell on it, it was too private. Apart from that, did she like him enough to do this off her own bat?

She looked down at the palms of her hands again and nodded toward them. Yes, oh yes, she liked him enough. . . .

The dressing-gown round her, a candle in her hand, she now tip-toed out of the room, along the landing and into the dressing-room. There was a clock on the mantelpiece and it said the time was twenty minutes to twelve. Would he be asleep? Well, if he was she wouldn't waken him.

Opening the communicating door, she stepped quietly into the room. It was in complete darkness except for the light from her own candle. She lifted it high above her head, and it showed him propped up on his pillows, his eyes wide and staring at her. His face looked pale in the light, his hair showing no gray at the temples looked black. He pulled himself slightly upward and said, "Trotter. . . . What is it?"

"I . . . I have come to keep you company, sir."

He was sitting bolt upright now, and after a moment his head drooped forward and he ran his fingers through his hair muttering as he did so, "Oh, Tilly! Tilly!" When he slowly raised his head and looked at her again, he said, "You're sorry for me?"

"It isn't only that, sir."

"No? You really mean that?"

"Yes."

He held out his hand now and when she placed hers in it he said, "On top of the clothes or underneath?"

She was pleased to hear a slight jocular note in the question and, turning slightly from him, she placed the candlestick on the side table, then deliberately with her free hand she turned the covers back and, taking her other hand from his hold, she turned her back on him, dropped her dressing-gown to the floor, sat on the edge of the bed, and slowly lifted her feet up and got under the bedclothes. And now sitting side by side with him, she turned her head slightly toward him but didn't look at him as she said, "You think me overbold?"

"Oh, Tilly! Tilly! Oh, my dear."

She was in his arms now and so quickly had he grasped her that they both fell back on to the pillows. And then they became still.

"Oh, Tilly. Tilly." His fingers came up and touched her chin. "I never thought, never dreamed you'd make the first move yourself. I . . . I thought I'd have to cajole you, maneuver you, and doubtless I would have at some future date even when my need of you wasn't as great as at this moment. Thank you, thank you, my dear one, for coming to me."

His fingers now moved up and followed the bone formation of her face and his eyes followed his hand,

and when his fingers touched her lids, he said, "You have the strangest, the most beautiful eyes I've ever seen in a woman. Do you know that, Tilly?"

There was an audible sound of her swallowing her spittle before she said, "No, sir."

"Don't call me sir any more, Tilly. . . . Do you hear?"

She was looking at him now.

"Don't call me sir any more, at least not when we're together, like this, and at other times omit it as often as, what shall we say, decorum allows. My name as you know is Mark. Say it, Tilly, Mark."

"I . . . I couldn't. If I. . . ." She gave the smallest of laughs here and repeated, "No, I couldn't, sir."

"Tilly, Tilly Trotter, this is an order, you will in future, give me my name. How can you love someone you call sir? . . . Tilly—" He waited for a moment. Then, his voice thick and from deep in his throat, he asked, "Do you care for me, just . . . just a little?"

She did not hesitate. "Yes. Oh yes, yes I care for you."

"Thank you, my dear. Thank you. Now I'm going to tell you something, Tilly, and you must believe me. . . . It's just this. I love you. Do you hear? I love you. The feeling I have for you I have never experienced in my life before, not for my first wife or my second wife, or for my children. From the first time I became aware of you I think I knew I was going to be bewitched." When she gave a slight movement he pulled her tightly to him and murmured, "The day I offered you the post in the nursery I had the feeling then because I just wanted to keep looking at you, and I wanted you to look at me. I didn't recognize it as love, but that's what it was, Tilly, love. I love you. . . . I love you. . . . Oh Tilly, I love you."

When she shivered within his embrace, his voice changing now, he said, "You know what you're about to do? It may have consequences and I may not be able to give you my protection, except in a monetary way. You understand that?"

She eased herself slightly back from him till she could see his face half reflected in the candlelight and she said, "I understand very little at this moment. All I know is that I want to make you happy."

"Tilly, my dear, my dear. Oh, you're like a gift from the gods. Do you know that? You, so young and beautiful, I . . . I find it hard to believe you're here. Tell me, does . . . does my condition not repel you?"

"You . . . you mean, the accident, your feet?"

"Just that."

"Aw . . . w!" The common exclamation had a sort of trill to it, and then she added quietly, "Not a bit. Not a bit. To me you're a wonderful man, all over."

And a moment later she proved her words, for when the stump of his leg gently eased itself between hers, she did not shrink either outwardly or inwardly, but now of her own accord she put her arms about him and when his mouth covered hers and his hand moved down over her hips and she responded to him he moaned his joy, and it was in this moment that her love for him was born. .